The Bedquilt and Other Stories by

DOROTHY CANFIELD FISHER

The Bedquilt and Other Stories by Dorothy Canfield Fisher

• Edited with an Introduction and •
Afterword by Mark J. Madigan

University of Missouri Press Columbia and London

University of Missouri Press, Columbia, Missouri 65201
Printed and bound in the United States of America

5 4 3 2 1 00 99 98 97 96

Library of Congress Cataloging-in-Publication Data

Fisher, Dorothy Canfield, 1879–1958.

The bedquilt and other stories / by Dorothy Canfield Fisher ; edited with an introduction and afterword by Mark J. Madigan.

p. cm.

Includes bibliographical references (p.)

ISBN 0-8262-1035-X (alk. paper)

1. United States—Social life and customs—20th century—Fiction. 2. World War, 1914–1918—France—Fiction. I. Madigan, Mark J., 1961– . II. Title.

PS3511.I7416A6 1996

813′.52—dc20 95-37923

CIP

∞ ™ This paper meets the requirements of the American National Standard for Permanence of Paper for Printed Library Materials, Z39.48, 1984.

Designer: Stephanie Foley
Typesetter: BOOKCOMP
Printer and Binder: Thomson-Shore, Inc.
Typefaces: University Roman and Caslon 224

The editor dedicates this volume to his grandparents Joseph and Jeannette Lavoie

In Memoriam

Contents

Acknowledgments

For permission to reprint Dorothy Canfield Fisher's work, I am indebted to her granddaughter, Vivian Scott Hixson, and the author's estate. I owe many thanks to the University of Missouri Press, especially to its Director and Editor in Chief, Beverly Jarrett, who offered early encouragement and wise counsel, and to my editor, Annette Wenda, whose guidance improved this volume in many ways. I am also grateful for the advice of my colleagues Paul Eschholz and Harry Orth at the University of Vermont and for the support of my Department Chair, T. Alan Broughton.

Last, and most important, I acknowledge and celebrate my parents, John and Jeanne Madigan, whose love and support has never faltered.

A Note on the Text

The copy-texts for the stories in this volume are drawn from *A Harvest of Stories,* a collection of Fisher's work that was edited by the author and published in 1956. The stories bear Fisher's revisions for inclusion in that volume. The sole exception is "An American Citizen," which was originally published in *The Crisis* and has not been heretofore reprinted. The places and dates of original publication of the stories are listed below:

"Prologue: What My Mother Taught Me" in *A Harvest of Stories.*
"The Bedquilt" in *Harper's Monthly Magazine* 113 (November 1906): 885–91.
"Flint and Fire" in *Harper's Monthly Magazine* 130 (April 1915): 723–34.
"The Heyday of the Blood" in *Hillsboro People.*
"Through Pity and Terror . . ." (originally titled "La Pharmacienne") in *Pictorial Review* 20 (September 1918): 14–16, 34–35, 58–59.
"An American Citizen" in *The Crisis* 19 (April 1920): 302–8; 20 (May 1920): 23–29.
"Gold from Argentina" in *Basque People.*
"The Saint of the Old Seminary" excerpted in *The Delineator* 118 (January 1931): 8–9. Full text in *Basque People.*
"Memorial Day" in *Fables for Parents.*
"The Knot-hole" in *The Yale Review* 32 (March 1943): 493–517.
"Sex Education" in *The Yale Review* 35 (December 1945): 252–64.
"The Washed Window" in *American Heritage* 7 (December 1955): 28–31, 115.
Essay: "How 'Flint and Fire' Started and Grew" in *Americans All: Stories of American Life Today,* ed. Benjamin A. Heydrick. New York: Harcourt, Brace and Howe, 1920.

Chronology

1873 (June) Flavia A. Camp and James Hulme Canfield marry.

1879 (February 17) DCF born in Lawrence, Kansas. Father is professor of political economy and sociology at University of Kansas; mother is artist. DCF spends summers at Canfield relatives' house in Arlington, Vermont.

1890 (winter) DCF makes first trip to Europe, accompanies mother to Paris; later attends French schools.

1891 Canfields move to Lincoln, Nebraska; father becomes chancellor of the state university where Willa Cather, who becomes a lifelong friend, is a student.

1894 Publishes story "The Fear That Walks by Noonday" (collaboration with Willa Cather) in University of Nebraska yearbook.

1895 Canfields move to Columbus, Ohio; father becomes president of Ohio State University, where DCF is enrolled as student.

1899 (spring) DCF graduates from OSU; father resigns presidency, becomes librarian of Columbia University, New York.

(fall) DCF begins graduate work in French at the Sorbonne in Paris.

1902 (March) First professional publication, *New York Times* article on "Holy Week in Spain."

1903 Turns down assistant professorship at Case Western Reserve University, Cleveland, Ohio.

1904 (spring) Receives Ph.D. from Columbia University.

(May) Dissertation, *Corneille and Racine in England,* is published by Columbia University Press.

(May) Meets John Fisher.

(fall) Accepts job as "secretary" at Horace Mann School, New York City. Publishes stories in magazines.

1905 (summer) Travels in Germany, Norway, and France.

1906 *Elementary Composition* (with George R. Carpenter) published by Macmillan.

1907 (May) Marries John Fisher, moves to Arlington, Vermont. *Gunhild* (novel) published by Henry Holt.

1908 (June) Meets Sarah Cleghorn.

1909 (March 29) Father dies.

(July 30) Daughter, Sarah (Sally), born.

1911 (winter) Meets Maria Montessori in Rome.

1912 *A Montessori Mother* published by Henry Holt. *The Squirrel-Cage* (novel) published by Henry Holt. Hires Paul Reynolds as literary agent.

1913 (December) Son, James (Jimmy), born. *A Montessori Manual* published by Richardson Co.

1914 *Mothers and Children* published by Henry Holt.

1915 *Hillsboro People* (stories) published by Henry Holt. *The Bent Twig* (novel) published by Henry Holt.

1916 *The Real Motive* (stories) published by Henry Holt. *Fellow Captains* (miscellaneous prose, with Sarah N. Cleghorn) published by Henry Holt. *Self-Reliance* published by Bobbs-Merrill.

(April) John Fisher leaves for France to aid in war relief.

(August) DCF travels with children to join her husband in relief work in France.

1917 *Understood Betsy* (young adult novel) published by Henry Holt.

(spring) DCF loses hearing in one ear.

1918 *Home Fires in France* (stories) published by Henry Holt.

1919 *The Day of Glory* (stories) published by Henry Holt.

(April 26) Fishers return to Arlington.

1921 Honorary Ph.D., Middlebury College. *The Brimming Cup* (novel) published by Harcourt, Brace. First woman elected to the Vermont State Board of Education.

1922 Honorary Ph.D., Dartmouth College. Honorary Ph.D., University of Vermont. *Rough-Hewn* (novel) published by Harcourt, Brace.

1923 *Raw Material* (stories) published by Harcourt, Brace.

1924 *The Home-Maker* (novel) published by Harcourt, Brace.

1925 *Made-to-Order Stories* (stories) published by Harcourt, Brace.

1926 Accepts position on Book-of-the-Month Club Committee of Selection; eyesight steadily diminishes as a result of professional reading. *Her Son's Wife* (novel) published by Harcourt, Brace. *Life of Christ* (translated from the Italian of Giovanni Papini) published by Harcourt, Brace.

1927 *Why Stop Learning?* published by Harcourt, Brace.

1929 Honorary Ph.D., Columbia University.

1930 (August 15) Mother dies. *The Deepening Stream* (novel) published by Harcourt, Brace.

1931 (spring) Honorary Ph.D., Northwestern University. Elected to the National Institute of Arts and Letters. *Basque People* (stories) published by Harcourt, Brace.

1932 *Tourists Accommodated* (play) published by Harcourt, Brace. *Work: What It Has Meant to Men through the Ages* (translated from the Italian of Adriano Tilgher) published by Harcourt, Brace.

1933 Daughter, Sally, marries John Paul Scott. *Bonfire* (novel) published by Harcourt, Brace.

1934 Honorary Ph.D., Rockford College.

1935 Honorary Ph.D., Ohio State University. Honorary Ph.D., Swarthmore College. Honorary Ph.D., Williams College.

1937 (June) Son, Jimmy, marries Eleanor Bodine.

1939 Honorary Ph.D., Mt. Holyoke College. Honorary Ph.D., University of Nebraska. *Seasoned Timber* (novel) published by Harcourt, Brace.

1940 *Nothing Ever Happens and How It Does* (children's stories, with Sarah N. Cleghorn) published by Beacon Press. *Tell Me a Story* (children's stories) published by University Publishing Co.

1943 *Our Young Folks* published by Harcourt, Brace.

(March) John Fisher suffers heart attack.

1945 (January 31) Son, Jimmy, dies in Philippines.

1946 *American Portraits* published by Henry Holt.

1949 *Four-Square* (anthology) published by Harcourt, Brace.

1950 *Our Independence and the Constitution* (children's history) published by Random House. *Paul Revere and the Minute Men* (children's history) published by Random House.

1951 Retires from Book-of-the-Month Club.

(February) Receives Constance Lindsay Skinner Award from Women's National Book Association. Honorary Ph.D., Marlboro College.

1952 *A Fair World for All* (children's history) published by Whittlesey House.

1953 Donates papers to the University of Vermont. *Vermont Tradition* published by Little, Brown.

(December 1) Suffers stroke.

1954 Honorary Ph.D., Smith College.

1956 *A Harvest of Stories* (anthology) published by Harcourt, Brace.

1957 *Memories of Arlington, Vermont* published by Duell, Sloan, and Pearce.

1958 (November 9) Dorothy Canfield Fisher dies of stroke.

1959 *And Long Remember* (children's history) published posthumously by Whittlesey House.

(June 1) Husband, John, dies of complications from influenza.

INTRODUCTION

The Short Stories of Dorothy Canfield Fisher

The past decade has been a remarkably fruitful one in Dorothy Canfield Fisher studies. The publication of a full-length biography, a collection of Fisher's letters, and the reissuing of several of her novels have helped introduce a new generation of readers to the work of one of America's most extraordinary women. This edition joins in the chorus of voices calling renewed attention to Fisher's life and career. The stories gathered here are the work of an uncommonly perceptive, prescient, and engaging writer. Their subjects range from New Englanders to the Basques of France to the struggles of African Americans to gain equal rights. Many received literary awards and were included in anthologies and textbooks. Most were originally published in popular magazines and literary journals, and all but one, "An American Citizen," were among the twenty-seven selected by the author for inclusion in *A Harvest of Stories,* a long-out-of-print compilation published in 1956, just two years before her death.

Measured against her output of more than two hundred stories, the selections in this volume provide a limited survey of what Fisher once referred to as a fifty-year "love affair" with the writing of fiction. But it is an arresting view nonetheless. In composing her stories, Fisher drew from a rich vein of personal experience, which is later discussed in this volume's Afterword. As a female artist in a male-dominated profession, she not only flourished, but also encouraged and opened doors for other women. With her own desire to write, she successfully balanced her duties as wife and

mother. Yet hers was not the charmed life and career it may have appeared to be. Chief among her personal disappointments was the death of her son in World War II, which brought so many tears that her optometrist feared she might go blind. The distillation of her experiences is contained in a body of work marked by far more than a technical facility with narrative. There is in Fisher's best writing a vigorous curiosity about human nature, and a judiciousness that is no less bracing for its acknowledgment of our inherent frailties.

While stylistic experimentation was never her primary concern, Fisher nonetheless contributed significantly to the genre of the short story. At her disposal were a storyteller's natural talent for plot development, an ear for the nuances of spoken language, and an eye for telling detail. Her stories are populated with an unusually broad range of characters—young, old, rich, poor, middle class, men, women, children, American, French, Spanish—all rendered convincingly. But Fisher's greatest strength lies in her ability to mine the commonplace for the revelatory. Her observation of life at hand is at once scrupulous in its detail and inviting of far-ranging interpretation.

Fisher related her observations of the human drama in direct language and with a desire to educate. With typical candor, she once declared in *The Home-Maker* that "Under its greasy camouflage of chivalry, society is really based on a contempt for women's work in the home." Such statements made Fisher's best-selling novel, which focuses on the restrictions of traditional gender roles within a marriage, one of the most controversial works of 1924, and led at least one reviewer to call it "extreme."[1] To those familiar with Fisher's fiction, however, *The Home-Maker* should have been anything but extreme. The topics she explores therein—women's rights, marital relations, domesticity, the bonds of family that both unite and constrict, the struggle to support oneself in a capitalist society, the artistic temperament—are the same ones that had been of consistent interest to her since she began publishing short stories in mass-market magazines nearly twenty years earlier. "The Bedquilt," for example, is, on the surface, a "quiet" tale about a

1. Dorothy Canfield, *The Home-Maker,* 312; F.M., "Feminism Triumphant."

New England spinster, which, on a deeper level, speaks as forcefully about the condition of women and "contempt for women's work in the home" as any line from *The Home-Maker.*

In this volume's opening essay, "What My Mother Taught Me," Fisher recalls the moment of inspiration for "The Bedquilt" at the Prado museum as she gazed into the eyes of one of the court dwarfs painted by Diego Velásquez:

> The subject of one of the first stories I wrote, "The Bedquilt," was as helplessly starved as the Spanish dwarf of what all human beings need for growth . . . was as humbled before her fellow-men through no fault of hers . . . as defenselessly given over to the careless mockery of those luckier than she. This by no glandular lack . . . by the social code of her time which decreed that plain women without money, who did not have husbands, who had never been admired by men, were only outcasts from the normal group . . . grotesque deformities, so that to look at them was to laugh at them!
>
> . . . A message received from the marvelously painted, dark, tragic eyes of Sebastian de Morra had forced me to look deep into the faded blue eyes of Aunt Mehetabel.

The significance to Fisher of that look into Aunt Mehetabel's eyes is hard to overstate. In fashioning the character of the elderly country woman, she felt the importance of her work as a writer for perhaps the first time. The effort to understand and communicate the complexity of the human condition, begun in earnest in "The Bedquilt," would be her authorial project for the next fifty years. That understanding is at once specific to the character of Mehetabel and more expansive as it argues that the attributes of all women need to be better recognized.

The character of Mehetabel and her talent for quilting are not only convincingly rendered, but also are an effective means of voicing provocative thematic concerns. For her heroine, Fisher chose neither a radical feminist nor an avant-garde artist, but rather a character with whom even the most conservative reader could sympathize. Moreover, in quilting, she chose a craft with deep roots in American history. By embodying her message of empowerment in the unassuming Aunt Mehetabel, Fisher subverted the negative criticism that greeted more strident female characters such as Kate Chopin's Edna Pontellier. While it is true that Mehetabel is eventually honored for the magnificent quilt she creates, her initial invisibility in the Elwell home serves as a powerful metaphor for the failure of a patriarchal society to acknowledge the special skills and qualities of the women it oppresses. As Elaine Showalter has written in her essay "Piecing and Writing," "The Bedquilt" is indeed a story that reverberates with larger implications. For Showalter, it is no less than "a parable of the woman writer, and her creative fantasies." More recently, Cecilia Macheski, in her anthology *Quilt Stories,* has called the tale "triumphant."[2]

Like "The Bedquilt," "Flint and Fire" and "The Heyday of the Blood" were published in Fisher's first volume of stories, *Hillsboro People.* Of that book, Fisher wrote to her publisher Henry Holt, "Every one of those stories looks to me like everything I write (when I'm serious) a desperate attempt to get at and report what is inside of people's hearts."[3] Fisher's "people" in this case are the country folk with whom she had grown intimately acquainted after many years of living in Vermont. What is "in their hearts" is usually difficult to discern. In "Flint and Fire," for instance, we find that beneath the stoic exterior of 'Niram Purdon lies a depth of feeling. Likewise, Gran'ther Pendleton in "The Heyday of the Blood" possesses an inner strength that defies all outward indications. In the tradition of Harriet Beecher Stowe and Mary E. Wilkins Freeman, Fisher showcases her command of New England dialect in each story. Yet, like the best work of those writers and the well-wrought Maine tales of Sarah Orne Jewett, Fisher's Vermont stories transcend the relatively narrow interests of regionalism or "local color."

"Through Pity and Terror . . ." (originally published as "La Pharmacienne") takes the reader far from the village of Hillsboro. The story, like all those in *Home Fires in France,* is based upon the author's firsthand experience of World War I. In August 1916 Fisher traveled with her two children across the Atlantic to join her husband, who had volunteered for the American Ambulance Corps in France. By the time

2. Elaine Showalter, "Piecing and Writing," 241; Cecilia Macheski, ed., *Quilt Stories,* 7.
3. Mark J. Madigan, ed., *Keeping Fires Night and Day: Selected Letters of Dorothy Canfield Fisher,* 43.

Fisher returned to Vermont in April 1919, she had founded a hospital for refugee children and a Braille press for blinded soldiers, among other charitable works. *Home Fires in France* was by any measure a successful book. As Alan Price notes in his study of Fisher's and Edith Wharton's war publications, the collection sold thirty thousand copies and went through six printings in six months.[4] Dedicated to General John Pershing, commander of the American Expeditionary Force in France and Fisher's one-time mathematics teacher, *Home Fires in France* contained the following "Publisher's Note": "This book is fiction written in France out of a lifelong familiarity with the French and two years' intense experience in war work in France. It is a true setting-forth of personalities and experiences, French and American, under the influence of war."

While Ernest Hemingway found occasion—however unfairly—to call the war writing of Fisher's longtime friend Willa Cather "plagiarized," Fisher brought to her own stories a genuine understanding of the French people, whose country was being ravaged by the war.[5] As able-bodied men left for the front, those who held together the French families behind the lines were women. Fisher's narratives are especially valuable for their presentation of the war from this point of view. About the valiant female protagonist of "Through Pity and Terror . . . ," Fisher wrote to her literary agent, Paul Reynolds:

> To my mind the study has value because nobody has said a word about the *processes* by which all this unexpected heroism has been evolved out of the French people. There has been a great deal of exclaiming and admiring, but I have a notion that most Americans don't *realize* by what hard and bitter and horrible phases the Frenchwomen have had to pass before they emerged from being just nice home-keepers into being guardians of the public weal, as they are to so great an extent in the deserted villages and towns. And I don't think American women realize at all how many of the little

4. Alan Price, "Writing Home from the Front: Edith Wharton and Dorothy Canfield Fisher Present Wartime France to the United States," 4.

5. Edmund Wilson, *The Shores of Light: A Literary Chronicle of the Twenties and Thirties,* 118.

> prettinesses of life the French women have had to leave behind, and leave behind forever—I don't think ever ever they can be so foolishly important as before.[6]

Fisher's involvement in the First World War made an indelible impression upon her and the subject was one that stimulated her imagination for many years after. In fact, her most fully developed consideration of the war did not appear until 1930, in her novel *The Deepening Stream.*

In addition to the inhumanity of war, Fisher sought to expose the effects of racism in her short fiction. At a time when Ku Klux Klan membership and lynchings were at their peak, the author's stories portrayed African Americans in a positive light. Fisher's family had been involved in the fight against racial prejudice for generations. Her great-grandmother tolled the bell of her church all day long upon word of John Brown's execution; her grandfather was with Henry Ward Beecher when he sailed for England in an attempt to sway the British in favor of the abolitionists; and her father subjected himself to public criticism when, as president of Ohio State University, he invited Booker T. Washington (the subject of "The Washed Window") to lunch at their home. Fisher later wrote to James Thurber that the luncheon was "the final affront to Ohio standards which set the pack on him so fiercely that he couldn't stay."[7] Fisher partook in the struggle as well, serving as a trustee of Howard University from 1945 to 1951 and using her position as a BOMC judge to promote the careers of African American writers such as Richard Wright.

"An American Citizen" predates by one year Fisher's treatment of racism in *The Brimming Cup.* In one of the novel's subplots, a retired business executive abandons his comfortable life in Vermont to fight against racial injustice in the South. To W. E. B. Du Bois, Fisher wrote about her reasons for presenting the first critique of racism in a modern best-seller:

> . . . I wish never to lose a chance to remind Americans of what their relations to the Negro race are, and might be, and so into this story

6. Ida H. Washington, *Dorothy Canfield Fisher: A Biography,* 159.
7. Madigan, *Keeping Fires,* 300.

> of Northern life and white people, I have managed to weave a strand of remembrance of the dark question. It is a sort of indirect, side-approach, a backing-up of your campaign from someone not vitally concerned in it personally, except as every American must be, which I hope may be of use exactly because it is not a straight-on attack, but one of a slightly different manner.[8]

If *The Brimming Cup* is more of an "indirect, side-approach" than a "straight-on attack," "An American Citizen" is closer to the latter—despite passages of stilted dialogue and, ironically, some stereotypical assumptions about African Americans. (For example, note the black protagonist's innate ability to "interest children" and his "racial easy-going good-humor.") Here, Fisher tells the story of Heywood Jefferson, whose fine character can blossom only when he is outside the United States. Through alcohol he attempts to escape the pain of being black in America, where he is as "caged" as he is in the hotel elevator he operates. In a remarkable passage early in the story, Fisher presents Jefferson's alternating feelings of rage and despair in his own voice. In response to a question about his apparent lack of ambition, he says: "Well, what would I do with my money? . . . What good would it do me? I'd be a Negro just the same, wouldn't I? I'd be punished and spit on, all the time, for being something I never asked or wanted to be, and that I'd stop being if I could."

Fisher later contrasts the hypocrisy of racism with the Declaration of Independence and confronts her Caucasian readers with the question, "Would you just as soon be a Negro as white?" Finally, she denies the white reader an opportunity to feel vindicated by the conclusion of "An American Citizen." In an ironic twist, it is Jefferson who liberates a white man from enslavement, undertaking an heroic action that whites would not risk for him. The story's title, then, refers to the African American and the democratic principles he lives by. In France, Jefferson is judged based on his intelligence and admirable behavior, while the U.S. constitutes the "depths" from which he has risen.

8. Ibid., 95.

The French setting of "An American Citizen" also is used in "Gold from Argentina" and "The Saint of the Old Seminary." Both were published in *Basque People,* a collection of eight stories drawn from the author's experience of living in the southwest corner of France during World War I. After her daughter, Sally, contracted typhoid fever in Paris, Fisher moved her children to the Basque town of Guethary to take advantage of its warmer climate. It was during this period of convalescence that the author grew to love the Basques, who, as biographer Ida H. Washington has stated, "reminded her of the independent Vermonters at home." Washington has observed that the characters of *Basque People* have much in common with the Vermonters of *Hillsboro People:* "The Basques, like the Vermonters, are pictured as defensive of their simple way of life and opposed to more sophisticated urban patterns. . . . The strong presence of the past, the independence, the material poverty, and the distrust of outsiders are reminiscent of Vermont traditions."[9]

Despite her deep affection for the Basques, Fisher's portrayal is not uncritical. The special appeal of "Gold from Argentina," for example, lies in its satirical presentation of the Basque villagers whose estimation of the Yturbe and Haratz families fluctuates according to their perceived monetary wealth. The story demonstrates with a wry sense of humor that greed knows no ethnic boundaries. In "The Saint of the Old Seminary," Fisher's readers are faced with a narrative situation similar in its ambiguity to that which confronts the citizens of Mendigaraya in the previous tale. Reading this story, one must judge the character of Tomasina against a background of conflicting evidence. Is the young woman a true martyr or a self-serving actress? When queried about the ending, Fisher refused to clarify the matter. To author Albert L. Guerard, she explained: "You should just see the number of letters that have come in from readers about that story . . . asking me about that same double interpretation. '*Which* one is the *real* one?' such letters ask. And my answer always is 'What do you mean, "real"?' "[10]

9. Washington, *Dorothy Canfield Fisher,* 89, 163–64.
10. Madigan, *Keeping Fires,* 317.

"Memorial Day" and "The Knot-hole" extend Fisher's meditation on war begun in *Home Fires in France.* The antiwar message of the former foreshadows the greatest tragedy of Fisher's life. Although the story bears the date "May 30, 1913" beneath its title, it was actually written not long before the advent of the Second World War, during which the author's son, Jimmy, was killed while serving as a medical doctor in the Philippines. The author's linkage of economic class issues and military service is particularly astute. Also notable is the story's conclusion, in which the buried soldiers, and presumably their admonitions, are forgotten, if ever heard.

In "The Knot-hole," Fisher's abhorrence of war and love of the French are made palpable through the suffering and courage of a group of POWs locked in a boxcar. She once wrote that it was "more like a groan of anguish than a story." The ending is a mix of foreboding and hopeful signs, as the protagonist Bergeron's voice is heard over the rumbling of the train headed back to Germany. The tale won second prize among the O. Henry Memorial Award stories of 1944, and in the introduction to that volume Carl Van Doren wrote, "It has great power in an honest, downright way, and I was much moved by it."[11]

"Sex Education," like "The Knot-hole," was an O. Henry Memorial Award Prize story, and one that editor Herschel Brickell cited as among his "special favorites" in the volume for 1946.[12] Its complex narrative structure makes it as much a story about storytelling as it is about sex, education, and sex education. Through the three versions of Aunt Minnie's tale, Fisher illustrates how stories evolve according to the demands of audience and purpose. While the ending casts the most important details of Minnie's youthful encounter with the minister in the cornfield into doubt, Fisher's message about sex education is clear: It is only when young people are given objective information—not threatening stories—that they will be able to make wise decisions.

The author's belief that environment and individual effort, rather than heredity, are the crucial elements in the formation of character is

11. Ibid., 239–40; Herschel Brickell, ed., *The O. Henry Memorial Award Prize Stories of 1944,* xii.

12. Herschel Brickell, ed., *The O. Henry Memorial Award Prize Stories of 1946,* xii.

emphasized in "The Washed Window." While it is a well-drawn and clever sketch intended to honor Booker T. Washington, what some readers may still find troubling is its glorification of manual labor and not intellectual capacity as the key to the young African American's success. It is important to remember, however, that Fisher befriended both leaders in the great turn-of-the-century debate over African American education, supporting Du Bois's efforts in favor of university schooling as well as Washington's push for vocational training.

Finally, in "How 'Flint and Fire' Started and Grew" the author reconstructs the genesis of her story in much the same manner as Poe's "Philosophy of Composition." Since she did not wish to imply that the artistic process could be reduced to a formula, Fisher was reluctant to write the piece but relented at her publisher's insistence. The essay provides a behind-the-scenes view of her creative methods. The dissatisfaction she expresses with the results of her literary efforts is typical. Throughout her career, Fisher was a harsh critic of her work and felt that her writing was indeed a "desperate attempt" to convey her ideas. Yet, just as the elderly protagonist of "The Heyday of the Blood" embraces life lived to its fullest—"Live while you live, and then be done with it!" he states succinctly—so, too, did Fisher approach her writing. The relative success or failure of her work was never so important as the challenge of the creative process itself, as the struggle to convey insight to others.

By the mid-1940s, Fisher had written her last novel and all but a handful of her short stories. In a letter of that period, she expressed her passion for the endeavor of creative writing:

> Articles and statements can be produced by the single effort of will, purpose, concentration.
>
> But fiction—that's more like falling in love, which can't be done by will-power or purpose, but concerns the *whole* personality, which includes the vast areas of the unconscious and sub-conscious, as well as those processes within the control of purposefulness. This element of the unknown puts into the writing of fiction an element of the uncontrollable. And fiction written *without* the whole person-

> ality is not fiction (that is, re-created human life, interpreted) but only articles or statements in narrative *form.*[13]

Likewise, in his essay "On Writing," Raymond Carver has suggested that "a writer who has some special way of looking at things and who gives artistic expression to that way of looking: that writer may be around for a time."[14] The same may be affirmed of Dorothy Canfield Fisher. Gifted with an ability to distinguish the enduring from the merely topical, she left a body of work, much of it written over a half-century ago, that is often startling in its contemporaneity. Whether writing about love, war, greed, race relations, women's rights, or the quilt of an aging country woman, Fisher brought to her short fiction a deep understanding of human beings and the world we inhabit. Above all else, these stories bear the imprint of her "special way of looking at things," a way of interpreting life as she knew it—with "her whole personality."

13. Madigan, *Keeping Fires,* 240.
14. Raymond Carver, *Fires,* 13.

Prologue

What My Mother Taught Me

When I was asked by my publishers to collect a bookful of stories from among the many I have written, I did not at once realize that even to begin this task—to justify selecting one, discarding another—would call for a long look into the years back of me. But it soon became clear that an author of fiction cannot reread page after printed page, written during half a century or more, without being forced into serious reflection on the past. By no means only a narrow, individual past. Even more on the timeless elements which always have been, are now, and always will be the reasons why anybody tells stories.

The earliest in date of the tales in this volume, "The Bedquilt," for instance, or "The Heyday of the Blood," were published more than fifty years ago. The latest, "The Washed Window," was written only last October. What has made an adult citizen, who was free to do any of a great many other things, keep up so long the baffling struggle with her own limitations in the effort to get stories told? For that, I meditated, there must have been some deeply rooted driving impulse, and not only a root-impulse, but food to nourish it in the places, persons, happenings of the outer world.

What was—what is—this impulse? It is to try with all one's might to understand that part of human life which does not lie visibly on the surface. And then to try to depict the people involved, and their actions, so that they may be recognizable men, women—and children.

To attempt this means to have one's primary interest concentrated on, and absorbed by, human beings and their doings. But why that one special concentration? Why not science, or music, or mathematics, philosophy, or any one of the myriad other aspects of existence in our cosmos?

Pondering this question as it affected my own case, "Better disregard internal motivation," I thought. "Nobody really knows anything about that. It can't be proved, one way or another. As for external influences, no doubt many of them were combined. Usually that's what happens. But I wonder if I cannot put my finger on one of them stronger than the others. . . ."

Of course I could. The moment I had formulated that question I knew the answer. I knew whose influence it was. My mother's! Let me tell you something about her.

She was a Vermonter of undiluted blood stream, was Flavia Camp Canfield; yet all her long life she set herself in word and deed against most of what was implicit in her inheritance. A few rebels and plenty of deviationists, of course, are to be expected in any society—especially in one like ours in Vermont, where fierce individualism rejects enforcement of a rigid party line for tribal customs. Still here, as elsewhere, there are preponderant tendencies—nine-times-out-of-ten accepted rules of thought and action.

These were anathema to my mother!

For example, though Vermonters may backslide, most of us never doubt the value of regularity and stability as essential cogwheels in the clockwork of daily life. Many a time my mother has told me how every Sunday, her grandfather, Deacon Barney of the Rutland Congregational Church, drove with his family from his farm, put his team in the church shed, sat in his pew through the service—and never missed once in half a century. If you only knew what weather an occasional Vermont Sunday can produce in January or February—! But you can guess again if you think she told that story with pride in her grandfather's remarkable resolution, stamina, and loyal adherence to a cherished faith. On the contrary, all she saw in it was a hidebound devotion to routine for the sake of routine. She herself preferred to miss trains rather than to put herself out to be punctual to the hour or the minute, or, indeed, to the day. For she detested the frozen rigidity (as it seemed to her) of set plans.

Our valley lies on a reasonably straight line between Montreal and New York. This fortunate situation brought it for many years a single-track railroad and two trains a day, one south, one north—both called "Flyers" with the poker-faced irony of our regional talk. As the distance is about equal in both directions, the schedule often called for them to meet and pass at Arlington. One morning, many years ago, my mother decided that she would go to New York to buy some artist's materials she needed (she was a painter), which could not be found in Vermont. I'll say they could not! They can now. So she asked a neighbor who was going to drive to the village to take her as far as the railway station. That day the train for New York was late, and the north-bound express was the first to come along. The next afternoon we had a postcard from her in Montreal, delighted to be doing her shopping 500 miles away from where she had planned to go when she left us.

Living all her life—well, for as much of her life as she could not avoid them—with people who made plans and carried them out, my mother developed an almost miraculous skill, eel-like and sinuous, for avoiding limiting certainties. At the start of a journey she was never willing to say when she would come back. She invoked reasonableness to explain this unwillingness—how could she tell beforehand? When she went away, as she constantly did (my father's half-rueful, half-amused phrase was that she had never found a place on the globe that seemed to her fit to live in for more than a fortnight), she always called back to us the same farewell phrase. Leaning out of the train window, or waving from the deck of a departing ship, "Expect me when you see me!" shouted my smiling mother, elated to be leaving her family tiresomely rooted in a tradition of stability.

It did not dim her elation that this uncertainty was sand in the house-machinery of those left behind. The door must always be left unbolted so that she could get in if she happened to take a notion to come home on a midnight train; a bedroom must be kept empty and ready to receive her; someone must always stay within sound of the telephone bell in case she should call up and ask to be met at Pittsfield, Massachusetts, where some oddity of her fancy and her disdain of railway timetables had landed her. Such precautions for the care of an absent member are minimum requirements in any traditional family code. Her family, like most others, cherished that code. But she did not. She would have died of ennui if she had been the one to stay at home and make such provisions for someone else. Or, rather, more accurately, it would have been inconceivable to her that she should be expected to make sacrifices to keep regular machinery running, when she disapproved of machinery as a part of pulsingly irregular human life.

No, do not jump to conclusions. These first strokes of a portrait-sketch of my mother's way of life do not mean what, probably, you take them for—a one-sided negative. She did not say a frowning "No" to aspects of human existence she did not wish to admit as valid. Rather she ignored them, did not see that they were there. She turned a glowing, ardent welcome to what she was willing to recognize.

She was a dedicated lover of art. As unswervingly as her deacon grandfather, she cherished a faith. The core of hers was an absolute certainty in the infallible, unique perfection of the Greeks in their great period. This was a theoretic creed. Born in 1844, before modern archaeology had more than scratched the surface of Hellenic civilization, and never crossing the Atlantic until after she was grown up and married, her devotion rested on decidedly unstable foundations. No matter! Dogmas need no material proof. This was her dogma. But her worship of the Greeks in no way blinded her to the achievements of their successors. Any art of the first rank was sacred to her. The best in fiction, in music, above all, in the art she herself tried to practice—painting—those were to her the true realities of life.

She never confused the pursuit of art with sipping absinthe in a bohemian café, or with the impermanent love affairs of the Left Bank. (At the remote date of which I write, Montmartre hadn't been discovered.) It was a new art-experience which gave her the gloriously pulsing emotion which for most people is associated with falling in love.

Falling in love was one of the things my mother had not much use for. Since that experience has nothing to do with the enjoyment of the first-rate best in art, it had no special interest for her. When there was talk of it (there often is talk of it, you may have noticed), my mother's delicately modeled face took on a rather grim, aloof look. People who did not know her intimately thought her expression was "the Puritan look." This idea caused considerable mirth among those who did know her. Nobody could have been further away from Puritanism. Her excitements—she had plenty of them—came in other ways.

Here is a report on one such typical excitement of hers. As it turned out, it was one of mine too. Many of hers did so turn out. We were in Paris that winter. My mother, as usual, was studying and painting in one of the well-known studios, Carlorossi's, it was, I remember. I was regularly enrolled as a student, attending lectures at the Sorbonne, and the École des Hautes Études. I had naïvely thought we were settled for some months. I was, you see, barely twenty, and still uninstructed by experience.

All at once the name of Velásquez roared through the Paris ateliers like a hurricane on the Florida coast. Of course he had been known and admired by an inner circle ever since he had been "discovered" by the Romantic School, in the early nineteenth century. But at this time his fame became a craze. Such crazes have always been frequent in that world. You must have seen many come and go just as this one did.

The word went around, excitedly (part of the creed of that world was that to be really alive, to be excited was essential)—"The greatest master of all time!" "Oh, yes, yes—of course, there *are* samples in the Louvre. The little Infanta in the Salle Carrée." "But you can't begin to guess his power until you see his work in Spain."

So my mother and I went to Madrid.

Everyone with a grain of common sense tried to head us off. They pointed out loudly that Spain and Russia alone in Europe were so backward that they still insisted on passports for foreign visitors. In those long-ago, politically tranquil days, none of us had ever seen a passport. My mother said easily, "Oh well, we'll get passports."

"But the language! Nobody speaks anything but Spanish."

"Dolly will soon learn Spanish. She always picks up new languages," said my mother. She herself was detached from the stupid, wasteful Tower-of-Babel multiplicity of languages, never bothered to learn a word of anything but her native Vermontese.

The French members of our circle who had friends or relatives forced by business to go to Spain, cried out that the sanitary arrangements south of the Pyrenees were of a filthiness beyond imagination. Everybody who went there, they said, fell desperately ill with prodigious intestinal troubles (yes, then, half a century ago, just as now, only more so!). To this warning, my mother did not respond, because she was already throwing her artist's materials into a suitcase—we called them valises or satchels in those days.

You wouldn't believe me if I told you all the details of that endless, rumbling, jolting trip from Paris to Madrid—the old-fashioned railway compartments (we always traveled third class not to waste money on non-essentials) had no toilet arrangements of any kind. Such needs were to be taken care of in the stinking, foul outhouses at the railway stations. No food, save what could be snatched from unwashed hands and counters during stops of the train. No water save what was sold by old women carrying bloated goatskins, walking up and down the platforms, screaming, "Quien quiere agua-a-a?" in a shrill refrain which rang in my ears for—well, it still does at times. No heat. On the dirty wooden floor of our compartment lay flat tin containers filled with water. Cold water. Looking back now after later experiences with Spain, I imagine that if we and our fellow-passengers had bribed the conductors, the water might have been—at intervals—hot. But those suffering travelers were too poor and too unsophisticated to think of that. And the season of the year of our hastily-decided trip was still so early that the cold was penetrating. I can close my eyes and see the bleak, snow-covered Pyrenees as we saw them by starlight from the windows of the stone-cold train.

By the time we had inched our endless way to Madrid, my mother was ill. Very. The people at the hotel looked at her, groaning, racked with pain, ashy-faced, bowed together weakly as she hung on my arm. Evidently they thought she was likely to die, and felt a superstitious fear against letting her into the house. But we pushed our way in and upstairs, behind a reluctant chambermaid, to a tile-floored room, as cold as the train we had left.

There was a fireplace in it. It was a black, empty, yawning, dust-filled cavity. But a fireplace. I hurried my mother into bed with a hot brick or two beside her. My considerable acquaintance with unheated European hotels had made me hope there would be soapstones or bricks on the back of the cookstove in the big kitchen, and I ran down and snatched them.

Then I began to argue with the hotel people about firewood. Nobody at the hotel spoke a word of French or English, it being a meager little inn, all that we could afford. But, as my mother predicted, I did learn Spanish, with as scared a speed as a chased cat climbs a tree. One of the first sentences I understood was that there was no firewood. I pointed out to the proprietors that if a fireplace had been built there must have been something to burn in it. No, the season had gone by for heat in bedrooms. Winter was over—or would be soon. No firewood in the fuel-merchants' shops. But how about sick people, new babies, very old people, I insisted, in what rags and scraps of Spanish I had, raising my voice belligerently to match their attempt to drown me out by vociferations. Finally to get rid of me, they admitted that sometimes one could buy a sack of dug-up dried tree roots, said to be combustible. Leaving my poor mother huddled in bed, looking and feeling deathly sick, I raced away to find a merchant who would sell tree roots.

One of the dangers which kind French friends had tried to impress upon my mother was that Spain was still medieval in its ideas about women. Any personable young female taken there, they explained, *must* be carefully protected, *must not* go out alone on the streets, "because, Mrs. Canfield, it is simply not *safe* for a respectable girl to leave the house by herself."

Having for years scurried along Paris streets without a companion, I had already discovered that pleasure-seeking men are repelled (as a dog by a pail of cold water) by a swift ejaculation of obviously sincere exasperation, the equivalent of "Oh! For goodness' sakes! I've got something else on my mind! Go along and find someone else." Hastily learning enough Spanish phrases for an approximation of these sentiments, I rushed here and there, up and down all kinds of Madrid streets and alleyways, by day and night; to the pharmacist's; to the doctor's; to the fuel merchant's; to the markets, trying to find something that could be made fit for an invalid to eat; to the householdware shops hunting for utensils in which I could cook that food over an open fire. It turned out, as I expected, that my mother had been accurate in her estimate of the perils of the late nineteenth-century equivalent of wolf-calls. I had some disagreeable but no alarming experiences, in my headlong, hurried errands.

With what doctoring could be found for her, with what nursing could be improvised, with a fire in her bedroom, with a diet she could digest, my mother slowly got better. As a matter of record, she lived for thirty-five years after this, to the venerable age of eighty-five. The instant she could stand on her feet, she had me take her to the Prado.

All this happened when I was just past twenty. I have now passed my seventy-seventh birthday. It must have been fifty-six years ago, and that was long before sight-seers had begun to swarm into Spain. It was also so early in the year that Baedeker warned tourists away, and sensible Spaniards were staying at home or hugging sunny street corners. If there were any other sight-seers, they were lost in the interstellar spaces of the Prado. My memory of that vast museum, on our first visit, and on all the other days we spent there, is of empty, long, and cold, cold, cold galleries. Each room had a *brasero* of burning charcoal as its sole means of heat. Over each *brasero* hovered an elderly uniformed guardian, fanning the red coals feebly with a turkey wing. His frozen old body was evil-smelling because nobody in his senses would take a bath in that weather, and because his unwashed person was wrapped, many layers deep, in equally unwashed woolens.

I don't suppose my mother with her unrivaled ability to ignore whatever seemed unessential to her saw or smelled any of that.

She saw Velásquez.

White-faced, her legs trembling under her with weakness and cold, her Victorian false front pinned crookedly on her head (before we had come out I had tried to straighten it in the hotel bedroom but she had waved me aside), she tottered into the Prado, hanging all her weight on my arm—the arm that was not carrying the campstool for her. When she could stagger no further, she sank down on the stool and gazed up. That first halt happened to be before the great canvas called "Las Meniñas."

How long did she gaze, ecstatic as a saint in prayer, enraptured as Adam and Eve when "Lo, Creation widened on man's view"? Hanging by her hands to the guardrail to keep from falling from her seat, she forgot for a while to breathe—then drew a deep lungful of air on a quivering a-a-ah, and forgot to breathe again. All her life was in her eyes, feasting on the luminous atmosphere which filled that seventeenth-century room, peopled by those exquisitely painted court figures.

When she came to the surface enough to move, it was to the antithesis of the Spanish court that she went, to the magnificent, Rembrandt-like "Aesop." Perhaps in the end this was her favorite canvas. There she sat, gazing into those rich browns, making little swimming motions with her arms as though drowning in pleasure. In front of the particularly luscious flesh, miraculously painted, of a young woman's back and shoulders—in "The Weavers," I think it was—she wiped tears of joy from her eyes. In front of the cheerful, vulgar, life-enjoying materialism of "Los Borrachos," she laughed out loud in sympathy. To the "Christ on the Cross" she gave but one fleeting glance. A too-zealously pious clergyman stepfather had set her, as a girl, against religious people, and to his memory she dedicated a lifelong anticlericalism. (Could this have been one reason for her feeling about Greek art?)

But she almost cried out, did fling up one arm as if to ward off the overpowering impression of artistic power, when she lifted her eyes to the two mighty equestrian portraits of Oliveres and Philip IV.

As you can see, I too remember those masterpieces, because by that time I had been following my mother's flickering course from one picture gallery to another for so many years that I had absorbed something of her burning conviction that masterpieces of great art are important beyond anything else in the world—beyond taking reasonable care of one's health in order not to be a burden; beyond, far, far beyond comfort—one's own or one's family's; beyond regret at seeing the disagreeable consequences of one's own actions weighing on other people. My mother's eyes were shocked wide open at that moment of her first contact with masterpieces new to her. Mine were, too. I too gazed, my heart shaken. Now after half a century I can still see, so deep was the impression made on me, the golden reflection of that splendor of art which I encountered in the course of living with my mother.

Of course my mother had to stay on in Madrid—no matter what the reasons were for going back to Paris. Among these reasons was my winter's work at the Sorbonne. She could not leave until she had made copies of some of the pictures she especially adored. For her excellent way of penetrating herself to the last fiber by a picture she loved was to make a careful, detailed copy of it, just as painters of the great centuries often did. A fine Velásquez copy of a Titian was one of the canvases in the Prado.

Did you ever, I wonder, carry through from beginning to end the complex undertaking of getting permission from a European Museum of Art for a foreigner to make copies? If not—and why should you have been forced to struggle through those labyrinths?—there's no use trying to tell you where the trail led which I followed in Madrid, pantingly learning more Spanish with every step, from one bureaucrat's office to another, in and out of the Prado. In fact I couldn't tell you if I wanted to, because all the times, all the cities, all the museums connected with that often-repeated process have rather run together into a blur in my memory. From the Prado struggle with entrenched red tape, the only detail I recall was that at one point I found myself improvising the birthday dates of my mother's parents. The museum and government authorities would not put their seal on the permission for her to copy, unless every line of every questionnaire was completely filled in. She herself had no idea of her parents' birthdays. "Oh, gracious, child, tell them anything that comes into your head," she said carelessly.

So we stayed on in Madrid for a long time. My mother fell ill occasionally. She was often ill all through her life, as why wouldn't she be? But after nursing and special food, she recovered from each attack and returned to her copyist's easel. Every day I was needed to carry back to the hotel that part of the paraphernalia of painting which copyists were not allowed to leave at the museum. And naturally the duration of each day's work was unpredictable, depending as it did on the ups and downs of my mother's health. A good deal of waiting around was part of my daily routine.

Some of those waiting hours I conscientiously spent in book study—Spanish, philology, the history of French and Italian literature, subjects on which I was supposed to be working at the Sorbonne. More of those marking-time weeks were wasted, as was natural to my age, dawdling, fidgeting or yawning vacantly. But since those pictures hung there before my eyes, I did look at them as no casual visitor to a gallery ever has time to look. One day I found myself noting broad lines of composition; on another my attention chanced to be fixed on detail; sometimes I could not see beyond the marvel of color. Once in a while, just because the clock seemed to stand still, and there was no reason for moving on, I stood before a picture until I sank deep into that rare, trancelike, timeless gaze, which penetrates by divination to the inner meaning which, perhaps, in spite of the theories of the professional technicians, is the core of every great artist's intention.

It was with this mesmerized gaze that I looked long at one of the Velásquez court dwarfs. There are several of these strange figures in the Prado. From one of them, a lack-witted, simpering moron, I turned away with a shudder. But another—was he called Sebastian de Morra?—that name sticks in my mind when I remember him—was not young. Above his dwarfed body, there looked out a full-grown man's face, terrible in its quiet sadness. I could not pass along that wall without stopping to meet his darkly shadowed eyes. It was as if he had a wordless message for me, a compelling one. In the end even the hard, adolescent crust over my shallow, undeveloped young heart was pierced with an involuntary, persistent compassion for human ills, which has been for me, as for everybody who admits that skeleton into his inner closet, a disquieting cause for heavy-heartedness.

Of course the superbly painted, horrible detail in Brueghel's "Triumph of Death" caught, shocked, and held my young eyes as sensational, materialistic horrors always do fix the attention of inexperience and ignorance. Many years went by before I saw the much more there is in Brueghel, but even then to look from corpses and hell-fires and gloating devils, up into the patient, steadfast understanding in the shadowed wise eyes of the ugly old Aesop—that gave the inexperienced girl a hint of what serene maturity might bring.

Weeks slipped by. I came and went in the Prado. I passed the time of day with the bored, elderly, underpaid guardians, rubbing their chilblained feet in their patched shoes. I explored the basement. It was tomblike, colder even than the upper floors. My mother never went down those stairs because only etchings, engravings, drawings—all black-and-whites—were in the glass showcases. She burned all her incense before color. I loitered long over the Goya drawings. It was there, I remember, that I saw for the first time the skeleton, his winding-sheet trailing from his frantic bones, struggling out of his tomb, propping up with one fleshless arm the lid of the coffin so that he could scrawl on it "Nada"—"Nothing."

But that black negation faded to less than a shadow in the life-giving warmth which streamed from the "Surrender of Breda" upstairs in the long gallery. Upstairs in the long gallery? In my memory forever, there, in front of a forest of slim lances, the conquering general with a sublimely gentle gesture of respect for human dignity accepts the sword from his defeated opponent.

After a while we moved back to Paris.

One more brush-stroke on this portrait of my Vermont-anti-Vermont mother, whose attitude towards life really—although at the time this was not obvious—was all the while pointing out for me a road I could follow with wholehearted acceptance, leading me on into the country where my nature could most deeply live.

Many years had passed since the trip to Madrid. During them the direction of my life—apparently through no volition of mine—had totally changed. I had turned away to the writer's world from the scholar's world where I had been contentedly working. This abrupt transfer had taken place so wholeheartedly that I had not tried to understand why it caused neither hesitation nor regret. The subjects, the plots of the many novels and stories I had written, seemed to be chosen by accident. I had not bothered my head to consider whether there might be some general underlying principle which made one kind of plot seem valueless to me, while I grudged no amount of hard, long-continued labor to the development of another.

Also by this time I had married, had children, and with my husband set up a home wherever we went. My mother, now nearly eighty, greatly disliked the routine drudgery of managing domestic arrangements. She equally disliked hotel life. Since my father's death she had divided her time, as the whim took her, between my brother's home and mine. Thus I was not at all surprised when I found myself in mid-December boarding a north-bound train for Rotterdam to meet the ship on which she had come from New York to spend the rest of the winter with us in Paris.

It goes without saying that my brother and his wife in New York had tried their conscientious best to persuade her not to take that trip at all. After a good many arguments, they had recognized the meaning of her mouth's set lines, and shifted their ground: "Not in midwinter, anyway," they pleaded. "Why not wait until good weather in spring?" Her face did not soften.

"Well, at least not alone. Plenty of women, young or old, would jump at the chance of earning a free passage to Europe in return for acting as companion—little personal services, you know, reading aloud, finding mislaid shawls, eyeglasses . . ." their baffled voices trailed off before her silence. My mother had recognized perfectly the real intention her children always had, she thought—not as we claimed, to make her life more comfortable and safe, but to make her less of a bother to others. She appeared to be turning their suggestion over in her mind. Finally she said, using the patient intonation of a mature, reasonable adult, trying to make ignorant children aware of the nature of things, "But that's out of the question. You see—I hate her already! How could I live with her?"

So she came alone. So I traveled from Paris to her port of debarkation, making the trip as quick a one as possible not to interrupt Christmas doings for my home and family. Someone was needed to get her through the customs and on the right train. There are, you may remember, a good many noble masterpieces in the Dutch art museums!—hence Dutch is one of the languages with which I have some enforced acquaintance.

As I waited for the fine, Holland-American liner to dock, I looked around at the clean, warmed, well-ordered customs office and thought of another time when I had helped my mother to get safely on land from a ship. That was in Naples, the wild, old pre-Mussolini days, when trains did not run on time and Naples was Naples. What ferocious screams from the dirty pirate-porters, profiting by the venality of the customs officials to snatch, overcharge, frighten. How helplessly and shamefully—to resist their bullying—I had let myself be dragged down to their level. How I had lost my self-respect, had screamed, shaken my fist, snatched back valises from their clutches, spat out threats. I felt sick at the memory of the foul, unswept paving stones from which all those trampling feet sent up a cloud of pulverized horse manure and ever-renewed rotten refuse. The insane bedlam of noise! The lice crawling visibly on those thick necks caked with sweat and dirt! The garbage smell of everything!

Now the Holland-American liner was there, warped quietly into its place. The gangplank was pushed out, making contact between dock and ship in one accurate gesture. A stream of clean, silent stewards filed down, carrying valises and suitcases. The passengers appeared.

There was my mother, stooped, tiny, looking so infirm in her old-lady blacks that a strong steward had been told off for her to lean on. Suiting his step with gentle kindness to her slow, uncertain progress, the big Hollander brought her to me, transferred her familiar weight to my arm (but I had the folding campstool ready for her to sit on) and took his departure. I noticed that my mother did not tip or thank him, but looked the other way. I recognized the signs. Something had evidently gone wrong on that crossing.

But when I asked her, "Yes, yes," she told me absently, the trip had been all right. It had been long enough for her to reread, yet once more, every word of *Portrait of a Lady.* She enjoyed, in books, what she loved in pictures—the best. Never, in all her life, did she read five minutes' worth of poor-quality writing. That was a golden part of what I inherited from her example.

But her old face, which the years had worn almost to translucence like a winter leaf, had a severe look.

I inquired farther, "Was the trip stormy?"

"Yes, rather," she replied casually. "To be expected on a midwinter crossing." But she was never bothered by storms, she reminded me. Enjoying intensity as she did, she liked their ferocity. Another joy—an epic one—which was part of what I learned from her.

What could be, I wondered, the reason for her cold look of disapproval. It continued during all the process of my seeing to the examination of her steamer trunk. She sat on her campstool gazing back at the ship and its personnel still treading up and down the gangplank, carrying baggage in unhurried, well-disciplined order.

I knew the reason as soon as we were outside in the comfortable cab, on our way to the station. As its door closed smoothly behind us, she broke out heatedly, "Of all the dreary, cold, inexpressive, cheerless people—! I hope I never have to see one of the race again as long as I live! They are like men walking in their sleep. Rembrandt *couldn't* have been a Dutchman! I don't believe it!"

The scene at Naples had so freshly hung before my memory that—it was, you see, some time since I had stepped into my mother's aura—I remarked, "Why, I was just thinking how deliciously peaceable and decent this debarkation has been, compared to the time at Naples."

My mother turned to me in amazement. "How *can* you compare that—that wonderful flood of light, that wild, free animation, that life, life, life—with these glum, congealed, *worthy* people! I'd a thousand times rather have my purse stolen by a smiling, dirty, charming pickpocket than have money put into it by a priggishly honest close-mouthed Hollander—or Swiss—or Vermonter!"

I said no more. The time had long passed—of course I mean it had never been—for discussion with my mother along lines on which our minds could really meet.

We looked out of the windows at the well-swept streets of Rotterdam, and very soon the smooth motion of the solidly constructed Dutch cab sent her off into the light, dozing sleep of old age.

The trip from the Rotterdam dock to the railway station is not long but in it I had time for considerable reflection about the bases of human life.

No, don't think that a cab in motion is an odd place for a grave, deep, inner effort to understand. The technique for thus using quiet intervals of any kind no matter how short is one of the skills acquired, out of necessity, by any woman trying to turn a house into a home. The sands of the sea are not more multifarious than the hurricane of details which constantly hurtles around her. A drive in a cab with a sleeping companion is, for her, essential silence.

Looking out unseeingly at stepped gable roofs and well-scrubbed white doorsteps, I drove my mental probe down, down, to inner depths where I hoped to find an honest answer to the honest question which for so many years had been at the back of my mind: "What are they all trying to say—the people who talk like that?"

For, long ago, I had realized that my mother did not by any means speak for herself alone. She was an extremist, to be sure, but she had plenty of company, much of it very brilliant. In my youth I had listened during innumerable studio bull-sessions to people talking just as she did. All my life I had read similar ideas, mordantly expressed in magazines representing one generation after another of the always recurrent rebel-youth movement. Briefly unhampered now, by material worries, since I could trust a Dutch cab driver to land us at the station in time for our train, and not to overcharge us, I tried to reach the bedrock of that abstract question.

I did not get far—although my speculations ranged very far and very wide. Yet like Peer Gynt with his onion, I came to no definite "yes," or "no." Every time I peeled off a layer marked, "On the one hand," I found below it another, distinctly labeled "On the other hand."

Before I could command my mind to honestly non-partisan reflection, I found myself (as often cheaply happens even to those who are trying to be fair) substituting a wisecrack for thought. "When they bring up, once again, their old threadbare notion that they would prefer having their pockets picked by a filthy thief who is laughing and charming, rather than . . . what they mean is that they can count on some tiresomely decent stupidly honest person feeling it his priggish duty to replace the stolen money."

But I knew at once that this was no more than petulant. "No," I thought. "They can't count on help—except occasionally from those who love them. Far more often they are rebuffed, like La Fontaine's grasshopper." When I first read that fable, a little nine-year-old in a French classroom, did I admire the prudent responsible ant? Not at all. I was revolted by his self-righteous cruelty. I still am.

I tried to penetrate to deeper motives. "What they think is, isn't it, that the only two alternatives open to us are, either to repudiate the whole idea of human responsibility, or else year by year to shut out any glimpses of the spaciousness of beauty, of poetry, of the deeper intuitions, "Brush your teeth, balance your checkbook, wash behind your ears, catch trains, watch the clock. . . . That's the way to make sure you have three square meals a day." On such terms I would be the first to agree that life's not worth living, no matter how conventionally virtuous. But, of course, the fallacy was obvious—those two extremes are not the only ways of life open to us. Bach, Wordsworth, Darwin, Einstein—I snatched up the great names at random, as representing their peers—they had all known that great wild pulse of intuition which Beethoven called his "raptus"; but they had also accepted their share of responsibility for others. After all Rembrandt *had* been a Dutchman, had lived his life in Holland, not in an artist's Utopia.

Unfortunately I was not battling by hook or by crook to beat down an opponent in a law suit. I was trying to search out the rights of the question, and I recognized at once that the example of those illustrious men had two sides. True, they had lived orderly lives. But did their *primary* interest lie in the quality of human relations? Certainly it did not. They and all others in their richly gifted group have unutterably longed to reach not a human but a non-human goal . . . the creative constructive ordering of elements such as colors and lines, musical sounds, mathematical conceptions, the mysteries of astronomy, theology, biology.

A little cast down now, I admitted, "Yes, nobody can feel responsible for the whole universe. We have to make a choice, shut our minds to many things, concentrate on the few which to us seem vital."

Something far away from thoughts fumblingly trying to take shape . . . something up there on the surface of things—it was the dimly perceived railway station just coming into view down the long street—warned me that I was near the end of the short truce with personal responsibility which gave me time to think . . . to try to understand the metes and bounds of such responsibility. It also supplied an example as I hastened to go on.

"I never bother my head, do I, about the train in which I am a passenger. I don't feel any duty toward the cylinders, pistons, connecting rods, under the steel flanks of the locomotive. Isn't this just the spirit in which my mother and those who speak her language brush off the intricate mechanisms which keep human relations going? They admit no obligation to understand human nature, to moderate it, to learn how to help it survive its self-secreted poisons. Why not, if they have other things to do?"

We were now, I saw dimly, not far from the station. Dull, banal thoughts began to trickle into my mind like water under a closed door. Had I the right change in Dutch coin, I wondered, to pay the driver?

Only a moment was left. Trying hard to concentrate, I continued my thoughts. "When I hear an engine laboring painfully on an upgrade, I know in a vague way that it cannot function without oil. But do I feel that I must share in the responsibility for providing the oil? Not in the least. How am I different from those who refuse to take seriously such qualities as self-discipline, fair play, thoughtfulness for others, promise-keeping? To them, humanity's pathetic aspiration to virtue is no more than useful . . . as a social lubricant."

The cab slowed down, swerved gently towards the curb. A last thought called out from the depths. "There is more to it than that. The more comes in because they themselves, like all of us, are human beings and live with men and women, not with locomotives, or colors, or musical notes."

The shift of the cab's wheels was enough to unbalance my mother's ancient, frail, sleeping body. It swayed, slowly tipped against me. Her head rested on my shoulder. The human touch moved my heart, and lifted my thoughts to a wider viewpoint. "Why, all this is metaphysics . . . or something. Not for me. Sort of self-righteous too. How did I get so deep in it?" I put my arm protectingly around her. "After all, what she's always done," I reflected, "is to reach for the only stars she sees. What better can any of us do than to reach for our own stars . . . and know which they are?"

The cab, with dreamlike smoothness, came to a halt. The motor stopped purring. My mother did not wake. We were poised in stillness.

In that silence occurred the miracle when thought and emotion crystallize. As by a flash of lightning, a vivid memory thrust me through and through. For the instant which is long enough for memory to unroll a piece of the past, I was not grown up, married, a mother, in a cab in Holland. I was again young—crassly young—and in Madrid, in the Prado, standing beside my artist-mother. She was lifted out of herself by the ethereal radiance of light-suffused air, presented on nobly painted canvases. I was looking at the same pictures. I too was exalted by them. But although she was the force which had brought me there, what I saw, even in my raw youth, was not what my mother saw.

The sad-faced dwarf, bearing with patience the ignominy of his misshapen body, was a victim of man's inability in the 17th century to cure glandular lacks which now our modern medical skill easily sets straight. The tragedy of the dwarf man, the dignity of that helplessly suffering face . . . they had opened my heart to share the sorrow of the victims of modern man's ignorant inability to mend flaws in the social structure and standards, which cause just as much misery as glandular lacks ever did centuries ago.

The subject of one of the first stories I wrote, "The Bedquilt," was as helplessly starved as the Spanish dwarf of what all human beings need for growth . . . was as humbled before her fellow-men through no fault of hers . . . as defenselessly given over to the careless mockery of those luckier than she. This by no glandular lack . . . by the social code of her time which decreed that plain women without money, who did not have husbands, who had never been admired by men, were only outcasts from the normal group . . . grotesque deformities, so that to look at them was to laugh at them!

I had never known, had never before thought, what had been the impulse which in my youth had inexplicably detached me from the study of phonetic changes in Old French, to which I had been set as a part of the training to earn my living; the impulse which had lifted me away from my textbooks to gaze, deeply sorrowing with her, into the patient remembered eyes of an insignificant old maid whom I had known in my careless childhood; the impulse which had forced me into facing the enormous difficulties of story telling, often enough too great for my powers to cope with.

Well, now I had a clue to that impulse. A message received from the marvelously painted, dark, tragic eyes of Sebastian de Morra had forced me to look deep into the faded blue eyes of Aunt Mehetabel. With that look the walls which keep a scholar's room windless and still, had fallen, leaving me in the heartsick turmoil of a compulsion to imagine and desperately to try to portray a human being not as what she seemed, but what she was . . . to convince people who in life hardly even noticed her existence that she shared in the human dignity of the instinct to create.

They were not all somber—far from it—those memories from the Prado . . . those early premonitions of the interests which were to govern my outlook on life. What had I seen in "Los Borrachos," The Topers, for example? The simple, close-to-earth satisfaction of workingmen, neither quarrelsome nor rapacious, eating and drinking on a holiday . . . a gusto in merely being alive. Perhaps some great-great-grandchild of that perception led to my writing "The Heyday of the Blood."

"How could they ever—the studio-people of my youth," I wondered, "have endured me at all, incorrigibly transposing their technical glories into mere human terms? The pure linear beauty of those slim lances clustered back of the two generals—he who had conquered—he who had been defeated . . . that noble triumph of color and composition had been transparent to my eyes. I had looked through it to the magnanimity of Spinola's courteous deference toward his beaten enemy—whom he could have ground brutally down in humiliation—whom he did not humiliate, but with radiant gladness respected. That, and not the beauty of the painting, had been a bulwark in my heart against those dark hours which come to the stoutest spirit when overpowering disgust for the despicable aspects of our human race batters at the inner door.

The driver climbed down from his seat. The flash-of-lightning memory dimmed. In my last glimpse of it, I saw that what had lifted me out of myself in the Prado was an idea which, expressed in the language of my mother's inner world, was irrelevant . . . even heretical: that art with its magical intuitions brings, and should bring, to the observer an enrichment of human life . . . of humanity's ceaseless Pilgrim's Progress through the years.

The driver opened the door of the cab. All that turmoil and searching sank down to the inner depths. I was at the Prado no longer. I was in front of the big modern railway station.

My mother woke up, refreshed by her nap, smiling cheerfully at the prospect of the long rail trip which would carry her away from the prison bars of bleak Dutch integrity. We got out of the cab. I paid the courteously silent driver the legal fare and the specified tip. A porter emerged from the railway station, ready to carry our bags. That would be another tip, I thought calculatingly.

It was at the moment when I looked down into my purse for the right Dutch coins, that I first became consciously aware that, for good or ill, for success or failure, my fate had been settled long ago. I was marching in the right regiment—the right one for me.

Because, whatever may be true for other branches of the arts, no novel—and no novel condensed into its bare essentials and written as a short story—is worth the reading unless it grapples with some problem of living. Beauty of description, a stirring plot, the right word in the right place . . . all these are excellent. But without that fundamental drive, they are only words—words—words. My task, I saw it clearly, was to go on as inner bent and outer circumstances had started me . . . to focus what powers I had on the effort to understand and to invite readers to join me in trying to understand what happens to and within our poor, fumbling, struggling human race. Nobody can hope to understand the whole human race. But everyone can make a beginning. The essential first step for any reader, and for any writer of fiction, humble or great, is to bend the utmost effort of mind and sympathy on the lives nearest at hand. More often than not those lives appear in no way remarkable, seem barren of all external drama.

What if they do?

Only those of our fellows whom we have really known and lived with can we, if we are fortunate, after long meditation see with the intuition of imagination. And only from achieving such intuition about lives we have shared comes the broader vision which lifts our eyes to those other men, women—and children, outside our personal circle . . . brings them so close that—if our own hearts are big enough—we can share their joys and sorrows—understand the meaning of their lives.

Once, in a Boston street, my father used to tell us, he chanced to ask a doleful, grizzled Irish immigrant, "What part of the Old Country do you come from?"

"I was born in Mayo—God help me!" said the old man.

As the porter picked up the bags and we turned into the station, I thought wryly: "I was born to be a teller of stories . . . God help me!"

Wryly, but gladly too. For in the obscure labyrinth of the inner world, it is comforting to be sure of anything.

The Bedquilt

Of all the Elwell family Aunt Mehetabel was certainly the most unimportant member. It was in the old-time New England days, when an unmarried woman was an old maid at twenty, at forty was everyone's servant, and at sixty had gone through so much discipline that she could need no more in the next world. Aunt Mehetabel was sixty-eight.

She had never for a moment known the pleasure of being important to anyone. Not that she was useless in her brother's family; she was expected, as a matter of course, to take upon herself the most tedious and uninteresting part of the household labors. On Mondays she accepted as her share the washing of the men's shirts, heavy with sweat and stiff with dirt from the fields and from their own hard-working bodies. Tuesdays she never dreamed of being allowed to iron anything pretty or even interesting, like the baby's white dresses or the fancy aprons of her young lady nieces. She stood all day pressing out a monotonous succession of dish-cloths and towels and sheets.

In preserving-time she was allowed to have none of the pleasant responsibility of deciding when the fruit had cooked long enough, nor did she share in the little excitement of pouring the sweet-smelling stuff into the stone jars. She sat in a corner with the children and stoned cherries incessantly, or hulled strawberries until her fingers were dyed red.

The Elwells were not consciously unkind to their aunt, they were even in a vague way fond of her; but she was so insignificant

a figure in their lives that she was almost invisible to them. Aunt Mehetabel did not resent this treatment; she took it quite as unconsciously as they gave it. It was to be expected when one was an old-maid dependent in a busy family. She gathered what crumbs of comfort she could from their occasional careless kindnesses and tried to hide the hurt which even yet pierced her at her brother's rough joking. In the winter when they all sat before the big hearth, roasted apples, drank mulled cider, and teased the girls about their beaux and the boys about their sweethearts, she shrank into a dusky corner with her knitting, happy if the evening passed without her brother saying, with a crude sarcasm, "Ask your Aunt Mehetabel about the beaux that used to come a-sparkin' her!" or, "Mehetabel, how was't when you was in love with Abel Cummings?" As a matter of fact, she had been the same at twenty as at sixty, a mouselike little creature, too shy for anyone to notice, or to raise her eyes for a moment and wish for a life of her own.

Her sister-in-law, a big hearty housewife, who ruled indoors with as autocratic a sway as did her husband on the farm, was rather kind in an absent, offhand way to the shrunken little old woman, and it was through her that Mehetabel was able to enjoy the one pleasure of her life. Even as a girl she had been clever with her needle in the way of patching bedquilts. More than that she could never learn to do. The garments which she made for herself were lamentable affairs, and she was humbly grateful for any help in the bewildering business of putting them together. But in patchwork she enjoyed a tepid importance. She could really do that as well as anyone else. During years of devotion to this one art she had accumulated a considerable store of quilting patterns. Sometimes the neighbors would send over and ask "Miss Mehetabel" for the loan of her sheaf-of-wheat design, or the double-star pattern. It was with an agreeable flutter at being able to help someone that she went to the dresser, in her bare little room under the eaves, and drew out from her crowded portfolio the pattern desired.

She never knew how her great idea came to her. Sometimes she thought she must have dreamed it, sometimes she even wondered reverently, in the phraseology of the weekly prayer-meeting, if it had not been "sent" to her. She never admitted to herself that she could have thought of it without other help. It was too great, too ambitious, too lofty a project for her humble mind to have conceived. Even when she finished drawing the design with her own fingers, she gazed at it incredulously, not daring to believe that it could indeed be her handiwork. At first it seemed to her only like a lovely but unreal dream. For a long time she did not once think of putting an actual quilt together following that pattern, even though she herself had invented it. It was not that she feared the prodigious effort that would be needed to get those tiny, oddly shaped pieces of bright-colored material sewed together with the perfection of fine workmanship needed. No, she thought zestfully and eagerly of such endless effort, her heart uplifted by her vision of the mosaic-beauty of the whole creation as she saw it, when she shut her eyes to dream of it—that complicated, splendidly difficult pattern—good enough for the angels in heaven to quilt.

But as she dreamed, her nimble old fingers reached out longingly to turn her dream into reality. She began to think adventurously of trying it out—it would perhaps not be too selfish to make one square—just one unit of her design to see how it would look. She dared do nothing in the household where she was a dependent, without asking permission. With a heart full of hope and fear thumping furiously against her old ribs, she approached the mistress of the house on churning-day, knowing with the innocent guile of a child that the country woman was apt to be in a good temper while working over the fragrant butter in the cool cellar.

Sophia listened absently to her sister-in-law's halting petition. "Why, yes, Mehetabel," she said, leaning far down into the huge churn for the last golden morsels—"why, yes, start another quilt if you want to. I've got a lot of pieces from the spring sewing that will work in real good." Mehetabel tried honestly to make her see that this would be no common quilt, but her limited vocabulary and her emotion stood between her and expression. At last Sophia said, with a kindly impatience: "Oh, there! Don't bother me. I never could keep track of your quiltin' patterns, anyhow. I don't care what pattern you go by."

Mehetabel rushed back up the steep attic stairs to her room, and in a joyful agitation began preparations for the work of her life. Her very first stitches showed her that it was even better than she hoped. By some heaven-sent inspiration she had invented a pattern beyond which no patchwork quilt could go.

She had but little time during the daylight hours filled with the incessant household drudgery. After dark she did not dare to sit up late at night lest she burn too much candle. It was weeks before the little square began to show the pattern. Then Mehetabel was in a fever to finish it. She was too conscientious to shirk even the smallest part of her share of the housework, but she rushed through it now so fast that she was panting as she climbed the stairs to her little room.

Every time she opened the door, no matter what weather hung outside the one small window, she always saw the little room flooded with sunshine. She smiled to herself as she bent over the innumerable scraps of cotton cloth on her work table. Already—to her—they were ranged in orderly, complex, mosaic-beauty.

Finally she could wait no longer, and one evening ventured to bring her work down beside the fire where the family sat, hoping that good fortune would give her a place near the tallow candles on the mantelpiece. She had reached the last corner of that first square and her needle flew in and out, in and out, with nervous speed. To her relief no one noticed her. By bedtime she had only a few more stitches to add.

As she stood up with the others, the square fell from her trembling old hands and fluttered to the table. Sophia glanced at it carelessly. "Is that the new quilt you said you wanted to start?" she asked, yawning. "Looks like a real pretty pattern. Let's see it."

Up to that moment Mehetabel had labored in the purest spirit of selfless adoration of an ideal. The emotional shock given her by Sophia's cry of admiration as she held the work towards the candle to examine it, was as much astonishment as joy to Mehetabel.

"Land's sakes!" cried her sister-in-law. "Why, Mehetabel Elwell, where did you git that pattern?"

"I made it up," said Mehetabel. She spoke quietly but she was trembling.

"No!" exclaimed Sophia. "Did you! Why, I never see such a pattern in my life. Girls, come here and see what your Aunt Mehetabel is doing."

The three tall daughters turned back reluctantly from the stairs. "I never could seem to take much interest in patchwork quilts," said one. Already the old-time skill born of early pioneer privation and the craving for beauty, had gone out of style.

"No, nor I neither!" answered Sophia. "But a stone image would take an interest in this pattern. Honest, Mehetabel, did you really think of it yourself?" She held it up closer to her eyes and went on, "And how under the sun and stars did you ever git your courage up to start in a-making it? Land! Look at all those tiny squinchy little seams! Why, the wrong side ain't a thing *but* seams! Yet the good side's just like a picture, so smooth you'd think 'twas woven that way. Only nobody could."

The girls looked at it right side, wrong side, and echoed their mother's exclamations. Mr. Elwell himself came over to see what they were discussing. "Well, I declare!" he said, looking at his sister with eyes more approving than she could ever remember. "I don't know a thing about patchwork quilts, but to my eye that beats old Mis' Andrew's quilt that got the blue ribbon so many times at the County Fair."

As she lay that night in her narrow hard bed, too proud, too excited to sleep, Mehetabel's heart swelled and tears of joy ran down from her old eyes.

The next day her sister-in-law astonished her by taking the huge pan of potatoes out of her lap and setting one of the younger children to peeling them. "Don't you want to go on with that quiltin' pattern?" she said. "I'd kind o' like to see how you're goin' to make the grapevine design come out on the corner."

For the first time in her life the dependent old maid contradicted her powerful sister-in-law. Quickly and jealously she said, "It's not a grapevine. It's a sort of curlicue I made up."

"Well, it's nice-looking anyhow," said Sophia pacifyingly. "I never could have made it up."

By the end of the summer the family interest had risen so high that Mehetabel was given for herself a little round table in the sitting room, for *her,* where she could keep her pieces and use odd minutes for her work. She almost wept over such kindness and resolved firmly not to take advantage of it. She went on faithfully with her monotonous housework, not neglecting a corner. But the atmosphere of her world was changed. Now things had a meaning. Through the longest task of washing milk-pans, there rose a rainbow of promise. She took her place by the little table and put the thimble on her knotted, hard finger with the solemnity of a priestess performing a rite.

She was even able to bear with some degree of dignity the honor of having the minister and the minister's wife comment admiringly on her great project. The family felt quite proud of Aunt Mehetabel as Minister Bowman had said it was work as fine as any he had ever seen, "and he didn't know but finer!" The remark was repeated verbatim to the neighbors in the following weeks when they dropped in and examined in a perverse Vermontish silence some astonishingly difficult tour de force which Mehetabel had just finished.

The Elwells especially plumed themselves on the slow progress of the quilt. "Mehetabel has been to work on that corner for six weeks, come Tuesday, and she ain't half done yet," they explained to visitors. They fell out of the way of always expecting her to be the one to run on errands, even for the children. "Don't bother your Aunt Mehetabel," Sophia would call. "Can't you see she's got to a ticklish place on the quilt?" The old woman sat straighter in her chair, held up her head. She was a part of the world at last. She joined in the conversation and her remarks were listened to. The children were even told to mind her when she asked them to do some service for her, although this she ventured to do but seldom.

One day some people from the next town, total strangers, drove up to the Elwell house and asked if they could inspect the wonderful quilt which they had heard about even down in their end of the valley. After that, Mehetabel's quilt came little by little to be one of the local sights. No visitor to town, whether he knew the Elwells or not, went away without having been to look at it. To make her presentable to strangers, the Elwells saw to it that their aunt was better dressed than she had ever been before. One of the girls made her a pretty little cap to wear on her thin white hair.

A year went by and a quarter of the quilt was finished. A second year passed and half was done. The third year Mehetabel had pneumonia and lay ill for weeks and weeks, horrified by the idea that she might die before her work was completed. A fourth year and one could really see the grandeur of the whole design. In September of the fifth year, the entire family gathered around her to watch eagerly, as Mehetabel quilted the last stitches. The girls held it up by the four corners and they all looked at it in hushed silence.

Then Mr. Elwell cried as one speaking with authority, "By ginger! That's goin' to the County Fair!"

Mehetabel blushed a deep red. She had thought of this herself, but never would have spoken aloud of it.

"Yes indeed!" cried the family. One of the boys was dispatched to the house of a neighbor who was Chairman of the Fair Committee for their village. He came back beaming, "Of course he'll take it. Like's not it may git a prize, he says. But he's got to have it right off because all the things from our town are going tomorrow morning."

Even in her pride Mehetabel felt a pang as the bulky package was carried out of the house. As the days went on she felt lost. For years it had been her one thought. The little round stand had been heaped with a litter of bright-colored scraps. Now it was desolately bare. One of the neighbors who took the long journey to the Fair reported when he came back that the quilt was hung in a good place in a glass case in "Agricultural Hall." But that meant little to Mehetabel's ignorance of everything outside her brother's home. She drooped. The family noticed it. One day Sophia said kindly, "You feel sort o' lost without the quilt, don't you, Mehetabel?"

"They took it away so quick!" she said wistfully. "I hadn't hardly had one good look at it myself."

The Fair was to last a fortnight. At the beginning of the second week Mr. Elwell asked his sister how early she could get up in the morning.

"I dunno. Why?" she asked.

"Well, Thomas Ralston has got to drive to West Oldton to see a lawyer. That's four miles beyond the Fair. He says if you can git up so's to leave here at four in the morning he'll drive you to the Fair, leave you there for the day, and bring you back again at night." Mehetabel's face turned very white. Her eyes filled with tears. It was as though someone had offered her a ride in a golden chariot up to the gates of heaven. "Why, you can't *mean* it!" she cried wildly. Her brother laughed. He could not meet her eyes. Even to his easy-going unimaginative indifference to his sister this was a revelation of the narrowness of her life in his home. "Oh, 'tain't so much—just to go to the Fair," he told her in some confusion, and then "Yes, sure I mean it. Go git your things ready, for it's tomorrow morning he wants to start."

A trembling, excited old woman stared all that night at the rafters. She who had never been more than six miles from home—it was to her like going into another world. She who had never seen anything more exciting than a church supper was to see the County Fair. She had never dreamed of doing it. She could not at all imagine what it would be like.

The next morning all the family rose early to see her off. Perhaps her brother had not been the only one to be shocked by her happiness. As she tried to eat her breakfast they called out conflicting advice to her about what to see. Her brother said not to miss inspecting the stock, her nieces said the fancywork was the only thing worth looking at, Sophia told her to be sure to look at the display of preserves. Her nephews asked her to bring home an account of the trotting races.

The buggy drove up to the door, and she was helped in. The family ran to and fro with blankets, woolen tippet, a hot soapstone from the kitchen range. Her wraps were tucked about her. They all stood together and waved goodby as she drove out of the yard. She waved back, but she scarcely saw them. On her return home that evening she was ashy pale, and so stiff that her brother had to lift her out bodily. But her lips were set in a blissful smile. They crowded around her with questions until Sophia pushed them all aside. She told them Aunt Mehetabel was too tired to speak until she had had her supper. The young people held their tongues while she drank her tea, and absent-mindedly ate a scrap of toast with an egg. Then the old woman was helped into an easy chair before the fire. They gathered about her, eager for news of the great world, and Sophia said, "Now, come, Mehetabel, tell us all about it!"

Mehetabel drew a long breath. "It was just perfect!" she said. "Finer even than I thought. They've got it hanging up in the very middle of a sort o' closet made of glass, and one of the lower corners is ripped and turned back so's to show the seams on the wrong side."

"What?" asked Sophia, a little blankly.

"Why, the quilt!" said Mehetabel in surprise. "There are a whole lot of other ones in that room, but not one that can hold a candle to it, if I do say it who shouldn't. I heard lots of people say the same thing. You ought to have heard what the women said about that corner, Sophia. They said—well, I'd be ashamed to *tell* you what they said. I declare if I wouldn't!"

Mr. Elwell asked, "What did you think of that big ox we've heard so much about?"

"I didn't look at the stock," returned his sister indifferently. She turned to one of her nieces. "That set of pieces you gave me, Maria, from your red waist, come out just lovely! I heard one woman say you could 'most smell the red roses."

"How did Jed Burgess' bay horse place in the mile trot?" asked Thomas.

"I didn't see the races."

"How about the preserves?" asked Sophia.

"I didn't see the preserves," said Mehetabel calmly.

Seeing that they were gazing at her with astonished faces she went on, to give them a reasonable explanation, "You see I went right to the room where the quilt was, and then I didn't want to leave it. It had been so long since I'd seen it. I had to look at it first real good myself, and then I looked at the others to see if there was any that could come up to it. Then the people begun comin' in and I got so interested in hearin' what they had to say I couldn't think of goin' anywheres else. I ate my lunch right there too, and I'm glad as can be I did, too; for what do you think?"—she gazed about her with kindling eyes. "While I stood there with a sandwich in one hand, didn't the head of the hull concern come in and open the glass door and pin a big bow of blue ribbon right in the middle of the quilt with a label on it, 'First Prize.'"

There was a stir of proud congratulation. Then Sophia returned to questioning, "Didn't you go to see anything else?"

"Why, no," said Mehetabel. "Only the quilt. Why should I?"

She fell into a reverie. As if it hung again before her eyes she saw the glory that shone around the creation of her hand and brain. She longed to make her listeners share the golden vision with her. She struggled for words. She fumbled blindly for unknown superlatives. "I tell you it looked like—" she began, and paused.

Vague recollections of hymnbook phrases came into her mind. They were the only kind of poetic expression she knew. But they were dismissed as being sacrilegious to use for something in real life. Also as not being nearly striking enough.

Finally, "I tell you it looked real *good,*" she assured them and sat staring into the fire, on her tired old face the supreme content of an artist who has realized his ideal.

Flint and Fire

My husband's cousin had come up from the city, slightly more fagged and sardonic than usual. As he stretched himself out in the big porch-chair he lost no time in taking up his familiar indictment of what he enjoys calling Vermonters' emotional sterility.

"Oh, I admit their honesty. They don't forge checks. And they're steady. Sure. They never burn their neighbors' barns. You can count on them to plug ahead through thrifty, gritty, cautious lives. But no more! No inner heat. Not a spark ever struck out. They're inhibition-bound! Generations of niggling nay-sayers have dried out all feeling from them except . . ."

I pushed the lemonade pitcher nearer him, clinking the ice invitingly. With a wave of my hand I indicated our iris bed, a more cheerful object for contemplation than the flat monotony of rural life. The flowers burned on their stalks like yellow tongues of flame. The strong green leaves, vibrating with vigorous life, thrust themselves up into the spring air.

In the field beyond them, as vigorous as they, strode Adoniram Purdon behind his team, the reins tied together behind his muscular neck, his hands gripping the plow handles. The hot sweet spring sunshine shone down on 'Niram's head with its thick crest of brown hair. The ineffable odor of newly turned earth steamed up around him like incense. The mountain stream at the fence-corner leaped and shouted. His powerful body answered every call made on it with the precision of a splendid machine. But there was no elation in the set face as 'Niram wrenched the plow around a

fixed rock, or as, in a more favorable furrow, the gleaming share sped along before the plowman, turning over a long, unbroken brown ribbon of earth.

My cousin-in-law followed my gesture. His eyes rested on the sturdy, silent figure, as it stepped doggedly behind the straining team, the head bent forward, the eyes fixed on the horses' heels.

"There!" he said. "There is an example of what I mean. Is there another race on earth which could produce a man in such a situation who would not on such a day sing or whistle, or at least hold up his head and look at all the earthly glories about him?"

I made no answer, but not for lack of material for speech. 'Niram's reasons for austere self-control were not such as I cared to discuss with my cousin. As we sat looking at him the noon whistle from the village blew. The wise old horses stopped in the middle of a furrow. 'Niram unharnessed them, led them to the shade of a tree, and put on their nose-bags. Then he turned and came toward the house.

"Don't I seem to remember," murmured my cousin under his breath, "that, even though he is a New Englander, he has been known to make up errands to your kitchen to see your pretty Ev'leen Ann?"

I looked at him hard; but he was only gazing down, rather cross-eyed, on his grizzled mustache. Evidently his had been but a chance shot. 'Niram stepped up on the grass at the edge of the porch. He was so tall that he overtopped the railing easily, and, reaching a long arm over to where I sat, he handed me a small package done up in yellowish tissue-paper. Without a nod or a good morning, or any other of the greetings usual in a more effusive culture, he explained briefly:

"My stepmother wanted I should give you this. She said to thank you for the grape juice." As he spoke he looked at me gravely out of deep-set blue eyes, and when he had delivered his message he held his peace.

I expressed myself with the babbling volubility of another kind of culture. "Oh, 'Niram!" I protested as I opened the package and took out a finely embroidered old-fashioned collar. "Oh, 'Niram! How *could* your stepmother give such a thing away? Why, it must be one of her precious family relics. I don't *want* her to give me something every time I do her just a neighborly favor. Can't a neighbor send her in a few bottles of grape juice without her thinking she must pay it back somehow? It's not kind of her. She has never yet let me do the least thing for her without repaying me with something that is worth ever so much more than the little I've done."

When I had finished my prattling, 'Niram repeated, with an accent of finality, "She wanted I should give it to you."

The older man stirred in his chair. Without looking at him I knew that his gaze on the young rustic was quizzical and that he was recording on the tablets of his merciless memory the ungraceful abruptness of the other's action and manner.

"How is your stepmother feeling today, 'Niram?" I asked.

"Worse."

'Niram came to a full stop with the word. My cousin covered his satirical mouth with his hand.

"Can't the doctor do anything to relieve her?"

'Niram moved at last from his Indian-like immobility. He looked up under the brim of his felt hat at the skyline of the mountain, shimmering iridescent above us. "He says maybe 'lectricity would help her some. I'm goin' to git her the batteries and things soon's I git the rubber bandages paid for."

There was a long silence. My cousin stood up, yawning, and sauntered away toward the door. "Shall I send Ev'leen Ann out to get the pitcher and glasses?" he asked in an accent which he evidently thought very humorously significant.

The strong face under the felt hat turned white, the jaw muscles set, but for all this show of strength there was an instant when the man's eyes looked out with the sick, helpless revelation of pain they might have had when 'Niram was a little boy of ten, a third of his present age, and less than half his present stature. That chance shot rang the bell.

"No, no! Never mind!" I said hastily. "I'll take the tray in when I go."

Without salutation or farewell 'Niram Purdon turned and went back to his work.

The porch was an enchanted place, walled around with starlit darkness, visited by wisps of breezes shaking down from their wings the breath of lilac and syringa, flowering wild grapes, and plowed fields. Down at the foot of our sloping lawn the little river, still swollen by the melted snow from the mountains, plunged between its stony banks and shouted to the stars.

We three—Paul, his cousin, and I—had disposed our uncomely, useful, middle-aged bodies in the big wicker chairs and left them there while our young souls wandered abroad in the sweet, dark glory of the night. At least Paul and I were doing this, as we sat, hand in hand, thinking of a May night twenty years before. One never knows what Horace is thinking of, but apparently he was not in his usual captious vein, for after a long pause he remarked, "It is a night almost indecorously inviting to the making of love."

My answer seemed grotesquely out of key with this, but its sequence was clear in my mind. I got up, saying: "Oh, that reminds me—I must go and see Ev'leen Ann. I'd forgotten to plan tomorrow's dinner."

"Oh, everlastingly Ev'leen Ann!" mocked Horace from his corner. "Can't you think of anything but Ev'leen Ann and her affairs?"

I felt my way through the darkness of the house, toward the kitchen, both doors of which were tightly closed. When I stepped into the hot, close room, smelling of food and fire, I saw Ev'leen Ann sitting on the straight kitchen chair, the yellow light of the bracket-lamp beating down on her heavy braids and bringing out the exquisitely subtle modeling of her smooth young face. Her hands were folded in her lap. She was staring at the blank wall, and the expression of her eyes so startled and shocked me that I stopped short and would have retreated if it had not been too late. She had seen me, roused herself, and said quietly, as though continuing a conversation interrupted the moment before:

"I had been thinking that there was enough left of the roast to make hash-balls for dinner"—Ev'leen Ann would never have used a fancy name like croquettes—"and maybe you'd like a rhubarb pie."

I knew well enough she had been thinking of no such thing, but I could as easily have slapped a reigning sovereign on the back as broken in on the regal reserve of Ev'leen Ann in her clean gingham.

"Well, yes, Ev'leen Ann," I answered in her own tone of reasonable consideration of the matter, "that would be nice, and your piecrust is so flaky that even Mr. Horace will have to be pleased."

"Mr. Horace" is our title for the sardonic cousin whose carping ways are half a joke, and half a menace, in our household.

Ev'leen Ann could not manage a smile. She looked down soberly at the white-pine top of the kitchen table and said, "I guess there is enough sparrow-grass up in the garden for a mess, too, if you'd like that."

"That would taste very good," I agreed, my heart aching for her.

"And creamed potatoes," she finished steadily, thrusting my unspoken pity from her.

"You know I like creamed potatoes better than any other kind," I concurred.

There was a silence. It seemed inhuman to go and leave the stricken young thing to fight her trouble alone in the ugly prison, her work-place, though I thought I could guess why Ev'leen Ann had shut the doors so tightly. I hung near her, searching my head for something to say, but she helped me by no casual remark. 'Niram is not the only one of our people who possesses to the full the supreme gift of silence. Finally I mentioned the report of a case of measles in the village, and Ev'leen Ann responded in kind with the news that her Aunt Emma had bought a potato-planter. Ev'leen Ann is an orphan, brought up by a well-to-do spinster aunt, who is strong-minded and runs her own farm. After a time we glided by way of similar transitions to the mention of his name.

" 'Niram Purdon tells me his stepmother is no better," I said. "Isn't it too bad?" I thought it well for Ev'leen Ann to be dragged out of her black cave of silence once in a while, even if it could be done only by force. As she made no answer, I went on. "Everybody who knows 'Niram thinks it splendid of him to do so much for his stepmother."

Ev'leen Ann responded with a detached air, as though speaking of a matter in China: "Well, it ain't any more than what he should. She was awful good to him when he was little and his father got so sick. I guess 'Niram wouldn't ha' had much to eat if she hadn't ha' gone out sewing to earn it for him and Mr. Purdon." She added firmly, after a moment's pause, "No, ma'am, I don't guess it's any more than what 'Niram had ought to do."

"But it's very hard on a young man to feel that he's not able to marry," I continued. Once in a great while we came so near the matter as this. Ev'leen Ann made no answer. Her face took on a pinched look of sickness. She set her lips as though she would never speak again. But I knew that a criticism of 'Niram would always rouse her, and said:

"And really, I think 'Niram makes a great mistake to act as he does. A wife would be a help to him. She could take care of Mrs. Purdon and keep the house."

Ev'leen Ann rose to the bait, speaking quickly with some heat: "I guess 'Niram knows what's right for him to do! He can't afford to marry when he can't even keep up with the doctor's bills and all. He keeps the house himself, nights and mornings, and Mrs. Purdon is awful handy about taking care of herself, for all she's bedridden. That's her way, you know. She can't bear to have folks do for her. She'd die before she'd let anybody do anything for her that she could anyways do for herself!"

I sighed acquiescingly. Mrs. Purdon's fierce independence was a rock on which every attempt at sympathy or help shattered itself to atoms. There seemed to be no other emotion left in her poor old work-worn shell of a body. As I looked at Ev'leen Ann it seemed rather a hateful characteristic, and I remarked, "It seems to me it's asking a good deal of 'Niram to spoil his life in order that his stepmother can go on pretending she's independent."

Ev'leen Ann explained hastily: "Oh, 'Niram doesn't tell her anything about—she doesn't know he would like to—he don't want she should be worried—and, anyhow, as 'tis, he can't earn enough to keep ahead of all the doctors cost."

"But the right kind of a wife—a good, competent girl—could help out by earning something, too."

Ev'leen Ann looked at me forlornly, with no surprise. The idea was evidently not new to her. "Yes, ma'am, she could. But 'Niram says he ain't the kind of man to let his wife go out working." Even while she drooped under the killing verdict of his pride she was loyal to his standards and uttered no complaint. She went on, " 'Niram wants Aunt Em'line to have things the way she wants 'em, as near as he can give 'em to her—and it's right she should."

"Aunt Emeline?" I repeated, surprised at her absence of mind. "You mean Mrs. Purdon, don't you?"

Ev'leen Ann looked vexed at her slip, but she scorned to attempt any concealment. She explained dryly, with the shy, stiff embarrassment our country people have in speaking of private affairs: "Well, she *is* my Aunt Em'line, Mrs. Purdon is, though I don't hardly ever call her that.

You see, Aunt Emma brought me up, and she and Aunt Em'line don't have anything to do with each other. They were twins, and when they were girls they got edgeways over 'Niram's father, when 'Niram was a baby and his father was a young widower and come courting. Then Aunt Em'line married him, and Aunt Emma never spoke to her afterward."

Occasionally, in walking unsuspectingly along one of our leafy lanes, some such fiery geyser of ancient heat uprears itself in a boiling column. I never get used to it, and started back now.

"Why, I never heard of that before, and I've known your Aunt Emma and Mrs. Purdon for years!"

"Well, they're pretty old now," said Ev'leen Ann listlessly, with the natural indifference of self-centered youth to the bygone tragedies of the preceding generation. "It happened quite some time ago. And both of them were so touchy if anybody seemed to speak about it, that folks got in the way of letting it alone. First Aunt Emma wouldn't speak to her sister because she'd married the man she'd wanted, and then when Aunt Emma made out so well farmin' and got so well off, why, then Mrs. Purdon wouldn't try to make it up because she was so poor. That was after Mr. Purdon had had his stroke of paralysis and they'd lost their farm and she'd taken to goin' out sewin'—not but what she was always perfectly satisfied with her bargain. She always acted as though she'd rather have her husband's old shirt stuffed with straw than any other man's whole body. He was a real nice man, I guess, Mr. Purdon was."

There I had it—the curt, unexpanded chronicle of two passionate lives. And there I had also the key to Mrs. Purdon's fury of independence. It was the only way in which she could defend her husband against the charge, so damning in her world, of not having provided for his wife. It was the only monument she could rear to her husband's memory. And her husband had been all there was in life for her!

I stood looking at her young kinswoman's face, noting the granite under the velvet softness of its youth, and divining the flame under the granite. I longed to break through her wall, to put my arms about her. On the impulse of the moment I cast aside the pretense of casualness.

"Oh, my dear!" I said. "Are you and 'Niram always to go on like this? Can't anybody help you?"

Ev'leen Ann looked at me, her face suddenly old and gray. "No, ma'am; we ain't going to go on this way. We've decided, 'Niram and I have, that it ain't no use. We've decided that we'd better not go places together any more or see each other. It's too—if 'Niram thinks we can't"—she flamed so that I knew she was burning from head to foot—"it's better for us not—" She ended in a muffled voice, hiding her face in the crook of her arm.

Ah, yes; now I knew why Ev'leen Ann had shut out the passionate breath of the spring night!

I stood near her, a lump in my throat, but I divined the anguish of her shame at her involuntary self-revelation, and respected it. I dared do no more than to touch her shoulder gently.

The door behind us rattled. Ev'leen Ann sprang up and turned her face toward the wall. Paul's cousin came in, shuffling a little, blinking his eyes in the light of the unshaded lamp, and looking very old and tired. He glanced at us as he went over to the sink. "Nobody offered me anything good to drink," he complained, "so I came in to get some water from the faucet for my nightcap."

When he had drunk with ostentation from the tin dipper, he went to the outside door and flung it open. "Don't you people know how hot and smelly it is in here?" he said roughly.

The night wind burst in, eddying, and puffed out the lamp. In an instant the room was filled with coolness and perfumes and the rushing sound of the river. Out of the darkness came Ev'leen Ann's young voice. "It seems to me," she said, as though speaking to herself, "that I never heard the Mill Brook sound so loud as it has this spring."

I woke up that night with the start one has at a sudden call. But there had been no call. A profound silence spread itself through the sleeping house. Outdoors the wind had died down. Only the loud brawl of the river broke the stillness under the stars. But all through this silence and this vibrant song there rang a soundless menace which brought me out of bed and to my feet before I was awake. I heard Paul say, "What's the matter?" in a sleepy voice, and "Nothing," I answered, reaching for my dressing-gown and slippers. I listened for a moment, my head ringing with frightening neighborhood tales I had been brought up on—that despairing Hilton boy who, when his sweetheart—the Raven

Rocks loomed up, with their hundred-foot straight drop to death—and the deserted wife—. There was still no sound. I stepped rapidly along the hall and up the stairs to Ev'leen Ann's room, and opened the door. Without knocking. The room was empty.

Then how I ran! Calling loudly for Paul to join me, I ran down the two flights of stairs, out of the open door, and along the hedged path that leads down to the little river. The starlight was clear. I could see everything as plainly as though in early dawn. I saw the river, and I saw—Ev'leen Ann!

There was a dreadful moment of horror, which I shall never remember very clearly, and then Ev'leen Ann and I—both very wet—stood on the bank, shuddering in each other's arms.

Into our hysteria there dropped, like a pungent caustic, the arid voice of Horace, remarking, "Well, are you two people crazy, or are you walking in your sleep?"

I could feel Ev'leen Ann stiffen in my arms, and I fairly stepped back from her in astonished admiration as I heard her snatch at the straw thus offered, and still shuddering horribly from head to foot, force herself to say quite connectedly: "Why—yes—of course—I've always heard about my grandfather Parkman's walking in his sleep. Folks *said* 'twould come out in the family some time."

Paul was close behind Horace—I wondered a little at his not being first—and with many astonished and inane ejaculations, such as people always make on startling occasions, we took our way back into the house to hot blankets and toddies. But I slept no more that night.

Some time after dawn, however, I did fall into a troubled unconsciousness full of bad dreams, and only woke when the sun was quite high. I opened my eyes to see Ev'leen Ann about to close the door.

"Oh, did I wake you up?" she said. "I didn't mean to. That little Harris boy is here with a letter for you."

She spoke with a slightly defiant tone of self-possession. I tried to play up to her interpretation of her role.

"The little Harris boy?" I said, sitting up in bed. "What in the world is he bringing me a letter for?"

Ev'leen Ann, with her usual clear perception of the superfluous in conversation, turned away silently, went downstairs and brought back the note. It was of four lines, and—surprisingly enough—from old

Mrs. Purdon, who asked me abruptly if I would have my husband take me to see her. She specified, and underlined the specification, that I was to come "right off, and in the automobile." Wondering extremely at this mysterious bidding, I sought out Paul, who obediently cranked up our small car and carried me off. There was no sign of Horace about the house, but some distance on the other side of the village we saw his tall, stooping figure swinging along the road. He carried a cane and was characteristically occupied in violently switching off the heads from the wayside weeds as he walked. He refused our offer to take him in, alleging that he was out for exercise and to reduce his flesh—an ancient jibe at his bony frame which made him for an instant show a leathery smile.

There was, of course, no one at Mrs. Purdon's to let us into the tiny, three-roomed house, since the bedridden invalid spent her days there alone while 'Niram worked his team on other people's fields. Not knowing what we might find, Paul stayed outside in the car, while I stepped inside in answer to Mrs. Purdon's "Come *in,* why don't you!" which sounded quite as dry as usual. But when I saw her I knew that things were not as usual.

She lay flat on her back, the little emaciated wisp of humanity, hardly raising the piecework quilt enough to make the bed seem occupied, and to account for the thin, worn old face on the pillow. But as I entered the room her eyes seized on mine, and I was aware of nothing but them and some fury of determination behind them. With a fierce heat of impatience at my first natural but quickly repressed exclamation of surprise she explained briefly that she wanted Paul to lift her into the automobile and take her into the next township to the Andrews farm. "I'm so shrunk away to nothin', I know I can lay on the back seat if I crook myself up," she said, with a cool accent but a rather shaky voice.

I suppose that my face showed the wildness of my astonishment for she added, as if in explanation, but still with a ferocious determination to keep up the matter-of-fact tone: "Emma Andrews is my twin sister. I guess it ain't so queer, my wanting to see her."

I thought, of course, we were to be used as the medium for some strange, sudden family reconciliation, and went out to ask Paul if he thought he could carry the old invalid to the car. He replied that, so far as that went, he could carry so thin an old body ten times around the town, but that he refused absolutely to take such a risk without authorization from her doctor. I remembered the burning eyes of resolution I had left inside, and sent him to present his objections to Mrs. Purdon herself.

In a few moments I saw him emerge from the house with the old woman in his arms. He had evidently taken her up just as she lay. The piecework quilt hung down in long folds, flashing its brilliant reds and greens in the sunshine, which shone so strangely upon the pallid old countenance, facing the open sky for the first time in years.

We drove in silence through the green and gold lyric of the spring day, an elderly company sadly out of key with the triumphant note of eternal youth which rang through all the visible world. Mrs. Purdon looked at nothing, said nothing, seemed to be aware of nothing but the purpose in her heart, whatever that might be. Paul and I, taking a leaf from our neighbors' book, held, with a courage like theirs, to their excellent habit of saying nothing when there is nothing to say. We arrived at the fine old Andrews place without the exchange of a single word.

"Now carry me in," said Mrs. Purdon briefly, evidently hoarding her strength.

"Wouldn't I better go and see if Miss Andrews is at home?" I asked.

Mrs. Purdon shook her head impatiently and turned her compelling eyes on my husband. I went up the path before them to knock at the door, wondering what the people in the house *could* possibly be thinking of us. There was no answer to my knock. "Open the door and go in," commanded Mrs. Purdon from out her quilt.

There was no one in the spacious, white-paneled hall, and no sound in all the big, many-roomed house.

"Emma's out feeding the hens," conjectured Mrs. Purdon, not, I fancied, without a faint hint of relief in her voice, "Now carry me upstairs to the first room on the right."

Half hidden by his burden, Paul rolled wildly inquiring eyes at me; but he obediently staggered up the broad old staircase, and, waiting till I had opened the first door to the right, stepped into the big bedroom.

"Put me down on the bed, and open them shutters," Mrs. Purdon commanded.

She still marshaled her forces with no lack of decision, but with a fainting voice which made me run over to her quickly as Paul laid her down on the four-poster. Her eyes were still indomitable, but her mouth hung open slackly and her color was startling. “Oh, Paul, quick! quick! Haven't you your flask with you?”

Mrs. Purdon informed me in a barely audible whisper, “In the corner cupboard at the head of the stairs,” and I flew down the hallway. I returned with a bottle, evidently of great age. There was only a little brandy in the bottom, but it whipped up a faint color into the sick woman's lips.

As I was bending over her and Paul was thrusting open the shutters, letting in a flood of sunshine and flecky leaf-shadows, a firm, rapid step came down the hall, and a vigorous woman, with a tanned face and a clean, faded gingham dress, stopped short in the doorway with an expression of stupefaction.

Mrs. Purdon put me on one side, and although she was physically incapable of moving her body by a hair's breadth, she gave the effect of having risen to meet the newcomer. “Well, Emma, here I am,” she said in a queer voice, with involuntary quavers in it. As she went on she had it more under control, although in the course of her extraordinarily succinct speech it broke and failed her occasionally. When it did, she drew in her breath with an audible, painful effort, struggling forward steadily in what she had to say. “You see, Emma, it's this way: My 'Niram and your Ev'leen Ann have been keeping company—ever since they went to school together—you know that's well as I do, for all we let on we didn't, only I didn't know till just now how hard they took it. They can't get married because 'Niram can't keep even, let alone get ahead any, because I cost so much bein' sick, and the doctor says I may live for years this way, same's Aunt Hettie did. An' 'Niram is thirty-one, an' Ev'leen Ann is twenty-eight, an' they've had 'bout's much waitin' as is good for folks that set such store by each other. I've thought of every way out of it—and there ain't any. The Lord knows I don't enjoy livin' any. I'd thought of cutting my throat like Uncle Lish, but that'd make 'Niram and Ev'leen Ann feel so—to think why I'd done it; they'd never take the comfort they'd ought in bein' married. So that won't do. There's only one thing to do. I guess you'll have to take care of me till the Lord calls me. Maybe I won't last so long as the doctor thinks.”

When she finished, I felt my ears ringing in the silence. She had walked to the sacrificial altar with so steady a step, and laid upon it her precious all with so gallant a front of quiet resolution, that for an instant I failed to take in the sublimity of her self-immolation. Mrs. Purdon asking for charity! And asking the one woman who had most reason to refuse it to her.

Paul looked at me miserably, the craven desire to escape a scene written all over him. "Wouldn't we better be going, Mrs. Purdon?" I said uneasily. I had not ventured to look at the woman in the doorway.

Mrs. Purdon motioned me to remain, with an imperious gesture whose fierceness showed the tumult underlying her brave front. "No; I want you should stay. I want you should hear what I say, so's you can tell folks, if you have to. Now, look here, Emma," she went on to the other, still obstinately silent, "you must look at it the way 'tis. We're neither of us any good to anybody, the way we are—and I'm dreadfully in the way of the only two folks we care a pin about—either of us. You've got plenty to do with, and nothing to spend it on. I can't get myself out of their way by dying without going against what's Scripture and proper, but—" Her steely calm broke. She burst out in a scream. "You've just *got* to, Emma Andrews! You've just *got* to! If you don't, I won't never go back to 'Niram's house! I'll lie in the ditch by the roadside till the poor-master comes to git me—and I'll tell everybody that it's because my twin sister, with a house and a farm and money in the bank, turned me out to starve—" A spasm cut her short. She lay twisted, the whites of her eyes showing between the lids.

"Good God, she's gone!" cried Paul, running to the bed.

Instantly the woman in the doorway was between Paul and me as we rubbed the thin, icy hands and forced brandy between the flaccid lips. We all three thought her dead or dying, and labored over her with the frightened thankfulness for one another's living presence which always marks that dreadful moment. But even as we fanned and rubbed, and cried out to one another to open the windows and to bring water, the blue lips moved to a ghostly whisper: "Em, listen—" The old woman went back to the nickname of their common youth. "Em—your Ev'leen Ann—tried to drown herself—in the Mill Brook last night . . . That's what decided me—to—" And then we were plunged into another desperate struggle with Death for the possession of the battered old habitation of the dauntless soul.

"Isn't there any hot water in the house?" cried Paul, and "Yes, yes; teakettle on the stove!" answered the woman who labored with us. Paul, divining that she meant the kitchen, fled downstairs. I stole a look at Emma Andrews' face as she bent over the sister she had not seen in thirty years, and I knew that Mrs. Purdon's battle was won. It even seemed that she had won another skirmish in her never-ending war with death, for a little warmth began to come back into her hands.

When Paul returned with the teakettle, and a hot-water bottle had been filled, the owner of the house straightened herself, assumed her rightful position as mistress of the situation, and began to issue commands. "You git right in the automobile, and go git the doctor," she told Paul. "That'll be the quickest. She's better now, and your wife and I can keep her goin' till the doctor gits here."

As Paul left the room she snatched something white from a bureau drawer, stripped the worn, patched old cotton nightgown from the skeleton-like body, and, handling the invalid with a strong, sure touch, slipped on a soft, woolly outing-flannel wrapper with a curious trimming of zigzag braid down the front. Mrs. Purdon opened her eyes very slightly, but shut them again at her sister's quick command, "You lay still, Em'line, and drink some of this brandy." She obeyed without comment, but after a pause she opened her eyes again and looked down at the new garment which clad her. She had that moment turned back from the door of death, but her first breath was used to set the scene for a return to a decorum.

"You're still a great hand for rickrack work, Em, I see," she murmured in a faint whisper. "Do you remember how surprised Aunt Su was when you made up a pattern?"

"Well, I hadn't thought of it for quite some time," returned Miss Andrews, in exactly the same tone of everyday remark. As she spoke she slipped her arm under the other's head and poked the pillow up to a more comfortable shape. "Now you lay perfectly still," she commanded in the hectoring tone of the born nurse; "I'm goin' to run down and make you a good hot cup of sassafras tea."

I followed her down into the kitchen and was met by the same refusal to be melodramatic which I had encountered in Ev'leen Ann. I was most anxious to know what version of my extraordinary morning I was to give out to the world, but hung silent, abashed by the cool casualness of the other woman as she mixed her brew. Finally, "Shall I tell 'Niram— What shall I say to Ev'leen Ann? If anybody asks me—" I brought out with clumsy hesitation.

At the realization that her reserve and family pride were wholly at the mercy of any report I might choose to give, even my iron hostess faltered. She stopped short in the middle of the floor, looked at me silently, piteously.

I hastened to assure her that I would attempt no hateful picturesqueness. "Suppose I just say that you were rather lonely here, now that Ev'leen Ann has left you, and that you thought it would be nice to have your sister come to stay with you, so that 'Niram and Ev'leen Ann can be married?"

Emma Andrews breathed again. She walked toward the stairs with the steaming cup in her hand. Over her shoulder she remarked, "Well, yes; that could be as good a way to put it as any, I guess."

'Niram and Ev'leen Ann were standing up to be married. They looked very stiff and self-conscious, and Ev'leen Ann was very pale. 'Niram's big hands, crooked as though they still held an axhelve or steered a plow, hung down by his new black trousers. Ev'leen Ann's strong fingers stood out stiffly from one another. They looked hard at the minister and repeated after him in low and meaningless tones the solemn and touching words of the marriage service. Back of them stood the wedding company, in freshly washed and ironed white dresses, new straw hats, and black suits smelling of camphor. In the background, among the other elders, stood Paul and Horace and I—my husband and I hand in hand, Horace twiddling the black ribbon which holds his watch and looking bored. Through the open windows into the stuffiness of the best room came an echo of the deep organ note of midsummer.

"Whom God hath joined together—" said the minister, and the epitome of humanity which filled the room held its breath—the old with a wonder upon their life-scarred faces, the young half frightened to feel the stir of the great wings soaring so near them.

Then it was all over. 'Niram and Ev'leen Ann were married, and the rest of us were bustling about to serve the hot biscuit and coffee and chicken salad, and to dish up the ice cream. Afterward there were no citified refinements of cramming rice down the necks of the departing pair or tying placards to the carriage in which they went away. Some of the men went out to the barn and hitched up for 'Niram, and we all gathered at the gate to see them drive off. They might have been going for one of their Sunday afternoon "buggy-rides" except for the wet eyes of the foolish women and girls who stood waving their hands in answer to the flutter of Ev'leen Ann's handkerchief as the carriage went down the hill.

We had nothing to say to one another after they left, and began soberly to disperse to our respective vehicles. But as I was getting into our car a new thought suddenly struck me.

"Why," I cried, "I never thought of it before! However in the world did old Mrs. Purdon know about Ev'leen Ann—that night?"

Horace was pulling at the door. Its hinges were sprung and it shut hard. He closed it with a vicious slam. "I told her," he said crossly.

The Heyday of the Blood

The older professor looked sharply at his assistant, fumbling with a pile of papers. "Farrar, what's the *matter* with you lately?" he asked, brusquely.

The younger man started, "Why—why—" his face twitched. He went on desperately, "I've lost my nerve, Professor Mallory, that's what's the matter with me.

"What do you mean—nerve?" asked Mallory, challenging impatience in his tone.

The younger man started, "Why—why—" His face twitched. He went trembling so that the papers he held fell on the floor. "I worry—I forget things—I take no interest in life. The psychiatrists tell me to relax, to rest. I try to but it's no good. I never go out—every evening I'm in bed by nine o'clock. I take no part in college life beyond my own work. I turned down that chance to organize a summer seminar in New York, you know—I'll never have such a splendid professional opportunity again!—If I could only sleep! Heavens, what nights I have! Yet I never do anything exciting in the evening. I keep seeing myself in a sanitarium, dependent on my brother—why, I'm in hell—that's what's the matter—"

Professor Mallory interrupted him, patiently now, as if he were quieting a frightened saddle-horse. "But don't your psychiatrists do more than just advise you to take it easy? What do they tell you about your case?"

The young man's face drew together in a spasm. "That's just it," he cried. "They won't tell me the truth. Not one. They won't speak

right out. They pretend to believe that a little rest and quiet is all I need. But I've read enough case histories to know I'm doomed by the craving for defeat. I've heard about the 'will to—' " He choked and stopped.

The older man looked at him speculatively. When he spoke again his voice was neither challenging nor patient. It had a relaxed, offhand quality. "Well, well," he said, "let's leave it at that. I can't advise you. All this is no field of mine. I don't know anything about psychiatry except what I read in the papers. I do know from there that psychiatrists pay a lot of attention to childhood impressions, and I should say they show their good sense in that. I've had childhood experiences of my own." He paused, hesitated, swung around in his swivel chair from his desk and said as if on an impulse, "I'd sort of like to tell you about one. You're not too busy?"

"Busy! I've forgotten the meaning of the word! I don't dare to put any pressure on myself."

"Very well, then; I mean to carry you back to the stony little farm in the Green Mountains, where I had the good luck to be born and raised. You've heard me speak of Hillsboro. The story is all about my great-grandfather, who came to live with us when I was a little boy."

"Your great-grandfather?" protested the other. "People don't remember their great-grandfathers!"

"Oh, yes, they do, in Vermont. There was my father on one farm, and my grandfather on another, without a thought that he was no longer young, and there was 'Gran'ther' as we called him, eighty-eight years old and just persuaded to settle back, let his descendants take care of him. He had been in the War of 1812—think of that, you mushroom!—and had lost an arm and a good deal of his health there. He had lately begun to get a pension of twelve dollars a month. For an old man he was quite independent financially, as poor Vermont farmers look at things; and he was a most extraordinary character. His arrival in our family was an event.

"He took precedence at once over the oldest man in the township, who was only eighty-four and not very bright. I can remember bragging at school about Gran'ther Pendleton, who'd be eighty-nine come next Woodchuck Day, and could see to read without glasses. He had been ailing all his life, ever since the fever he took in the war. He used to remark triumphantly that he had now outlived six doctors who had each given him but a year to live, 'and the seventh is going downhill fast, so I hear!' This last was his never-failing answer to the attempts of my conscientious mother and anxious, dutiful father to check the old man's reckless indifference to any of the rules of hygiene.

"Our parents had never been stern or harsh with us, but we children never dreamed of questioning their firm decisions. Neither did Gran'ther Pendleton question them. He ignored them, this naughty old man, who would give his weak stomach frightful attacks of indigestion by stealing out to the pantry and devouring a whole mince pie because he had been refused two pieces at the table—this rebellious, unreasonable, whimsical old madcap brought a high-voltage electric element into our quiet, orderly life. He insisted on going to every picnic and church sociable, where he ate all the indigestible dainties he could lay his hands on, stood in drafts, tired himself to the verge of fainting away by playing games with the children, and returned home, exhausted, animated, and quite ready to pay the price of a day in bed, groaning and screaming out with pain as heartily and unaffectedly as he had laughed with the pretty girls the evening before.

"The climax came, however, in the middle of August, when he announced his desire to go to the county fair, held some fourteen miles down the valley from our farm. Father never dared let Gran'ther go anywhere without going with the old man himself, but he was perfectly sincere in saying that it was not because he could not spare a day from the haying that he refused pointblank to consider it. The doctor who had been taking care of Gran'ther since he came to live with us said that it would be crazy to think of such a thing. He added that the wonder was that Gran'ther lived at all, for his heart was all wrong, his asthma was enough to kill a young man, and he had no digestion; in short, if Father wished to kill his old grandfather, there was no surer way than to drive fourteen miles in the heat of August to the noisy excitement of a county fair.

"So Father for once said 'No,' in the tone that we children had come to recognize as final. Gran'ther grimly tied a knot in his empty sleeve—a curious way he took to express strong emotion—put his one hand on his cane, and his chin on his hand, and withdrew himself into that incalculable distance from the life about him where very old people spend so many hours.

"He did not emerge from this until one morning toward the middle of fair-week, when all the rest of the family were away—Father and the bigger boys on the far-off upland meadows haying, and Mother and the girls blackberrying in the burnt-over lot, across the valley. I was too little to be of any help, so I had been left to wait on Gran'ther, and to set out our lunch of bread and milk and huckleberries. We had not been alone half an hour when Gran'ther sent me to extract, from under the mattress of his bed, the wallet in which he kept his pension money. He counted it over carefully, sticking out his tongue like a schoolboy doing a sum. 'Six dollars and forty-three cents!' he cried. He began to laugh and snap his fingers and sing out in his high, cracked old voice:

" 'We're goin' to go a skylarkin'! Little Jo Mallory is going to the county fair with his Gran'ther Pendleton, an' he's goin' to have more fun than ever was in the world, and he—'

" 'But, Gran'ther, Father said we mustn't!' I protested, horrified.

" 'But I say we *shall!* I was your gre't-gran'ther long before he was your feyther, and anyway I'm here and he's not—so, *march!* Out to the barn!'

"He took me by the collar and pushed me ahead of him to the stable, where old white Peggy, the only horse left at home, looked at us amazed.

" 'But it'll be twenty-eight miles, and Peg's never driven over eight!' I cried, my established world of rules and orders reeling.

" 'Eight—and—twenty-eight!
But I—am—*eighty*-eight!'

"Gran'ther improvised a sort of whooping chant of scorn as he pulled the harness from the peg. 'It'll do her good to drink some pink lemonade—old Peggy! An' if she gits tired comin' home, I'll git out and carry her part way myself!'

"I thought this the funniest idea I'd ever heard and laughed loudly as together we hitched up, I standing on a chair to slip the check-rein in place, Gran'ther doing wonders with his one hand. Then, just as we were—Gran'ther in a hickory shirt not very clean, an old hat flapping over his wizened face, I bare-legged, in my faded everyday old clothes—we drove out of the grassy yard, down the steep, stony hill that led to the main valley road. Along the hot, white turnpike, deep with dust, we joined the farm teams on their way to the fair. Gran'ther exchanged hilarious greetings with the people who constantly overtook old Peg's jogging trot. Between times he regaled me with spicy stories of the hundreds of thousands—they seemed no less numerous to me then—of county fairs he had attended in his youth. He was horrified to find that I had never been even to one.

"'Why, Joey, how old be ye? 'Most eight, ain't it? When I was your age I had run away and been to two fairs an' a hangin'.'

"'But didn't they lick you when you got home?' I asked shudderingly.

"'You *bet* they did!' cried Gran'ther with gusto.

"I felt the world expanding into an infinitely larger place with every word he said.

"'Now, this is somethin' *like!'* he exclaimed, as we drew near to Granville and fell into a procession of wagons all filled with country people in their best clothes, who looked with friendly curiosity at the ancient, shriveled cripple, his face shining with sweat and animation, and at the small boy beside him, his bare feet dangling high above the floor of the battered buckboard, overcome with the responsibility of driving a horse for the first time in his life, and filled with such a flood of new emotions and ideas that he must have been quite pale."

Professor Mallory leaned back and laughed aloud at the vision he had been evoking—laughed with so joyous an abandon and relish in his reminiscences that the face of his listener relaxed a little.

"Oh, that was a day!" went on the professor, still laughing and wiping his eyes. "Never will I have another like it! At the entrance to the grounds Gran'ther stopped me while he solemnly untied the knot in his empty sleeve. I don't know what kind of harebrained vow he had tied up in it, but with the little ceremony disappeared every last trace of restraint, and we plunged head over ears into the saturnalia of delights that was an old-time county fair.

"People had little cash in those days, and Gran'ther's six dollars and forty-three cents lasted like the widow's cruse of oil. We went to see the fat lady, who, if she was really as big as she looked to me then, must have weighed at least a ton. My admiration for Gran'ther's daredevil qualities rose to infinity when he entered into free-and-easy talk with her, about how much she ate, and could she raise her arms enough to do up her own hair, and how many yards of velvet it took to make her gorgeous, gold-trimmed robe. She laughed a great deal at us, but she was evidently touched by his human interest, for she confided to him that it was not velvet at all, but furniture covering; and when we went away she pressed on us a bag of peanuts. She said she had more peanuts than she could eat—a state of unbridled opulence which fitted in for me with all the other superlatives of that day.

"We saw the dog-faced boy, whom we did not like at all; Gran'ther expressing, with a candidly outspoken cynicism, his belief that 'them whiskers was glued to him.' We wandered about the stock exhibit, gazing at monstrous oxen, and hanging over the railings where the prize pigs lived to scratch their backs. In order to miss nothing, we even conscientiously passed through the Woman's Building, where we were very much bored by the serried ranks of preserve jars.

"'Sufferin' Hezekiah!' cried Gran'ther irritably. 'Who cares how gooseberry jell *looks*. If they'd give a felly a taste, now—'

"This reminded him that we were hungry, and we went to a restaurant tent, where, after taking stock of the wealth that yet remained of Gran'ther's hoard, he ordered the most expensive things on the bill of fare."

Professor Mallory suddenly laughed out again. "Perhaps in heaven, but certainly not until then, shall I ever taste anything so ambrosial as that fried chicken and coffee ice cream! I have not lived in vain that I have such a memory back of me!"

This time the younger man laughed with the narrator, settling back in his chair as the professor went on:

"After lunch we rode on the merry-go-round, both of us, Gran'ther clinging desperately with his one hand to his red camel's wooden hump, and crying out shrilly to me to be sure and not lose his cane. The merry-go-round had just come in at that time, and Gran'ther had never experienced it before. After the first giddy flight we retired to a lemonade-stand to exchange impressions, and finding that we both alike had fallen completely under the spell of the new sensation, Gran'ther said that we 'sh'd keep on a-ridin' till we'd had enough! Nobody could tell when we'd ever git a chance again!' So we returned to the charge, and rode and rode and rode, through blinding clouds of happy excitement, so it seems to me now, such as I was never to know again. The sweat was pouring off from us, and we had tried all the different animals on the machine before we could tear ourselves away to follow the crowd to the race track.

"We took reserved seats, which cost a quarter apiece, instead of the unshaded ten-cent benches, and Gran'ther began at once to pour out to me a flood of horse talk and knowing race track aphorisms, which finally made a young fellow sitting next to us laugh superciliously. Gran'ther turned on him heatedly.

" 'I bet-che fifty cents I pick the winner in the next race!' he said sportily.

" 'Done!' said the other, still laughing.

"Gran'ther picked a big black mare, who came in almost last, but he did not flinch. As he paid over the half-dollar he said: 'Everybody's likely to make mistakes about *some* things; King Solomon was a fool in the head about women-folks. I bet-che a dollar I pick the winner in *this* race!' and 'Done!' said the disagreeable young man, still laughing. I gasped, for I knew we had only eighty-seven cents left, but Gran'ther shot me a command to silence out of the corner of his eyes, and announced that he bet on the sorrel gelding.

"If I live to be a hundred and break the bank at Monte Carlo three times a week," said Mallory, shaking his head reminiscently, "I could not know a tenth part of the frantic excitement of that race or of the mad triumph when our horse won. Gran'ther cast his hat upon the ground, screaming like a steam calliope with exultation as the sorrel swept past the judges' stand ahead of all the others, and I jumped up and down in an agony of delight which was almost more than my little body could hold.

"After that we went away, feeling that the world could hold nothing more glorious. It was five o'clock, and we decided to start back. We paid for Peggy's dinner out of the dollar we had won on the race—I say 'we,' for by that time we were welded into one organism—and we still had a dollar and thirty-seven cents left. 'While ye're about it, always go the whole hog!' said Gran'ther, and we spent twenty minutes in laying out that money in trinkets for all the folks at home. Then, dusty, penniless, laden with bundles, we stowed our exhausted bodies and our uplifted hearts into the old buckboard, and turned Peg's head toward the mountains. We did not talk much during that drive, and though I thought at the time only of the carnival of joy we had left, I can now recall every detail of the trip—how the sun sank behind Indian Mountain, a peak I had known before only through distant views; then, as we journeyed on, how the stars came out above Hemlock Mountain—our own home mountain behind our house, and later, how the fireflies filled the darkening meadows along the river below us, so that we seemed to be floating between the steady stars of heaven and their dancing, twinkling reflection in the valley.

"Gran'ther's dauntless spirit still upheld me. I put out of mind doubts of our reception at home, and lost myself in delightful ruminatings on the splendors of the day. At first, every once in a while, Gran'ther made a brief remark, such as, "Twas the hind-quarters of the sorrel I bet on. He was the only one in the hull kit and bilin' of 'em that his quarters didn't fall away'; or, 'You needn't tell *me* that them Siamese twins ain't unpinned every night as separate as you and me!' But later on, as the damp evening air began to bring on his asthma, he subsided into silence, only broken by great gasping coughs.

"These were heard by the anxious, heartsick watchers at home, and, as old Peg stumbled wearily up the hill, Father came running down to meet us. 'Where you be'n?' he demanded, his face pale and stern in the light of his lantern. 'We be'n to the county fair!' croaked Gran'ther with a last flare of triumph, and fell over sideways against me. Old Peg stopped short, hanging her head as if she, too, were at the limit of her strength. I was frightfully tired myself, and frozen with terror of what Father would say. Gran'ther's collapse was the last straw. I began to cry loudly, but Father ignored my distress with an indifference which cut me to the heart. He lifted Gran'ther out of the buckboard, carrying the unconscious little old body into the house without a glance backward at me. But when I crawled down to the ground, sobbing and digging my fists into my eyes, I felt Mother's arms close around me.

"'Oh, poor, naughty little Joey!' she said. 'Mother's bad, dear little boy!'"

Professor Mallory stopped short.

"Perhaps that's something else I'll know again in heaven," he said soberly, and waited a moment before he went on: "Well, that was the end of our day. I was so worn out that I fell asleep over my supper, in spite of the excitement in the house about sending for a doctor for Gran'ther, who was, so one of my awe-struck sisters told me, having some kind of 'fits.' Mother must have put me to bed, for the next thing I remember, she was shaking me by the shoulder and saying, 'Wake up, Joey. Your great-grandfather wants to speak to you. He's been suffering terribly all night, and the doctor thinks he's dying.'

"I followed her into Gran'ther's room, where the family was assembled about the bed. Gran'ther lay drawn up in a ball, groaning so dreadfully that I felt a chill like cold water at the roots of my hair; but a moment or two after I came in, all at once he gave a great sigh and relaxed, stretching out his legs, laying his one good arm down on the coverlet. He looked at me and attempted a smile.

" 'Well, it was wuth it, warn't it, Joey?' he said, and closed his eyes peacefully to sleep."

"Did he die?" asked the younger professor, leaning forward.

"Die? Gran'ther Pendleton? Not much! He came tottering down to breakfast the next morning, as white as an old ghost, with no voice left, his legs trembling under him, but he kept the whole family an hour and a half at the table, telling them in a loud whisper all about the fair, until Father said really he would have to take us to the one next year. Afterward he sat out on the porch watching old Peg graze around the yard. I thought he was in one of his absent-minded fits, but when I came out, he called me to him, and, setting his lips to my ear, he whispered:

" 'An' the seventh is a-goin' downhill fast, so I hear!" He chuckled to himself for some time over his familiar battle-cry, wagging his head feebly, and then he said: 'I tell ye, Joey, I've lived a long time, and I've larned a lot about the way folks is made. The trouble with most of 'em is, they're 'fraid-cats! As Jeroboam Warner used to say—he was in the same regiment with me in 1812—the only way to manage this business of livin' is to give a whoop and let her rip! If ye just about half-live, ye just the same as half-die; and if ye spend yer time half-dyin', someday ye turn in and die all over, without rightly meanin' to at all—just a kind o' bad habit ye've got yerself inter.' Gran'ther fell into a meditative silence for a moment. 'Jeroboam, he said that the evenin' before the battle of Lundy's Lane, and he got killed the next day. Some live, and some die; but folks that live all over die happy, anyhow! Now I tell you what's my motto, an' what I've lived to be eighty-eight on—' "

Professor Mallory stood up and, laying a hand on the younger man's shoulder, said: "This was the motto he told me: 'Live while you live, and then die and be done with it!' "

"Through Pity and Terror..."

When the war broke out, Madeleine Brismantier was the very type and epitome of all which up to that time had been considered "normal" for a modern woman, a *nice* modern woman. She had been put through the severe and excellent system of French public education in her native town of Amiens, and had done so well with her classes that when she was nineteen her family were about to feed her into the hopper of the system of training for primary teachers. But just then, when on a visit in a smallish Seine-et-Marne town, she met the fine, upstanding young fellow who was to be her husband. He was young too, not then quite through the long formidable course of study for pharmacists, who are in France next to being doctors. It was not until two years later, when Madeleine was twenty-one and he twenty-five, that they were married, and Madeleine left Amiens to live in Madriné, the town where they had met.

Jules Brismantier's father had been the only pharmacist there all his life, and Jules stepped comfortably into his father's shoes, his business, and the lodgings over the pharmacy. If this sounds grubby and "working-class" to your American ears, disabuse yourself; the home over the pharmacy was as well-ordered and well-furnished a little apartment as ever existed in a "strictly residential portion" of any American suburb. The beds were heirlooms, and were of mahogany, there were several bits of excellent furniture in the small, white-paneled salon, and three pretty, brocade-covered chairs which had come down from Madeleine's

great-grandmother; there was a piano on which Madeleine, who had received a good substantial musical training, played the best music there is in the world, which is to say, German (Jules, like many modern young Frenchmen, had a special cult for Beethoven); and there was a kitchen—oh, you should have seen that kitchen, white tiles on the walls and red tiles on the floor and all around such an array of copper and enamel utensils as can only be found in well-kept kitchens in the French provinces where one of the main amusements and occupations of the excellent housewives is elaborate cooking. Furthermore, there was in the big oaken chests and tall cupboards a supply of bedding which would have made us open our eyes, used as we are to our (relatively speaking) hand-to-mouth American methods. Madeleine had no more than the usual number of sheets, partly laid aside for her, piece by piece, when the various inheritances from aunts and cousins came in, partly left there in the house, in which her mother-in-law had died the year before Madeleine's marriage, partly bought for her (as if there were not already enough!) to make up the traditional wedding trousseau without which no daughter of a respectable bourgeois family can be married. So that, taking them all together, she had two hundred and twenty sheets, every one linen, varying from the delightfully rough old homespun and home-woven ones, dating from nobody knew when, down to the smooth, fine, glossy ones with deep hemstitching on the top and bottom, and Madeleine's initials set in a delicately embroidered wreath. Of course she had pillow slips to go with them, and piles of woolen blankets, fluffy, soft and white, and a big puffy eiderdown covered with bright satin as the finishing touch for each well-furnished bed. Madeleine pretended to be modern sometimes, and to say it was absurd to have so many, but in her heart, inherited from long generations of passionately homekeeping women, she took immense satisfaction in all the ample furnishings of her pretty little home. What woman would not?

Now, although all this has a great deal to do with what happened to Madeleine, I am afraid you will think that I am making too long an inventory of her house, so I will not tell you about the shining silver in the buffet drawers, nor even about the beautiful old walled garden, full of flowers and vines and fruit trees, which lay at the back of the pharmacy. The back windows of the new bride's home looked down into the treetops of this garden, and along its graveled walks her children were to run and play.

For very soon the new family began to grow: first, a little blue-eyed girl like Madeleine; then, two years later, a dark-eyed boy like Jules—all very suitable and as it should be, like everything else that happened to Madeleine. She herself, happily absorbed in her happy life and in the care of all her treasures, reverted rapidly to type, forgot most of her modern education, and became a model wife and mother on the pattern of all the other innumerable model wives and mothers in the history of her family. She lived well within their rather small income, and no year passed without their adding to the modest store of savings which had come down to them because all their grandmothers had lived well within *their* incomes. They kept the titles relative to this little fortune, together with what cash they had, and all their family papers, in a safe in the pharmacy, sunk in the wall and ingeniously hidden behind a set of false shelves. They never passed this hiding place without the warm, *sheltered* feeling which a comfortable little fortune gives—the feeling which poor people go all their lives without knowing.

You must not think, because I speak so much of the comfortableness of the life of this typical French provincial family, that there was the least suspicion of laziness about them. Indeed, such intelligent comfort as theirs is only to be had at the price of diligent and well-directed effort. Jules worked hard all day in the pharmacy, and made less money than would have contented an American ten years his junior. Madeleine planned her busy day the evening before, and was up early to begin it. The house was always immaculate, the meals always on time (this was difficult to manage with Madeleine cooking everything and only a rattle-headed young girl to help) and always delicious and varied. Jules mounted the stairs from the pharmacy at noon and in the evening, his mouth literally watering in anticipation. The children were always as exquisitely fresh and well-cared-for as only European children of the better classes used to be, when household help was available at preindustrial pittance payments. Their hair was always curled in shining ringlets and their hands clean, as those of our children are only on Sunday mornings. Madeleine's religion was to keep them spotless and healthful and smiling; to keep Jules' mouth always watering in anticipation; to help him with his accounts in the evenings, and to be on hand during the day to take his place during occasional absences; to know all about the business end of their affairs and to have their success as much at heart as he; to keep her lovely old garden flowering and luxuriant; to keep her lovely old home dainty and well ordered; and, of course, to keep herself invariably neat with the miraculous neatness of French women, her pretty, soft chestnut hair carefully dressed, her hands white and all her attractive person as alluring as in her girlhood.

Madeleine saw nothing lacking in this religion. It seemed to her all that life could demand of one woman.

In the spring of 1914, when Raoul was five years old and Sylvie eight, Madeleine was once more joyfully sorting over the tiny clothes left from their babyhood. All that summer her quick fingers were busy with fine white flannel and finer white nainsook, setting tiny stitches in small garments. Every detail of the great event was provided for in advance. As usual in French families, in all good families everywhere, the mother-to-be was lapped around with tenderness and indulgence. Madeleine was a little queen-regnant whose every whim was law. Of course she wanted her mother to be with her, as she had been for the arrival of Sylvie and Raoul, although her mother was not very well, and detested traveling in hot weather; and she wanted the same nurse she had had before, although that one had now moved away to a distant city. But Madeleine did not like the voice of the nurse who was available in Mandriné, and what French daughter could think of going through her great, dreadful hour without her mother by her to comfort and reassure her and to take the responsibility of everything! So of course that special nurse was engaged and her railway fare paid in advance, and of course Madeleine's mother promised to come. She was to arrive considerably in advance of the date, somewhere about the middle of August. All this was not so unreasonable from a money point of view as it sounds, for when they made up the weekly accounts together they found that the business was doing unusually well.

All through the golden July heats Madeleine sewed and waited. Sometimes in the pharmacy near Jules, sometimes in the garden where Raoul and Sylvie, in white dresses, ran and played gently up and down the paths. They played together mostly and had few little friends, because there were not many "nice" families living near them, and a good many that weren't nice. Of course Madeleine kept her children rigorously separated from these children, who were never in white but in the plainest of cheap gingham aprons, changed only once a week, and who never wore shapely, well-cut little shoes, but slumped about heavily in the wooden-soled, leather-topped "galoches" which are the national footgear for poor French children. Like many good mothers in France (are there any like that elsewhere?) Madeleine looked at other people's children chiefly to see if they were or were not "desirable" playmates for her own; and Sylvie and Raoul were not three years old before they had also learned the art of telling at a glance whether another child was a nice child or not, the question being settled of course by the kind of clothes he wore.

July was a beautiful month of glorious sun and ripening weather. For hours at a time in her lovely green nest, Madeleine sat happily, resting or embroidering, the peaches pleached against the high stone walls swelling and reddening visibly from one day to the next, the lilies opening flaming petals day by day, the children growing vigorously. Jules told his pretty wife fondly that she looked not a day older than on the day of their marriage ten years before. This was quite true, but I am not so sure as Jules that it was the highest of compliments to Madeleine.

The last week of July came, the high-tide moment of lush growth. Madeleine was bathed in the golden, dreamy content which comes to happy, much-loved women in her condition. It was the best possible of worlds, she had the best possible of husbands and children, and she was sure that nobody could say that she had not cultivated her garden to be the best possible of its kind. The world seemed to stand still in a sunny haze, centered about their happiness.

Drenched in sunshine and peace, their little barque was carried rapidly along by the Niagara river of history over the last stretch of smooth, shining water which separated them from the abyss.

I dare not tell you a single word about those first four days in August, of the incredulity which swiftly, from one dreadful hour to the next, changed to black horror. Their barque had shot over the edge, and in a wild tumult of ravening waters they were all falling together down into the fathomless gulf. And there are not words to describe to you the day of mobilization, when Jules, in his wrinkled uniform, smelling of moth-balls, said goodby to his young wife and little children and marched away to do his best to defend them.

There are many things in real life too horrible to be spoken of, and that farewell is one.

There was Madeleine in the empty house, heavy with her time of trial close upon her; with two little children depending on her for safety and care and cheer; with only a foolish little young maid to help her; with such a terrible anxiety about her husband that the mere thought of him sent her reeling against the nearest support.

The first hint came when the Mayor in person, venerable and white-bearded, appeared to gather up the weapons in all the houses. To Madeleine, wondering at this, he explained that he did it, so that *if* the Germans came to Mandriné he could give his word of honor there were no concealed arms in the town.

It was as though thunder had burst there in the little room. Madeleine stared at him, deathly white. "You don't think . . . you don't think it possible that the Germans will get as far as *this!*" It had not once occurred to her that not only Jules in the Army but she and the children might be in danger. Monsieur le Maire hastened to reassure her, remembering her condition, and annoyed that he should have spoken out. "No, no, this is only a measure of precaution, to leave nothing undone." He went away, after having taken Jules' shotgun and little revolver, and even a lockless, flintless old musket which had belonged to some of the kin who had followed Napoleon to Russia. As he left, he said, "Personally I have not the faintest idea they will penetrate as far as Mandriné—not the *faintest!*"

Of course when Jules left, *no* one had the faintest idea that his peaceful home town would see anything of the war. That horror, at least, was spared the young husband and father. But during the fortnight after his departure, although there were no newspapers, practically no trains, and no information except a brief, brief announcement, written by hand, in ink, posted every day on the door of the Town Hall, the air began to be unbreathable, because of rumors, sickening rumors, unbelievable ones . . . that Belgium was invaded, although not in the war at all, and that Belgian cities and villages were being sacked and burned; that the whole north country was one great bonfire of burning villages and farms; then that the Germans were near! Were nearer! And then all at once, quite definitely, that they were within two days' march.

Everyone who could got out of Mandriné, but the only conveyances left were big jolting farm wagons full of household gear; wagons which went rumbling off, drawn by sweating horses lashed into a gallop by panic-stricken boys, wagons which took you, nobody knew where, away! away! which might break down and leave you anywhere, beside the road, in a barn, in a wood, in the hands of the Germans . . . for nobody knew where they were. The frightened neighbors, clutching their belongings into bundles, offered repeatedly to take Madeleine and the children with them. Should she go or not? There was nobody to help her decide. The little fluttering maid was worse than nothing, the children were only babies to be taken care of. After her charges were all in bed, that last night, Madeleine wrung her hands, walking up and down the room, literally sick with indecision. What ought she to do? It was the first great decision she had ever been forced to make alone.

The last of the fleeing carts went without her. During the night she had come to know that the first, the most vital of all the needs of the hour was the life of the unborn baby. She was forced to cling to the refuge she had. She did not dare leave it for the unknown until she had her baby safely in her arms.

And perhaps the Germans would not come to Mandriné.

For two days the few people left in town lived in a sultry suspense, with no news, with every fear. M. le Curé had stayed with his church; M. le Maire stayed with the town records, and his white-haired old wife stayed to be with her husband (they had never been separated during the forty years of their marriage); good fresh-faced Sister Ste. Lucie, the old nun in charge of the little Hospice, stayed with some bedridden invalids who could not be moved; and there were poor people who had stayed for the reason which makes poor people do so many other things, because they could not help it, because they did not own a cart, nor a wheelbarrow, nor even a child's perambulator in which to take along the old grandfather or the sick mother who could not walk. Soeur St. Lucie promised to come to be with Madeleine whenever she should send the little maid with the summons.

Madeleine sickened and shivered and paled during these two endless days and sleepless nights of suspense. There were times when she felt she must die of horror at the situation in which she found herself, that it was asking too much of her to make her go on living. At such moments she shook as though in a palsy and her voice trembled so that she could not speak aloud. There were other times when she was in an unnatural calm, because she was absolutely certain that she was dreaming and must soon wake up to find Jules beside her.

The children played in the garden. They discovered a toad there, during that time, and Madeleine often heard them shouting with laughter over its antics. The silly little maid came every few moments to tell her mistress a new rumor . . . she had heard the Germans were cannibals and ate little children, was that true? And was it true that they had a special technique for burning down whole towns at once, with kerosene pumps and dynamite petards? One story seemed as foolish as the other to Madeleine, who hushed her angrily and told her not to listen to such lies. Once the little maid began to tell her in a terrified whisper what she had heard the Germans did to women in Madeleine's condition . . . but the recital was cut short by a terrible attack of nausea which lasted for hours and left Madeleine so weak that she could not raise her head from the pillow. She lay there, tasting the bitterness of necessity. Weak as she was, she was the strongest of their little band. Presently she rose and went back to her work, but she was stooped forward like an old woman.

She told herself that she did not believe a single word the terror-stricken little maid had told her; but the truth was that she was half dead with fear, age-old, terrible, physical fear, which had been as far from her life before as a desire to eat raw meat or to do murder. It was almost like a stroke of paralysis to this modern woman.

For two whole days the town lay silent and helpless, waiting the blow. On the morning of the third day the sound of clumsily clattering hoofs in the deserted street brought Madeleine rushing downstairs to the door of the pharmacy. An old farmer, mounted on a sweating plow horse, drew rein for an instant in the sun and, breathing hard, gave the news to the little cluster of white-faced women and old men who gathered about him. Madeleine pressed in beside her poorer neighbors, closer to them than at any time in her life, straining up to the messenger, like them. What he had to tell them loomed threateningly in their ears. The Germans were in the next town, Larot-en-Multien, only eight miles away. The vanguard had stopped there to drink and eat, but behind them was an antlike gray horde which pressed steadily forward with dreadful haste and would be in Mandriné within two hours.

He gathered up his reins to go on, but paused to add a brief suggestion as to what they might expect. The Germans were too hurried to burn or to destroy houses; they were only taking everything which was easily portable. They had robbed the church, had taken all the flour from the mill, all the contents of all the shops, and when he left (the sight of the shining plate-glass windows of the pharmacy reminded him) they were just in the act of looting systematically the pharmacy of Larot, taking down all the contents of the shelves and packing them carefully into a big camion.

He rode on. The women dispersed, scurrying rapidly each to her dependents, children, or sick women, or old men. The Mayor hurried away to carry a few more of his priceless town records to the hiding place. The priest went back to his church. For an instant Madeleine was left alone in the empty street, echoing to disaster. She looked at the pharmacy, shining, well ordered, well stocked, useful, *as Jules had left it.*

At the call to action her sickness vanished like a passing giddiness. Her knees stiffened in anger. They should not carry off everything from the Mandriné pharmacy! What could the town *do* without remedies for its sick? The first breath from the approaching tornado annihilating all in its path crashed through the wall which had sheltered her small, comfortably arranged life. Through the breach in the wall she had a passing glimpse of what the pharmacy was; not merely a convenient way for Jules to earn enough for her and the children to live agreeably, but one of the vital necessities of the community life, an important trust which Jules held.

And now Jules was gone and could not defend it. But she was there.

She ran back into the shop, calling for her little maid in a loud, clear voice such as had not issued from her throat since Jules had gone away. "Simone! Simone!"

The maid came running down the stairs and at the first sight of her mistress expected to hear that her master had returned or that the French troops were there, so like herself did Madeleine seem, no longer stooping and shivering and paper-white, but upright, with hard, bright eyes. But it was no good news which she brought out in the new ringing voice. She said: "The Germans will be here in two hours. Help me quickly hide the things in the cellar . . . you know, the further room . . . and we can put the hanging shelves over the door so they won't know there is another part to the cellar. Bring down the two big trays from the kitchen. We can carry more that way. Then light three candles up and down the cellar stairs. It won't do for me to fall, these last days."

She was gathering the big jars together as she spoke, and taking out the innumerable drawers.

In a moment the two women, one who had been hardly strong enough to walk, the other scarcely more than a child, were going slowly down the cellar stairs, their arms aching with the weight of the trays, and then running back upstairs. Shelf after shelf was cleared of the precious remedies that meant health, that might mean life, in the days to come. The minutes slipped past. An hour had gone.

From her attic windows where she could see the road leading to Larot-en-Multien, a neighbor called down shrilly that dust was rising up in thick clouds at the lower end. And even as she called, silently, composedly, there pedaled into the long main street five or six men in gray uniforms on bicycles, calm and sure of themselves, evidently knowing very well that the place had no defenders. Madeleine saw the white hair of M. le Curé and the white beard of M. le Maire advance to meet the invaders.

"We can't do any more here," she said. "Down to the cellar now, to mask the door. No, I'll do it alone. Somebody must be here to warn us. We mustn't be caught down there." She turned to go, and came back. "But I can't move the hanging shelves alone!"

Simone ventured, "Mlle Sylvie? Could she watch and tell us?"

Madeleine hesitated. Sylvie, like her mother at her age, had been asked to do very little with herself except to be a nice little girl.

Then, "Sylvie! Sylvie!" called her mother with decision.

The little girl came running docilely, her eyes wide in wonder.

Madeleine bent on her a white, stern face of command. "The Germans are almost here. Simone and I have been hiding papa's drugs in the cellar and we've not finished. Stay here . . . pretend to be playing . . . and call to us the moment you see the soldiers coming. *Do you understand?"*

Sylvie received her small baptism of fire with courage. Her chin began to tremble and she grew very white. This was not because she was afraid of the Germans. Madeleine had protected her from all the horrid stories which filled the town, and she had only the vaguest baby notions of what the Germans were. It was her mother's aspect, awful to the child, which terrified her. But it also braced her. She pressed her lips together and nodded. Madeleine and the maid went down the cellar stairs for the last time.

When they came back, the troops were still not there, although one could see beyond the river the cloud of white dust raised by their myriad feet. The two women were covered with earth and cobwebs, and were breathing heavily. Their knees shook under them. Taking the child with them, they went up the stairs to the defenseless home. They found five-year-old Raoul just finishing the house-and-farmyard which he and Sylvie had begun. "If only I had three more blocks to do this corner!" he lamented.

Twenty minutes from that time they heard heavy, rapid footsteps enter the shop below and storm up the stairs. There was a loud knocking, and the sound of men's voices in a strange language.

Madeleine went herself to open the door. This was not an act of bravery but of necessity. There was no one else to do it. She had already sent the children to the most remote of the rooms, and at the sound of those trampling feet and hoarse voices Simone had run away, screaming. Madeleine's fingers shook as she pushed back the bolt. A queer pulse began to beat very fast in the back of her dry throat.

The first German soldiers she had ever seen were there before her. Four or five tall, broad, red-faced men, very hot, very dusty, in gray, wrinkled uniforms and big boots, pushed into the room past her. One of them said to her in broken French: "Eat! Eat! Drink! Very thirsty. Quick!" The others had already seized the bottles on the sideboard and were drinking from them.

Madeleine went into the kitchen and brought back on a big tray everything ready-cooked which was there: a dish of stew, cold and unappetizing in its congealed fat, a long loaf of bread, a big piece of cheese, a platter of cooked beans. . . . The men drinking at the sideboard cried aloud hoarsely and fell upon the contents of the tray, clutching, cramming food into their mouths, into their pockets, gulping down the cold stew in huge mouthfuls, shoveling the beans up in their dirty hands and plastering them into their mouths, already full. . . .

Someone called, warningly, from below. The men snatched up what bottles were at hand, thrust them into their pockets, and still tearing off huge mouthfuls from the cheese, the bread, the meat they held, and masticating them with animal noises, turned and clattered down the stairs again, having paid no more attention to Madeleine than if she had been a piece of the furniture.

They had come and gone so rapidly that she had the impression of a vivid, passing nightmare. For an instant she continued to see them. Everywhere she looked, she saw yellow teeth, gnawing and tearing at food; bulging jaw-muscles straining; dirty foreheads streaked with perspiration, wrinkled like those of eating dogs; bloodshot eyes glaring in physical greed.

"Oh, les sales bêtes!" she cried out loud. "The dirty beasts!"

Her fear left her, never to come back, swept away by a bitter contempt. She went, her lip curling, her knees quite strong under her, to reassure Simone and the children.

The house shook, the windows rattled, the glasses danced on the sideboard to the thunder of the innumerable marching feet outside, to the endless rumble of the camions and artillery. The volume of this wild din, and the hurried pulse of haste which was its rhythm, staggered the imagination. Madeleine scorned to look out of the window, although Simone and the children called to her from behind the curtains: "There are millions and millions of them! They are like flies! You couldn't cross the street, not even running fast, they are so close together! And how they hurry!"

Madeleine heard someone come up the stairs and enter the hall without knocking. She found there a well-dressed man with slightly gray hair who informed her in correct French, pronounced with a strong accent, that he would return in one hour bringing with him four other officers and that he would expect to find food and drink ready for them. Having said this in the detached, casual tone of command of a man giving an order to a servant, he went away down the stairs, unfolding a map.

Madeleine had all but cried an angry refusal after him, but, as brutally as on a gag in her mouth, she choked on the sense of her defenselessness in the face of physical force. This is a sensation which moderns have blessedly forgotten, like the old primitive fear of darkness or of thunder. To feel it again is to be bitterly shamed. Madeleine was all one crimson flame of humiliation as she called Simone and went into the kitchen.

They cooked the meal and served it an hour later to five excited, elated officers, spreading out maps as they ate, laughing, drinking prodigiously and eating so rapidly such vast quantities of food that Simone was sure she was serving demons and not human beings and crossed herself repeatedly as she waited on table. In spite of all their haste they had not time to finish. Another officer came up the stairs, thrust his head in through the door, and called a summons to them. They sprang up, in high feather at what he had said, snatching at the fruit which Simone had just set on the table. Madeleine saw one of her guests crowd a whole peach, as big as an apple, into his mouth at once, and depart, choking and chewing, leaning over so that the stream of juice which ran from his mouth should not fall on his uniform.

Simone shrieked from the kitchen, "Oh, madame! The garden! The garden!"

Madeleine ran to a window, looked down, and saw long rows of horses picketed in the garden. Two German soldiers were throwing down hay from the gable end of the Mandriné livery stable which overlooked the wall. The horses ate with hungry zest, stamping vigorously in the flowerbeds to keep off the flies. When they had finished on the hay, they began on the vines, the little, carefully tended fruit trees, the bushes, the flowers. A swarm of locusts could not have done the work more thoroughly.

As she stood there, gazing down on this, there was always in Madeleine's ears the incessant thundering rumble of the passing artillery. . . .

Through the din there reached her ears a summons roared out from below: "Cellar! Cellar! Key!"

She was at white heat. She ran downstairs, forgetting all fear, and, raising her voice to make herself heard above the uproar outside, she shouted with a wrath which knew no prudence: "You low, vile thieves! I will not give you one thing more!"

Her puny defiance to the whirlwind passed unnoticed. The men did not even take the time to strike her, to curse her. With one movement they turned from her to the cellar door, and, all kicking at it together, burst it open, trooped downstairs, returning with their arms full of bottles, and ran out into the street.

And all the time the very air shook, in almost visible waves, to the incessant thundering rumble of the artillery passing.

Madeleine went upstairs, gripping the railing hard, her head whirling. She had scarcely closed the door behind her when it was burst open and five soldiers stormed in, cocked revolvers in their fists. They did not give her a look, but tore through the apartment, searching in every corner, in every closet, pulling out the drawers of the bureaus, tumbling the contents on the floor, sweeping the cupboard shelves clear in one movement of their great hands, with the insane haste which characterized everything done that day. When they had finished they clattered out, chalking up something unintelligible on the door. Raoul and Sylvie began to cry wildly, their nerves undone, and to clutch at their mother's skirts.

Madeleine took them back into their own little room, undressed them and put them to bed, where she gave them each a bowl of bread and milk. All this she did with a quiet air of confidence which comforted the children. They had scarcely finished eating when they fell asleep, worn out. Madeleine heard Simone calling for her and went out in the hall. A German soldier, desperately drunk, held out a note which stated that four Herr-Lieutenants and a Herr-Captain would eat and sleep there that night, dinner to be sharp at seven, and the beds ready.

After delivering this he tried to put his arm around Simone and to drag her into the next room. Simone struggled and screamed, shriek after shriek, horribly. Madeleine screamed too, and snatching up the poker, flung herself on the man. He released his hold, too uncertain on his feet to resist. Both women threw themselves against him, pushing him to the door and shoving him out on the narrow landing, where he lost his balance and fell heavily, rolling over and over, down the stairs.

Madeleine bolted the door, took a long knife from the kitchen table, and waited, her ear at the keyhole, to see if he tried to come back.

This was the woman, you must remember, who less than a month before had been sitting in the garden sewing on fine linen, safe in an unfathomable security.

The man did not attempt to return. Madeleine relaxed her tense crouching attitude and laid the knife down on the table. The perspiration was streaming down her white cheeks. It came over her with horror that their screams had not received the slightest response from the outside world. No one was responsible for their safety. No one cared what became of them. It made no difference to anyone whether they had repelled that man, or whether he had triumphed over their resistance. . . .

And now she must command her shaking knees and hands to prepare food for those who had sent him there. Of all the violent efforts Madeleine had been forced to make, none was more racking than to stoop to the servility of this submission. She had an instant of frenzy when she thought of locking the door and defying them to enter, but the recollection of the assault on the thick oaken planks of the cellar door, and of its splintering collapse before those huge hobnailed boots, sent her to the kitchen, her teeth set in her lower lip. "I never will forgive them this, never, never, never!" she said aloud passionately, more passionately than she had ever said anything in her life, and she knew as she spoke that it was not of the slightest consequence to anyone whether she would or not.

At seven the meal was ready. At half-past seven the four officers entered, laughing, talking loudly, jubilant. One of them spoke in good

French to Madeleine, complimenting her on her soup and on the wine. "I told my friends I knew we would find good cheer and good beds with Madame Brismantier," he told her affably.

Astonished to hear her name, Madeleine looked at him hard, and recognized, in spite of his uniform, a well-to-do man, reputed a Swiss, who had rented a house for the season, several summers back, on a hillside not far from Mandriné. He had professed a great interest in the geology of the region and was always taking long walks and collecting fossils. Jules had an amateur interest in fossils also, and this, together with the admirably trained voice of the Swiss, had afforded several occasions of social contact. The foreigner had spent an evening or two with them, singing to Madeleine's accompaniment. And once, having some valuable papers left on his hands, he had asked the use of the Brismantier safe for a night. He had been very fond of children, and had had always a jolly greeting for little Raoul, who was then only a baby of two. Madeleine looked at him now, too stupefied with wonder to open her lips. A phrase from "An die ferne Geliebte," which he had sung very beautifully, rang in her ears, sounding faint and thin but clear, through the infernal din in the street.

She turned and went back into the kitchen. Standing there, before the stove, she said as though she had but just known it, "Why, he was a spy, all the time!" She had not thought there were such people as spies outside of cheap books.

She was just putting the roast on the table when someone called loudly from the street. The men at the table jumped up, went to the window, leaned out, exchanged noisy exultant words, cursed jovially, and turned back in haste to tighten the belts and fasten the buttons and hooks which they had loosened in anticipation of the feast. The spy said laughingly to Madeleine: "Your French army runs away so fast, madame, that we cannot eat or sleep for chasing it! Our advance guard is always sending back word to hurry faster, faster!"

One of the others swept the roast from the table into a brown sack, all crammed their pockets full of bread and took a bottle under each arm. At the door the spy called over his shoulder: "Sorry to be in such a hurry! I will drop you a card from Paris as soon as the mails begin again."

They clattered down the stairs.

Madeleine bolted the door and sank down on a chair, her teeth chattering loudly. After a time during which she vainly strove to master a mounting tide of pain and sickness, she said: "Simone, you must go for Sister Ste. Lucie. My time has come. Go by our back door, through the alley, and knock at the side door of the Hospice . . . you needn't be gone more than three minutes."

Simone went downstairs, terribly afraid to venture out, even more afraid to be left alone with her mistress. Madeleine managed to get into the spare bedroom, away from the children's room, and began to undress, in an anguish of mind and body such as she had not thought she could endure and live. But even now she did not know what was before her. In a short time Simone came back, crying and wringing her hands. A sentry guarded the street and another the alley. They had thrust her back into the house, their bayonets glittering, and one had said in French, "Forbidden; no go out till daylight." She had tried to insist, to explain, but he had struck her back with the butt end of his rifle. Oh, he had hurt her awfully! She cried and cried, looking over her shoulder, tearing at her apron. It was evident that if there had been any possibility for her to run away, she would have done it, anywhere, anywhere . . .

Madeleine's little boy was born that night. She, who of course must needs have her mother to take all the responsibility, and the nurse whose voice was agreeable to her, went through her fiery trial alone, with no help but the foolish little Simone, shivering and gasping in hysteria. She was nothing but a pair of hands and feet to be animated by Madeleine's will power and intelligence. In those dreadful hours Madeleine descended to the black depths of her agony but dared never abandon herself even to suffer. At every moment she needed to shock Simone out of her panic by a stern, well-considered command.

She needed, and found, strange, unguessed stores of strength and resolution. She felt herself alone, pitted against a malign universe which wished to injure her baby, to prevent her baby from having the right birth and care. But she felt herself to be stronger than all the malignity of the universe. Once, in a moment's lull during the fight, she remembered, seeing the words zigzag like lightning on a black sky, a sentence in the first little history-book she had studied as a child—"The ancient Gauls said they feared nothing, not enemies, not tempest, not death. Until the skies fell upon their heads, they would never submit." . . . "They were my ancestors!" said the little Gaulish woman, fighting alone in the darkness. She clenched her teeth to repress a scream of pain and a moment later told Simone, quite clearly, in a quiet tone of authority, just what to do, again.

Outside, all night long, there thundered the rumbling passage of the artillery and camions.

In the morning, when Sylvie and Raoul awoke, they found Simone crouched in a corner of their mother's room, sobbing endlessly from sheer nervous exhaustion. But out from their mother's white, white face on the pillow looked triumphant eyes. She drew the covers down a little and lifted her arm. "See, children, a little new brother."

As she spoke she thrust out of her mind, with a violence like that with which she had expelled the ruffian from the door, the thought that the little brother would probably never see his father. It was no moment to allow herself the weakness of sorrow. She must marshal her little forces. "Come, Sylvie dear. Simone is all tired out; you must get us something to eat, and then you and Simone must bring in all you can of what is left in the kitchen and hide it here under mother's bed." She had thought out her plan in the night.

During the next days Madeleine was wholly unable to stand on her feet. From her bed she gave her orders—desperate, last-resort orders to a defeated garrison. The apartment was constantly invaded by ravenously hungry and thirsty men, but her room was not entered. The first morning the door had been opened brusquely, and a grayhaired under-officer entered. He stopped short when he saw Madeleine's drawn white face on the pillow, with the little red, bald head beside her. He went out as abruptly as he had gone in and chalked something on the door. Thereafter no one came in; although not infrequently, as though to see if the chalked notice were true, the door was opened suddenly and a head thrust in. This inspection of a sick woman's room could and did continually happen without the slightest warning. Madeleine was buffeted by an angry shame which she put aside sternly, lest it make her unfit to nurse her baby.

They lived during this time on what happened to be left in the kitchen, after that first day of pillage, some packages of macaroni, tapioca, and cornstarch, part of a little cheese, some salt fish, two or three boxes of crackers, a little sugar, a little flour. They did unsavory cooking over the open fire till their small supply of wood gave out. The children submitted docilely to this régime, caused by their mother's fierce command not for an instant to go out of her sight. But the little maid, volatile and childish, could not endure life without bread. She begged to be allowed to go out, to slip along the alley to the Hospice and beg a loaf from Sister Ste. Lucie. There must be bread somewhere in town, she argued, unable to conceive of a world without bread. And in the daytime the sentries would let her pass.

Madeleine forbade her to leave the room, but on the third day when her mistress was occupied with the baby she slipped out and was gone. She did not come back that day or the next. They never saw or heard of her from that moment.

Madeleine and the children continued to live in that one room, shaken by the incessant rumble of the passing artillery wagons and by the hurrying tread of booted feet. And now there was the low growl of distant cannon, to the south. *To the south!* Far in towards the heart of France. Now and again, there were incursions into the other rooms of their home, and as long as there were loud voices and trampling and clattering dishes, the children crept into bed beside Madeleine and the baby, cowering together under the poor protection of their mother's powerless arms. They never dared speak above a whisper during those days. They heard laughing, shouting, cursing, snoring in the rooms all around them. Once they heard pistol shots, followed by a great splintering crash of glass and shouts of wild mirth.

Madeleine lost all count of the days, of everything but the diminishing stock of food. She tried repeatedly to sit up, she tried to put her feet to the floor, but she felt her head swim and fell back in bed. She had little strength left to struggle now. The food was almost gone, and her courage was almost gone. As though the walls of the room were closing in on her, the approach of the spent, beaten desire to die began to close in on her. What was the use of struggling on? If she could only kill the children and herself . . .

One morning Sylvie said in a loud, startled whisper: "Oh, *Maman,* they are going the other way! Back towards Larot . . . and yet they are still hurrying as fast as ever . . . faster!"

Madeleine felt her hair raise itself on her scalp. She sat up in bed. "Sylvie, *are you sure?"*

The child answered, always in her strained whisper, "Yes, yes, I am sure." Her mother sprang out of bed with a bound and ran to the window.

It was true. The dust-gray tide had turned. They were raging past the house, the horses straining at the heavy artillery wagons, lashed into a clumsy canter by the drivers, leaning far forward, urging; the haggard men, reeling in fatigue, stumbling under their heavy packs, pressing forward in a dogtrot; the officers with red angry faces, barking out incessant commands for more haste . . . and their backs were turned to Paris!

The Frenchwoman, looking down on them, threw her arms up over her head in a wild gesture of exultation. They were going back!

She felt as strong as ever she had in her life. She dressed herself, set the wretched room in some sort of order, and managed to prepare an edible dish out of soaked tapioca and sugar. The children ate it with relish, comforted by their mother's new aspect.

About two o'clock that night Madeleine awoke to an awful sense of impending calamity. Something had happened, some tremendous change had come over the world. She lay still for a long moment. Then she realized that she heard nothing but the beating of her own heart, that the thunder of the trampling feet had stopped. She got out of bed carefully, trying not to waken the children, but Sylvie, her nerves aquiver, called out in a frightened whisper, *"Maman, Maman!* What is it?" She caught her mother's arm, and the two went together to the window. They leaned out, looked to right and left, and fell to weeping in each other's arms. Under the quiet stars, the village street was perfectly empty.

The next morning Madeleine made the children swallow a little food before, all together, the baby in his mother's arms, they ventured out from their prison-room. They found their home gutted and sacked and sullied to the remotest corner. The old brocade on the chairs in the salon had been split to ribbons by sword-slashes, the big, plate-glass windows over the mantels had each been shattered into a million pieces, all the silver was gone from the drawers, every piece of linen had disappeared, the curtains had been torn down and carried away, and every bit of bedding had gone, every sheet, every blanket, every eiderdown quilt. The mattresses had been left, each having been cut open its entire length and sedulously filled with filth.

The kitchen, emptied of all its shining copper and enamel utensils, was one litter of splintered wood, remnants of furniture which had been cut up with the ax for fuel. Madeleine recognized pieces of her mahogany beds there. Through the kitchen window she looked down into the walled space which had been the garden and saw it a bare, trampled stable-yard, with heaps of manure. She looked at all this in perfect silence, the children clinging to her skirts, the baby sleeping on her arm. She looked at it, but days passed before she really believed that what she saw was real.

A woman's voice called quaveringly from the landing: "Madame Brismantier, are you alive? The Germans have gone." Madeleine stepped to the landing and saw old Sister Ste. Lucie. Her face which had always been so rosy and fresh was as gray as ashes under her black-and-white coif. She leaned against the wall. At the sight of the sleeping baby in Madeleine's arms, the gray face smiled, the wonderful smile which women, even those vowed to childlessness, give to a new mother. "Oh, your baby came," she said. "Boy or girl?"

"Yes," said Madeleine, "he came. A boy. A nice little boy." For one instant the two women stood there in that abomination of desolation, death all around them, looking at newborn life—and smiling.

Then Soeur Ste. Lucie said: "There is nothing in the pharmacy, I see. I thought maybe they might have left something, by chance, but I see everything has been taken away or smashed to pieces. You don't happen to have any supplies up here, do you? We need bandages horribly at the Hospice, for the wounded. There are forty there."

Madeleine knew the minute size of the little Hospice and exclaimed: "Forty! Where do you put them?"

"Everywhere. On the floor, up and down the hall, in the kitchen. But we haven't a thing except hot water to use for wounds. All the sheets were torn up two days ago, what hadn't been stolen! If I only had a little iodine, or any sort of antiseptic. The wounds are too awful, all infected, and nothing . . ."

Without knowing it Madeleine took a first step forward into a new life. "There's plenty of everything," she said. "I hid them all in the far room of the cellar."

"God grant 'they' didn't find them!" breathed the nun.

Madeleine lighted a candle, left the sleeping baby in charge of Sylvie, and went with Soeur Ste. Lucie down into the cellar. They found it littered and blocked with emptied and broken bottles. A strange hoarse breathing from a dark corner frightened them. Lifting her candle, Madeleine brought to view a German soldier, dead-drunk, snoring, his face swollen and red. The older woman said, "We should be sure his gun is not available." They looked for the weapon, found nothing, not even his bayonet in its sheath. They turned from him then as from an object of no importance and went across the cellar. With a long sigh of relief they saw that the hanging shelves were still there, untouched. Madeleine's device was successful.

As they looked for bandages and antiseptics among the heaped-up supplies from the pharmacy, Soeur Ste. Lucie told Madeleine very briefly what had been happening. Madeleine listened in a terrible silence. Neither she nor the nun had strength to spare for exclamations. Nor could any words of theirs have been adequate. M. le Maire was dead, shot in front of the Town Hall, on the ground that there had been weapons found in one of the houses. "You know in the Bouvines' house they had some Malay creeses and a Japanese sword hanging up in M. Bouvines' study, things his sailor uncle brought back. The Mayor had never thought to take those down, and they wouldn't give him time to explain. M. le Curé was dead, nobody knew or ever would know why—found dead strapped to a bed in an attic room of a house occupied by some German officers. Perhaps he had been forgotten by the person who had tied him there. . . ." The nun's voice died away in sobs. She had been brought up under M. le Curé's protection all her life and loved him like a father.

Madeleine sorted bandages in silence, her throat very dry and harsh. Later Soeur Ste. Lucie went on, trying to speak more collectedly: "The worst of trying to care for these wounded is not being able to understand what they say."

"How so?" asked Madeleine, blankly.

"Why, I don't speak German."

Madeleine gave a violent start—and stood motionless, her hands full of bandages. "Are they *Germans?* Are we getting these things for *German soldiers?"*

Soeur Ste. Lucie said gravely, "I felt that way too, at first. But—are we not taught to do good to our enemies?" Madeleine stared silently at her. The religious went on, "If it were our army in Germany—if your husband were terribly wounded like these men—how would you wish German women to—?"

Of these words Madeleine heard little at the time, although they were to come back to her, again and again. But one image evoked by the words burned before her eyes—her Jules, wounded—French soldiers in Germany—would they, if the tide had swept the other way—would Frenchmen be stamping into strangers' houses, snatching the food away from the—was it *war* itself not only—.

She cried out as if in a fury of anger, "Oh, of course we'll have to give them the antiseptics and bandages." She could not have named the impulse which drove her to say this, nor could she have explained why she said it, with an intonation so unsuited to the words—with wrath. It was nothing but self-respect, a bare meager minimum of the most ordinary self-respect. . . .

But she could not think. Her head ached, her back ached as though it were being beaten with hammers. She gave up her attempt to think.

"Here," said Soeur Ste. Lucie, staggering with exhaustion. "The baby is only a few days old. You're not fit to be doing this."

Madeleine, who had lain flat on her back for two weeks after the birth of the other two children, shook her head. "No, no, I can do it as well as you. You look fearfully tired."

"I haven't had my clothes off for ten days," said the old nun.

At the street door, with her basket of bandages on her arm, Soeur Ste. Lucie stood looking around her at the desolate filth-strewn shop, the million pieces of glass which had been its big windows covering the floor, its counter hacked and broken with axes. She said: "We haven't any mayor and the priest is dead, and we haven't any pharmacy and the baker is mobilized, and there isn't one strong, well man left in town. How are we going to live?"

Madeleine took another step, hesitating, along the new road. She leaned against the counter to ease her aching body and put back her hair to look around her at the ruin of her husband's business. She said in a faint voice: "I wonder if I could keep the pharmacy open. I used to help Jules with the accounts. I know a little about where he bought and how he kept his records. I wonder if I could—enough for the simpler things?"

"You have already," said the nun, as she went away, "and the first things you have given out are bandages for your enemies. God will not forget that."

Madeleine received this with an impatient shrug. She was not at all glad that her first act had been to help the suffering among her enemies. She had hated doing it. Only some confused sense of decency had forced her to it. She would have been ashamed not to. That was all. And yet to help those men who had murdered M. le Maire, so blameless, and M. le Curé—so defenseless! . . . No, these were not the same men who lay bleeding to death in the Hospice to whom she had sent bandages. *They* had not murdered . . . as yet!

Her head throbbed feverishly. She renounced again the effort to think, and turned to the urgent needs of the moment. It seemed to her that she could not breathe till she had set the pharmacy as far as possible in the order Jules had left it. This intense feeling was her only refuge against her certainty that Jules was killed, that she would never see him again. Without an attempt to put in order even a corner of the desolated little home, she began toiling up and down the cellar stairs carrying back the glass jars, the pots, the boxes, and bottles and drawers. In her dazed condition it seemed to her that somehow she was doing something for Jules in saving his pharmacy which he had so much cared for, that she was almost keeping him from dying by working with all her might for him there. . . .

In the middle of the morning she went upstairs and found that Sylvie, with Raoul's help, had cleared the kitchen of the worst of the rubbish. In a pot-closet under the sink they had found two old saucepans which had not been stolen. Madeleine made a fire, stoically using her own broken-up furniture, and, putting a few potatoes (the last of their provisions) on to boil, sat down to nurse the hungry baby.

"*Maman* dear," said Sylvie, still in the hoarse whisper of the days of terror. She could not speak aloud for weeks. "*Maman* dear," she whispered, "in the salon, in the dining room, I wanted to try to clean it, but it is all nasty, like where animals have been."

"Hush!" said her mother firmly. "Don't think about that. Don't look in there. It'll make you sick if you do. Wait here till I finish feeding the baby. Then don't go away, tend the fire, watch the baby, and play with Raoul." She outlined this program with decision and hurried back downstairs. If she could only get the pharmacy to look a little as it had when Jules had left it, it seemed that Jules would seem less lost to her.

She shoveled the incredible quantity of broken glass back through the shop into what had been her garden, hardening herself against a qualm of horror at the closer view of the wreckage there.

She went back to her work hastily, knowing that if she stopped for an instant to look, she would be lost.

At noon she climbed the stairs, and with the children lunched on potatoes and salt.

She was putting the last of the innumerable drawers back in its place, after having tried it in all the other possible places, when a poorly dressed, rough-haired, scrawny small boy came into the shop.

Madeleine knew him by sight, the six-year-old grandson of Madame Duguet, a bedridden, old, poor woman on Poulaine Street. He said that he had come to get those powders for his grandmother's asthma. She hadn't slept any for two nights. As he spoke he wound the string about a top and prepared to spin it, nonchalantly. Looking at his cheerful, dirty little face, Madeleine felt herself a thousand years old, separated for always and always from youth which would never know what she had known.

"It was my husband who took care of your grandmother's asthma powders. I wouldn't have any idea where to look for them," she said. The little boy insisted. He was so young he was astonished that a grown person did not know everything. "*He* always kept them. *Grandmère* used to send me twice a week to get them. *Grandmère* will scold me awfully, if I don't take them back. She's scolding all the time now, because the Germans took our soup kettle and our frying pan. We haven't got anything left to cook with."

The memory of her immensely greater losses rose burningly to Madeleine's mind. "They took *all my sheets!"* she cried impulsively—"every one!"

"Oh," said the little boy indifferently, "we never had any sheets, anyhow." This did not seem an important statement to him, apparently; but to Madeleine, emerging from her old world into new horizons, beaten upon by a thousand new impressions, it rang loudly. The Germans, then, had only put her in the situation in which a woman, like herself, had always lived . . . and within a stone's throw of these well-filled linen-closets of hers! There was something strange about that, something which she would like to ponder, if only her head did not ache so terribly. The little boy said, insistently, *"He* always gave me the powders, right away!"

Through obscure mental processes, of which she had only the dimmest perceptions . . . *Jules* had always given the powders . . . how strange it was that precisely a bedridden woman who had most need of them should have owned no sheets . . . there came to her a great desire to send that old woman the medicine she needed. "You go outside and spin your top for a while," she said to the child; "I'll call you when I'm ready."

She went upstairs. Holding her skirts high to keep them out of the filth on the floor, she picked her way to the bookcase. Books were scattered all about the room, torn, cut, trampled on, defiled; but for the most part those with handsome bindings had been chosen for destruction. On the top shelf, sober in their drab, gray-linen binding, stood Jules' big record-books, intact. She carried down an armful of them to the pharmacy, and opened the latest one, the one which Jules had put away with his own hand the day he had left her.

The sight of the pages covered with Jules' neat, clear handwriting brought scalding tears to her eyes. Her bosom heaved. She laid down the book, and, taking hold of the counter with all her strength, she forced herself to draw one long, regular breath after another, holding her head high.

When her heart was beating quietly again, quietly and heavily, breast, she opened the book and began studying the pages.

Jules set everything down in writing, it being his idea that a pharmacist had no other defense against making those occasional mistakes inevitable to human nature, but which must not occur in his profession.

Madeleine read: "March 10, sold 100 quinine pills to M. Augier. Stock low. Made 100 more, using quinine from the Cochard Company's laboratories. Filled prescription. . . ." Madeleine's eyes leaped over the hieroglyphics of the pharmaceutical terms and ran up and down the pages, filled with such items, looking for the name Duguet. She had almost given up when she saw, dated July 30, 1914, the entry: "Made up fresh supply Mme Duguet asthma powders, prescription 457. Dr. Millier. Drawer No. 17."

Madeleine ran behind the counter and pulled out No. 17. She found there a little pasteboard box marked "Duguet."

"Oh, boy, little boy!" she called. She did not know his name. He had lived all of his six years close to her home, and she did not know his name.

When the child came in she asked, "Did your grandmother ever get any other medicine here?"

"No," said the grandson of the bedridden woman, "she hasn't got anything else the matter with her."

"Well," said the pharmacist's wife, "here is her medicine." She put the box in his hand.

"But we never get more than four at a time," he told her. "She never has the money to pay for more. Here it is. Granny hid it in her hair so the Germans wouldn't get it. She hid all we have. She's got more than *five francs,* all safe."

He put a small silver coin in her hand and departed.

The mention of the meager sum of hidden money made Madeleine think of her own dexterously concealed little fortune. She had noticed at once on entering the shop that the arrangement of false shelves which concealed the safe had not been detected, and was intact. She pushed the spring; the shelves swung back and disclosed the door of the safe just as usual. She began to turn the knob of the combination lock. It worked smoothly and in a moment the heavy door swung open. The safe was entirely empty, swept clear of all the papers, titles, deeds, bonds which had covered its shelves.

As actually as though he stood there again, Madeleine saw the polite pseudo-Swiss geological gentleman, thanking Jules for the temporary use of his excellent safe.

She felt the very ground give way under her feet. A cold, cold wind of necessity blew upon her. The walled and sheltered refuge in which she had lived all her life was cast down and in ruins. The realization came to her, like something indecent, that *she,* Madeleine Brismantier, was now as poor as that old bedridden neighbor had been all her life . . . *all her life. . . .*

Somehow, that had something to do with those sheets which she had had and the other woman had not . . . her mind came back with a mortal sickness to the knowledge that she had now nothing, nothing to depend upon except her own strength and labor—just like a *poor* woman. She *was* a poor woman!

Somebody was weeping and tugging at her skirts. She looked down blindly. It was Raoul, her little son. He was sobbing and saying: "Sylvie said not to come, but I couldn't stand it any more. I'm hungry! I'm hungry, and there isn't a thing left upstairs to eat! I'm hungry! I'm hungry!"

Madeleine put her hand to her head and thought. What had happened? Oh, yes, all their money had been stolen, all . . . but Raoul was hungry, the children must have something to eat. "Hush, my darling," she said to the little boy, "go back upstairs and tell Sylvie to come here and look out for the shop while I try to find something to eat."

She went down the silent, empty street, before the silent, empty houses staring at her out of their shattered windows. Not a soul was abroad. At the farm, in the outskirts of town, she saw smoke rising from the chimney and went into the courtyard. The young farmer's wife was there, feeding a little cluster of hens, and weeping like a child. She stared at the newcomer for a moment without recognizing her. Madeleine looked ten years older than she had a fortnight ago.

"Oh, madame, we had three hundred hens, and they left us just these eight that they couldn't catch! And they killed all but two of our thirty cows; we'd raised them ourselves from calves up. They killed them there before the very door and cooked them over a fire in the courtyard, and they broke up everything of wood to burn in the fire, all our hoes and rake handles, and the farm wagon and . . . oh, what will my husband say when he knows!"

Madeleine had a passing glimpse of herself as though in a convex mirror, distorted but recognizable. She said, "They didn't hurt you or your husband's mother, did they?"

"No, they were drunk all the time and they didn't know what they were doing mostly. We could hide from them."

"Then your husband will not care at all about the cows and pigs and farm wagons," said Madeleine very firmly, as though she were speaking to Sylvie. The young farmer's wife responded automatically to the note of authority in Madeleine's voice. "Don't you think he will?" she asked simply, reassured somewhat, wiping away her tears.

"No, and you are very lucky to have so much left," said Madeleine. "I have nothing, nothing at all for my children to eat, and no money to buy anything." She heard herself saying this with astonishment.

The young wife was horrified, sympathetic, a little elated to have one whom she had always considered her superior come asking her for aid; for Madeleine stood there, her empty basket on her arm, asking for aid, silently, helplessly.

"Oh, we have things left to *eat!*" said the farmer's wife. She put some eggs in Madeleine's basket, several pieces of veal left from the last animal killed which the Germans had not had time entirely to consume, and, priceless treasure, a long loaf of bread. "Yes, the wife of the baker got up at two o'clock last night, when she heard the Germans go by, and started to heat her oven. She had hidden some flour in barrels behind her rabbit hutches, and this morning she baked a batch of bread. It's not so good as the baker's of course, but she says she will do better as she learns."

Madeleine turned back down the empty, silent street before the empty silent houses with their wrecked windows. A child came whistling along behind her, the little grandson of the bedridden Madame Duguet. Madeleine did what she had never done before in her life. She stopped him, made him take off his cap, and put into it a part of her loaf of bread and one of the pieces of meat.

"Oh, meat!" cried the child, overjoyed. "We hardly ever had meat!"

He set off at a run.

As she passed the butcher shop, she saw an old man hobbling about on crutches, attempting to sweep up the last of the broken glass. It was the father of the butcher. She stepped in, and stooping, held the dustpan for him. He recognized her, after a moment's surprise at the alteration in her expression, and said, "Merci, madame." They worked together silently a moment, and then he said: "I'm going to try to keep Louis' business open for him. I think I can till he gets back. The war *can't* be long. You, madame, will you be going back to your parents?"

Madeleine walked out without speaking. She could not have answered him if she had tried. In front of the Town Hall she saw a tall old woman in black toiling up the broad stone steps with a large package under each arm. She went to help. It was the white-haired wife of the old mayor, who turned a ghastly face on Madeleine to explain: "I am bringing back the papers to put them in place as he always kept them. And then I shall stay here to guard them and to do his work till somebody else can come." She laid the portfolios down on a desk and said in a low, strange voice, looking out of the window: "It was before that wall. I heard the shots."

Madeleine clasped her hands together convulsively, in a gesture of horror, of utter sympathy, and looked wildly at the older woman. The wife of the Mayor said: "I must go back to the house now and get more of the papers. All the records must be in order." She added as she sat down at her husband's desk, "And you? Will you be going back to live with your mother at Amiens?"

Madeleine made no answer.

The Mayor's wife went on, "We will need a pharmacy. There will be no doctor, you know. You could do a great . . ." Her voice failed her.

Again Madeleine said nothing.

In the stillness they heard the banging of a shutter, hanging by one hinge in front of a broken window.

There was another sound. Their eyes met as they held their breath to listen. It was the distant growl of cannon, and it was to the north . . . to the *north!*

A sob of relief broke from Madeleine. "But . . . do you think . . . will they perhaps come back?"

The white lips in the old face were trembling. But the words of the Mayor's widow were—almost—steady. "Perhaps . . . perhaps not." She looked down at the Mayor's desk. It was covered with broken glass and plaster. She lifted a hand to sweep it clear, dropped her hand, and said, "But . . . but it is now that we have our work to do."

Madeleine stooped for her basket. "Yes, I shall keep the pharmacy open," she said. "I used to help my husband. I already know about the simple things. I can study my husband's books on pharmacy at night, after the children are in bed. There will be much I can learn."

She went out at the broken door, and down the broad stone steps. When she was once more on the paving stones of the street, she stood motionless for a moment, gazing into a new, terrifying, and pleasureless life.

Something stern and mighty rose within her and swept her to meet it. She turned her face toward her ruined home and felt a wind blowing coldly along the deserted street. It was savagely cold. She shuddered. Would she ever be warm again? But she held her head up and walked steadily forward.

An American Citizen

I.

I would not have noticed her among the other uniformed American women on board the steamer, if it had not been for a troubled look of uneasiness in her honest eyes, which contrasted with the healthy, kind, fixed certainty of themselves and their standards shining out from the honest eyes of the other serious-faced American women who made up her "unit," just returning home for a well-earned rest after two years continuous service in war relief. Indeed, the difference between them was so great that once the cynic of our party, who had seen her staring darkly out to sea, said of her mockingly,

"There's one who looks as gloomy as though her shell had been penetrated by the awful thought that perhaps French amenities in everyday life and French daily pleasure in small pleasantnesses, may mean more civilization than bath-tubs and open plumbing."

But he was wrong, as usual. Something deeper, even more impersonal, was in question, as I learned later on in the voyage when I had come to know and greatly respect her. One evening, quite late, she stopped her restless pacing about the deck, and dropped into the chair beside me. I felt touched to sympathy by the long sigh she drew, and said, clumsily trying to invite a confidence which might perhaps relieve her, "You seem to be troubled about something. I'd be so glad if I could help." She turned her head towards me, quickly, and looked at me hard,

shaking her head. "I don't see what anybody can do about it," she said. Then she added, unexpectedly, "What part of the States do you come from?"

"Vermont," I answered, not seeing why she should be interested in that.

She moved her head restlessly and said, "Oh, well, I suppose one American is very much like another. I know I am, and I'm from New Jersey!"

As I was silent, quite at sea, she went on, "I wonder if it would make things any clearer to me if I should just tell you all about it! Perhaps it would!"

Her voice was so sincerely troubled that I took her hand in mine, as assurance of my interest. She began her story.

II.

And I now set it down here just as she told it to me, wishing to shift it to other American shoulders, as she shifted it to mine.

"I had been brought up," she began, "like all public school American children, to salute the flag every morning, to believe that America was the only country where Liberty prevailed, and to read in my little American history textbook, how our fathers had fought to found that new thing,—a country where all men are free.

"Up to the time (I was fourteen years old then) that I encountered Jefferson Heywood, I had no idea that there might be shadows in the bright day of American freedom. Of course, Jeff was not the first Negro I had ever seen. I had been brought up near a lot of them, had played with little colored children quite as much as with white. But the black flame in Jeff's bloodshot eyes was very different from the light-hearted, giggling fun of my little black play-fellows, or from the easy-going good humor of Uncle Harry, the bald-headed old Negro who used to come once a week to shake our rugs and do other things too heavy for the maid. And, especially, the bitter carelessness of Jeff's accent when he said, 'Yes, I've been off on a jag again,' was very different from the humble and repeated, 'Yas'm,' of Uncle Harry when my mother took him to task for being half-seas over.

"When I came to know him, Jefferson belonged to a very different world from the family-like atmosphere of the small town where I had spent my early childhood. He ran the elevator in the ramshackle old building in New York where one of my grown-up cousins had a studio, and although he had come originally from a small town in Virginia, with the same innocent rusticity as my own small town, it was evident that in New York he had become an integral part of vicious, big-city life. He drank and gambled to everybody's certain knowledge.

"With his habits and his quite apparent hostility to white people, he would not have been kept a day in any other building than the battered, shabby rabbit-warren which sheltered so many impecunious artists. The owners of the building were only waiting for a sufficiently big rise in the price of land to tear down the dingy old place and put up an apartment house. Everybody who rented a studio there was told that he might be turned out at a day's notice, and all the service of the building was done in the same hand-to-mouth precarious method. Jeff always managed somehow to be able to run his elevator and the superintendent of the building, expecting to lose his own job from one day to the next, asked nothing more of the powerfully built, sullen Negro who looked so malevolently from under his black brows at the white people he took up and down in his creaking cage.

"A child finds studio life very tiresome, especially if she has had a good deal of it, and I used, while waiting for my cousin to get ready to go home, to wander up and down the dirty, unswept corridors of the building and to stand at the windows, looking down idly on the noisy, futile bustle of the New York street, feeling dreadfully vacant-minded and bored, and longing for somebody to talk to. In course of time I drifted towards Jeff's cage, (I was still child enough to enjoy riding up and down in the elevator), and towards the casual acquaintance with him which gave me my first doubts of the golden perfection of American institutions.

"All Negroes know how to interest children, and Jeff shared his race's capacity to charm childhood. I still remember the stories he used to tell me of his fishing exploits in his Virginia village, of his happy boyhood with his widowed mother, of the way they celebrated Christmas in his town. Occasionally also he used to tell stories of his school, where he had learned to speak so correctly; of his grave, dignified, well-instructed school-teacher; and of the industrial school where later he went to learn the trade of carpenter. I remember (because it afterwards came back to me, vividly) his explanation about the old blind mare, Nancy, who came frequently into these reminiscences. I said one day, 'But, Jeff, how did it happen that you had a horse, all your own?'

"His eyes deepened. 'I was going by one day when the white man that owned her was beating her up because she couldn't go straight. It made me kind of crazy to see. . . .' He paused, made a grimace, and passed over the details to the end of the story. 'I worked two summers for that white man, to buy her off'n him. She lived seven years after that. Happy years, too. My mother liked her mighty well, too.' He added, on another note, 'They died the same winter.'

"I glimpsed vaguely through this dry outline of emotions deeper than the words showed, and was silent a moment. Jeff said presently, 'Colored folks have got a fellow-feeling for creatures that get jumped on and can't help it.' And as I found no comment to make on this, our interview of that day ended.

"This was the only reference he ever made to the deep grievance of his life, until one day, emboldened by much talk with him, I ventured, priggishly enough, to try to be a small mentor for him and made a childish and ill-advised effort to serve up to him, at second hand, some of the good counsels I had heard my mother give to Uncle Harry.

"The conversation which followed I have never forgotten. He said, listlessly, 'Why, Miss Ma'gret, I'm an American Negro. What else is there for me to do but to get drunk and gamble?'

"I was astonished beyond the extent of my capacity for astonishment, sincerely unable to make the faintest guess at the meaning of his words. 'Why, Jeff,' I said earnestly, with a simplicity I find now rather touching, 'if you didn't get drunk, you could get a better job and earn more money and save up and. . . .'

" 'Well, what would I do with my money?' he asked me. 'What good would it do me? I'd be a Negro just the same, wouldn't I? I'd be punished and spit on, all the time, for being something I never asked or wanted to be, and that I'd stop being if I could.'

"Reminiscences of abolitionist ancestors stirred vaguely in my head, and with the proper canting accent, I pronounced the cant phrase, 'Well, I'm sure that is nothing to be ashamed of, or to regret.'

"*'Isn't it!'* he blazed out suddenly, and then in a voice which brought the words home to me, like a thunderclap, *'Would you just as soon be a Negro as white?'*

"He had so fiercely focused on me in one burning flash the hidden flame of his heart that he succeeded for just an instant in forcing me to take in, actually and intimately, the meaning of his words. For just an instant I realized the meaning of the possibility that I might have been born black and not white . . . and I gave a vivid reflex gesture of physical recoil, which made Jeff laugh sardonically . . . although he had visibly winced.

"I was horrified at the confession he had startled out of me. I swallowed hard and tried to think of something defensive to say. Various smug reflections came to my mind and I brought out the one which seemed to me most unanswerable. 'Oh, Jeff, there are lots of nice things Negroes can do. Look at Peter Ruffner.' (He was the elevator man for the night shifts.) 'He's saving up his money and studying to pass the Civil Service examinations, and he's going to get a job in the Customs House and own a little home and he's bringing up his children so nicely and—'

"Jeff answered me, with a grunt of scorn, 'Yes, Pete's giving himself a lot of trouble, and what'll he get? No matter how much he succeeds, the poorest, little, low-down street-mick, if he's white, will look down on Pete . . . and *you know it.* And if Pete went home to Georgia, not if he had a million dollars, they wouldn't let him eat in the same restaurant with the most worthless white folks, nor pray to God in the same church. Not if he'd found out how to cure cancer, would he be allowed to vote like the white drunkards nor live on the same street. There isn't a white convict in a penitentiary who would change place with Pete, to have his freedom and his job and his savings-bank book and his home, if he had to get inside Pete's black skin to do it . . . and you know that, too. Don't you suppose *we* know the reason why nobody on earth would be willing to change places with an American Negro? Do you suppose I'd want to bring a child into this world to live through that—much as I'd like having a son!'

"I was shocked and silenced, more by the dreadful deep quiver of acrimony in his voice than by what be said. I shrank a little back, as though I saw heat-waves quivering over molten metal; and hung my head.

"Of course, like everyone else, I had been perfectly familiar with the daily unprovoked, personal indignities in the life of an American Negro, but I seemed never to have seen them before.

"Well, I have not forgotten them since.

"Somebody came in and asked to be taken up to the fifth floor. Jeff carried us both up, and me back again to the ground floor before I could think of anything to say. Then I brought out miserably, only because I could not endure the silence, 'Well, they don't all feel like that. Look at Booker Washington. Seems to me you're unreasonable, Jeff.'

" 'Does it?' he said indifferently, as though he cared very little about my opinion.

"There was another silence. Then he added, 'Well, maybe I wouldn't get so sore if it wasn't for all the Declaration-of-Independence-business and everybody-being-equal that white folks are always shooting off. I reckon it's that, that makes me take to drink.'

"I had no occasion to speak to Jeff for some time after that. In fact, he got so drunk for once, that he could not run his elevator, and was absent for many days. I thought about him a great deal, most uncomfortably, and during the morning exercises in my patriotic school, found the words sticking in my throat as I tried to pronounce in unison some of the accustomed phrases of satisfaction in belonging to the country of freedom. Yes, Jeff had cast a shadow which was not to lift.

"He was so long in coming back to his work that one day I asked the superintendent about him. He said impatiently that Jeff had been off on a terrible bat, but would be back soon. He went on, 'But you don't want to have anything to do with him. If I was your cousin, I wouldn't let you ride up and down in the elevator. He's just as bad a nigger as any I ever saw, and I've seen a-plenty. He's the kind that carries a razor in his hip pocket, and don't you forget it!'

When Jeff came listlessly back to work, with the curious ashy color of a man who has been sick, I told him what the superintendent had said about his concealed weapon, half hoping to have the thrill of seeing him show it to me. He laughed scornfully, 'No, I don't carry a razor, but it's not because I'm not a bad nigger, all right. If I could kill what ails me with a razor, I wouldn't be long doing it. But suppose I cut Mr. Superintendent all to hash with a razor, would it keep me from being treated like a dog?' He laughed again, and said, 'No, my razor is a whiskey-bottle. That comes the nearest to killing what's the matter with me.'

"He looked so ill and wretched as he spoke, that he made me feel wretched, myself. It seemed to me, child as I was, that life was an infinitely more puzzling matter than I had dreamed it might be.

"As it happened, it was almost the last time I saw him there, for soon after, the old building really was torn down, as had been threatened so often, and all the inhabitants of the old rookery were dispersed to the four corners of the earth. But what could not be dispersed was the puzzled uncertainty which Jeff's talks had left in my mind."

She paused, and I murmured, helplessly in sympathy with her feeling, "Oh, yes, life is puzzling, horribly, distractingly puzzling."

III.

She went on, "I was sent that next winter to a boarding school in France, and suffered acutely from the indoor confinement of this life, so that it was with a bird's joy in freedom that I found myself, the next summer, spending the vacation on the Breton seacoast, where I went to visit one of my school-mates. She was as wild as I with physical exuberance long repressed, and we raced up and down the broad yellow beach and risked our necks on the rocky cliffs, every moment that the weather allowed us to be out of doors.

"It was only when one of the big tempests of the region kept everybody indoors, that we took cognizance of the dull adult life of the house and neighborhood. This was about the usual life in cosmopolitan seaside towns, full of vain idle women, sensual vacationing men and malicious gossip. The old aunt of Marcelle, my little school-friend, was an invalid who could not walk, but in the miraculous way of some shut-in-people she knew all the talk of the small, uncharitable settlement better than any one of us who ran about freely among the actors of the sordid little comedies and tragedies. She not only knew all that was happening that summer, but all that ever had happened, apparently, and she was fond of imparting her information. It was she, I remember, one stormy afternoon when Marcelle and I were kept indoors by the weather,—it was she who gave to a caller the story of our next-door neighbors, a strange combination of personalities which had vaguely aroused even my child's interest, naturally dull to the curious and inexplicable doings of grown-ups.

"The story was not at all meant for little girls, nor did Marcelle and I really listen to it, I believe, except with that sort of preoccupied attention which children give to ugly, grown-up talk. At least I find there are many gaps in it which I can't fill. Perhaps those were the times when Marcelle's aunt lowered her voice to a mysterious whisper and spoke in her interlocutor's ear. All that I really understood from this half-heard story was that the big, burly, red-faced Hollander, M. Stekkar, whom we glimpsed through the iron grating of the garden gate, lounging about in a purple dressing-gown, had somehow, some awful power over the shabby, thin, gray-faced man, M. Levreau, who never went anywhere without his silent little boy, and who stumbled so as he walked.

" 'They were partners together, out in some God-forsaken place in the far East,' said Marcelle's aunt, 'where Stekkar made his money: Java, or Borneo, or somewhere where white men have little law over them. And this poor wretch—they say he was a handsome, fine fellow in those days,—married, and they say he came to blows when Stekkar tried to . . .' here the voice went off into sibilant whispers and I lost the thread, until it rose again with, 'And Stekkar was so furious at that, they say he almost died of his rage, and he swore he'd get even with Levreau for the humiliation, and Levreau laughed and said he wasn't afraid. And then Stekkar bided his time, and the year after . . . well, some say Levreau really did embezzle a lot of the money, and some say Stekkar arranged the accounts to look as though he did . . . and then he put the clamps on. Off Levreau would be sent to prison, arrested right there, leaving the young wife, and a baby about due, there on the island with Stekkar. And then Levreau,' the old woman gloated over the spectacular character of her tale, glanced sideways at the little girls, and lowered her voice again. We heard no more until, ' . . . the feeling ran high out there, even among the natives, so they say, after the wife's death, and so Stekkar sold out, retired, and brought Levreau and the baby here to live, and here he gets all his interest in life out of torturing Levreau. You see, he's got a death-grip on him, on account of the child. Levreau would have given himself up, long ago and gone to prison, whether he was guilty or not, if it wouldn't have meant leaving the little boy to old Stekkar, on account of that signed agreement I told you about. So there he is, a rat in a trap.

"'Stekkar has the legal right any day to call in the gendarmes and have him put behind bars. And he knows it and daren't do anything on account of little Jean. Well, there's little enough left of him to do anything! The treatment he has had . . . they say that when Stekkar is more than usually drunk, he makes him . . .' A particularly sibilant whisper followed this, accompanied by upturned eyes of horror on the part of her listener . . . 'and he has taken to drugs, too. Oh, he's nothing but a walking corpse, physically and morally. Stekkar'll get the child all right, before long, in any case. They say he's beginning on him now. Our maid, Madeleine, was talking to old Nanette, the other day, the charwoman who was working there, and she said she saw old Stekkar take little Jean out of his bed, right before his father, and . . .'

"The visitor broke in here, crying, 'In God's name, why doesn't the father take his son and run away . . . just escape! There are plenty of forgotten corners of France where . . .'

"'He's too broken down to try,' said Marcelle's aunt. 'Stekkar *has* him as a horse-breaker has an animal with a broken spirit. And, anyhow, since the drugs have worked on him so, he's not more than half there any of the time. To drug himself till he can't feel anything Stekkar tries to make him feel, that's *his* escape, and his only one, in this life.'

"At this point the sun showed for a moment through a rift in the clouds and Marcelle and I, feeling fairly stifled in the malarial atmosphere of grown-up gossip and indoor air, clamored to be allowed to take a sandwich apiece and go down to the beach. A few moments later, the great, clean, roaring voice of the sea had drowned out the human voice with its gruesome tale of human doings.

"And yet, I must have taken in, even then, something of the story, for I remember looking with scared pity at M. Levreau the next time

I met him in the street. His ravaged gray face was lowered towards the ground, as he made his painful halting way towards the house, his heavy market-basket weighing him down to one side and making his uneven gait more unsteady. The hollow-eyed little boy at his side, clung hard to the bony hand, and trotted anxiously along in unsmiling silence.

"Fourteen-year-olds have, however, a liberal allowance of self-preserving concentration on their own affairs, and our strange neighbors played a very small part in the life of the two romping tomboys. Most of the summer had passed before we gave them more than a passing thought, half aversion, half compassion.

"I had plenty of other things to think of, things that bothered my fourteen-year-old mentality to the verge of utter bewilderment. My troubles began on the day when Marcelle and I came in from the beach and found a new group of guests, evidently familiars of the house; a handsome, white-haired father, a magnificently oriental-looking mother, two elegant young lady daughters, velvet-eyed and languorous, and a grave, noble-looking son, with thoughtful, kind, dark eyes and long, slim, delicate hands . . . all of these things yes, but also unmistakably with Negro blood. 'Light-colored mulattoes,' I diagnosed them with one glance of my American eyes, experienced in such appraisings.

"I glanced around at the family in astonishment . . . didn't they *know* that their guests were *colored people?* What ought I to do? How could I enlighten them? Perhaps I ought to go and whisper in Marcelle's ear and let her devise some way of telling her mother.

" 'Here, my dear,' said Marcelle's mother, holding out her hand to me, 'Come, I want to introduce you to our friends, Monsieur and Madame Perez. They are Americans, too, like you, only they have lived in Europe so long that we claim them as of us entirely. Madame, this is a little American school-friend of my Marcelle, but from North America . . . it *is* North America, isn't it, dear? The Perez were from South America originally.'

"The Perez smiled down, out of their kind, soft, dark eyes, on the awkward crimson-faced child, who, bewildered and ill at ease, stared at them unhappily. Perhaps Marcelle's family *did* know that their guests were . . .

"The conversation flowed on, urbane, various, facile, and closed over the head of the child, who sat miserably trying to readjust her notions of things. I was suffering the sick uncertainty that comes to children with the first sharp encounter with totally new standards. The quite matter-of-fact ignorance of Marcelle's family, that there *was* any other standard than their own, inconceivable to me, gave me a dizzy feeling. I did not know what I really felt about it; I did not even know what I thought I ought to feel, and I hated the moral distress that this uncertainty gave me.

"But after they had gone, I had a staggering blow, compared to which these little pushings and shovings were as nothing. Marcelle's mother and aunt broke out into panegyrics of their visitors, who were, I gathered, very wealthy, very artistic, very gifted, very charitable, very distinguished, and, said Marcelle's aunt, forgetting my nationality, 'There's such a *fineness* about them, none of that crudeness you see in most other Americans. Sometimes I think it is their colored ancestry that gives them that refinement. I've noticed that Americans with a little colored blood often seem more gently bred than . . .'

"But at this point Marcelle's mother remembered I was there and made a quick change of subject.

"Not that I was capable of protesting. I was sunk in a stupor of astonishment so extreme that I had no words. As I look back on the situation now, there was a comic element in my stupefaction, but I felt none at the time, only a sore, hurt surprise, as though my mind had suffered an attack from a quarter which in the nature of things should have been secure.

"It was not long after this, when I was still revolving my new impressions furtively, that, loitering on the beach with Marcelle, we came upon Jefferson Heywood, towering up above the Breton fishermen like a black portent. He certainly looked like one to the little American girl who gazed at him open-mouthed, quite sure that it was physically impossible that he, of all people, should be there. He had preserved all the insolent self-possession which had been his old defense and showed neither the slightest surprise nor discomfiture at being recognized, although he was evidently very drunk again.

" 'Hello there, Miss Ma'gret,' he said. 'It's a long way from here to the old elevator, isn't it?'

" 'Well, *Jeff!*' I ejaculated. 'How in the world did you get here?' "

IV.

" 'Oh, I fell from bad to worse,' he said easily, 'till I got into the last berth anybody ever takes. I'm a stoker on a transatlantic liner. They've *got* you for the length of the trip, and no matter how big a jag you start with, it don't last you more'n a couple of days after you leave port.' He turned away, with his old offensive indifference, and slouched off down to the beach, to put his great shoulders to a fishing boat that was being hauled up on the sand.

" 'Somebody you used to know in America?' Marcelle asked, as we went up the hill to the house.

" 'Yes, he's a sailor now, on an American ship.'

" 'What a fine, strong-looking man he is!' said Marcelle, glancing back at him, as he strained powerfully at the boat.

"I looked at her in the genuine American astonishment, inexplicable to a European, that anyone should speak of a Negro, just as though he were anyone else. I tried to acquiesce, feeling myself very far away from my old surroundings. 'Yes, he's strong-looking,' I said, and heard, myself, the flatness of my accent.

"The next days seemed to me to be pervaded with the Perez family. They came to tea again, they came to play tennis, they came in the evening to make music with Marcelle's mother, the Perez sisters singing together so sweetly, in voices so rich and poignant that Marcelle's bad-tempered old aunt was moved to wipe her eyes, an action I had never thought to see her take. They were even there on the afternoon when Marcelle's mother came bursting in from the street, exclaiming over such an exciting scene, as the market-people had just told her about . . . 'Disgraceful to allow such people as Stekkar to live near respectable people!' And relishing in advance the pleasant importance of being the narrator of dramatic happenings, she sat down to tell us about it.

" 'You know how old Stekkar has been mistreating that miserable man, worse and worse of late . . . in one of his fits. Well, today, Levreau went to the market, as usual, and was a little later than usual in coming back. Stekkar tore out to find him, bare-headed in his dressing gown, his face that horrid purple-red he is when he's been drinking more than usual. And when he found him, he rushed right at him, yelling out something in English, and struck him such a blow that Levreau fell down, all in a heap, and little Jean with him. Levreau screamed terribly, so people say who saw it, and then cowered together, his face hidden under his arms. Stekkar stood over him, sort of frothing at the mouth, kicking at him once in a while, and yelling out things in English . . . you know they talk English together, mostly.

"'Nobody dared do anything, you know what a big strong beast Stekkar is! Some of the women had run for the gendarmes to come and stop it, when an American sailor from one of the ships that docked the other day, came along, eating a banana. When he heard the English words, he turned around and looked.' She had a vivid dramatic gesture here, 'And they say when he saw Stekkar standing over that wretched thing . . . why, the market-people say he was awful to look at. They say his hair seemed to rise up, and his whole forehead came right down over his eyes, and his jaw bulged like a great dog's. They say he jumped right over the applewoman's counter, and landed on top of Stekkar, and flung him down just by giving him one great slap on the side of his head, such a slap that you could have heard it a mile. And then he kicked him, and helped that miserable creature, Levreau, up to his feet and stood over Stekkar until he hobbled away, back to the house. They say he snarled so, when Stekkar tried to get up, that the market-women turned white to hear it. And when finally, after he'd gotten clear away, Levreau had with little Jean, the American gave Stekkar such a talking-to that people could hardly bear it not to know what he was saying. You know how they all hate that Hollander. And then he let him up and walked off beside him, towering over him, and threatening him till it did your heart good to hear. They said the American was a giant.'

"Marcelle looked at me, envying me, a fellow-countryman, of such prowess. 'Are all American men so big and strong?' she asked. 'We met one the other day, Margaret and I, who was a perfect Hercules.'

"'*American!* Why, that man was a *Negro!*' This simon-pure North American exclamation burst from me before I could stop it.

"'Was he?' said Marcelle's mother casually. 'Maybe it was the same one. I remember now, they said this other American was black, too.

Most likely it *was* the same one. We don't see so many foreigners off here.'

"From this distance I am almost sorry for the little American girl so very far from anybody who could understand the confusion of her mind.

"That night contained as dreadful a moment as ever I have passed in my life. About one o'clock in the morning, Marcelle and I (and I suppose the whole household) were wakened by horrid screams of terror and pain, coming from the house next door. I sat up in bed, shuddering, and found Marcelle clinging to me, crying out, 'Oh, he'll kill them!'

"And then almost as quickly as they had come, they ceased, leaving the air quivering to their violence. We heard rough voices in the distance, and then complete silence.

"Even ignorant and inexperienced little girls can get glimpses of abominable possibilities in life, that are perhaps more dreadful than anything life can really show, because of their very nightmare vagueness. My horror and disgust that night, as my little friend and I clung to each other, buried for the moment, leagues deep, in my vigorous young zest in living. I remember thinking passionately that living was such a horrid, awful affair, I didn't at all know whether I wanted to go on with it!

"But, of course, ultimately I dropped off to sleep, and woke to bright sunshine and a bunch of letters from America, and good old Madeleine, bringing in our hot chocolate and crisp rolls. And I was again only fourteen years old, with only a child's curiosity about the extraordinary happenings next door.

"It seemed, from what Madeleine had gathered of the gossip already buzzing, that old Herr Stekkar had been worse than usual, had somehow hurt Levreau, his spine it was thought, so that he could not walk or even stand up. And then the American . . . they called Jeff 'The American'—just like that—had come right in over the locked gate of the garden, had slammed old Stekkar into temporary insensibility, and when he had come to himself, Levreau and little Jean had disappeared, together with the American.

"None of our most brightly colored penny melodramas had anything in it more thrilling than that. There were even that morning, the police.

They walked around a great deal in the Stekkar garden and made out from Jeff's tracks what he had done and where he had been, which everybody knew already. Old Herr Stekkar's roars of rage could be heard in our garden, where we listened to them with a pleasant excitement, coming as they did, from the other side of a twelve-foot wall.

"But that was the end of it. The police could find no trace of Jeff or Levreau or little Jean. I don't believe they tried very hard, for nobody in the region had the slightest interest in serving the interests of hideous old Stekkar, and Jeff's actions met with a great deal of outspoken sympathy among the hard-headed Bretons.

"And there was an end of the vacation, and of Jeff and any thought of him for many long years. Marcelle and I went back to school, and that was the winter I had typhoid fever, and my parents came over and took me home to America, when I got over it."

The narrator came to a pause here, during which I had time to take in the awful significance of the weak and wretched man's life of which she had been telling me. I am not fourteen years old, nor anywhere near it, but I, too, found myself shuddering at the glimpse I had had of that human misery. "Yes, oh, yes," I cried, "isn't life too dreadful!"

V.

The American woman drew a long breath and went on, "It's impossible to tell you how entirely all this seemed to leave no trace behind it in my life. Nothing ever occurred to bring Jeff, or the Breton fishing-village, or even (after schooldays were over) Marcelle to my mind. This is not saying that I had forgotten them. They all remained there, a confused, dark mass of little-understood facts, which seemed to bear on nothing else in my life.

"I think if a choice could have been made of all the innumerable memories of my life, some twenty years later, that not one could have been further from my consciousness, on the day, only about two months ago, when, walking to spare the under-nourished little Spanish horse, I toiled up the long slope towards the pass in the Pyrenees, which was to lead me down into the remote little Basque village on the other side.

"They had telegraphed from the main office in Paris that I was to go there, rent the big empty convent, and fix it up to receive within a fortnight's time, a convoy of sixty scrofulous refugee children.

"They were always asking impossible things like that, and, of course, since it was a question of sick children, it had to be done. I had my plan of action ready in my mind, as, in the little cart once more, I went rattling down the slope into the sleepy medieval village. This was by no means the first time I had done this sort of thing, and I knew beforehand the series of preparations to be made. First, the sewerage system. . . . Was it at least passable? And could the dormitories be ventilated with an approach to modern ideas? And the lease. . . . I ran over the various legal points to remember . . . and the question of whether we or the Sisters should pay for the whitewashing of the walls.

"At this I wondered, as I looked down at the small, remote settlement, if I would find there any able-bodied man who could do the whitewashing, and manufacture the beds; for, of course, I would have to have the beds made by a carpenter, out of planks and wire-netting. It would be out of the question to bring furniture over that tremendous mountain-pass by horse-power. And in any case, there was no furniture in the whole region to buy, everything having been bought up by the thousands of refugees from the war-zone who crowded into that safe corner of France.

"The village was the quintessence of all Basque villages; whitewashed houses with red-painted beams, clean sunny empty street, and before each house the shady, atrium-like entrance of the carefully trimmed and trained plane-trees. There were only two buildings of any size, the big fortress-like church with its grave-yard all around and its two gigantic pyramidal box-trees; and up on the hill a barrack-like building, which could only be the convent I had come to rent.

"An hour later I was finishing the last of the negotiations with the Mother Superior, ' . . . and did you say that there is a workman in town who could do the whitewashing and make the beds for me?'

" 'There's a very good workman,' she answered, 'the sexton of the church. He is a carpenter and would make the beds in his shop, and I think he might do the whitewashing.'

"As I turned away, she asked me, 'Madame is American?' and when I said I was, she said, 'The man I'm speaking of is an American, too, although he has lived here for twenty years.'

"I supposed, of course, he was a Basque returned from Argentina. A great many Basques and Béarnais go there to make their fortunes and return to live out the end of their lives in the Pyrenees. The untraveled Basques always call these compatriots of theirs 'The Americans,' so I asked, 'Is he from North or South America?'

"She hesitated, evidently vague as to the difference, and shrugged her shoulders, passing on to the more important matter of locating his house, the third one after the church, the one with the big stone bench by the door. 'His shop is at one side of the courtyard, and probably you will hear his hammer or his saw.'

"Of course, you know by this time what I was infinitely far from imagining, as I went rather wearily along the street towards the small, whitewashed, red-shuttered house, gleaming behind the thick shade of its plane-trees; and of course you can feel nothing of the very ecstasy of astonishment which I felt when the big, gray-haired, massively built man left his carpenter's bench and came to greet me. I recognized him in spite of his gray hair, and his Basque costume of blue *béret,* neat blue shirt, broad red sash and loose velveteen trousers. But he did not at all recognize in the tired, middle-aged woman before him, the little girl with whom he had had so casual an acquaintance so long ago.

"When I exclaimed, sitting down hastily on the stone bench because my very legs failed me, in amazement, 'Why, if you're not Jefferson Heywood!' he was obliged to look at me a long time, hard, before he said, speaking rather slowly, as though his English were rusty, 'Oh, yes, you used to ride up and down in my elevator, back in New York.'

"He had evidently forgotten seeing me on the Breton beach. Perhaps he had been too drunk that day to remember the momentary encounter. I did not, of course, remind him of it. He said, quietly, 'Yes, ma'am, I've been living here for twenty years. And I like it fine. They're very good people around here!'

"I said, 'Yes, I know and like the Basques, too.'

" 'They've been very good to us,' he said.

"We went into the low-ceilinged room, with the shining, red brick floor, and found, seated in a wheel-chair, an old, old man, or so he seemed, with his thin white hair and deeply lined, wax-like face. He was neatly dressed in the Basque fashion, with the blue *béret* on his head.

"He greeted me gently, without surprise (it was evident that his faculties were not very acute), mildly glad to see a visitor, but not specially interested in me. It was when his eyes rested on Jeff's black face that his countenance came to life with a sort of curious shining, confident look, such as I had thought only happy children have.

"I stayed to supper with them (Jeff cooking and serving it deftly), and heard from them both, all about their life there, of which my unsuspected knowledge of the episode in Brittany cast a dramatic light.

" 'No, Madame,' said Jeff's companion, 'we are not either of us Basques,' (as though it were not apparent to every eye that Jeff was not a Basque!) 'but we wanted a quiet place to live, and somehow we found this, and we've stayed ever since.'

" 'But you're dressed like Basques,' I said.

" 'Yes, Madame; we came to like our Basque neighbors so much we wanted to be like them. And then it is hard to get other clothes here, so far from the railroad.'

" 'You see, my friend's an invalid,' said Jeff, 'and we had to have a place where he could be quiet.'

" 'I've never taken a step since we came here to live,' said the other. " 'M. Heywood has taken care of me as though I had been a child. M. Heywood is the best man in the world,' he added, in a voice which shook a little.

"After this he showed me, wheeling himself about the tiny house, the innumerable proofs of Jeff's patient ingenuity. He had made the wheeled chair for the invalid, had arranged his bed so that he could pull himself from it into his chair, although there were many days, he told me, when he was too weak to sit up. That was why Jeff had given him the sunny front-room for his bedroom. He made me put my head on his pillow, so that I could see the view he had on shut-in days. An austere, snow-capped peak, serenely exalted above the pleasant, green slopes of the pastures on its lower flanks, looked down a silent benediction on the quiet end of the life-scarred man.

"He showed me Jeff's little bedroom, at the back of the house, nothing but a closet with an iron bed in it. 'He says he doesn't need much of a bedroom, because he's not in it much. He's the hardest worker in all the village, and even Sundays he doesn't rest, because he's sexton of the church, and the *chantre,* too. He's the one who sings the responses to the priest in the mass. He has a beautiful voice.'

"About that time I felt that my capacity for astonishment had given out, and that I must take a moment in which to recover my lost sense of reality. I made an excuse and went out into the garden, where Jeff was digging potatoes. I sat down on the wheelbarrow and burst out, 'Good gracious, Jeff, are you really here, and yourself, or am I dreaming all this?'

"Jeff's answer gave me a more vivid and intimate impression of his escape from bitter nervous tension, even than all that I had seen there, for his answer was a real unctuous Negro chuckle, such as I had never heard from him in the old days.

"I went on, 'But look here, what kind of a fraud are you? I bet anything you were brought up to be a Methodist. How can you sing the responses in a Catholic Church?'

"His answer was a corollary to the chuckle. 'He said, with racial easy-going good-humor, 'Oh, yes'm, I got converted and all. They are a right good kind of folks around here. I reckon their religion is likely to be all right. And, anyhow, I take a lot of comfort in their music.'

"He hummed in a deep bass voice, rich and mellow, *Confitebor tibi, in cithara, Deus, Deus meus . . .'* and added, as he shook some potatoes loose of the soil, 'Yes'm, I like the music. The priest has taught me most all of what he uses in the different services.'

"He stood up, took off his *béret* (how strange it looked on his woolly, gray head!) looked up to the snow-covered mountains, and said very seriously, 'You see, it's different now from what it ever was with me. I got something to do now. My friend in there has had some awful bad treatment from a low-down white man, and I'm making it up to him. And he had a little boy who wouldn't have had any sort of a chance either, if things hadn't changed. You know I always wanted a boy of my own, that I could bring up without thinking he was going to have to go through what I did, back there in the States.' He brought out of his pocket a photograph and handed it to me with a look of indescribable pride.

"I saw a tall young soldier, with a sensitive, intelligent face and fine eyes, who stood erect and vigorous, his rifle in his hand, and smiled straight at you. Underneath, in a bold handwriting, full of personality, was inscribed, 'To my dear foster-father, from his loving, grateful Jean.' Jeff said, 'He's one of the best boys who ever lived. I've worked hard and taken care of his father, and given him as good an education as anybody in this country's got. He's a chemist, and when the war's over, he's got a fine job waiting for him as chemical expert in a big factory. He wants his father and me to go to live with him. But I don't think we'd better. He's engaged to be married. They'd better have their home to themselves. He writes me every single week, Jean does, and so does his girl. They say they're going to name the first boy Jefferson Heywood Levreau.'

"As he talked, my eyes must have grown wider as I took in the happy horizons opened by what he said. He stopped short as though he knew of what I was thinking. We exchanged a long look, full of things we could not say, both of us thinking of the old days, so bitter for him, when I had first known him.

"When he spoke, his voice shook me with the unforgettable emotion that comes only a few times in a life, when one hears another human being open his heart wide and speak out. He said, 'There's one of the chants—when the priest first told me what it meant, I thought it must have been meant for me. *"From the depths, from the black depths, oh, Lord, hast Thou lifted me out!"'*

"His lower lip was quivering. He said no more."

The American woman beside me also said no more. This was evidently the end of her story.

It was my turn to draw a long, long breath. "Well," I said unsteadily, "your story makes me sure of one thing, at least . . . that life is as beautiful as it is dreadful and puzzling."

"Beautiful!" she cried, quivering. "How *can* you say that? When it was of our own country, of our own America that he spoke when he said 'the depths'!"

I saw that the tears were on her cheeks.

Gold from Argentina

Up the steep slope to Mendigaraya toiled an automobile, and this was remarkable, for Mendigaraya lies high in the Pyrenees, is geographically fifteen miles from a railroad, spiritually two centuries from the modern world, and does all of its business by oxcart. The only contact with the twentieth century known to that region is through the occasional departure of one of the poorest boys, starved out, who emigrates to South America, and through the very infrequent return of one years later, either as a ragged failure or as a pot-bellied, well-to-do man in store clothes and suspenders, accompanied by a heathenish wife with a hat on her head. (Any Basque woman used to covering her sleek black hair with a mantilla would as soon go out on the street in her chemise as in a hat. And no Basque mountaineer, his lean, agile body sashed in red, ever gets enough to eat or can stop work long enough to acquire corpulence.)

Unless they come back to visit their old homes the emigrants are seldom heard of after their departure. Basques poor enough to be driven to emigrate can rarely read and write. Even if they could their families could not read their letters. For the most part they disappear forever, the strong, handsome young men, despairing at the grinding narrowness of the lives before them, who pluck up courage to take the plunge, and, hiding their homesick panic under a pale bravado of gaiety, set off down the long stony road leading to St. Jean-de-Luz and the railroad.

But of course one never knows; this car might be bringing a returned "American," as Basques who have lived in Argentina are always called. What other possible reason could an automobile have for coming to Mendigaraya? The little boys in blue berets, playing *pelota* up against the wall of the church, halted their nimble sandaled feet and stared at the strange vehicle panting into the far end of the village street. The girls, drawing water at the fountain, stopped their chatter and turned their long, lustrous eyes toward it in wonder.

The automobile turned the one corner of the street and stopped short, stalling with a grunt of astonishment, for it found itself in an impasse, low, whitewashed, red-beamed houses before it, set thick all around a small public square of beaten earth, shaded by pollarded plane trees. There was no way out between the houses, not even an alleyway. Mendigaraya is at the end of the road and does not mind admitting it.

The door of the car opened, and a man stepped out, instantly known, by all the Basque eyes looking at him, to be a foreigner. He had stiff leather shoes on his feet, and his stumping, wooden-legged gait was that of a city-dweller. He looked about him, saw that one of the houses announced by a faded sign that it was both the city hall and the post office, and knocked on its door.

The elderly postmaster, who was also the town clerk and who had, like everybody else in town, been staring from a window at the automobile, lost no time in opening the door. The stranger stepped in and introduced himself as a lawyer from St. Jean-de-Luz, come to get some legal information from the town records of Mendigaraya. The two men sat down together after the town clerk had shut the upper half of the door at the back of his office, through which a too-friendly cow was thrusting a pretty head. The questioning began. Was anything known in Mendigaraya about the Yturbe and the Haratz families? Of course, there were Yturbes everywhere. What were those in this town?

Well, everything was known about them—two landless, moneyless, unimportant clans, not very bright, not very honest, not very clean, not very industrious—good-natured, easy-going, with never a penny's worth of property between them, and extremely prolific, as such clans are apt to be the world around. They were not bad people, seldom got into prison for anything, and were rather convenient to have around, as they furnished the necessary hired men and domestic servants for other people with more energy and brains. They were, in short, the kind of people who, since the fantastic invention of universal suffrage, can be counted on to vote for the candidate with the loudest voice.

The lawyer from St. Jean-de-Luz listened attentively to this piece of town lore and asked if two of the grandmothers in the clan had not been sisters.

Yes, that was true; two Bidaranty girls they had been, from a scrub family, exactly like the ones they had married into. Yes, they were both still living, although very old now. There was one now, this minute, over across the square. The lawyer turned in his chair, settled his glasses on his nose, and looked hard through the window at an old crone, her head tied up in a rusty black handkerchief, creeping feebly about, stooping to pick up fallen twigs and putting them in a gunnysack which she dragged along with one hand. That was Granny Haratz, about seventy-seven now, useful for gathering fuel for the cooking fire, and for nothing else. Her sister, Grandmother Yturbe, spent her time in the pastures, watching the cows to see that they did not wander, the usual work given to members of the community whose time was worth nothing.

And had those sisters ever had a brother?

Ah, that the town clerk did not know. He was a newcomer to Mendigaraya, having lived there only thirty-seven years. But the town records would show. They did. Yes, there had been an elder brother, Jean Manuel Bidaranty, who, sixty-two years ago, at the age of nineteen, had gone to South America. Here was the record of his birth, his baptism, all the data about his securing his passport.

The lawyer pulled from his black leather portfolio a packet of documents, compared names, dates, ages. Evidently—he remarked after a time—evidently the same man.

He folded his documents together and returned them to his serviette, remarking that he had just received word from a lawyer in Buenos Aires that M. Bidaranty was dead.

How strange, thought the town clerk, to hear one of such a tribe as the Bidarantys called a *monsieur!*

The lawyer went on to say that, dying, M. Bidaranty had willed what property he had to his two sisters. Now that the identification was complete, there were only some legal formalities to be finished. They would take perhaps a month—perhaps two—possibly as long as three. Inheritances were long in getting themselves settled. And then he would transfer the property to the two heiresses.

The town clerk had listened to this, open-mouthed, his eyes wider and wilder with every breath he drew. He now asked in a faint voice if it would be indiscreet to inquire whether M. Bidaranty had left much?

No, the lawyer told him, it would not be in the least indiscreet. No secret about it. Quite a tidy little sum. About three million dollars.

He reached for his hat and stepped toward the door. The town clerk sat stricken, numb to his marrow.

"Good day," said the lawyer pleasantly, opening the door, "and many thanks for your assistance."

He stepped out.

The town clerk came to life with a convulsive shudder and cried after him in a cracked voice, "Did you say dollars? Or francs?"

"Dollars," said the lawyer, conversationally, and, stepping into his car, disappeared.

The town clerk never saw the same man again.

Mendigaraya reeled from the shock. The news flared up and down the narrow valley like fire in dry weeds, and in a twinkling burned away a number of false ideas about the Yturbe and Haratz families. Everybody saw now what he had not chanced to note before, that the Yturbes had great natural distinction of manner, and that the younger Haratz girls had wonderful hair and eyes. Everybody remembered what respected citizens they had always been, and there was a universal feeling among the better people of the town that it was not suitable for members of such good old families to be in menial positions. Generous friends, whose fathers were—now—reported to have been the intimate friends of their fathers, rushed to help them out of their temporary difficulties. Before long one of the grandsons was taken into partnership by the village grocer. Three of the granddaughters, servant girls, were sought in marriage by sons of well-to-do farmers who worked their own land and owned many head of cattle. Another grandson, who had been stableboy for the doctor in the next town—the doctor who had once been almost elected to the Chamber of Deputies—was taken into the doctor's family on the most familiar terms and was already a great favorite with the doctor's marriageable daughter. An Yturbe boy! Think of it!

The two old ladies, now dressed in black silk presented to them by friendly neighbors, were removed from the earth-floored huts in which they had always lived and borne their numerous children, into salubrious new quarters in an elegantly furnished house, with sheets on the beds, wax flowers in glass bells on the mantelpieces, and actually—almost the only one in the village—a cast-iron two-holed cookstove in the kitchen. Of course the bewildered, docile old women never did any cooking on the stove, the fire on the hearth being so much handier.

This house was thrown open to them in a burst of humanity by the only landed proprietor thereabouts, a wealthy Frenchman who owned four of the houses in town and had three farms to rent. He was on the point of settling, rent free, on one of his farms, a widowed daughter of Mme Yturbe, when a sudden thought struck him, waking him up in the night, piercing to his vitals.

By dawn the next morning his son, a well-to-do horse-trader, as shrewd as himself, was dispatched down the road to St. Jean-de-Luz with instructions to see that lawyer in person and find out the truth about this wild story, which, after all, as the proprietor had suddenly remembered, rested on nothing more than the uncorroborated say-so of the town clerk, who, judging from the state of extreme agitation in which he had been found after the visit of the lawyer, might easily have misunderstood the whole business.

The horse-dealer left at six one morning. By nine, everybody in the village (with the natural exception of the Yturbe and Haratz families) knew why he had gone. They were all shuddering at the danger they had unwittingly been in and were thanking Providence that they had for a townsman so sagacious a person as the proprietor. During the two days of his son's absence the village went into a trance of suspended animation.

On the evening of his return the village notables assembled at his house to hear his report. It threw them into an ague. He had not, it is true, been able to see the lawyer, who had gone to Bordeaux and would not be back for a fortnight more. And, shrewd son of a worldly-wise Gallic father, he had been far too knowing to confide in a mere jackanapes of a lawyer's clerk. But he had heard—what had he not heard!

All St. Jean-de-Luz was talking of it. He had heard from everybody that the whole story was a hoax, an infamous practical joke. Jean Manuel Bidaranty had returned from South America years ago, a poor vagabond, like all the other Bidarantys, had earned a scanty living in a fishing village farther up the coast, and when he died, had not left enough money to bury him. Everybody knew all the details of the true story—had heard in just which cemetery his poor wooden cross was to be found, had been told the full name of the fisherman who had employed him. Three million dollars nothing! Of all the preposterous tales! Nobody but backwoods simpletons would have believed for an instant such a preposterous story.

The assemblage of village notables, headed by the almost-Deputy himself who had gathered to hear the news, turned with one accord to rush out and denounce the wretched impostors. But the well-to-do Frenchman called them back in an agonized voice. They had no more *proof* of this last story than of the first. Suppose the Yturbes and Haratz families were not wretched impostors at all, but really valid heirs to three million dollars. It would not do to be in too great haste. The story did sound madly impossible, and thanks be to God and all the saints, there was still time to draw back. But *suppose it should be true!*

The group of notables glared upon each other with tortured faces. Superior, upper-class people as they were, they expected as a matter of course to dominate any situation in which they found themselves and to extract from it whatever profit there might be, naturally the due of the refined and cultivated. But this situation—! Until the lawyer came back, what would be safe for them to do? To *do?* How could they even know what to feel, utterly at sea as they were, with no data on which an intelligent person could form a judgment? Were those Haratz girls really handsome, or were they common slatterns? Were the Yturbe boys promising lads or the scum of the earth? How could anybody know? Were ever human beings put into so hideous a situation as the townspeople of those two families?

Shut into this suspense, in the intolerable position of having nobody to blame, their nerves gave way, and they turned on each other. Before that first meeting had broken up, they had begun to quarrel fiercely, twitting each other with old scandals, raking up forgotten family skeletons, which, by the customary conspiracy of silence among gentry, had been kept dark lest the lower classes learn of them. Their exasperation found a real relief in this wrangling, which, after the fashion of wrangling, rose in intensity and fury from day to day. What else could they do to fill those long slow days of waiting?

The apoplectic French proprietor, meeting Mme Haratz in her black silk dress on the street, put up his hand to doff his hat to her, snatched it down again indignantly, put it up again falteringly, and glared upon her in an uncertainty so violent that he felt something give way in his brain and fell to the ground in the first of the paralytic seizures which finally carried him off. People were as tense as fiddle strings. If wheels sounded in the street everyone leaped to his window and was enraged to see that it was only the miller with an oxcart loaded with bags of corn.

Even in their confusion, however, there was one thing which was almost at once obvious to them all. Whatever happened, they could prevent the others from exploiting those dumb ignorant peasants. They were revolted by each other's sordid calculations. Secretly, one by one, they went to warn the Yturbe and Haratz families. It was a Christian duty, they told Mme Haratz, to let her know that the doctor's mother had died in an insane asylum and that the doctor often showed signs of the same malady, homicidal mania. Did Mme Yturbe perhaps know that the proprietor of their house had been accused of poisoning his first wife? And did the Haratz girls know that the young men who had shown such mercenary haste in seeking them out after it was known they were heiresses were not at all what they should be—were drunkards—thieves—had illegitimate families in other villages—had served terms in prison—walked in their sleep? And had the Yturbes happened to hear that it was the persecutions of the grocer that had driven his former partner to suicide?

To these revelations of the criminal, diseased, and depraved character of their neighbors, the Yturbe and Haratz families listened, pale-cheeked, panic-struck, credulous. They doubted not a word of it. It fell in perfectly with their conception of life, founded on tremulous notions of witchcraft and black art. Never, never had they dreamed that the people around them were so dangerous, so savage, so adroit—but now that they knew it, it seemed quite understandable.

They held a council of their own, at night, behind locked doors—cowering together, starting at every sound, constantly sending one of the boys to make sure no one was listening at the windows. What could they do? How could they escape from the perils around them? How could they, poor, ignorant, bewildered, helpless folk as they were, hold their own against these upper-class, highly educated assassins, crooks, robbers, and maniacs who surrounded them, as they had all seen a flock of sheep surrounded by wolves?

No idea of resistance crossed their minds. Never in the memory of man had any one of them been able to defend himself against property owners, who could read and write and cipher, and knew how to get the law on you if you didn't do as they wished. Open resistance would not have the faintest shadow of success. And even if fighting could have saved them, there was not a drop of fighting blood in the lot of them.

But—like an inspiration it came to them—there are other ways of escape for creatures who dare not fight. With a huddled, sheeplike rush, once the idea was conceived, they made their plans. The night was a dark one. There were plenty of strong arms to carry the children. They could be far, far on their way before dawn. For at least twenty-four hours, perhaps longer, no one could guess where to look for them. And it would take a good day, after that, to find them. Fifteen miles, while long and hard for the soft feet of well-to-do folk, does not seem far to people used to working hard for their living. And it was all downhill to St. Jean-de-Luz.

Four days later the son of the proprietor once more came back from a trip to St. Jean-de-Luz. He was gray with fury. They had gone. The whole tribe. To Buenos Aires. To where Jean Manuel had lived. They had found the lawyer just returned to his office, and had asked him, so he said, if they had the right to go? If there was money enough to pay for their tickets? If anyone could get the law on them if they did go?

Would they inherit that money if they went to South America as well as if they stayed here?

The lawyer had said yes to all these questions. He would, he told them, send all necessary identification to the Buenos Aires lawyer who had the matter in hand. He had bought their tickets for them and helped them get off. After all, why not, he had said impudently to the man from Mendigaraya, if that was what they wanted?

No, it had not been a hoax about the money. All solid fact. Just as the lawyer had said at first. Incredible. True.

The Saint of the Old Seminary

School was over for the day. The children's little hemp-soled *espadrilles* padded softly on the floor as they filed out before Mlle Etchegaray. Her tired, kind eyes looked at each one in turn. Well-dressed pale French children from bourgeois homes, with intelligent, irregular faces; Spanish children, ragged, dirty, Murillo-beautiful, their heads crusted with filth from the dens of the Old Seminary; dark little Basques carrying their heads high with pride in being Basque—Mlle Etchegaray gave to each one the look that really sees. For twenty-five years parents in Mendiberria had counted on Mlle Etchegaray's ability to see what was there—and to report it. Did someone say, "Isn't your Jeanne getting stoop-shouldered?" the first defensive answer of Jeanne's mother would be, "Why, Mlle Etchegaray hasn't said anything to us about it!"

After the last bobbing head had vanished, the teacher set herself to straighten her desk before going wearily up the stairs to her lodging. But this afternoon—as usual—she was denied even a few minutes of restful solitude. Footsteps approached. At the door Juanito Tuán's father appeared. Not happy and elated as he should have been. Not in the least. Could something have gone wrong with that scholarship for Juanito? After all the trouble she had taken with the inspector to get it!

The Tuáns were Spanish, but old Enrique left off, today, all his usual formalities of greeting.

"He won't go," he announced tragically.

He evidently expected the teacher to know the reason without being told. She did.

With the hot-blooded lack of moderation which endeared her to the Basques and Spaniards of Mendiberria she said intensely, "I wish that Tomasina had choked to death on her mother's milk!"

Enrique Tuán's deeply lined swarthy face took for an instant an appeased look.

But Mlle Etchegaray corrected herself conscientiously—characteristically: "No, I take that back. Tomasina is the only child I ever had in my classes whom I really couldn't endure. But perhaps I wouldn't hate her so much for her posing and lying if she weren't young and beautiful, while I am ugly and old and a spinster. No, I don't wish she had died, but I do wish to Heaven she would land her French sergeant, marry him, and have whatever it is she wants him for—leave off her mantilla, and wear hats, change her *espadrilles* for leather slippers, smoke cigarettes, be as French as she likes—only where we wouldn't have to see her—off in France somewhere." Officially, of course, Mendiberria became French territory several centuries ago, but the Basques refuse to take that annexation seriously.

Old Enrique, looking down at his blackened shoemaker's hands, said: "He'll never marry her. He's as ambitious as she. If only he could *get* his promotion and be stationed somewhere else along the frontier, and never show his face here again!"

"You mean—leave Tomasina for your Juanito? Tomasina for your daughter-in-law! You must be crazy! You know Tomasina!"

The old Spaniard fixed a somber gaze on her, his face working. In the silence she could hear his teeth grinding together.

"If Juanito wants her," he said finally, and leaned against the wall, wiping his forehead.

Emerging into the market place an hour later, Mlle Etchegaray turned toward the Tuán shop. Old Enrique sat at his bench, his hammer tapping fast, but the shop itself was empty. No customers sat on the brightly varnished benches which were the pride of the workman risen to proprietor; no foot pressed the strip of real carpet down the center; the pasteboard boxes of shoes on each side rose to the ceiling with no attendant to admire them. Mlle Etchegaray knew where to look, across the square at the Martinez vegetable stand. A tall slender boy leaned against the doorjamb there, gazing at a girl in a brightly flowered dress who was bending over a display of cabbages and tomatoes and with pretty, sinuous, self-conscious gestures rearranging them unnecessarily on the sloping boards of her stall. Old Enrique was watching them. His hands continued to tap blindly at the shoe he was resoling, but his blazing eyes cried, "Look out! Don't push me beyond what I can endure!"

Mlle Etchegaray stepped close to his open window and proffered hastily all she had to give.

"I came down to have a talk with Juanito. I thought it might do some good to make him understand what a marvelous opportunity this scholarship is, what a wonderful life he would have as a doctor, what a shame it would be to miss—"

Young laughter rippled through the air. Tomasina and Juanito were standing close together now, looking into each other's eyes, laughing. The girl's black hair glistened in the sun. She turned at the waist, flexible and firm, and leaned to tease a parrot, brooding misanthropically on his perch. With a grating scream he pounced at her finger. But she drew away with a flash and now, holding her hand high above her head, shook it at him tauntingly as if she had castanets between her fingers. Then, curving her white neck, she turned her eyes again on the boy. The magnetism of that glance could be felt all across the square.

Steps sounded, heavy, leather-soled French steps. Mlle Etchegaray hastily looked another way, and moving forward, gazed through the dusty window of the pharmacist's shop at the familiar fly-specked bottles there. Presently she heard other steps behind her, not leather-soled, the soft scuff of *espadrilles.* Juanito walked slowly past, not seeing her. He went into the shop without a glance at his father and sank down on one of the grand new benches, gazing at his feet.

Young laughter rippled through the air. Tomasina and Sergeant Brugnol were standing close together, looking into each other's eyes and laughing. The girl's black hair glistened in the sun. She poured her personality into her eyes so that once again it could be felt across the square. But Sergeant Brugnol, though his fair face wore a dazzled expression, was evidently able to remind himself that he had other things to do than to chat with the market-gardener's daughter. Lingering and turning back after several starts to leave her, he finally, in spite of her animation, lifted his cap in the citified French way, scorned and envied by wearers of tight-fitting berets, and went on down the street.

Tomasina's animation vanished. She watched him out of sight, her face dark and forbidding. The cobbler's hammer tapped away like an insistent, unwanted thought. When Mlle Etchegaray went into the shop, Juanito looked up at her, startled, with so wan an expression of misery that she only asked for a pair of shoestrings and went her way, passing, as she did so, a group of tourists in their outlandish clothes. A guide was talking to them in their outlandish language. A good many tourists came to Mendiberria. Their guides told them that Charlemagne—or was it Henry the Fourth?—had done something or other there, in the public square. Mendiberria people were of the opinion that the autobus company invented this unlikely story to get more trade.

Along with all the Basques and most of the Spanish in town, Mlle Etchegaray was indignant over the news of the discovery by the French of the secret path used by the Orthez smugglers and of the capture of their whole convoy in the night. As a schoolteacher she was a functionary of the French government, but she shared to the full the opinion of her high-spirited race that no government has a right to lay down a frontier across another people's territory. It was Basque on both sides, wasn't it? A pity it would be if a Basque couldn't walk over the mountain to his uncle and take him a twist of tobacco without having the top of his head shot off by murderous frontier guards. Of course, the four Orthez brothers did rather more than this, with their regular trips, loaded with bales of silks and tobacco and lace and what not; but their business was based on sound Basque principles. They were nice boys too, thought Mlle Etchegaray, fidgeting restlessly about her quarters over the schoolroom—steady, decent young fellows, real Basques. It was a horror to think of their being taken off to a French prison.

Another stick in the fire of her wrath was that Sergeant Brugnol must be delighted. It is part of the French campaign against smuggling to have the guards and their officers always from a distant part of

France. Sergeant Brugnol, a big-boned Fleming from near the Belgian frontier, would have said confidently that the black-haired, neatly-made Southerners of Mendiberria were quite ignorant of him personally (all except that pretty little trick at the Martinez vegetable stand). But everybody in town knew that he was ambitious and joked about his burning desire to make a spectacular *coup* that would force his superiors to promote him. Mlle Etchegaray walked to the window to see if the guards and their prisoners were visible yet in the road down from the mountain and turned away quickly lest she should see what she was looking for.

As for the traitor who had given him the information—at the thought, the schoolteacher flung violently on the floor the book she chanced to have in her hand. A spy among them! It made her sick, as falsity always did. Who could it be? The Orthez boys had no enemies. She could imagine no one in Mendiberria capable of such treachery. The little shepherd boy who had run so fast down the mountain knew no more than that, as the Orthez band came along the path they always used, bent under their usual bales, suddenly the French frontier guards were all about them. From the pasture above he had heard men's voices shouting, scuffles on the stony path, Sergeant Brugnol's voice giving commands. He had run away then, all the way down to Mendiberria, knowing that certain people there would pay him well for a warning.

Mlle Etchegaray decided that a violent counter-irritant was what she needed. Little Maria Benevente was once more out of school. There was nothing for it but to go down to the Old Seminary again to see what the matter was. She had been putting it off—not that she was a timid woman. Quite the contrary. But the Old Seminary! She was the only respectable woman in town who ever went near it. "Oh, well, in broad daylight they wouldn't cut anybody's throat," she reassured herself. And as for dirt and germs, they could be washed off. "I'll just spray my nose and throat with a disinfectant and go."

But she did not see the Old Seminary that day, nor think of it for many days to come. As she stepped out of the schoolhouse door she saw the men with their drawn faces, hurrying to tell her. A boy from an upland farm, running fleetly by short-cut paths, had brought into town the news that Juanito Tuán, the only child of old Enrique, the widower, had been with the Orthez boys, had resisted arrest, had attacked the officer in command, and had been shot dead. They were bringing his body down on a stretcher. Someone must go to tell his father, so that his first intimation of the catastrophe should not be Juanito's dead body with a bullet hole through the temple.

Mlle Etchegaray broke in on their agitated story with frantic exclamations of unbelief—"But Juanito stopped going with the Orthez boys all of three years ago. Why should he join them now? It *must* be a mistake." The excited men cried her down: Yes, yes, it was Juanito. He had asked Pedro Orthez to let him make one more trip . . . people in the know had heard that much, before the party set out for Spain. And this second farm boy had picked up a little more from one of the guards: instead of surrendering with the others, Juanito had seemed to go crazy when he saw the French officer—had thrown off his bundle of lace and silk—had leaped straight at the sergeant, who shot in self-defense. There was no possible doubt.

Quick! She must go to tell old Enrique. Who else could? There was no other woman to whom the old cobbler ever spoke. He was a mad freethinker who would drive Father Casimiro out of the house if he tried to go. Quick! The guards with their prisoners and Juanito's corpse might arrive at any moment. She still cried out that it was too dreadful, it could not be true. The men, waving their arms, urged her to be quick. Some of them were weeping with rage and sorrow. They all talked at once, motioning her to hurry.

The clamor of their voices rose so loud that a group of tourists, passing in an autobus, looked out and smiled to see how those excitable Latins scream and gesticulate over nothing.

A few days after the funeral of Juanito Tuán, Mlle Etchegaray, going down to see if there was anything she could do for his father, found the Tuán shop still tight closed. But as she stood an instant before it the door opened and Enrique motioned her to come in quickly. He shut the door behind her, and shaking one fist in the air, dragged her to a long crack in one of the shutters and bade her look. She saw, coming across the square toward them, like a picture of Youth Triumphant brilliantly painted by the sun, the blond officer of the frontier guard, the man who had shot Juanito dead, arm in arm with Tomasina Martinez in her best flowered silk. Her splendid eyes were flashing, her small head held proudly under a gala white lace mantilla. Smiling, looking deep into the other's blue eyes, her smooth scarlet lips moving in low intimate talk, she came closer and closer, unconscious of the fierce gaze upon her. They passed, brushing against the closed shutters. The murmur of their young voices came into the darkness like the hum of bees. They were gone.

Mlle Etchegaray choked down her impulse to shout aloud her indignation at the sight of Tomasina flaunting on the arm of the man who had killed Juanito. First of all she must find some words to quiet the infuriated old man beside her. She reminded him hastily that Tomasina, now she was grown up, was just what she had been as a child—a lying, cheating, play-acting fraud, of too little account for decent people to bother with, adding dryly, "She's not worth even hating. She would have made Juanito miserable. She will make this Frenchman miserable."

Old Enrique cut her short.

"She will make no man miserable any more," he said solemnly. Seeing the fear whitening the teacher's face, he said dryly, "No, I shall not need to touch her."

She was the last person to know what he meant to do. The examination for the *certificats d'étude* approaching now, everything else dropped from her mind.

It was said in Mendiberria that during the last fortnight before those examinations their teacher would not know if the house over her head were on fire. One after another, till late at night, she coached the children who were coming up. Everybody left her alone at such times, the honor of the town being involved. Sometimes mothers of the children with whom she was working came in silently to set down a covered dish of cooked food, but nobody stopped to gossip.

She had her usual success that year and emerged as usual to find everything in her two-roomed lodging in disorder and the supplies in her tiny kitchen almost exhausted. Basket on arm, she went down to the market place. Enrique Tuán was working quietly at his bench, deftly splitting a thick piece of leather with his thin sharp leather-cutting knife. He was as gray as a corpse, lean and gaunt, but collected and self-possessed. As she passed he looked up at her and nodded, his eyes tired and old, quite emptied of their frenzy. She went across to buy some vegetables and found there stout Mme Martinez, who waited on her silently, sighing heavily.

"Is Tomasina sick?" asked the schoolteacher.

"Non! oh, *non,* Mademoiselle!" cried her mother, putting both hands up to cover her face. Mlle Etchegaray said no more.

She usually stood on her professional dignity and waited till people told her local news of their own accord, but now she hurried into the bakeshop and asked the baker, point-blank, "Why isn't Tomasina at the Martinez stall?"

"She knows better than to show her face where we can see it," said the baker, folding his arms over his apron. And then, seeing her blankness, "Why, Mlle Etchegaray, hadn't you *heard?*"

No, she had heard nothing, she told him impatiently; he knew as well as she that it was the time of final examinations.

"Well, there was a letter from Tomasina to her darling Juanito . . . she'd never forget how sweet it was of him to go across the mountains once more and bring back the Spanish lace she simply yearned for. Only she couldn't bear the thought that he might be in danger and . . ." The baker half closed his eyes and went on in the monotonous singsong of a school child repeating a well-studied lesson, " 'Now, here is my plan for your safety. If you will tell me where the Orthez boys' secret path between the high peaks runs, I am sure I can drop enough hints to a certain blond booby . . . you know who . . . so that he will think he has solved the riddle, and will waste a cold night watching for you miles away from where you really are. Be sure to burn this letter, because if it should be found, both of us might get into trouble. Forever faithfully yours, Tomasina.' The dirty . . ." He spat, wiped his mouth on his hand and went on. "Juanito didn't burn the letter. The lovesick simpleton pinned it to his shirt right over his heart. That's where old Enrique found it . . . over the boy's dead heart. Enrique didn't waste any time passing it around so that every one of us could read it . . . pointing out every false, lying trick. We all knew every word of it . . . how she teased him into going, into telling her the path he would follow . . . and then sold him out to get a stand-in with Sergeant Brugnol." He stopped, out of breath, his face crimson with anger.

"Yes, it does look pretty dark," said the schoolteacher faintly. "But we must try to be fair. Have you thought that perhaps Tomasina really did her best to throw the sergeant off the track . . . to protect Juanito . . . only somehow her plan failed?"

"Her plan *didn't* fail," roared back the baker. "Enrique bribed Brugnol's housekeeper to pass out the sergeant's map case through the shutters at two o'clock the next night. We looked it over—fourteen of us—at Enrique's home. It took only a few minutes to convince us. Then he returned it to the housekeeper. On that map there was a cross marked at the very spot of the ambush. And on the margin, the words, 'near midnight' and 'HERE' in exactly the same handwriting as 'Here is my plan for your safety' in Tomasina's letter to Juanito. Oh, her plan succeeded all right! And everyone knows about it. Why the very kids in the street, when they're caught cheating at knuckle-bones, just grin and say 'Forever faithfully yours!' "

Mlle Etchegaray found no words to answer. She was literally cold at the recollection of Tomasina as she had last seen her, triumphant on the arm of . . .

The baker was thinking of that too. He went on: "The first day after Enrique had told all this, she tried to come to the café with her Frenchman, dressed up the way she had been ever since, with her silk dress and leather slippers and white mantilla. It wasn't so white by the time she got out. We men did no more than turn our backs on them. But the boys, Juanito's friends, had rotten eggs in their pockets. She hasn't been seen out of the house since."

"She can't stay in the house the rest of her life," said Mlle Etchegaray.

"She might go jump off the cliff on Izcohébie hill then," suggested the baker, changing the position of some rolls on his counter.

"Does the French sergeant go to see her?"

"No, he's got his promotion and gone. But he'd dropped her before that, as soon as he heard the story. Even sneaking customs guards have *some* sense of decency, I suppose. Besides, Brugnol has been around. No doubt he figured that a bitch like that would sell *him* out as soon as she had a chance of catching a richer man. She's done for herself this time, Tomasina has. She's caught where not even she can find a way to wriggle out."

II.

If Mlle Etchegaray had been the last to learn that Tomasina had done for herself, she was the first to know of the way out which Tomasina had found.

When she came back in the autumn after the two months of the summer vacation, she brought with her an old cousin from her home village to help her get through the rush of the first two weeks. Cousin Anna did the marketing, and so Mlle Etchegaray, never going down to *la place,* heard no more about Tomasina than from the babble of the children who told her that twice during the summer the girl had tried to return to her work on the square, "but a half an hour of what she got there sent her back to the house." Her father's hair was now quite white. Her mother began to cry if anyone spoke to her. The neighbors said that Tomasina had been like a wildcat at first: everybody on the street could hear her screaming at her parents. But since her last sortie there had been absolute silence. One little boy turned from his ball game a moment to say hopefully, "Maybe she's dead."

Little Maria Benevente was again not in school. "I'd better go to look her up while Cousin Anna is here," thought Mlle Etchegaray. "It's all very well not to be timid. But when a person has to make a visit to the Old Seminary, two are better than one."

As they went down the muddy, rutted lane, Cousin Anna asked, "I never happened to hear why they call that frightful old tenement house the 'Old Seminary.' "

"Because it is. It had been a seminary, crammed with boys learning how to be priests, from I don't know what date up to the time of the separation of Church and State. Then of course the Church had to vacate it."

"Oh!" said Cousin Anna, who was a good Clerical. "What a shame!"

"Guess again!" said the schoolteacher, stepping wide to avoid a pile of filth. "It was the best piece of good luck they ever had. All the sympathizers with the Church, oppressed by the wicked government, turned their purses inside out. Money just poured in—from as far as

South America, a lot of it. They built themselves the New Seminary. You know it, that splendid big château on the West Road. Bathrooms they have now, and hot and cold water and a handball court of their own. They owe a vote of thanks to the government for getting them out of the medieval rookery where they'd been. Nothing succeeds like being oppressed."

Cousin Anna looked her disapproval, sternly. Presently she said: "But I don't see what call the Municipal Council had for letting the Old Seminary fall into such frightful neglect."

Mlle Etchegaray laughed grimly. "It was the old familiar story. The Municipal Council was split. You know how much bad feeling there always is. They never could get a vote to do anything. So year after year it stood idle, unguarded, open to the weather, doors unlocked, plundered of everything that could be torn loose. And little by little—I hope they're rejoiced to see it—it's been lived in by riffraff, toughs, bums, most of them Spanish, drifted over the frontier because Spain was too hot for them. By and by they began to bring their women-folks. You can imagine what they were like. It's their children I have at school."

Cousin Anna interrupted her here by an exclamation: "Heavens! What's that horrible smell!" She buried her nose in her handkerchief.

"The Old Seminary," said Mlle Etchegaray, fiercely. "A good many of the children in my class live in that smell and bring it with them when they come to school."

They were at the entrance and turned in now between tall, battered stone posts which had once been handsomely carved. From them hung a few splinters of what were once gates. The two women had been seen, and from out the long leprous, tumbledown building before them a crowd of children poured out to meet them. "Mademoiselle! Mademoiselle!" they shrieked, enchanted to see the revered ruler of the classroom come visiting. Around them eddied gusts of the fetid odor of sweaty, unwashed, excreting human beings, moldy rags, and decayed refuse.

Mlle Etchegaray said heatedly in Basque to her horrified old cousin, "Don't you dare show a thing of what you're feeling. And take that handkerchief down from your nose this instant!"

The children were all about them now, many even of the little ones drooping under baby brothers and sisters, all of them, babies and children alike, indistinguishably filthy, ragged, their heads matted with eczema sores, their hands and legs and feet and faces crusted with dirt and scabs of mange, their fingernails like black claws, their smiling lips and soft, brilliant eyes lovely as those of cherubim. Mlle Etchegaray's heart, as so many times before, dissolved in a wild, indignant tenderness. She looked more grenadier-like than ever. But the children knew her. They caught at her hands; they looked at her adoringly.

"I've come to see Maria Benevente," she said.

"The Beneventes live in the stable now," they cried, proud to be guides. "We will show you. And her mother had another baby just now."

The procession moved across the foul, garbage-strewn paving stones of the courtyard, under the eyes of sluttish black-haired women and rowdy-looking men dressed in grimy rags, leaning out of holes which had been window frames before the woodwork of the house had been torn out to make cooking fires.

"Here's where the Beneventes live," said the children, stopping before what looked like the entrance to a vegetable cellar.

Cousin Anna gasped and stepped back, but Mlle Etchegaray drew her firmly into the blackness. They found themselves standing on an earthen floor at one end of a long, narrow shed. At the far end a square hole in the stone wall let in rays of daylight that slanted down upon a woman lying on a mattress, the small round head of a tiny baby tucked into the crook of her arm. The same light showed, kneeling before a large wooden trough set on the ground, a woman washing clothes. The swish of the water as she lifted a cloth from it came to their ears. Hearing someone enter, she turned her head to peer into the dark, wringing out the cloth as she did so. Something about the gesture, very free, very graceful, was familiar to Mlle Etchegaray. She took a long step forward as if to see and stopped short with a smothered exclamation.

The other drew her hands quietly from the soapy water, rose to her feet, and wiping her hands on her apron with a servant's gesture, came forward, her large dark eyes fixed intently on the schoolteacher's.

"Yes, Mlle Etchegaray, it is Tomasina," she said in a humble, earnest voice. "God has been very good to me. Just when I thought the burden of my sin more than I could bear, He sent the blessed St. Teresa to me to show me how to expiate it. She told me to leave behind my great misery and led me here. I saw her stand—glorious!—in the courtyard here, beckoning me in."

"I'd have died without her this morning, and the baby too," said the woman from the bed. "See how clean she has made everything. Isn't it beautiful?" She put her hand on the coarse white sheet which covered her.

Tomasina stood before Mlle Etchegaray, her eyes dropped, her hands, reddened and swollen by washing, put together on her breast in the attitude of prayer. She was dressed like the poorest, in cheap black cotton, with an apron of coarse gray stuff. Her hair was hidden under a black cotton kerchief drawn tightly around her head.

Mlle Etchegaray looked at her in a stunned silence.

Cousin Anna's heart was outraged by such unresponsiveness. "I don't know what you've done that's wrong," she said warmly, laying her hand on Tomasina's shoulder, "but I'm sure it is glorious to do what you are doing now."

Tomasina's heavy white eyelids fluttered. She murmured, "God has been good to me, a sinner," but she did not look up.

Mlle Etchegaray, gazing at her in the twilight, still said nothing.

She kept the same silence before the flurry of talk that ran around town as the news spread. Everybody else exclaimed and speculated, but Mlle Etchegaray made no comments save by the shrugged shoulders and widespread hands of professed ignorance.

At first everybody echoed Enrique's contemptuous comments, "What's the girl up to *now?*"

"It's just another of her tricks. She'll soon get tired of it."

"Wouldn't it make you laugh to think of Tomasina Martinez being visited by the saints!" (The story of her vision was soon well known.) "Somebody in Heaven must have given St. Teresa the wrong address."

"Father Casimiro isn't any too enthusiastic, I hear. He asked her why she didn't go into a convent. She says she told him she needed a much harder penance. That's *one* way to put it! You couldn't get her into a convent! She wants to be the whole thing, wherever she is!"

But as months went on, another note began to sound. First one, then another voiced a protest against Enrique's implacable bitterness.

"After all, Enrique, what more could anybody do for a penance? Nobody scrubs floors and washes children's heads and lays out the dead and takes care of old women with cancer just to show off. That's not play-acting!"

"You're being an audience for her this minute!" said Enrique sourly.

Later: "She has put a statue of St. Teresa up in a shrine on the wall of the courtyard just where she saw her vision. And after each piece of her work she goes out there to pray, rain or shine, kneeling on the paving stone."

"Where she can be seen," said Enrique.

Mlle Etchegaray never commented on such reports, but now she asked, "Where did she get a statue? I thought Father Casimiro didn't—"

"Oh, she doesn't have Father Casimiro for her confessor any more! She gets up at four o'clock in the morning and walks clear down the valley to St. Pé, to the priest there. He gave her the statue."

The next time the schoolteacher met Father Casimiro on the street she surprised the mild, absent-minded old priest by stopping to shake hands with him and in the most cordial manner to pass the time of day. He was not used to such friendliness from one of the anticlericals.

The tone of the general talk in town became more and more respectful: "Those people in the Old Seminary seem to think a great deal of Tomasina. They get her in to settle their quarrels, it seems, and have her take care of their money—the better ones, that is, with families. Some of the tough men use terrible language to her, they say. She never answers a word, just stops whatever work she is doing, puts her hands together on her breast, and begins to pray. Some of them were drunk the other day, I hear, and when she started to sweep the courtyard they began to yell foul words at her. She knelt down to pray for them, and one of them struck her over the head with his stick. They say when she fell the women burst out of the house, dozens of them, screaming like tigresses, and landed on the men as if they'd tear their eyes out. There was a free-for-all fight, about ten women to every man, and the men drunk. They ended by making the fellow who had struck her come to ask her pardon. But she wouldn't let him, took him out before St. Teresa's shrine, and bade him make his excuses there, on his knees, to the saint. She's had her head tied up ever since."

"She thinks a bandage looks like a halo," growled Enrique.

The winter wore on, and one day a mother bringing a child to school stopped to tell Mlle Etchegaray of a dramatic happening that was in everybody's talk: "A couple of drunks from the Old Seminary got to fighting with knives in the market place yesterday, and one of the children ran quick to get Tomasina. The moment the fighters saw her come up to them they stopped and looked foolish and went off, different ways. It was the first time she's been out on the street there since—you know when. Her face was as *white—!* they say, and shining! Like a lighted window, somebody told me. People stood back to let her pass, and some of the Frenchmen took off their hats. She didn't look at a soul, kept her head bent over her clasped hands, praying all the time."

"Did Enrique Tuán see her?" asked Mlle Etchegaray.

"Yes, she passed just in front of his shop. He looked at her like a demon. People didn't like it. It's about time he stopped saying those awful things about her anyhow. It's not Christian to keep up your grievance so long. Down in St. Pé they are all talking about her. Their priest says she is wonderful. They think it very queer, the people in her own town not appreciating her more."

Later: "Who do you think came today to our doors, begging, with a basket on her back, but Tomasina Martinez! She was begging for food and clothes for a poor family. My husband said, 'Tomasina! You begging!' She answered in a little voice as clear as a bird's, 'God is good to me, a sinner, to let me serve his poor.' Our Jeannot—you know what a tender-hearted little fellow he is—burst out crying and ran after her to ask her blessing."

She came thus to Mlle Etchegaray's door, begging for her poor. Mlle Etchegaray had always, ever since she had been in Mendiberria, given everything she could possibly spare, food, clothing, and money, to those of her school children who came from the Old Seminary. But she did not tell Tomasina this. After a moment's hesitation she said soberly she would see what she could do and went off to ransack the shelves of her tiny pantry. Tomasina, left alone, did not stir from where she stood in the middle of the floor. She bent her black coifed head over her clasped hands and began to pray.

Mlle Etchegaray, coming back, saw this picturesque tableau of piety and was unexpectedly set upon by an emotion which translated itself—before she could restrain it—into a small smile. Tomasina opened her eyes, caught the smile on the schoolteacher's lips. She closed her eyes more tightly and raised her prayers to a murmur. She never went again to the schoolhouse to beg.

But Juanito Tuán's father came. As spring approached and doors were opened, he sat many times of an evening on the doorstep of the schoolhouse, talking half to the schoolteacher, correcting arithmetic papers back of him, and half to the blackness before him.

"She is a devil, that girl, simply a devil. It must be Satan himself who tells her how to fool people. First she killed Juanito, and now she makes everybody forget him. Nobody but his poor old father remembers him, and what have I done? I am the one who has pushed her up to where she always wanted to be. My son is dead and done for, and his friends taking off their hats to the woman who killed him. This business of begging now—that she's invented to keep people thinking about her—I see them, man after man, stepping back to let her pass. And the Municipal Council giving in to her, when they never would even let you put the case to them!" (Tomasina had suddenly appeared before the Council, and speaking with such sweetness and devotion about her poor that even the most skeptical were moved, had prevailed on them to clean and repair the Old Seminary.) "Is Juanito any less dead because she puts on all these airs? He lies rotting in his grave, and his father has put his murderess where she gets what she wants. I did it! I!"

Sometimes the tired teacher, bending over the same mistakes in subtraction which she had corrected for a quarter of a century, heard him run wildly down the path in the darkness, weeping and crying, "I did it! I! I!"

But the next evening she would hear his voice again from the doorstep, moaning: "She says she is happy! That false, murdering woman says she is happier now than ever in her life. People who won't let me so much as say Juanito's name to them tell me, 'Look at her face as she goes along praying. Isn't that a beautiful happiness on it?'

How did she get that happiness they all admire? By killing my boy. Yes, it was a fine thing for her and her soul when she killed Juanito. He lies in his grave so that she can be happy. 'Perhaps,' I tell people, 'you would like to have her murder *your* boy, so that she could repent even more gloriously.' "

Sometimes he interrupted his dreary muttering to call back: "Mademoiselle, *you* know, don't you, that all this saint business is just because there wasn't any other way she could get out of her hole?" She took these questions as part of his monologue and did not answer, but once he got up and came into the lighted schoolroom, his bloodshot eyes blank with their long gaze into darkness, his gray hair shaggy with neglect, the dirt deep in the creases of his swarthy face, which he no longer remembered to wash. "See here!" he said challengingly. "You know as well as I, don't you, that all this is no more than just another way—the only way she had left—for Tomasina to go on being Tomasina?"

At first the gaunt schoolteacher only lifted her eyebrows and shoulders and spread out her hands in the gesture of professed ignorance. When she spoke, it was slowly, with long spaces between her three words: "I don't know," she said.

People began coming up from the village of St. Pé to pray for special favors before the St. Teresa of the Old Seminary and to ask Tomasina to pray with them. One woman had left her little girl very sick with a sore throat to come up to ask Tomasina to intercede for her. At the very hour—so the story went around—that Tomasina left the floor she was scrubbing and went down on her knees on the stones of the courtyard, the little girl in St. Pé smiled, said, "Oh, Grandmère, I feel so much better!" and when the mother reached home the fever had gone and the child was almost well.

"I know which book of pious stories that comes out of," growled Enrique. "It had a blue cover. That was the third story in it. I had it read to me when I was a boy, and so had she."

But fewer and fewer people would listen to Enrique. He might at least, they thought, not say such things to visitors who had come from another town all the way to a shrine in Mendiberria. They murmured, too, at Father Casimiro's passive, ungracious attitude. It was because he was getting old, they said. A younger priest would have helped Tomasina more, would have appreciated her, as the priest of St. Pé did. One day an autobusload of pilgrim excursionists drove all the way around from Lourdes, addressed themselves (naturally) to the priest of the parish, and said they would like to see the holy woman of whom they had heard and to pray with her before her shrine. Father Casimiro told them that he had not one but many holy women in his parish, and that he thought holiness was best practiced without too many spectators. And sent them away. Only think what a priest like the one at St. Pé would have done with such an opening!

The next autumn, when Mlle Etchegaray came back once more from her two months' vacation, she found the Tuán shop shut. Enrique paid so little attention to his work now, she heard, that people didn't give the cantankerous old man their custom. He scarcely seemed to notice whether he had work or not, going aimlessly up and down the streets as if he were looking for someone, sitting by Juanito's grave, his hand laid on it, and standing opposite the entrance to the Old Seminary, watching Tomasina.

Here for a time he was, by gusts, violent and abusive, calling out such jibes as "Tomasina! Tomasina! Why do you always choose the two times when the men are coming and going to work to be out sweeping the courtyard?" or accosting visitors with the suggestion that they go to Father Casimiro for an account of what was happening at the Old Seminary: "After all, *he* is the priest of this parish!" Or he shouted, the tears running down his cheeks, "Juanito! Juanito! Ask her who Juanito was!" Tomasina had once suddenly crossed the road, knelt in the mud before the dirty old man, and folding her hands in the gesture of prayer, her lovely face shining with the white fire of exaltation, said gently and humbly to him, "Punish me as you wish. It will be what I deserve." The old man had broken from his tears into dreadful laughter then, and looking from her to the deeply moved group of pilgrims back of her, cried out, "Always where there's somebody to see, my girl!"

But he had been made to understand not too gently by the authorities of the town that this sort of rowdyism would not be permitted. After this he stood silent, skeleton-thin and ragged, the incarnation of dirt and misery, tears running down his cheeks as though from a never-exhausted reservoir. When his half-starved old body could endure no more he shuffled back to Juanito's grave and sat beside it, resting, his hand laid across it as though to try to reach his son. And when he could stand again, he returned to his place across the road from Tomasina. Sometimes one of the many visitors to the shrine of the Old Seminary saw him standing thus, forlorn and emaciated, took him for a beggar, and offered him alms. Never more than once!

He seemed not to take his eyes from Tomasina. He saw her followed by adoring children, transformed by the cleanliness and care she gave them, kneeling with them before the statue of St. Teresa like their young spiritual mother; he saw her sweetly teaching the same children to play without the Stone Age ferocity that had been their habit; he saw the men and women in the tenement, lifted from their misery of poverty by the gifts of pilgrims to their shrine, consult and obey her; he saw many of the expressive, emotional Spanish women kneel to kiss her hand, although she always drew back with a pained look and motioned them to St. Teresa; he saw people coming to pray beside her, not only from St. Pé and the villages down the valley and beyond, but her own townspeople, women who had known and loved Juanito as a little boy, but who now, pale and anxious, thought of nothing but the sick person for whom they were praying. Exhausted, he went to sit by Juanito's grave and returned to see the young priest from St. Pé with a visiting priest come to look into Tomasina's story and listen to the girl, kneeling before the shrine, describe once more the vision that had brought her there. He saw an autobus of pilgrims from Lourdes, this time not consulting Father Casimiro, stop at the entrance of the lane and discharge a crowd of visitors who, after praying at the shrine, left Tomasina's hands full of offerings of which she kept not a penny for herself. He saw finally, one day, a delegation of students file into the courtyard and kneel before the shrine. Afterward the priest who was their leader asked Tomasina with deference if she could tell them of her vision. Old Enrique saw her leave the huge pan of potatoes she was peeling and come humbly forward, wiping her stained hands on her apron, her beautiful face like alabaster under the severe folds of her black headkerchief. He saw her listeners absorbed, transported, their sensitive young lips parted. They were of Juanito's age at the time of his death, as big as men, as simple-hearted as boys. He saw Tomasina's eyelids raised once, only once, and saw her young audience thrill to the magnetism of her great eyes, deep with emotion.

After they went away, he walked steadily across the street and into the courtyard, drawing out his long leather-cutting knife, and without a word, without a change of expression on his sad old face, stabbed Tomasina to the heart.

III.

Mlle Etchegaray was leaving Mendiberria. Not for the summer. For always. The day after Father Casimiro had departed for his new parish far up in the mountains, she had put in her application to be transferred to another school. She had gone to see the old priest off at the station, a great bouquet of flowers for him in her unbeliever's hand, and had, amazingly, asked him for his blessing. He had shown no surprise at this. He was perhaps too much broken by the shock of his transfer to a strange parish to have vitality enough left to be surprised at anything.

The day she was to leave town, Mlle Etchegaray set out on the road to the Old Seminary. It was marked from afar by a sun-gilded cloud which hung quivering over the crowd like dust at a fair. Like a fair it was lined with booths, selling souvenirs. Behind the booths were people she knew, old students of hers, very animated and active now, as they counted out change and called attention, leaning over their counters, to the attractions of their wares. Many of the booths were selling eatables too, for the crowds of pilgrims needed to be fed. She saw the baker bustling about, setting out hundreds of rolls fresh from the oven. His was one of the largest and finest of the booths.

As she came nearer the building the movement of the crowd became slower. They inched themselves forward slowly and stood for long periods without advancing at all. Visitors were being admitted to the courtyard by groups of forty at a time. Up and down the waiting line moved vendors of souvenirs on foot, some selling relics, although that was forbidden by both the Church and the municipal authorities. "A piece of wood from the broom used by the martyr the day of her death," a woman would say, drawing her relic furtively from under her shawl and speaking in a low voice, "guaranteed authentic." Everyone now crowded to one side to allow an excited group to pass, returning from the shrine. The news flew about, pervasive as the dust: "A cure! That woman in the middle hadn't walked for ten years!" Some well-tailored North American women with loud voices laughed and called back and forth to each other as they took snapshots.

A smartly dressed young man fought his way down the line, asking, "Which is Mlle Etchegaray? I was told the schoolteacher was here." When he reached her he said, speaking in her ear in a furtive tone like that of the vendors of relics, that he was a reporter from a left-wing newspaper in Paris, sent down to make an investigation, and to report along modern scientific lines on all this furor. He looked at her knowingly, with a smile of secret understanding. "I've been told that you—a highly intelligent, thinking person—can give me the real inside facts of the matter, and I'd like to make an appointment to get some stuff from you that will—"

"The facts?" said Mlle Etchegaray, breaking in on his whispering with her natural tone. "So far as that goes, I can tell you the facts right here. A girl of this town who had done a great wrong gave the rest of her life to self-inflicted penance for it, devoting herself to the poorest miserables, from whom the rest of us held aloof. She served them to the hour of her death, and since then has been serving them and all other poor by her example, which has caused the founding of a national organization of girls of good family to give part of their superfluities and time to the needy. She was killed by an insane man who died in prison shortly after. There have been many authentic cures made on the place where she died, and people love her memory for them. She has brought much prosperity to her townspeople, as you can see for yourself. The former priest of the parish was too old and too infirm to take charge of the complex situation always caused by a sudden influx of pilgrims, and has been sent to a smaller parish more within his powers. Those are the facts, if facts are what you are looking for." She added conscientiously, "I have forgotten to say that she was very beautiful."

"But—but—" The smart young man was disconcerted. "I was told that you knew all about—"

Mlle Etchegaray lifted her shoulders and spread out her hands. "I know nothing whatever about anything," she told him, passing forward with the crowd into the courtyard.

When she came out, half an hour later, she turned away from the crowd, off into the waste country covered by gorse, its thorny, graceless branches hung with yellow bloom. She walked a long time there, following aimlessly one after another of the wandering sheep-tracks through it, her head sometimes bent, sometimes lifted to look up at the mountain where Juanito was killed, sometimes turned to look back at the Old Seminary. Presently, picking a few of the harsh, spiky sprays of blossoming gorse, she went to lay them on the neglected, unmarked grave of old Enrique.

Memorial Day
May 30, 1913

Anyone watching from the cemetery could have seen the distant little cloud of dust in the valley which announced the approach of the first car. But no one was watching from the cemetery. A thrush was absorbed in his liquid song. The dead lay quiet. The grass and trees and all things living thrust their roots deeper into the warm moist earth and lifted their heads towards the spring sun. There was no one among the living or the dead who cared in the least that the first Model T Ford was approaching from the village.

Presently it appeared, and ground slowly in low speed up the steep sandy road, a small American flag standing stiffly at attention beside its radiator cap. Similar flags lay flat on the wreaths of flowers held by the little country boys who filled the car to the brim. When it stopped at the gate of the cemetery, the little boys spilled themselves out. Like the grass and trees and other growing things, they were quivering and glistening with vitality. Their small bodies were clad in their Sunday clothes, their hair was smoothly brushed back from their round, well-soaped faces. Everyone wore a necktie. Everyone carried on his arm a wreath to decorate a soldier's grave.

"Now, don't go and get everything mixed up, the way the boys did last year," cautioned the middle-aged citizen who was driving their car. He was chairman of the committee for the annual ceremony of remembering the dead soldiers, and responsible for the careful spending of the small sum voted at Town Meeting for

this purpose. He slammed the car into reverse to turn it around, calling out, "Keep your minds on what you're doing." The car was now pointed downhill ready to return to the valley. He turned off the switch and continued, "Now, boys, *listen* while I tell you what to do. Be sure not to bother with any graves except those that have the G.A.R. standard on them. They're kind of rusty now, but you can make them out if you look sharp. If last year's flag is still left in the socket, take that out, but don't leave it lying around. Put it in your pocket. And then stick in your this-year's flag. But be sure about it. We haven't any flags to waste."

The little boys listened seriously. "Lay your wreath down near the head of each grave," the chairman told them. He had a second thought, "No, lean it against the tombstone. It shows up better there." The little boys nodded. They walked on. It made them feel important to be walking. They were at the age when boys usually skip or trot.

More cars came slowly up the hill. From them more clean-faced little boys with wreaths clambered out. From others, mothers and fathers emerged, extra wreaths over their arms. Like the cleaned-up little boys, they were carefully dressed in holiday clothes, suitable for the beautiful spring weather. Their faces were good-humored and comfortable. In one of the cars sat the elderly minister in black broadcloth, who had come to "say a few words and pronounce the benediction." His hair was white, his pale, broad face had a genial, pleasant expression.

Inside the cemetery there was no dust. It was not thought decorous for cars to roll in over the weedy gravel of those driveways—except for funerals, which were of course serious occasions. Now there were ten or twelve little boys. They walked forward. The smaller ones once in a while gave a skipping hop to keep up with the bigger ones. Their mothers and fathers sauntered beside them, the wreaths over their arms, their eyes dreamily fixed on the quiet valley below, its small white homes peaceful in the sunshine.

When they reached the older part of the cemetery where the grayer, weather-beaten tombstones stood, they separated into groups and began to look for those graves where a limp last-year's flag drooped from the small metal standard.

JOHN HEMINWAY ANDREWS
Died in Camp Fairfax, Virginia
In the Twenty-second Year
of his Life.

A round-cheeked little boy stopped with a wreath at this first grave he saw. He did not read the inscription, although, in spite of many summers' and winters' weathering, it was still legible. He had not been told to read the inscription. He did what he had been told to do, took out of its socket the limp and grizzled flag, leaned over the grave and set his wreath against the tombstone.

Instantly a silent scream burst up from the grave. The first of the soldiers had awakened.

All the year around, they rested quietly in their graves. They had been country men, at home under the open sky. Neither the furious rages of winter nor the heat of the summer suns could disturb their sleep. Year by year, the shroud of their oblivion was thicker and softer. . . . If only little boys could be kept away from their grassy beds . . . little boys with clear eyes and small harmless hands. At the touch of those small hands, the dead men who had been small and harmless little boys themselves awoke in the old agony to what they were trying to forget.

It had been in an army hospital in Camp Fairfax that John Andrews had died in 1863, screaming his heart out while surgeons were amputating his leg without anesthetics. When he awoke, it was always in the midst of that shriek. But now it was at the little boy he screamed to tell him—to let him know—to warn him. He was horrified by the child's rosy calmness, by his awful unawareness. Yet he could never think of words to warn him. He could only shriek silently from his grave, till the trees quivered to it, till the clouds echoed it back, till the thrush was silenced. But none of the little boys ever heard him. Nor did this one.

He looked carefully at the standard to make sure that it had on it the letters the man had told them about—G.A.R. He had no idea what the letters meant. Older people always take for granted that children know.

But, unless children are told—in words, or in what they live through—they do not know. And if they have lived through it—it is too late.

Yes, the rusty letters were the right ones, he could see them plainly. He stuffed the dingy old flag into his pocket. It was the first time he had been old enough to be included among the boys who placed wreaths on Decoration Day. He wanted to make no mistake with the flag. Sure that he had it right, he turned away to his father with a gesture which said, "Well, that's *one* disposed of." His father smiled indulgently at his small son's brisk competence.

A little distance away from him was a bigger, older boy, who was already placing his second wreath and flag. He had been quicker about it because this was not his first trip to the cemetery on Decoration Day. He knew what to do. He took the old flag from the standard, set in the new one, and leaned up against the tombstone his wreath of already-drooping lilacs. His mother had told him not to take longer than he need because they were going on a picnic afterwards. Fishing, too. It had turned out lovely weather. As she sorted out the fishing tackle, her little son had heard her say to his father that it certainly was handy, having Decoration Day come after the opening of fishing season.

Under the matted shaggy old grass of the grave he had just decorated lay a dead man who had been very poor and who had gone away to war because he had been offered five hundred dollars to take a rich man's place. With the money he and his young wife had planned to buy a small farm. It would provide a home for his children and his wife, where he could take good care of them all as they grew up. Very dear to him were his three sons, so like this little boy who now bent his round child-face over the old grave. The dead man had not been able to think of any other way to earn so large a sum as five hundred dollars.

He had killed other men because he had been told to, killed and maimed men whom he had never seen before, who had never done anything to him: and then one of them had maimed and killed him. He had died in battle, an expression of astonishment on his face. He had never been very bright and had not at all understood what was happening to him. The last thing he remembered was the unknown face of the unknown man who was killing him, although they had never seen each other before. Death had sealed that stranger's face upon his eyes, so that when, with a start, once a year, he awoke from his sleep, he saw two faces . . . the set, strange features of the man who was driving a bayonet into his side, and a little boy's face, clear and harmless, like the face of one of his own little boys. He had died without a sound, but now as the child leaned upon his breast to set the wreath in place, he broke into a groan.

But no one ever heard him. This little boy brushed his hands together lightly to dust them off, and was about to turn away when he saw a tiny fly buzzing in terror in a spider's web. That was a groan he could hear. He stooped over the helpless, trapped little living victim, broke the threads and freed the small flying creature. It spun up into new life with a joyful, whirring beat of gauzy wings.

At this act of pity, the soldier in his grave groaned "Misery! Misery!" straining to be heard, till the blades of grass growing over him shook.

The little boy, having correctly placed his wreath and flag, ran down the weedy gravel path to slip his hand into his mother's. Now they could go fishing.

A thin little boy had halted beside another grave. His clothes were threadbare and faded. And not very clean. This was the first year he had been included in the Decoration Day celebration at the Old Burying Ground. He had never been in any cemetery before, and looked around him admiringly at the tombstones; some were plain weather-beaten slabs, some were sort of little elegant playhouses, stone ornaments all around. It was like the village in the valley, he thought, with its many houses—only here so small.

He had seen little—of anything—except his own run-down home. His father was very poor and could not do much for his children. Yet this was not the father's fault. All that he had done was, when he was a very young man, to marry because he pitied and loved her, a pretty young girl with a gentle smile. She was hired girl on the next farm. After they were married, she remained pretty and gentle and he still loved her, but she had turned out to be, as country people say, "not quite all there," and there must have been something amiss with the health of her family. So she never could really take care of the house or the children. Her husband did what in most families the wife did, as well as what in most families the husband and father does. She "forgot things." In the middle of plowing or haymaking, he often left his work and went back to the house to make sure she had not forgotten something important. Of course neither the farming nor the housework was done well and the children were sickly.

But the farmer never told anybody why, because he didn't want to complain of his smiling, gentle wife who was like his oldest child. He didn't want other people to criticize her. So they criticized him.

The little boy knew very well, although no word had ever been spoken to him about this, that his father was looked down on by the neighbors because "things weren't kept up as they should be." The shutters were unpainted, hung first by a hinge and then fell off and lay on the grass to rot. The porch steps had broken boards, which had been broken ever since the little boy could remember. The neighbors said, "Wouldn't you think he'd have gimp enough to—" Their cows got sick, more often than other people's, and sometimes one died. People said, "Wouldn't you think that he'd realize—" Their kitchen was always in a clutter and sometimes when you stepped in from outside, it didn't smell as it should. People said, "Wouldn't you think—?"

The little boy saw his silent father at Town Meeting, or where men gathered, looking humble and defeated among the others whose wives were "all there." He could see without being told that his father had nothing to be proud of and never would have. His heart almost burst with his longing to get for his father something to be proud of. There was in the village street a great old house, well-painted, with green shutters, lilac bushes, peonies and green grass smooth around it—much grander than any other. One of the little boy's earliest memories was looking wistfully up at it, and feverishly trying to hope that someday when he grew up, he could earn money and buy it and take his father and mother to live in it. He imagined his father standing in its front door, proud and looked-up to.

But how could he even hope? He was so small for his age that although he was ten, he was often taken for seven or eight. He tried to help his father on the farm, but he was not only little and strengthless—he had a sore on his knee that did not heal. He told no one about it because he feared if he did someone would tell his father he ought to be taken to the doctor. There would be no money to pay the doctor and his father would never have left a debt unpaid. It would be dreadful to owe money and not to be able to pay. The sore on his knee was not so very big. Maybe it would heal of itself. His gentle, smiling mother never noticed it. If the teacher at school asked him why he limped, he told her he had just stubbed his toe.

He limped a little now as he walked about among the graves, but in his sober little face his eyes shone with happiness. It was the first time in all his life that he had held a proud position of trust. He had ridden in an automobile, with flags on it, with other boys, well and strong, whose fathers kept up their farms and whose mothers were clean and knew how to keep house neatly. And just like anyone, he was now laying wreaths on the graves—trusted—nobody watching him to see that he did it right. He walked carefully and glanced down at his knee once in a while to be sure that the oozing matter from his sore had not soaked through the cheap material of his trousers.

He chose a grave—one with a fine great monument, marked with the name of Captain Elijah Hatwell on it. He was not going to take a plain, little slab when he could just as well have a fine one.

The dead man under the fine marble monument had been a country boy too. Not sickly—strong, broad-chested and always tall for his age. He had left the life in the valley and on the mountain which he had loved, and gone to war because he had thought it his duty to defend his country's unity and to free black men held as slaves. He had not been taken unawares. He knew why he had enlisted. Year after year, on this day when his dead comrades lost their courage, he had kept a righteous silence. He had winced at the touch of little boys' hands, but had been sternly mute. Yet year after year, his silence had worn thinner. He had stirred in a growing restlessness. Those few moments when the people from the valley strolled in over the graveled paths of the cemetery—with easy, quiet pulses, talking together of the day as a holiday!

Yet their little boys were beside them!

It must be that they did not *know!* But he still kept his silence. If they did not know there was no way to tell them.

If he could only think of a word so short that even as it was cried out, one out of all those sauntering people might understand.

But what was it—that one word? What one word—?

The little boy with the unhealing sore on his knee replaced the faded flag in the rusted standard with a new one, leaned his wreath against the fine marble monument and stood to admire the tall urn on top. The monument towered among the small slabs like the great old house in the village street that was so much better than any other.

The sickly little boy knew now that he would never own that fine house, would never take his father and mother there to live. But looking up at that richly ornamented tombstone, his heart leaped. Why, yes—*this* he could do!

He put his clawlike little hands together in front of his chest. Once in a while a kind neighbor family stopped to take him to Sunday school. So he knew how to pray. He bowed his head over his folded hands. His face shining with joyful hope, he prayed, "Jesus, please—make me grow up to be a soldier. Dear Lord Jesus, let me be a fine soldier and after I die have a grand tombstone. And then my father will have something to be proud of."

The desperately silent, dead soldier under the fine tomb had begun to hope that this year he would be passed by, had felt himself already sinking back into blessed blackness. The murmured prayer of the little boy startled him from his gaze into oblivion. He had no time to prepare himself, to stiffen, to resist. The child's helpless, empty ignorance of all that the soldier knew drove to his vitals like the bullet that had killed him, and as instinctively as he had screamed then, he screamed now . . . the thing the little boy did not know, and that he knew. "Blood! Blood! Blood!" he shrieked noiselessly.

It was the word he slept to forget. All eternity would be too short a sleep to forget that word. Awake now, with a living little boy standing beside him, his scream of "Blood! Blood! Blood!" rose from his grave like a scarlet spray and fell back in dripping red drops upon the child's bowed, praying head.

The little boy heard voices and a shuffling of feet on the gravel. Near the entrance of the cemetery the exercises were going on. The light breeze brought some of the phrases to his ears: " . . . over our fair land . . . the last meed of true devotion . . . with unflinching heroism to defend the right . . ."

Turning their backs on the scattered graves where they had left their wreaths, the little boys straggled towards the entrance. In front of them a group of people stood about the minister who was finishing his few remarks with a solemn dip of his voice intended as the transition to the benediction: " . . . unfailing grateful remembrance of our fallen heroes," he said and stopped to draw breath.

Back of the little boy, the dead soldiers had all taken up the cry of the last awakened, the strongest, the best, the one who had always till now been silent. Now they knew what it was that must be said and heard. "Blood! Blood! Blood!" they screamed after the harmless little boys, trotting lightheartedly through the flickering tree-shadows.

The minister slid into the benediction: "And now . . ." He raised his hand and lifted his face. The little boys knew what to do when a minister prayed. They stood still and looked down at their shoes.

" . . . the peace of God which passeth all understanding . . ."

"Blood! Blood! Blood!" screamed the dead soldiers soundlessly.

The exercises were over. The little boys swarmed up over the sides of the automobiles and perched three deep on the seats. Some of them took off their neckties and put them in their pockets. The little sick boy's face shone. Someone had carelessly given him a flag to keep (they were bought by the dozen anyhow, and one more or less . . .). He had never had a flag of his own before. He waved it with all his might as the Ford turned and started back down the hill. It had been the happiest day of his life. For once he had been an accepted part of things. He thought with pride of the great stone monument where he had laid a wreath. Perhaps his monument after he had been killed would be like that. He imagined his father standing proudly by it, admired by other men. A throb of pain from his knee made him look down with apprehension. No, it had not soaked through his trouser, yet.

The dust cloud settling in the distance marked the departure of the last car. The dead soldiers lay silent, fumbling with their dead hands to draw up over them once more the blessed black of oblivion. Nothing else in all the world could reach them to rend asunder that sheltering pall . . . if only no little boys came near them, little boys with clear eyes and honest faces and kind, harmless hands. Raw and shaken, the dead soldiers huddled down under the shreds of their forgetfulness.

The thrush rolled his rounded liquid note into the silence. The trees and grass and all the rooted living things quivered and glistened with vitality. In the hot sun the flowers of the wreaths, their life oozing from their amputated stems, began to hang their heads and die. The little new paper-crisp American flags, bought at wholesale, stood stiffly at attention. The last cloud of dust blew away in the distance. The cemetery lay quiet.

The soldiers, having been remembered, were now once more forgotten.

The Knot-hole

In the spring of 1940, a new little son or daughter was on the way, so our dear Emilie-Anne, my goddaughter, wrote me. She made a pretense of knowing as well as I how foolish it was for people living in a country at war to have babies. The pretense was thin. Lianne (as we who had known her from her chubby childhood called her) was obviously as lightheaded with joy and pride as any other young mother-to-be. It was really, she explained, not so crazy as it seemed to us in the United States. True, her husband was at the front, on the Maginot Line, like other French soldiers and officers. But during that quiet winter they had regular furloughs at home. Like vacations. By not taking the next furlough when the time came for it, he would have an extra long one, due in late October, when the baby would arrive.

Yes, yes, even so—can you remember those months of the phony war?—even so did the men of the French Army plan confidently for regular vacations from war. From the military leaders down to the sergeants and privates, even so did the French Army feel that this war would naturally repeat the pattern of the static, trench fighting of the First World War. And even so, in all unfearing ignorant confidence, did the wives go out at intervals, when they could, to spend a week end in some farmhouse, not too far from the front for Army husbands to dash back for an hour or so. Lianne was, when she wrote me, in such a week-end, temporary home. She was, she told me, cheerfully, that very minute looking out of the little rustic window, expecting to see him

appear. She said that she and Jean-Jacques felt so strongly about family unity that no effort was too great to be sure their little four-year-old boy did not forget his father. I smiled as I read this. We all knew that the reason for her expensive, uncomfortable trips to the farmhouse near the front was that Jacqui's young father and mother were crazy about each other.

There was no danger that Jacqui would forget his father. Jean-Jacques was the kind of bluff, good-humored, vital young man no boy would resist. In peace times he was a teacher of physics in a small-town high school, a great favorite with his students. In war times he was in an artillery battalion, as great a favorite with his Army comrades. He was one of those who know how to take hold of life by the right end.

In due time another letter came from Lianne. In that first dreamlike winter of the war, mail from France was slow but almost regular. The family plans were made for the event, she reported. In July she was to go South to stay with her mother in the old, white-washed, thatched cottage on the farm from which Lianne's grandfather had gone out, eighty years before, to his modest success in the big world. She wrote that they all thought it would be pleasant to have little Paul, or small Thérèse, whichever it was, born in the same room where she had been born, looking out on the hollyhocks at Voillac.

There were medical details in that letter—the last one she wrote from her home near the high school where her husband had taught—the intimate report on this and that detail of her pregnancy which a younger-generation friend makes to an affectionately solicitous older woman. She was, on the whole, she wrote, getting along better than before Jacqui was born. Her doctor said that if she would take things very calmly, relax, go up and down stairs as little as possible, and keep her mind tranquil, she would have no such trouble as with the birth of her first child. Her husband being first in her thoughts, she always passed along his news. He hoped, it appeared, that the new baby would be a girl, exactly like her mother. "But *I* want another boy. There can't be too many like my Jean-Jacques." There had been, her husband had written, some sickness among the horses in his battalion. But that was now past. Jean-Jacques was an intellectual but he was as good with horses as any army vet.

I was surprised. *"Horses?"* I thought. I knew as little about military equipment as most women of my age, but by that date I had seen hundreds of photographs of high-speed tanks, tearing Poland to pieces.

Lianne's cleaning woman had gone to live in another town, she wrote. Since the doctor had forbidden any stooping or lifting for her, she would need to find another helper.

On this trivial homely note, ended that last letter. It was written in April. By the time it came to me, May was drawing to a close. Do you need any reminder of what was happening late in May of 1940?

My desperate feeling is that if you have forgotten—all is lost. We are doomed if we forget. So I assume that you remember the appalling uproar of clanking tanks, screaming dive-bombers, and the sledge-hammer pound-pound-pound of hundreds of thousands of hobnailed boots, which in May of that year shook the earth under us, here, on the other side of the Atlantic from invaded France.

From Lianne nothing. Nothing. Not a word.

Like everybody else of that period, I was naïvely astonished by the failure of the world's postal system to carry letters to their addresses. Of course I did the frantic things which we were all doing then—I wrote and telegraphed to the American Consul in Lianne's home city, "Could any news be had of Madame Jean-Jacques Bergeron? She was last heard from at . . ." I wrote and telegraphed to the Consul in the nearest city to Voillac. And to the Consul in the city where her parents lived. And to other friends in France. And to French-American charitable organizations to which I had long belonged. I beat wildly on what I thought were doors. And then I saw that my knocking fell on unbroken walls. No doors. No windows. No echo from my outcry.

Not a word from Lianne. Not a word.

Then weeks and weeks later—three months after it had been written, a short letter. It must have been mailed on one of the very last days when a French post office was free to accept a letter for the world outside. It had been scrawled in pencil, in a cowshed where Lianne and Jacqui were spending the night. With her little boy, she was trying to reach Voillac. On foot. They had been tramping and hiding and trudging on for eight days before she could get together a piece of paper, a pencil, an envelope, a stamp to let us know that she and Jacqui were alive. She did not know as much of her family. No news of parents, of her husband's parents, of her sister, of her sister's husband—nothing.

And nothing, nothing, nothing of her husband! Her last letter from him, written hastily, was sent just as the horses were being put to the caissons to start the battalion to join the battle of Flanders.

Horses! I laid the letter down, shuddering. The quiet grass of a Vermont field lay before my eyes. Across it, as I read, there thundered the tornado of motorized war, hurling itself down in steel to meet those horses.

Silence again.

"No. Sorry, no telegram can be accepted for places inside occupied France."

"No, no change in the mail situation. We are informed that no letters are being sent to occupied France. It would be no use to mail them."

Then a letter. A letter! A system had been arranged for excluding letters from France as rapidly as a prison door is slammed shut and locked behind a man brought in by the police. But for a time there were, infrequently, cracks in those prison walls through which a letter in a crumpled soiled envelope could be pushed out—a cautious letter, unsigned, undated, not a name mentioned—short, hurried, a hoarsely whispered message, like what might be caught by the ears of tense watchers at the mouth of a mine, after a cave-in. Hardly loud enough to be heard, for even sound itself was a danger. A spoken word, a mere sob, might be enough to bring down more crashing tons of savagery upon human flesh and blood.

Letters could not reach those in that great prison but they could—by efforts and risks not to be imagined—send out at long, irregular intervals, one of those whispered, anonymous, secret messages. Often those which came to me were not even set down in their own handwriting, as familiar to me as their dear faces. But every word ringingly, unmistakably personal. Reading one left me trembling and wet with cold sweat.

From the first of these contraband letters, I learned that Lianne had not reached Voillac and her mother. She never did. Three days distant from the cowbarn where she had written me, the fleeing refugees had been stopped. It was their first encounter with the words "By Order" which came to cover the sky, to hang like black curtains before every door, every window, to smother all mouths, to blind all eyes. "By Order" the tragic mass of footsore women, children, old people, were halted in a town none of them had ever seen. Even in this smuggled-out letter, she dared not tell me the name of the town, since she was not sure into whose hands the message might fall.

Because her husband had been a teacher, Lianne and her little boy were directed by the distracted old Mayor of the town to the school. There were seven classrooms and a small office which had been that of the *Directeur.* The building had been meant to provide space for daytime classroom teaching for a hundred and fifty children. In it now, living, sleeping, cooking, being sick, being born, dying, were more than five hundred men, women, children, and babies.

Jacqui was with her. She underlined this. It was a triumph. In the rout, under the scream of the machine-guns in the dive-bombers, many of the fleeing mothers had been separated from their children, she wrote. "Day and night, my son has not once been out of reach of my arm. He and the baby to come are Jean-Jacques' children. I must keep them safe until their father is here to take care of us again. We sleep on the floor. There are so many, we take turns lying down. An old lady beside me died last night. Jacqui is being a good boy."

No news from her husband. No news of what inconceivable horror could be happening to France. All communications cut. To those thousands of French citizens not a word of what was being done to France. People around her told her that Jean-Jacques certainly had been killed in battle. But she would not let him die. *He was alive.* She knew he was alive.

These few secret letters which straggled out after long gaps usually came in the same mail. Probably held for some tramp freighter into which a sailor might smuggle them. In the same mail with this bulletin of news from Lianne was a letter from her mother at Voillac, frantically anxious about her daughter. "We know nothing of Lianne and Jacqui except that her town and home were obliterated by bombs. None of the refugees who have passed this way has heard of her." I, in Vermont, knew that Lianne was alive. Her mother in France, three hours' drive from her, did not. I could not tell her. "No, very sorry, the situation has not changed since you last inquired. No telegrams accepted for occupied France."

Silence. Silence. The calendar turned over one blank leaf after another, day after day, towards the month, the week, when Lianne's baby was to be born. That month, that week passed, another week, more weeks, another month went by.

Then, dated three months before, another scribbled, penciled note came in. It was a muffled scream of joy. "Jean-Jacques is alive. A prisoner. He is alive. The news was on a printed card. *But his name is in his own handwriting.* He is alive."

Then not a whisper, not a breath. For months.

Sometime in 1941, the German conquerors began the system of prisoner-of-war short messages. Do you remember them, the yellow printed slips marked "prisoner-of-war service"? The people of a great nation, prisoners of war! A message of twenty-five words, carefully innocuous and personal, was allowed "By Order." This was sent by the writer to the Paris Red Cross headquarters, then German of course. There the cards were held long enough to make any code-concealed information out of date, and sent to the Swiss Red Cross. In Switzerland, after a prescribed delay, they were sent to our own American Red Cross, and thence on to the persons to whom they were addressed. Mostly they arrived four to five months after they were written.

When one came, you were allowed, "By Order," to write twenty-five words on the back and return it, along the same five- or six-month long route. Of those twenty-five words every one must count. Every one did count. Pondered on for days as they were, factual, disjointed, so expressed as—first of all—to pass the Censor, those telegraph-short sentences lay like crusted scars on the flimsy yellow paper. It was later they began to bleed again, in the anguished hearts of those who read them.

Through this channel I learned that little Anne-Marie had arrived (she was already six months old by that time), that Lianne was in charge of the two- and three- and four-year-olds of the refugee group crowded into that old school building (she had been a kindergarten teacher before her marriage), that she and Jean-Jacques in his German prison were allowed "By Order" to write each other nine words a week, or thirty-six words a month.

The next message reported that Jean-Jacques now knew that he had a little girl. "He loves her wildly, he writes." So did Lianne. "Anne-Marie sweetest baby. Strong and well. I am nursing her much longer than I did Jacqui. Kindergarten full of children."

The twenty-five words of the message after that ran, "Am passionately excited. Reason to hope J. J.'s release. Jacqui is thinner. I dread weaning baby. Have heard from my parents. Kindergarten full of children."

Then, astonishing, unimaginable—a letter. A real letter though not in Lianne's handwriting. Once in a while this happened. Somebody about to try to escape "over the line" memorized messages given him by those left in the occupied zone. Not the most modern Gestapo sound-detecting machines could locate a memorized message in a man's mind. This was postmarked from near Marseille. It had been transcribed from memory by someone almost illiterate, to judge from the crudely penciled scrawl. Strange to hear echoes of Lianne's young voice, of her own turns of phrase, in this unfamiliar handwriting.

I soon knew it by heart, as well as did the unknown messenger who sent it. It took me straight into the crowded old building, to stand by the emaciated young mother, desperately trying to go on nursing her baby, trying to feed two lives on the only food there was—turnips, chestnuts, apples—and, inestimable privilege, because she was a nursing mother, every day a pint of whole, not skimmed, milk.

It was midwinter. She was still wearing the same dress she had on when, in June, she was driven from her home by bombs, wore the same summer-thin underwear and stockings. In her care were forty little boys and girls, all day, every day. Her task was to keep them—so I interpreted the imperfectly comprehended phrases of that letter—from the dismal idleness and barbarian quarreling into which closely confined, undernourished children sink without skilled direction.

There were places where the transcriber—perhaps a sailor? perhaps a cook?—confused the message so that it meant nothing. I suppose none of it meant anything to the near-illiterate who risked his life to pass it on to me. I suppose he (or she) had tried to memorize too many messages. Yet I could make out that Lianne wished to let me know that she was trying to do for the children what her husband was doing for his fellow-prisoners in the German camp. "Jean-Jacques study-classes, chorus, dramatic club, care for the sick, not allowed to say where he is, but climate cold, very damp."

Then for a sentence or two it was quite clearly remembered, clearly enough set down. "We still find each other, *we do meet* as we both try to keep life human, not animal-like. No equipment for kindergarten, but songs, poetry, games, keep clean, run and play outdoors—but mostly how to live without hurting each other." Then a blurred passage, with names I did not know, names I was sure Lianne had not put in—probably a passage from some other memorized letter—and then, like the clearing of radio reception, Lianne's words came through again, "Jacqui thin. All children thin except those still nursing. They lose weight terribly when weaned. I still nurse Anne-Marie. Loveliest baby. Fair, like Jean-Jacques' family. Beautiful expression in blue eyes. Everyone speaks about this. If only I have milk enough to keep on nursing her."

One item in this message never would have passed the Censor, if she had tried to write it on one of the prisoner-of-war cards. "Man escaped from *Oflag* where J. J. is, hiding in village here. I have talked with him. I touched a man who had seen my husband. He said he would have cut his throat without J. J.'s help and example."

A last paragraph, a long one, alas, so badly written, so blurred on the too-thin paper that I could make out almost nothing of it:—something about a photograph of the baby having been taken by a relief worker from a neutral country.

No signature. None was needed.

No other letter ever came through. Only the widely spaced-out, telegraph-short messages on official cards. "Hoping every day to see J. J. come in. He is soon to be released. Jacqui is thin. Still nursing Anne-Marie. Kindergarten not so full."

"Many children too weak for kindergarten. Jacqui very thin. Have had official word to expect J. J. soon. Have you received photograph of baby?"

Then one in which not even the twenty-five words were used. "Have weaned Anne-Marie. I had no more milk for her."

That was an open wound from which the blood gushed out as I read. "I had no more milk for her." Misery! Misery! My heart broke with the young mother's, I laid my old-woman's hand in horrified pity on the thin, drying, empty breast, with her I was shamed by the hungry baby.

After that, the short messages were mostly about Jean-Jacques' release and return to France. Over and over this seemed about to happen. "Two weeks ago card from J. J. with news they hear the order for their return has come in. They must be on their way now."

"Intense suspense. Every time the door opens, I think it is J. J. Anne-Marie does not grow. Very few children in kindergarten. Jacqui good."

Then, astounding, incredible—a cablegram delivered at my door. The yellow envelope, just as though there were no war. I cried out, "From France? Did you say a cablegram from *France*? Why, I thought they were not allowed." I tore it open. I was shaken to the heart by the naïve idea that Lianne had been allowed "By Order" to let me know that her husband was released, was with her.

LITTLE ANNE-MARIE DIED LAST NIGHT. NO SUFFERING. FADED AWAY.

Later that day, in answer to my rage of pain, of astonishment, of stupefaction, someone told me, "Oh, yes, hadn't you heard—cablegrams from France which announce a death are allowed by the Germans."

Silence. Silence. Silence.

Months later a battered envelope came in, postmarked from some undecipherable place in Africa. It had been addressed to me in Lianne's own handwriting. No letter in it. Only a small snapshot of a baby's head, fair, with a great candid rounded forehead, and innocent wide eyes. This came four months after the baby died.

Silence. Silence.

Then I heard at last. Not from Lianne. From Jean-Jacques. At second hand. No, at third hand. A Swedish war-relief worker (Sweden was a neutral country) who had been in France passed through the United States. He had not seen Jean-Jacques, but he had been in close and continued secret contact with a Frenchman, an escaped prisoner, hiding in France. This man had promised Jean-Jacques that if he did make that escape from the boxcar, and ever met an American, he would try to get word to the godmother of Bergeron's wife.

My Swedish informant told me in such detail that, almost at once, I broke my tense listening, to ask him wonderingly how the escaped French prisoner happened to talk at length—how had they had time, wherever had they found a place safe enough to talk where they were sure of no enemy ears? He told me, "The man was still frightfully shaken. I could see that. Everything we saw, or did, reminded him of those days in the boxcar. He told me about them over and over. They were just behind him you see. He still could think of nothing else. And every time he spoke of it, some new detail would come out. He was no peasant, you see, wordless in pain. He was a skilled scientist, a professionally trained laboratory worker in chemistry—and, like all educated French people, highly cultivated too. He had plenty of words at his command. I think now he would have gone insane if he hadn't been able to tell it all."

I asked again how they had time. And the place?

The worker from Sweden told me, "We were part of a group helping people marked down by the Gestapo but not yet caught, to escape over the Pyrenees. We waited, the two of us, night after night, for months, in a shepherd's abandoned hut, at the end of a mountain path. When we heard the first sounds of an escaping party, we went out to guide them over the hidden twisting way through the rocks of the pass, into Spain.

"They were never there before midnight. Often, if there were old people or children among them, much later. Some nights no one came at all. We had time enough, we two, and nothing else to do but talk. No light, of course, in the hut. We were safe enough. No listeners there. We could say what we pleased. I could ask all the questions I wished. I heard his story over and over, till I could tell it myself."

II.

He often began his story by saying wonderingly that he probably would never know why he had been put with those in the boxcar. They were not the ones who had been with him the preceding two years of his prison life. He had never seen one of them before.

Perhaps the reason was only that there had been room—if you could call it room—for one more. Perhaps when he was taken from his *Oflag,* the official intention had been to have him shot as a reprisal for something done somewhere else. There were always reprisals of this kind—no connection with the men shot. Then, perhaps—as he puzzled it out—perhaps in the jungle-growth of orders and counterorders in every prison office, someone might have picked up the wrong *dossier* from a desk, got an order for disposing of him, meant for another prisoner.

All he knew was that he and twenty others had been taken away from their prison in a closed truck. When it halted and they were herded out, they were beside a railway track. Not in a station. In the open country. He thought the train was a long one. But it was black night. He could see only the boxcar to which he was pushed. He had no idea what happened to the other prisoners with him in the truck. He never saw or heard of one of them again. His brother was among them.

An armed guard unlocked the sliding door to the car, opened it a crack, and two others shoved him in. The door was slammed shut behind him.

He felt that the blackness was full of men, but he did not, not as strongly as usual in prisons, smell them, for there was a sizable opening in the roof of the car down from which poured a current of fresh spring air which diluted the prison stench of unwashed bodies in dirt-encrusted clothes. He could not see the opening in the roof, but as he strained his eyes to get some idea of where he was, he caught a glint of distant stars immeasurably high above them. Nearer, seen through the roof-opening, a small yellowish glow. He knew what that was. A guard's lighted cigarette.

He flung one arm up to shield his face from blows, and tried to get his back against the wall. Prison technique. But the shove which had pushed him in had sent him stumbling several steps from the door, and when he tried to step back, he felt human bodies there.

Then a voice spoke. It was a French voice. It said neutrally, "We are from *Oflag* (he gave the number of the prison camp), confined there since June, 1940. For the last four months we have been told every day that we would be sent back to France. We have been two days and two nights in this car. Of that time it has rolled for about eleven hours. We do not know where we are."

The voice trembled, whispered in his ear, *"We think we are being repatriated."*

He heard the men about him breathe deeply. There was a silence. The voice went on. "My name is Bergeron. High-school teacher of physics. Of the — Field Artillery Battalion. Will you tell us who you are?"

The newcomer had been in prison camps for two years, was experienced in prison ways, and knew, he said, before the end of the first sentence that the speaker was the man who set the tone for the group. He knew too that he was safe from violence. He drew a long breath, dropped his arm, gave his name, the number of the prison camp he came from, the regiment to which he had belonged, his occupation in civilian life.

The rules of the place were explained to him. There were too many in the car for them all to lie down to sleep at the same time. So they took turns. The sick and crippled ones had twice the lying-down time given to the others. When it was not your turn to lie down, you had your choice of sitting on the floor or standing. The best sitting places were those around the edge where you could lean back against the side walls of the car. These were also shared turn and turn about. So far, the guards on the roof allowed them to talk—at least most of the time. Silence was enforced when, as nearly as they could judge, the train was in or near a railway station, or a town, where their voices might be heard. But where they were allowed to talk freely, as now, they supposed—

"The train is standing on a siding in the midst of the empty country," the newcomer broke in to tell them.

"Yes, we had guessed that." Bergeron's voice went on explaining the organization of the day. "One of us is a priest. There are morning and evening prayers in one of the corners of the car. No talking by others at that time. One of us was a medical student. He does what he can for our sick and gives a health inspection each morning. Four buckets make up the sanitary arrangements for forty men. With covers," said the voice, ironically. "They are, you know, a very cleanly nation. These buckets are emptied each day. After dark, four of us, each one roped to a guard and carrying a spade, carry them out, dig a hole and empty them. They are never washed out, there is no water for that. Only one cupful for each man, night and morning."

"Roped?" the newcomer had asked quickly.

"Roped."

"And did you say 'a *spade*'?"

There was a silence. He felt the men move closer to him. Then Bergeron's low voice said—and now it was not quietly firm, it was rough, agitated, anxious, "You understand—didn't you hear me?—*we think we are being repatriated*—on our way home! Our release will be, of course, conditional on absolute obedience to rules. There must be no . . . no . . ."

The newcomer hastily assured the invisible men around him that he understood. There would be no . . .

Towards the last of this talk the train had begun to move again. He had to raise his voice to make his pledge heard above the clatter of the freight car wheels. There was a muffled stirring as of animals at night in a barn. They sat down as best they could. Someone near him coughed rackingly, and from the other end of the car came an echoing series of other dreadful, deep coughs. Tuberculosis, he thought, forebodingly. He was given one of the favored places, where he could lean his head against the wall. As he relaxed against it, he said gratefully to the darkness, "Thanks."

"It is your turn," explained Bergeron's voice.

My Swedish informant had been speaking as tensely as I had been listening. To hear this in Vermont was incredible!

He shifted his position, drew a breath, went on, "The French prisoner did not, of course, tell it to me, up there in the shepherd's hut, as I am now telling it to you, all in one piece. But it ended by coming together in my mind, because I heard it so many times. I came to know just what would remind him of one or another part of it. Dawn for instance. How many dawns did we see together! He never saw the blackness fade to gray without telling me over again about the first dawn in the boxcar."

It was like this, he would say. First I noticed that over our heads the open hatchway was gray. I looked up at it. And when I looked down it was light enough in the car to see the men. There was no surprise for me in what I saw. I had known what they would be. For two years I had been with men like that, gray-faced, thin, their clothes faded, stained, patched, ragged, a stubble of beard on their sunken cheeks. They were sitting or lying down. The bare boards of the floor passed on to their bony frames every jar of the freight car. Yet many, even of those who were sitting up, were asleep, sagging to and fro, their heads fallen on their chests. Those who were awake braced themselves against the incessant shaking by locking their hands around their knees. A rank stench came from the four buckets at the end of the car.

Yet when my eye caught that of Bergeron—I knew at once which one he was, a gaunt, big-boned man, his eyes gray-blue—he saluted me from across the car with a nod, and a brisk wave of the hand. He was standing, wide awake, an alertness in his face very different from the sodden dullness of the usual prisoner's expression. For the moment he said nothing, not to disturb those who slept. But later, when those who had been sitting through the night were on their feet, yawning and stretching their stiff arms and legs, Bergeron came over to me to say, "One more night gone. Every one brings us nearer home—we hope." I noticed that no sour snarl rose from the other men such as, in the prison I had come from, had instantly quenched any attempt to speak cheerfully. All of them, even the sick ones, hoped.

The day began. Those which followed were exactly like it. The only variation was the color of the sky up there above the hatchway, which we saw beyond the rifle butt and the gray-green trousers of the guard seated in a sort of sentry box on the roof. Sometimes that bit of sky was blue and sun-flooded. Sometimes it was covered with lowering gray clouds. Once in a while the slow rattling car jolted for a time under green tree branches. When this happened, every man clutched at his neighbor and pointed to make him look up. Even the sleepers, by rule never to be disturbed during their turn to lie down, wanted to be awakened to see this. Sometimes rain poured in streams down through the hatchway. This, as far as possible, we used hastily as it fell, to clean the skin on our faces and hands and feet. It was, I saw, not only the fresh air from the roof-opening which lessened the fetid prison smell. Sometimes a square patch of sunshine lay on the floor, actual bright sunshine. It was big enough for several men to sit in. This privilege was shared in turn by all, with a double turn for the sick. Some of them, at the suggestion of the medical student, took off their clothes when their turn came for the sun bath. The white bodies they showed then were thin, but not strengthless except for the six or seven sick and crippled men.

This was probably because of the twice-a-day exercises. These were compulsory. As Bergeron had explained, the prisoners were never let out of the crowded car (except for the nightly sortie of the four who emptied the soil-buckets). They would all have been half paralyzed if they had not taken some exercise. These lasted half an hour, twice a day, for each of the three squads into which the men were divided. There was no room to take more than three or four steps in what space could be cleared. But for their first steps on French ground they were determined to be able at least to walk out of the car steadily on their own feet. The coats were laid down—the thin, threadbare coats—to soften a little the boards of the floor, and the men, by fours, rolled, stretched, kicked, did somersaults (those who could), walked on their hands, or did simple bending exercises, rhythmic, taken in time to an accompaniment of folk-tunes whistled by the spectators. A squad of helpers, directed by the medical student, massaged the sick, carefully flexed and gently moved the arms and legs—what there was left of them—of the crippled.

The food was—well, everyone now knows what prison food is— a little bread, often moldy, floating in what looked and tasted like tepid dishwater. Sometimes a few "eyes" of grease floated on the water. The prisoners, especially the sick ones, mortally dreaded the coming of these rations. But they were so famished that when the sickening food appeared, there was a deadly moment when they became starving animals. The frantic reflex instinct to fight for all they could grab was barely held in check by the rigid self-discipline of the group. At such instants, when the ground-swell of bestiality rose under our feet, Bergeron stopped it, "Now! Now! Turn and turn about is the rule here."

I had not meant to interrupt the narrative of the Swedish relief worker, not even for one question, but at this my wonder broke out. "Is it often that such rigid group discipline . . . ?"

"I asked the French prisoner that question too," said my informant. "It seemed to me a natural one. He scorned me for not knowing the answer. 'That depends, of course,' he said impatiently, 'on who sets the tone. When those who do are like animals, the group is like a pack of wolves—or hogs. When the leaders are human— Why should it be different with prisoners than with other men? It's always like that, everywhere.'

"What they liked best, the Frenchman told me, were the long talks between those who were awake, sitting or crouched near each other."

This talk was personal, casual, wandering, just what came into our heads. Mostly it was of what we would do when we were at home again. As the car jolted slowly on, most of us were surer and surer we were being repatriated. Not all. The coughing, sweating sick did not hope to live till they were free in France. Several older men, of the kind who always believe the worst, insisted that we were being taken to the Russian front, where we would be forced into front-line fighting. They said the trip was taking far too long for a short journey to France from Germany. This point was continuously argued. A younger man, a university undergraduate, had figured out from the stars wheeling over the open hatchway that the general direction of their course was south. But it was impossible to make any real calculations, because the car stood motionless more often and for longer periods than it moved.

Two or three times we could not keep ourselves from talking over, in the lowest of our whispers, what the chances of escape would have been—if we had not been going home anyhow—for at least one or two of us, during the night sorties with the soil-buckets. Those ropes. A spade in each prisoner's hand. A spade has a sharp edge. The darkness. Quick, concerted action. Of course it could have been done only once, would have meant a chance for only one or two men. Reprisals for the others. But it would have been worth it. But this whispered talk was idle speculation. As it was, it would only spoil the chances for all of us.

Mostly we talked as though we were certain that we were being taken back to France. Had we not been told over and over at the *Oflag* that any day we were likely to start home? Had not the *Oflag* been full of widespread rumors of this or that astute way in which *Le Maréchal* would secure the return of the prisoners? Most of us pushed away our doubts and sent our hearts flying forward.

A favorite subject for these rambling talks was the manner of each one's home-coming as it would be if he could have that as he wished. One man said he would send word ahead, and have all the village at the station to meet his train. With the band. He had played the piccolo in the band. Another young fellow would not let even his parents know he was coming. He planned to take the night train to his town, slip away from the station by the back road, turn up the lane to his father's barn, step in, take a milking stool, and be there, milking, his head dug against the cow's flank, when his father opened the door and came in for the morning chores. The farm boy's dream description made us all, even the city gutter-sparrows, even the death-struck sick, feel against our cheeks that warm, living, hairy flank, and smell the barn odors—straw, milk, earth, manure, fresh hay.

Another man said, "All I want is to get drunk—one long, glorious, blind drunk after another. It would be like heaven to be drunk-sick again."

"A hot bath—a hot bath a week long!"

"Girls! Girls! Girls!"

"The heel of a loaf of real white bread, French bread, and a whole Brie cheese . . ."

The young priest saw himself walking up the steps to his country church, and into its incense-fragrant dimness. A mechanic murmured, "To stand in my own garage again, to lift the hood of a car brought in for repairs, to lean over the engine, listening to hear what's the matter with it."

A young research worker from the botanical laboratory of the Jardin des Plantes tried to make us feel the brimming peace it would bring him to lean once more over his high-powered microscope. At this, someone said with the acrid savagery that was like the usual prison-camp talk, "Boy, you won't find any high-powered microscope there. It'll be in Berlin. Four hundred million francs a day drained off from France to pay for the occupation."

But Bergeron had quickly broken in on this bitterness to describe yet once more what his own home-coming would be. Not the little house which had been his home. That house, like all that town, was now nothing but bombed, burned rubble-cinder. But he would be going home, although to a wholly unknown town, because his wife and little son were there. He knew from his wife's nine-word messages through the prisoner-of-war service, just where he would find her—with thirty or forty children in a kindergarten improvised in an old school building, crammed with refugees.

He described over and over just how he would open the door to that crowded room. Quietly. He would not knock. Then he would stand there, looking at his wife and his little boy and those French children she had been taking care of, keeping them decent, saving them from becoming animals. At first she would think the door had been opened by one of the children. She would not turn her head. And then . . .

Bergeron talked a great deal about his wife. He was proud of her.

All the men were unnerved with the incredible prospect of seeing our own again after two years of prison, none more so—in spite of his self-control—than Bergeron. Whenever he spoke of his family his voice roughened and shook, and sometimes it broke.

One of the other men explained to me, one day, in a whisper, that Bergeron had a baby daughter born seven months after the battle of Flanders. He had been taken with an almost dreadful affection for this child of his he had not seen—his wife wrote the baby was like an angel—but of course all women thought that. Night after night the man in prison had waked up wild with a joyful dream that he had held his little daughter in his arms. When his wife had to wean her, he had worried frantically lest she suffer from the coarse, scanty food. Madame Bergeron had nursed her as long as she had any milk. His fellow prisoners had heard all about this again and again, till no one but other family men would listen.

When the rumor began to circulate back in the *Oflag,* that the prisoners were to be sent back to France, Bergeron had almost gone off his head at the thought he would see his baby girl. But three weeks before they had been put on the train, a telegram had been handed him—yes, a telegram!—saying the little girl had died.

He had been broken by this. Could not eat, could not sleep, never spoke, kept his hands clasped over his eyes. His fellow prisoners had thought he would die. He seemed dying before their eyes. But ten days before their departure he had received from his wife one of those brief, officially-allowed messages, "I promise you I will be here with Jacqui when you come back to me."

Then he rose and lived again.

He used to tell us in those long rambling talks in the boxcar, "I always knew my wife was lovely. I never knew she was so strong." He used to say, "My wife does honor to humanity, by her work with those homeless children. It is called a kindergarten. What it really is, is teaching French children they can live together like civilized beings. Not like wild beasts. She upholds human dignity, my wife does." He often said, too, "She would not be allowed 'By Order' to send in the message, in plain words, 'Never give up!' but really in everything she writes me that is what I have heard her say all these two years."

No matter how deep we were in these memories, in these forward looking hopes, Bergeron never forgot, when the time came, to get stiffly to his feet, motioning those with him to rise, letting the waiting ones move to the better places where they could lean back against the wall.

Then one night the car came to a halt and did not go on. For two days it was stationary. The sky seen through the hatchway was gray-blue, with small clouds. Several men said it looked like a French sky. A graybeard with one arm amputated, answered grimly, "Or Russian."

The guards on the train became bored with nothing to do. We could hear them calling idly back and forth to each other. Sometimes the gray-green trousered legs of the guard at the hatchway disappeared for a few moments. We could hear him clambering down the ladder at the end, and then a sound of several men talking and laughing together, as if he had been joined by others from the other cars. Sometimes there was the measured sound of counting—*ein, zwei, drei*—the numbers pronounced in louder and louder voices, ending in a great burst of laughing and hooting, as though some kind of game were being played, watched from above by those who stayed on guard on the roof, rifles cocked.

During those two days inside the boxcar, we went through the routine planned to keep us alive till we were freed. We ate the dreadful daily slop; we exercised; we played what finger and guessing games we could invent; with no tools but our cups, which were examined and checked every time the food was handed in, we could construct nothing. We took turns at lying down. We said our prayers or were respectfully silent when others prayed. We told the same stories over and over. We imagined again what we would do on the day we reached home. There were occasional brief outbursts of rough, wild, obscene talk when somebody's nerves snapped under the suspense. But we crowded close around the man who had broken, to steady him, to keep the guards from knowing that a Frenchman had given way. A few of the more thoughtful men talked sometimes with Bergeron about plans for serving their country and the country's youth more creatively than ever before—once they were free to do something creative. We ground our teeth in our struggle to remain human.

Over and over someone would say, in a hope that ebbed and rose as we breathed, "It *may* be only a little longer now . . ."

Every hour was exactly like the one which preceded it. In that windowless prison how could anything happen to make one hour, one minute, one day different from another?

And then one of the men darted from the other end of the car with the quick, astonished step of a man to whom something has happened. He put his lips to Bergeron's ear, whispered and turned back to where he had been. With a startled look, Bergeron sprang up and followed him.

In a rush we were all on our feet. There was nothing different to be seen. There could be nothing different. We knew that. But we were like stampeded cattle. The break in the monotony beat on our taut nerves as if a trumpet had shouted, as if—we did not know what, only that one among us had moved swiftly as if—incredibly—something had happened.

Crowding, pushing, shoving to see what it was, the stronger ones using their fists to be ahead of the others, we were a mob. Dehumanized. Bergeron turned, held us back with an upraised arm. "Turn and turn about is the rule here," he said sharply, in a phrase now so thickly encrusted with associations of order that we halted. With a cautious glance up at the guard's legs and the rifle butt at the hatchway's edge, he said, "Before I take another step, I will tell the man nearest me what Carrière said to me. He will tell the next man. And so on. Till we all know. It may be nothing, you understand. Nothing. If it is anything, we will all share it alike. Don't let the guard suspect anything."

He leaned to whisper in the ear of the nearest man, who turned to whisper to the next one. When it came to me, I heard, "Carrière thinks he has found a knot in one of the planks of the wall, loose enough to work out of its hole. He came to ask Bergeron if he thought it safe to do this. We might look through it and see something. But it may be a trap. A guard may be standing just outside. Or the car may be double-planked. In that case the hole would not go through to the outside." I passed this on to the man back of me. We were all on our feet, craning our necks, even those whose turn it was to lie down.

We watched Carrière stooping, the fingers of one hand picking slowly, delicately, at a place on the plank siding. After a time, he looked around at Bergeron, asking a question with upraised eyebrows. Bergeron assumed the responsibility, gave a nod of assent. Carrière brought his fingers together and slowly drew out the knot. The sunlight shone through in a long beam. The hole was as big as a man's thumb. In the light from it Carrière's prison-pale face was chalky. He looked at Bergeron for orders.

Bergeron turned his face to glance up at the hatchway. At the end of the car where we were, we could not be seen by the guard unless he stooped his head down through the hole. There was not a sound inside the car. Bergeron motioned the men to make a screen with their standing bodies around Carrière, said to him, all but soundlessly, "You were the one who found it. The first look belongs to you."

Carrière stooped and put his eye to the hole. The silence in the car was so entire that we could hear the guard on the roof clear his throat raucously, and spit. Our hearts rose at the casual, ugly, unself-conscious sound. It could mean nothing but that there was no guard waiting outside. We gazed tensely at the back of Carrière's bent head. Would he never look away? What was he seeing?

Then he stood up and turned towards us. Tears were streaming down his cheeks. His mouth worked. He put his bent arm up before his eyes and stumbled away to lean against the wall, his shoulders shaking.

"Your turn next, Fayolle," said Bergeron steadily, motioning to the man who stood nearest.

So all of us looked in turn. I had not liked Carrière crying. It made me sick to see one of us, who had endured so much, in tears. But every man was half-blinded by tears when he turned away to let the next one see. I was resolved to be calm.

But when my turn came, what I saw—oh! it was France I saw there under the gentle French sunshine—a narrow green meadow; next to it, on one side, a rolling, half-plowed brown field, two great work horses, nodding their heads as they stepped strongly forward throwing their shoulders against the tall collars; on the other side, a long, straight, white road bordered with slim poplar trees leading to a gray village in the distance, with red roofs and a white church tower; on the road a farm cart with two high wheels slowly approaching, the metal trimming on the harness winking in the sun; between the railroad tracks and the meadow, a slow-moving, dark-green little brook bordered with silvery pollarded willows—the earth, the grass, the water, the very sky of home. . . .

Bergeron was the last one to take his turn to look at France. We watched his tall form stoop, we gazed at the back of his head, seeing through it what he saw. We stood in a long orderly file beside him, eager for our second look at France.

When Bergeron stood up and turned towards us, his face was white. His lips moved. In a rhythm we all knew as we knew our own pulses, his hand began to beat time. He began to sing in a low clear voice—we knew the words—we sang with him in the same hushed voice: *"Amour sacré de la patrie"*—and *"Liberté, Liberté chérie—"*

"Nicht singen!" shouted the astounded guard, shoving the barrel of his gun down the hatchway.

We gave a convulsive start. We had not known we were singing. We were like men wakened roughly from a dream, who for an instant do not know where they are. Bergeron motioned for silence. He looked as startled as we. He, too, had not known what he was doing. For an instant, even he had forgotten the tense self-control which had focused all our faculties on one thing—to do nothing which might risk losing our release. . . .

Carrière, who had been stooping at the knot-hole to look, stood up now, and again whispered into Bergeron's ear. Bergeron whirled, stooped, looked out through our tiny window, and continued looking. Carrière tiptoed around our circle, telling us in a whisper, "I was looking out while you were singing. An old man sitting in that cart beside the driver stood up and looked this way, as if he had caught the sound."

We were terribly affected by this. To have made ourselves known to a fellow countryman, not a prisoner, still living on the sacred soil! But Bergeron turned back to us, shaking his head. "It couldn't have been," he said. "We were singing too low. Nobody could have heard. They were still a long way off. I watched closely as the cart jogged by. Neither of them so much as turned his head this way."

For the next day there was not one hour of the twenty-four when one of us was not feasting his eyes on the look of France. Even at night, someone was watching the golden lamps in the village, or the French stars in the French sky. The car had now stood still for three days.

Small as the hole was, it was possible, by shifting one's position a little lower, higher, to one side or the other, to take in perhaps a quarter of what we could have seen through a window. The far end of the car where the hole was, and where one man after another was perpetually stooping to look out, was not visible to the guard up at the edge of the open hatchway. We always kept a cluster of sitting or lounging men directly under him. Of course, twice a day when the slop food was brought in, the gnarled wood-brown knot, preciously preserved, was carefully inserted into the hole. Since only one could look at a time, we shared with the others whatever we had seen. "An old woman pushing a wheelbarrow was going along the road when I was looking out. The way her black headkerchief was tied made me think we are in the *Ile de France.*" Yes, the others who had seen that stooped old figure agreed that the kerchief's twist did look like the center of France. "My grandmother tied her kerchief on with that knot at the back."

The first morning the watcher at the hole whispered, "School children," and stood back to let the fathers among us take quick looks at five little boys and girls in black aprons, clattering along in their wooden-soled *galoshes,* their leather school bags swinging. There was something special about the way those children stepped, set their feet down on the ground—we felt it in our own feet. They were our children; we were again children clattering to school along a white, straight, poplar-shaded road. Thus to possess with our eyes the longed-for home scenes swept us beyond what we knew was real. We were not prisoners; we were out there, walking freely on the French road as the early sun sent long rays down through the thin mist.

An hour or so after they had passed, something exciting began. An old workingman, very shabby, his shoulders stooped under a faded blue blouse, carrying a long-handled spade, plodded his way slowly out from the village along the road. When he reached the sagging, weather-beaten gate to the meadow just across the little stream from the tracks, he stopped and pushed it open. How many times had each of us in imagination laid his hands on that gate to push it open! We touched, handled, smelled, felt everything we looked at, as we pored over that piece of our home country, framed in the knot-hole. Each one of us, as we took our turn to look, told what he did. "He is going into the meadow. He has shut the gate behind him. He has stopped, as if to get his breath. He has his lunch with him in a package. He has put his package down on a stone. He is going to stay all day. He has begun to spade. To turn under the sod."

At first, we wondered at anyone, let alone an old man, spading away in the open country, in a meadow. That was land for plowing, not spading. The guards evidently wondered, too. Presently, one of our watchers at the knot-hole reported that a green-gray uniform went out from the train towards the meadow, stood on the side of the little stream, and shouted something across to the old workman. The words were French, but the heavy voice sounded as writing looks which is done with a coarse pen in thick ink. But as we listened tensely, holding our breaths, we heard another voice—purely French, the clearly spoken vowels, the resonant consonants, the rise and fall of the familiar speech tune as accurate to our ears as, to our eyes, the tracing of fine lines made with a drawing pen. The sound of it was music, poetry. It took an instant for us to hear the prosaic words it uttered. "Potatoes," it explained. He was preparing a patch of ground to plant potatoes.

The watcher of the moment whispered back to us, "The guard isn't satisfied. He keeps standing there. He is going to order the old man off."

But he did not. He stood uncertainly for a while, calling something back to—we supposed—another guard on the train. There was an exchange of hoarse German. A moment of suspense. Finally, so our watcher reported, the guard came back, leaving the old man there. A long breath of relief went around the car. "What is he doing now?" we asked the watcher.

"He has gone back to spading. He is shaking out the earth from a sod." We felt, sifting through our own hands, the soil of our motherland. We smelled the fresh healing fragrance of earth newly turned over.

All day we shared what that free man did out there under the gray-blue home sky. Through that hole, which any one of us could have closed by putting a thumb into it, we flung our hearts, our senses, our souls. We stooped stiffly with the old man, we slowly spaded with him. With him we turned under what was alive, so that that something of more value could take root and grow. We stopped with him to rest, sitting down on a stone sucking a cold pipe meditatively. He evidently had no more tobacco than we. The stone happened to be so placed that when he dropped down on it to rest, he faced the railway track. Several times that day we saw his lifted glance run along the roofs of the cars indifferently, and drop from there to the ground, to his work, to his shoes, to the grass. He leaned to knot a loose shoelace, to finger a clod, he sat up again, looking off towards the horizon. He yawned, took his dead pipe out of his mouth, lifted his faded blouse to stuff it into his pocket, took up his spade again.

He did not get on very fast with his job, it seemed to some of us who knew about farm work. The farmer's son, every time it was his turn to look, whispered to us, "Listen, fellows, I don't believe he *is* a workingman. I never saw anybody try to spade with that kind of a push from the shoulders. You do it with your back and legs."

At the end of the first day, he had spaded only one strip across that narrow field. But he was old. How old? We all made a guess. Sixty, perhaps? Probably had served as Territorial in the last war. "I've got an uncle sixty-one, looks about like that."

The next morning began the fourth day since the car had stirred. Bergeron had insisted it would do no good to question the guards, since they probably knew no more than we. But on this fourth day he was overborne, and a man who spoke a little German was delegated to ask the guards who brought in the morning pail of food, "Why? Why so long waiting?"

The guards looked at each other, hesitated, said nothing, turned back to the door. The older one went out. The younger one went after him, stopped, said in broken French, "Not know. Hear that—"

The older guard shouted at him angrily. He stepped out and began to slide the door shut. Through the crack he called a word or two more, hurriedly. But strain our ears as we might, we could make nothing out of them. His accent was too heavy. They sounded like nothing we had ever heard.

All that they told us was that some reason for the delay existed.

We did not even try to guess what it might be. We sat motionless, sickened by frustration, by the intimate humiliation of total helplessness. Silently we looked down fixedly at the pale brown liquid in our tin cups, the drops of grease congealing as it cooled.

Bergeron lifted his cup and began resolutely to eat. But he was breathing very fast as though he had been running with all his might. He swallowed down what was in his cup and got up. "If no one else wants a turn at our lookout, I'll take mine now," he said.

He stooped to look. Over his shoulder he whispered, "The old man is certainly looking at our car. He *keeps* looking. He darts his eyes up and down the train. Perhaps the guards are all down on the ground on the other side playing that gambling game." We looked up at the hatchway. Our guard was not there. A whisper ran about from mouth to mouth, "Make him a signal! Let the old man know—" One of us went close to Bergeron and whispered this in his ear. He looked up at the hatchway, saw that it was still empty, nodded to us, put his thumb through the knot-hole, and slowly turned it up. Everyone's heart began to pound. Bergeron withdrew his thumb, stooped again to look and gave a great start. "The old man is running this way," he reported on a sharply indrawn whisper.

There was an instant in which we did not breathe. Then Bergeron let his breath out in a gasp and murmured, "He has turned back. He evidently saw a guard. He has picked up his spade. He has gone on working."

We pulled Bergeron back to whisper urgently, utterly at a loss, "What does it mean—what do you think—?" His gaze was darkly inturned in thought. "Perhaps he *did* hear us singing. And he must have seen my signal," he said. And then, shaking his head, "But there is nothing he—nothing anyone can do. He will be shot if he tries."

"Tries what?"

He lifted his shoulders. "There is nothing he could even try."

After that, we never took our eyes from the old man in the blouse. Late that day the watcher at the hole reported, "He has taken out a white handkerchief. He is unfolding it to wipe his forehead."

"A *white* handkerchief?" went rapidly around among us. "That's no workingman."

But what—what—? We could not think what.

We only never took our eyes from him. . . .

Late that afternoon, our guard was again not at the hatchway. We had for some time heard the thick voices talking and laughing together down on the side of the train away from the road. Then, as sometimes happened, the brawling sound of a quarrel broke out. One of the players had perhaps cheated. We had heard them before this, shouting angrily at each other. Now the noise was louder than usual, more voices joining in, as if the guards still up on the cars were leaning over the side and taking part in the row.

"Bergeron! Quick! Here!" the man at the knot-hole called in a loud whisper. Bergeron sprang to the hole. He saw the old man in the field racing towards us. He had something white in his hand. He sprang across the little brook. Looking fearfully up and down the train, he darted to our car. A paper, rolled up, was pushed through the knot-hole. We rushed to see.

Bergeron unrolled it, and held it up to the ten or eleven men near enough to read it. A question in one word, "French?" Bergeron scribbled on it "French" and thrust it back. The man outside darted a look up and down the train, took the paper and wrote feverishly. The tiny white roll came back through the hole. Bergeron held it up. On it was written, "Courage, Faith, Hope."

The thronging men leaning over Captain Bergeron's shoulder read the words at a glance, and motioned him fiercely to send an answer. "Tell him—" "Say that we—" Their pulses pounded with the answer that must go back, to say what must be said. "Tell him that we—" There were no words.

Bergeron was stretched on the rack with them, brains and hands paralyzed by the longing to speak, by the need for haste. The pencil in his hand hung suspended over the paper while his eyes plunged into those around him.

From somewhere in the car, a voice—we never knew whose—perhaps several at once—called hoarsely, *"Never give up."*

Bergeron's hand set the three words down all in one rushing line and pushed the paper through the hole.

He saw the old man read it at a glance, look up, his face convulsively working. He nodded over and over—his lips said soundlessly, "Yes, yes, yes, yes." He thrust the paper in under his blouse, and clasped one hand closely on it over his heart. With his other arm he made a long gesture towards the town. He was gone, racing back to the field.

The brawling voices were dying down. We heard our own guard climb up to the roof of our car. We saw his legs and the rifle butt. He hawked and spat. We sank back limply. The man at the knot-hole reported in a whisper, "The old man is sitting on the stone. He keeps his left hand pressed closely over his heart. He is looking straight at us." We took hasty turns to meet that long gaze.

When twilight began to fall he went away towards the village, taking his spade with him.

The next morning before dawn the man who was at the lookout said, "*Pst! Pst!*" Several of us went at once. "It seems to me I make out people walking by on the road," he said.

We all looked in turn. Yes, people were certainly passing there, dim shapes at first, which might be anything. As the light grew stronger, the shapes became men—old men—and women, boys, more women—children, big girls, little boys, small girls. They did not come together or abreast. Sometimes singly, sometimes by family groups, sometimes two or three. At times, the road would be quite empty all the long way to the gray houses with the red roofs. Then, from the end of the village street we would see a group, or a couple of people coming out towards us. They did not look—not more than once—at the train. They only walked by on the long white road bordered with poplars. As they approached the train, each one looked at it once, turning his full face towards us. Then as they passed on, everyone pressed his hand over his heart and held it there. Even the little children.

Not one of us needed to be told what it meant. The old man had answered "Yes!" to our message. He had understood it. He had pointed to the town. He had meant he would tell them. They were telling us that they understood, that they would not forget.

We saw that our guard stood up several times as if to look. We heard the others shouting questions back and forth. But there was nothing for them to see except groups of quiet people—men, women, children, blacksmith, priest, shopkeeper, fine lady, old farmers—quietly walking along a dusty white country road, their eyes straight before them. They were still passing when twilight thickened so that our eyes could no longer see them.

None of us slept much that night. It would have been a waste of the first moments of happiness we had known for two years. We talked in low tones, each one adding to the common store what he had seen of the procession. "There was a little girl with curly fair hair exactly like my Claire. The old blacksmith with the leather apron—my grandfather looked like that." "The tall dark-haired good-looking girl in the blue dress—one of my girls at home walks just as she did."

Would we see them again, we wondered, the next day when dawn came?

About midnight the door to the car slid open a little—yet it was long before the time for food. And hours before, the soil-buckets had been emptied. A flashlight played on us, sitting there, silent, our hands clasped around our knees. We were counted. The alien voices mechanically pronounced the numbers, *ein, zwei, drei*— The alien hand turned the flashlight on the paper and made a check mark.

The flashlight was held to another paper. The voice began to read aloud rapidly, rattling off the words drily. But they were not of the alien tongue. They were our men. We heard the words, "Sabotage. Reprisals." The door slid shut with a bang. In the smothering black stillness, the lock rattled loudly.

We were being sent back.

We were being sent back to prison.

We were being sent back to Germany.

One of us began to shriek out curses as if he had been stabbed. His screams stopped with a strangling choke. Bergeron had sprung upon him. Bergeron's voice sounded out in a cry as sharp as if he also had been stabbed—"Order! No screaming. We are men!"

We heard the other man struggling frantically to breathe through the hand pressed over his mouth. We heard Bergeron, too, fighting to breathe, when, after an instant, his voice came—breaking, dying, as he tried with long gasps to draw air into his lungs. "We have pledged ourselves to—" he said, "all those people. We gave them our promise. They promised us—" He gave up trying to speak. We heard his panting—loud, rough, strangling, as if he had been struck a terrible blow in the chest. Or was it our own struggle to breathe that we heard?

When he spoke again, his voice was under control. "We have been home," he said. "We have been home to France. We have made a promise to France."

The car jolted to and fro and began to roll slowly. On each side of me in the dark, I could hear groaning. But not loud. . . .

After a long time, Bergeron's voice said in my ear, in a faint whisper, "Now about those ropes—"

Sex Education

It was three times—but at intervals of many years—that I heard my Aunt Minnie tell about an experience of her girlhood that had made a never-to-be-forgotten impression on her. The first time she was in her thirties, still young. But she had then been married for ten years, so that to my group of friends, all in the early teens, she seemed quite of another generation.

The day she told us the story, we had been idling on one end of her porch as we made casual plans for a picnic supper in the woods. Darning stockings at the other end, she paid no attention to us until one of the girls said, "Let's take blankets and sleep out there. It'd be fun."

"No," Aunt Minnie broke in sharply, "you mustn't do that."

"Oh, for goodness' sakes, why not!" said one of the younger girls, rebelliously, "the boys are always doing it. Why can't we, just once?"

Aunt Minnie laid down her sewing. "Come here, girls," she said, "I want you should hear something that happened to me when I was your age."

Her voice had a special quality which, perhaps, young people of today would not recognize. But we did. We knew from experience that it was the dark voice grownups used when they were going to say something about sex.

Yet at first what she had to say was like any dull family anecdote; she had been ill when she was fifteen; and afterwards she was run down, thin, with no appetite. Her folks thought a change of air

would do her good, and sent her from Vermont out to Ohio—or was it Illinois? I don't remember. Anyway, one of those places where the corn grows high. Her mother's Cousin Ella lived there, keeping house for her son-in-law.

The son-in-law was the minister of the village church. His wife had died some years before, leaving him a young widower with two little girls and a baby boy. He had been a normally personable man then, but the next summer, on the Fourth of July when he was trying to set off some fireworks to amuse his children, an imperfectly manufactured rocket had burst in his face. The explosion had left one side of his face badly scarred. Aunt Minnie made us see it, as she still saw it, in horrid detail: the stiffened, scarlet scar tissue distorting one cheek, the lower lip turned so far out at one corner that the moist red mucous-membrane lining always showed, one lower eyelid hanging loose, and watering.

After the accident, his face had been a long time healing. It was then that his wife's elderly mother had gone to keep house and take care of the children. When he was well enough to be about again, he found his position as pastor of the little church waiting for him. The farmers and village people in his congregation, moved by his misfortune, by his faithful service and by his unblemished character, said they would rather have Mr. Fairchild, even with his scarred face, than any other minister. He was a good preacher, Aunt Minnie told us, "and the way he prayed was kind of exciting. I'd never known a preacher, not to live in the same house with him, before. And when he was in the pulpit, with everybody looking up at him, I felt the way his children did, kind of proud to think he had just eaten breakfast at the same table. I liked to call him 'Cousin Malcolm' before folks. One side of his face was all right, anyhow. You could see from that that he *had* been a good-looking man. In fact, probably one of those ministers that all the women—" Aunt Minnie paused, drew her lips together, and looked at us uncertainly.

Then she went back to the story as it happened—as it happened that first time I heard her tell it. "I thought he was a saint. Everybody out there did. That was all *they* knew. Of course, it made a person sick to look at that awful scar—the drooling corner of his mouth was the worst. He tried to keep that side of his face turned away from folks. But you always knew it was there. That was what kept him from marrying again, so Cousin Ella said. I heard her say lots of times that he knew no woman would touch any man who looked the way he did, not with a ten-foot pole.

"Well, the change of air did do me good. I got my appetite back, and ate a lot and played outdoors a lot with my cousins. They were younger than I (I had my sixteenth birthday there) but I still liked to play games. I got taller and laid on some weight. Cousin Ella used to say I grew as fast as the corn did. Their house stood at the edge of the village. Beyond it was one of those big cornfields they have out west. At the time when I first got there, the stalks were only up to a person's knee. You could see over their tops. But it grew like lightning, and before long, it was the way thick woods are here, way over your head, the stalks growing so close together it was dark under them.

"Cousin Ella told us youngsters that it was lots worse for getting lost in than woods, because there weren't any landmarks in it. One spot in a cornfield looked just like any other. 'You children keep out of it,' she used to tell us almost every day, *'especially you girls.* It's no place for a decent girl. You could easy get so far from the house nobody could hear you if you hollered. There are plenty of men in this town that wouldn't like anything better than—' She never said what.

"In spite of what she said, my little cousins and I had figured out that if we went across one corner of the field, it would be a short cut to the village, and sometimes, without letting on to Cousin Ella, we'd go that way. After the corn got really tall, the farmer stopped cultivating, and we soon beat down a path in the loose dirt. The minute you were inside the field it was dark. You felt as if you were miles from anywhere. It sort of scared you. But in no time the path turned and brought you out on the far end of Main Street. Your breath was coming fast, maybe, but that was what made you like to do it.

"One day I missed the turn. Maybe I didn't keep my mind on it. Maybe it had rained and blurred the tramped-down look of the path. I don't know what. All of a sudden, I knew I was lost. And the minute I knew that, I began to run, just as hard as I could run. I couldn't help it, any more than you can help snatching your hand off a hot stove. I didn't know what I was scared of, I didn't even know I *was* running, till my heart was pounding so hard I had to stop.

"The minute I stood still, I could hear Cousin Ella saying, 'There are plenty of men in this town that wouldn't like anything better than—' I didn't know, not really, what she meant. But I knew she meant something horrible. I opened my mouth to scream. But I put both hands over my mouth to keep the scream in. If I made any noise, one of those men would hear me. I thought I heard one just behind me, and whirled around. And then I thought another one had tiptoed up behind me, the other way, and I spun around so fast I almost fell over. I stuffed my hands hard up against my mouth. And then—I couldn't help it—I ran again—but my legs were shaking so I soon had to stop. There I stood, scared to move for fear of rustling the corn and letting the men know where I was. My hair had come down, all over my face. I kept pushing it back and looking around, quick, to make sure one of the men hadn't found out where I was. Then I thought I saw a man coming towards me, and I ran away from him—and fell down, and burst some of the buttons off my dress, and was sick to my stomach—and thought I heard a man close to me and got up and staggered around, knocking into the corn because I couldn't even see where I was going.

"And then, off to one side, I saw Cousin Malcolm. Not a man. The minister. He was standing still, one hand up to his face, thinking. He hadn't heard me.

"I was so *terrible* glad to see him, instead of one of those men, I ran as fast as I could and just flung myself on him, to make myself feel how safe I was."

Aunt Minnie had become strangely agitated. Her hands were shaking, her face was crimson. She frightened us. We could not look away from her. As we waited for her to go on, I felt little spasms twitch at the muscles inside my body. "And what do you think that *saint,* that holy minister of the Gospel, did to an innocent child who clung to him for safety? The most terrible look came into his eyes—you girls are too young to know what he looked like. But once you're married, you'll find out. He grabbed hold of me—that dreadful face of his was *right on mine*—and began clawing the clothes off my back."

She stopped for a moment, panting. We were too frightened to speak. She went on, "He had torn my dress right down to the waist before I—then I *did* scream—all I could—and pulled away from him so hard I almost fell down, and ran and all of a sudden I came out of the corn, right in the back yard of the Fairchild house. The children were staring at the corn, and Cousin Ella ran out of the kitchen door. They had heard me screaming. Cousin Ella shrieked out, 'What is it? What happened? Did a man scare you?' And I said, 'Yes, yes, yes, a man—I ran—!' And then I fainted away. I must have. The next thing I knew I was on the sofa in the living room and Cousin Ella was slapping my face with a wet towel."

She had to wet her lips with her tongue before she could go on. Her face was gray now. "There! that's the kind of thing girls' folks ought to tell them about—so they'll know what men are like."

She finished her story as if she were dismissing us. We wanted to go away, but we were too horrified to stir. Finally one of the youngest girls asked in a low trembling voice, "Aunt Minnie, did you tell on him?"

"No, I was ashamed to," she said briefly. "They sent me home the next day anyhow. Nobody ever said a word to me about it. And I never did either. Till now."

By what gets printed in some of the modern child-psychology books, you would think that girls to whom such a story had been told would never develop normally. Yet, as far as I can remember what happened to the girls in that group, we all grew up about like anybody. Most of us married, some happily, some not so well. We kept house. We learned—more or less—how to live with our husbands, we had children and struggled to bring them up right—we went forward into life, just as if we had never been warned not to.

Perhaps, young as we were that day, we had already had enough experience of life so that we were not quite blank paper for Aunt Minnie's frightening story. Whether we thought of it then or not, we couldn't have failed to see that at this very time, Aunt Minnie had been married for ten years or more, comfortably and well married, too. Against what she tried by that story to brand into our minds stood the cheerful home life in that house, the good-natured, kind, hard-working husband, and the children—the three rough-and-tumble, nice little boys, so adored by their parents, and the sweet girl baby who died, of whom they could never speak without tears. It was such actual contact with adult life that probably kept generation after generation of girls from being scared by tales like Aunt Minnie's into a neurotic horror of living.

Of course, since Aunt Minnie was so much older than we, her boys grew up to be adolescents and young men while our children were still little enough so that our worries over them were nothing more serious than whooping cough and trying to get them to make their own beds. Two of our aunt's three boys followed, without losing their footing, the narrow path which leads across adolescence into normal adult life. But the middle one, Jake, repeatedly fell off into the morass. "Girl trouble," as the succinct family phrase put it. He was one of those boys who have "charm," whatever we mean by that, and was always being snatched at by girls who would be "all wrong" for him to marry. And once, at nineteen, he ran away from home, whether with one of these girls or not we never heard, for through all her ups and downs with this son, Aunt Minnie tried fiercely to protect him from scandal that might cloud his later life.

Her husband had to stay on his job to earn the family living. She was the one who went to find Jake. When it was gossiped around that Jake was in "bad company" his mother drew some money from the family savings-bank account, and silent, white-cheeked, took the train to the city where rumor said he had gone.

Some weeks later he came back with her. With no girl. She had cleared him of that entanglement. As of others, which followed, later. Her troubles seemed over when, at a "suitable" age, he fell in love with a "suitable" girl, married her and took her to live in our shire town, sixteen miles away, where he had a good position. Jake was always bright enough.

Sometimes, idly, people speculated as to what Aunt Minnie had seen that time she went after her runaway son, wondering where her search for him had taken her—very queer places for Aunt Minnie to be in, we imagined. And how could such an ignorant, homekeeping woman ever have known what to say to an errant willful boy to set him straight?

Well, of course, we reflected, watching her later struggles with Jake's erratic ways, she certainly could not have remained ignorant, after seeing over and over what she probably had; after talking with Jake about the things which, a good many times, must have come up with desperate openness between them.

She kept her own counsel. We never knew anything definite about the facts of those experiences of hers. But one day she told a group of us—all then married women—something which gave us a notion about what she had learned from them.

We were hastily making a layette for a not especially welcome baby in a poor family. In those days, our town had no such thing as a district-nursing service. Aunt Minnie, a vigorous woman of fifty-five, had come in to help. As we sewed, we talked, of course; and because our daughters were near or in their teens, we were comparing notes about the bewildering responsibility of bringing up girls.

After a while, Aunt Minnie remarked, "Well, I hope you teach your girls some *sense.* From what I read, I know you're great on telling them 'the facts,' facts we never heard of when we were girls. Like as not, some facts I don't know, now. But knowing the facts isn't going to do them any more good than *not* knowing the facts ever did, unless they have some sense taught them, too."

"What do you mean, Aunt Minnie?" one of us asked her uncertainly.

She reflected, threading a needle, "Well, I don't know but what the best way to tell you what I mean is to tell you about something that happened to me, forty years ago. I've never said anything about it before. But I've thought about it a good deal. Maybe—"

She had hardly begun when I recognized the story—her visit to her Cousin Ella's Midwestern home, the widower with his scarred face and saintly reputation and, very vividly, her getting lost in the great cornfield. I knew every word she was going to say—to the very end, I thought.

But no, I did not. Not at all.

She broke off, suddenly, to exclaim with impatience, "Wasn't I the big ninny? But not so big a ninny as that old cousin of mine. I could wring her neck for getting me in such a state. Only she didn't know any better, herself. That was the way they brought young people up in those days, scaring them out of their wits about the awfulness of getting lost, but not telling them a thing about how *not* to get lost. Or how to act, if they did.

"If I had had the sense I was born with, I'd have known that running my legs off in a zigzag was the worst thing I could do. I couldn't have been more than a few feet from the path when I noticed I wasn't on it. My tracks in the loose plow dirt must have been perfectly plain. If I'd h' stood still, and collected my wits, I could have looked down to see which way my footsteps went and just walked back over them to the path and gone on about my business.

"Now I ask you, if I'd been told how to do that, wouldn't it have been a lot better protection for me—if protection was what my aunt thought she wanted to give me—than to scare me so at the idea of being lost that I turned deef-dumb-and-blind when I thought I was?

"And anyhow that patch of corn wasn't as big as she let on. And she knew it wasn't. It was no more than a big field in a farming country. I was a well-grown girl of sixteen, as tall as I am now. If I couldn't have found the path, I could have just walked along one line of cornstalks—*straight*—and I'd have come out somewhere in ten minutes. Fifteen at the most. Maybe not just where I wanted to go. But all right, safe, where decent folks were living."

She paused, as if she had finished. But at the inquiring blankness in our faces, she went on, "Well, now, why isn't teaching girls—and boys, too, for the Lord's sake don't forget they need it as much as the girls—about this man-and-woman business, something like that? If you give them the idea—no matter whether it's *as* you tell them the facts, or as you *don't* tell them the facts, that it is such a terribly scary thing that if they take a step into it, something's likely to happen to them so awful that you're ashamed to tell them what—well, they'll lose their heads and run around like crazy things, first time they take one step away from the path.

"For they'll be trying out the paths, all right. You can't keep them from it. And a good thing too. How else are they going to find out what it's like? Boys' and girls' going together is a path across one corner of growing up. And when they go together, they're likely to get off the path some. Seems to me, it's up to their folks to bring them up so when they do, they don't start screaming and running in circles, but stand still, right where they are, and get their breath and figure out how to get back.

"And anyhow, you don't tell 'em the truth about sex" (I was astonished to hear her use the actual word, taboo to women of her generation) "if they get the idea from you that it's all there is to living. It's not. If you don't get to where you want to go in it, well, there's a lot of landscape all around it a person can have a good time in.

"D'you know, I believe one thing that gives girls and boys the wrong idea is the way folks *look!* My old cousin's face, I can see her now, it was as red as a rooster's comb when she was telling me about men in that cornfield. I believe now she kind of *liked* to talk about it."

(Oh, Aunt Minnie—and yours! I thought.)

Someone asked, "But how *did* you get out, Aunt Minnie?"

She shook her head, laid down her sewing. "More foolishness. That minister my mother's cousin was keeping house for—her son-in-law—I caught sight of him, down along one of the aisles of cornstalks, looking down at the ground, thinking, the way he often did. And I was so glad to see him I rushed right up to him, and flung my arms around his neck and hugged him. He hadn't heard me coming. He gave a great start, put one arm around me and turned his face full towards me—I suppose for just a second he had forgotten how awful one side of it was. His expression, his eyes—well, you're all married women, you know how he looked, the way any able-bodied man thirty-six or -seven, who'd been married and begotten children, would look—for a minute anyhow, if a full-blooded girl of sixteen, who ought to have known better, flung herself at him without any warning, her hair tumbling down, her dress half unbuttoned, and hugged him with all her might.

"I was what they called innocent in those days. That is, I knew just as little about what men are like as my folks could manage I should. But

I was old enough to know all right what that look meant. And it gave me a start. But of course the real thing of it was that dreadful scar of his, so close to my face—that wet corner of his mouth, his eye drawn down with the red inside of the lower eyelid showing—

"It turned me so sick, I pulled away with all my might, so fast that I ripped one sleeve nearly loose, and let out a screech like a wildcat. And ran. Did I run? And in a minute, I was through the corn and had come out in the back yard of the house. I hadn't been more than a few feet from it, probably, any of the time. And then I fainted away. Girls were always fainting away; it was the way our corset strings were pulled tight, I suppose, and then—oh, a lot of fuss.

"But anyhow," she finished, picking up her work and going on, setting neat, firm stitches with steady hands, "there's one thing, I never told anybody it was Cousin Malcolm I had met in the cornfield. I told my old cousin that 'a man had scared me.' And nobody said anything more about it to me, not ever. That was the way they did in those days. They thought if they didn't let on about something, maybe it wouldn't have happened. I was sent back to Vermont right away and Cousin Malcolm went on being minister of the church. I've always been," said Aunt Minnie moderately, "kind of proud that I didn't go and ruin a man's life for just one second's slip-up. If you could have called it that. For it *would* have ruined him. You know how hard as stone people are about other folks' letdowns. If I'd have told, not one person in that town would have had any charity. Not one would have tried to understand. One slip, *once,* and they'd have pushed him down in the mud. If I had told, I'd have felt pretty bad about it, later—when I came to have more sense. But I declare, I can't see how I came to have the decency, dumb as I was then, to know that it wouldn't be fair."

It was not long after this talk that Aunt Minnie's elderly husband died, mourned by her, by all of us. She lived alone then. It was peaceful October weather for her, in which she kept a firm roundness of face and figure, as quiet-living country-women often do, on into her late sixties.

But then Jake, the boy who had had girl trouble, had wife trouble. We heard he had taken to running after a young girl, or was it that she was running after him? It was something serious. For his nice wife left him and came back with the children to live with her mother in our town. Poor Aunt Minnie used to go to see her for long talks which made them both cry. And she went to keep house for Jake, for months at a time.

She grew old, during those years. When finally she (or something) managed to get the marriage mended so that Jake's wife relented and went back to live with him, there was no trace left of her pleasant brisk freshness. She was stooped and slow-footed and shrunken. We, her kins-people, although we would have given our lives for any one of our own children, wondered whether Jake was worth what it had cost his mother to—well, steady him, or reform him. Or perhaps just understand him. Whatever it took.

She came of a long-lived family and was able to go on keeping house for herself well into her eighties. Of course we and the other neighbors stepped in often to make sure she was all right. Mostly, during those brief calls, the talk turned on nothing more vital than her geraniums. But one midwinter afternoon, sitting with her in front of her cozy stove, I chanced to speak in rather hasty blame of someone who had, I thought, acted badly. To my surprise this brought from her the story about the cornfield which she had evidently quite forgotten telling me twice before.

This time she told it almost dreamily, swaying to and fro in her rocking chair, her eyes fixed on the long slope of snow outside her window. When she came to the encounter with the minister she said, looking away from the distance and back into my eyes, "I know now that I had been, all along, kind of *interested* in him, the way any girl as old as I was would be in any youngish man living in the same house with her. And a minister, too. They have to have the gift of gab so much more than most men, women get to thinking they are more alive than men who can't talk so well. I *thought* the reason I threw my arms around him was because I had been so scared. And I certainly had been scared, by my old cousin's horrible talk about the cornfield being full of men waiting to grab girls. But that wasn't all the reason I flung myself at Malcolm Fairchild and hugged him. I know that now. Why in the world shouldn't I have been taught *some* notion of it then? 'Twould do girls good to know that they are just like everybody else—human nature *and* sex, all mixed up together. I didn't have to hug him. I wouldn't have, if he'd been dirty or fat and old, or chewed tobacco."

I stirred in my chair, ready to say, "But it's not so simple as all that to tell girls—" and she hastily answered my unspoken protest. "I know, I know, most of it can't be put into words. There just aren't any words to say something that's so both-ways-at-once all the time as this man-and-woman business. But look here, you know as well as I do that there are lots more ways than in words to teach young folks what you want 'em to know."

The old woman stopped her swaying rocker to peer far back into the past with honest eyes. "What was in my mind back there in the cornfield—partly anyhow—was what had been there all the time I was living in the same house with Cousin Malcolm—that he had long straight legs, and broad shoulders, and lots of curly brown hair, and was nice and flat in front, and that one side of his face was goodlooking. But most of all, that he and I were really alone, for the first time, without anybody to see us.

"I suppose, if it hadn't been for that dreadful scar, he'd have drawn me up, tight, and—most any man would—kissed me. I know how I must have looked, all red and hot and my hair down and my dress torn open. And, used as he was to big cornfields, he probably never dreamed that the reason I looked that way was because I was scared to be by myself in one. He may have thought—you know what he may have thought.

"Well—if his face had been like anybody's—when he looked at me the way he did, the way a man does look at a woman he wants to have, it would have scared me—some. But I'd have cried, maybe. And probably he'd have kissed me again. You know how such things go. I might have come out of the cornfield halfway engaged to marry him. Why not? I was old enough, as people thought then. That would have been nature. That was probably what he thought of, in that first instant.

"But what did I do? I had one look at his poor, horrible face, and started back as though I'd stepped on a snake. And screamed and ran.

"What do you suppose *he* felt, left there in the corn? He must have been sure that I would tell everybody he had attacked me. He probably thought that when he came out and went back to the village he'd already be in disgrace and put out of the pulpit.

"But the worst must have been to find out, so rough, so plain from the way I acted—as if somebody had hit him with an ax—the way he would look to any woman he might try to get close to. That must have been—" she drew a long breath, "well, pretty hard on him."

After a silence, she murmured pityingly, "Poor man!"

The Washed Window

Older people in Arlington have a special interest in the last house you pass as you leave our village to drive to Cambridge. It was built and lived in for many years by our first local skilled cabinetmaker. In the early days nearly every house had one good piece of professionally made furniture, brought up from Connecticut on horseback or in an oxcart. These were highly treasured. But the furniture made here was, for the first generation after 1764, put together by men who just wanted chairs, beds, and a table for the family meals—and those as fast as they could be slammed into shape.

For many years Silas Knapp lived in that last house practicing his remarkable skill. Nearly every house of our town acquired in those years one or two pieces of his workmanship. They are now highly prized as "early nineteenth-century, locally-made antiques."

He not only made many a fine chest of drawers and bedside stand there: he also brought up a fine family of children. You may never have noticed this house as you drove by, but once, some twenty or thirty years ago, a great American leader, who chanced to pass through Vermont, asked to be shown the old Knapp home. He had been delivering an important address to a large audience in Rutland. When he stood in front of the small low old house he took off his hat and bowed his gray head in silence. Then he explained to the person who had driven him down to Arlington, "For me it is a shrine."

This is the story back of his visit to the plain little early nineteenth century artisan's house which to him was a shrine. Viola Knapp was one of the Vermont girls who "went South to teach," taking along with her the attitude towards life she had been brought up to respect. She married there—as the saying goes, "married well"—an army officer of good family. It was a happy, lifelong mating. Viola Knapp Ruffner and her husband, General Ruffner, lived here and there in various cities and towns and brought up a family of five children. It was while the Ruffners were living in West Virginia that—but I'll set the story down as I heard it in my youth, about sixty years ago, from the lips of the distinguished American educator who, as a boy, had been a student of Viola Knapp Ruffner. In his later years, he became one of my father's valued friends.

This is about as he used to tell it to us with many more details than I ever half told in print. "I never knew exactly how old I was when I first saw Mrs. Ruffner, for in the days of slavery, family records—that is, black-family records—were seldom kept. But from what I have been able to learn, I was born, a slave, on a Virginia plantation, about 1858. In my youth, my home was a log cabin about fourteen by sixteen feet square. We slept on frowsy piles of filthy rags, laid on the dirt floor. Until I was quite a big youth I wore only one garment, a shirt made out of agonizingly rough refuse-flax. We slaves ate corn bread and pork, because those foods could be grown on the plantation without cash expense. I had never seen anything except the slave quarters on the plantation where I was born, with a few glimpses of the 'big house' where our white owners lived. I cannot remember ever, during my childhood and youth, not one single time, when our family sat down together at a table to eat a meal as human families do. We ate as animals do, whenever and wherever an edible morsel was found. We usually took our food up in our fingers, sometimes from the skillet, sometimes from a tin plate held on our knees, and as we chewed on it, we held it as best we could in our hands.

"Life outside our cabin was as slovenly and disordered as inside. The white owners made no effort to keep things up. They really could not. Slaves worked; hence any form of work was too low for white people to do. Since white folks did not work, they did not know how work should be done. The untaught slaves, wholly ignorant of better standards, seldom got around to mending the fences, or putting back a lost hinge on a sagging gate or door. Weeds grew wild everywhere, even in the yard. Inside the big house, when a piece of plastering fell from a wall or ceiling, it was a long time before anybody could stir himself to get it replastered.

"After the end of the Civil War, when we were no longer slaves, my family moved to a settlement near a salt mine, where, although I was still only a child, I was employed—often beginning my day's work at four in the morning. There, we lived in even more dreadful squalor, for our poor rickety cabin was in a crowded slum, foul with unspeakable dirt—literal and moral. As soon as I grew a little older and stronger, I was shifted from working in the salt mine to a coal mine. Both mines were then owned by General Lewis Ruffner.

"By that time I had learned my letters and could, after a fashion, read. Mostly I taught myself, but with some irregular hours spent in a Negro night school, after an exhausting day's work in the mines. There were no public schools for ex-slaves; the poor, totally unequipped, bare room where colored people, young and old, crowded in to learn their letters was paid for by tiny contributions from the Negroes themselves.

"About that time I heard two pieces of news, which were like very distant, very faint glimmers in the blackness of the coal mine in which nearly all my waking hours were spent. One was about a school for colored students—Hampton Institute it was—where they could learn more than their letters. The other was that the wife of General Ruffner was from Vermont and that she took an interest in the education of the colored people who worked for her. I also heard that she was so 'strict' that nobody could suit her, and that the colored boys who entered her service were so afraid of her, and found her so impossible to please, that they never stayed long. But the pay was five dollars a month, and keep. That was better than the coal mine—and there was also the chance that she might be willing to have me go on learning. I got up my courage to try. What could be worse than the way I was living and the hopelessness of anything better in the future?

"But I can just tell you that, great, lumbering, muscle-bound coal-mining boy that I was, I was trembling when I went to ask for that work. The Ruffners had just moved into an old house that had been empty for some time, and they were not yet established, their furniture not unpacked, the outbuildings not repaired. When I first saw her, Mrs. Ruffner was writing on an improvised desk which was a plank laid across two kegs.

"I falteringly told her I had come to ask for work. She turned in her chair and looked at me silently. Nobody had ever looked at me like that, not at my rags and dirt but as if she wanted to see what kind of person I was. She had clear, steady gray eyes, I remember. Then she said, 'You can try.' After reflection, she went on, 'You might as well start in by cleaning the woodshed. It looks as though it hadn't been touched for years.'

"She laid down her pen and took me through a narrow side-passage into the woodshed. It was dark and cluttered with all kinds of dirty, dusty things. A sour, moldy smell came up from them. Great cobwebs hung down from the rough rafters of the low, sloping roof. Stepping back for a moment, she brought out a dustpan and a broom. A shovel leaned against the woodshed wall. She put that in my hand and said, 'Now go ahead. Put the trash you clean out, on that pile in the yard and we'll burn it up later. Anything that won't burn, like broken glass, put into that barrel.' Then she turned away and left me.

"You must remember that I never had done any work except rough, unskilled heavy labor. I had never cleaned a room in my life, I had never seen a clean room in my life. But I was used to doing as I was told, and I was dead set on managing to go ahead with learning more than I would in that poor beginner's schoolroom. So I began taking out things which anybody could see were trash, like mildewed rags, which fell apart into damp shreds the minute I touched them. There were also, I remember, some moldy heaps of I don't know what, garbage maybe, that had dried into shapeless chunks of bad-smelling filth. In one corner was the carcass of a long-dead dog, which I carried out to the pile of trash in the side yard. Glass was everywhere, broken and unbroken empty whiskey bottles, bits of crockery ware. These I swept with the broom and picking up my sweepings in my hands (I had no idea what a dustpan was for) carried them outside.

"The shed looked to me so much better that I went in to find Mrs. Ruffner. She was still writing. I told her, 'I cleaned it.' Pushing back her chair she went out to the woodshed with me.

"She made no comment when she first opened the door and looked around her with clear gray eyes. Then she remarked quietly, 'There's still some things to attend to. Those pieces of wood over there you might pile up against the wall in the corner. They would do to burn. Be sure to clean the floor well before you start piling the wood on it. And here's another pile of rotten rags, you see. And that tangle behind the door. You'd better pull it all apart and see what's there. Throw away the trash that's mixed with it.' She turned to go back, saying, 'Just keep on till you've got it finished and then come and see me.'

"She didn't speak kindly. She didn't speak unkindly. I looked at the woodshed with new eyes and saw that, sure enough, I'd only made a beginning. I began to pull at the odds and ends in that dusty mess behind the door. And to my astonishment I felt I was perspiring. The work wasn't hard for me, you understand. It was like little boy's play compared to the back-breaking labor I had always done. And it wasn't that I minded carrying around in my bare hands things slimy with rot or having liquid filth drip on my ragged pants. I was used to dirt, and my hands were as calloused as my feet. What made me sweat was the work I had to do with my mind. Always before, when somebody had given me a piece of work to do, he had stood right there to do all the thinking. Here his orders would have been, 'Pull that piece of sacking out. That stick, put it on top of the woodpile. Those dried-up chicken bones, scrape them up from the dirt and throw them in the trash pile.' All I would have had to do was to plod along, doing what I was ordered. Now I was the one to give the orders.

"Now that I was really thinking about what I was doing, I was amazed to see how little I had done, how much more there was to do than I had seen.

"I stooped to pull apart the grimy, mud-colored tangle heaped up back of the door. As I stirred it, a snake crawled out from under it and wriggled towards the door. A big fellow. I wasn't surprised. I was used to snakes. I dropped a stone on his head and carried his long, black body out to the trash pile in the yard.

"Now I had come to a corner where chickens evidently roosted every night. Everything was covered with their droppings, like smearings of white paint. I thought nothing of handling them, and taking up the body of one I found lying still and dead in the midst of the rubbish. More rotted rags, a stained, torn pair of pants, too far gone even for me to wear, still smelling foul. Some pieces of wood, not rotten, fit for fuel. Everything I came to had first to be pulled loose from the things it was mixed up with, and enough of the dirt shaken off to let me make out what it was. And then I had to think what to do with it. No wonder that the sweat ran down my face. To see, I had to wipe my eyes with the back of my hands.

"Finally, the last of the refuse was taken apart and cleared away and the litter and filth which had dropped from it to the floor was swept together and carried out to the trash pile. I kept looking over my shoulder for somebody to make the decisions, to tell me what to do. 'Throw that away. Save that. Put it with the firewood. Toss that into the barrel with the broken glass.' But there was nobody there to give me orders. I went in to get Mrs. Ruffner. 'I got it done,' I told her.

"Laying down her pen, she came again to see. I felt nervous as, silent and attentive, she ran those clear eyes of hers over what I had been doing. But I wasn't at all prepared to have her say again, 'That's better, but there's a great deal still to do. You haven't touched the cobwebs, I see.' I looked up at them, my lower jaw dropped in astonishment. Sure enough, there they hung in long, black festoons. I had not once lifted my head to see them. 'And how about washing the window? Here, step in here and get a pail of water for that. Here are some clean rags. You'll have to go over it several times to get it clean.'

"She went back into the house and I stood shaken by more new ideas than I could tell you. I hadn't even noticed there was a window, it was so thick with dust and cobwebs. I had never had anything to do with a glass window. In the dark cabins I had lived in, the windows were just holes cut in the walls.

"I set to work once more, the sweat running down my face. Suppose she wouldn't even let me try to do her work. I never could get into Hampton! What if I just never could get the hang of her ways? Stricken, scared, I began again to clean that woodshed! I went over and over every corner of it. Once in a while I stopped stock-still to *look* at it, as I had never looked at anything before, trying really to see it. I don't know that ever in my life afterwards did I care about doing anything right, as much as getting that little old woodshed clean.

“When I came to what I thought was the end, I stopped to get my breath. I looked up at the slanting roof. The rafters were not only cleared of cobwebs but bare of dust; the floor was swept clean, not a chip, not a thread, not a glint of broken glass on it. Piles of firewood against the walls. And the window! *I* had washed that window! Five times I had washed it. How it sparkled! How the strong sunshine poured through it! Now the woodshed was no rubbish pile. It was a room. To me it looked like a parlor. I was proud of it. Till then I had never been proud of anything I had done.

“Then for the third time I went to call Mrs. Ruffner to inspect. Big boy as I was, twice her size, my hands were shaking, my lips twitching. I felt sick. Had I done it right this time? Could I ever do anything right?

“I watched her face as she passed my work in review, looking carefully up, down, and around. Then she turned to me and, looking straight into my eyes, she nodded and said, ‘Now it’s clean. Nobody could have done it any better.’

“She had opened the door through which I took my first step towards civilized standards of living.”

He drew a long breath and went on, “For a year and a half I lived with those standards around me, working for Mrs. Ruffner. What I learned from her! It was like breathing new air. I could never say in words what she taught me, for it was not taught in words but in life. She never pronounced such abstract expressions as ‘frankness’ and ‘honesty’—they radiated from her, like sunlight streaming silently through a clean window, as she spoke of the tasks she set me. They were so simple she took them for granted, but they were revelations to me. I have repeated ever so many times the story of what Mrs. Ruffner taught me by the way she lived in her home—lessons of as great a value to me as any education I ever had in all my life. To anybody seeing me from the outside, I would, I suppose, have seemed to be learning only how to clean a filthy yard, how to keep a fence in repair, how to hang a gate straight, how to paint a weather-beaten barn.

“And then how to study—how to learn from the books she helped me secure, the books she took for granted and which, for me, were revelations. She took my breath away by suggesting, casually, that I begin to have a library of my own. Me!

"It was an old dry-goods box. I knocked the boards out of one side, used them for shelves, and with Mrs. Ruffner's backing to steady me, began with incredulous pride to set up, side by side, one and another of the battered, priceless printed volumes which, under Mrs. Ruffner's roof, I had come to own. I owning books!

"And yet, after all, later on when the way ahead was darkly blocked, it was that woodshed which pushed open the door.

"It would take too long to tell you all the piled-up difficulties I had to climb over to reach my goal of a real school with real, full-time classroom study. All sorts of things happened as I made my way over the long distance which separated me from Hampton. And when I actually stood before that three-story, brick school building, it looked as though I would not be allowed to enter it as a student. My trip had been longer, harder, had cost more than I had dreamed it could. I was nearly penniless, footsore, dusty, gaunt, unwashed.

"The teacher who was in charge of admitting or turning away students gave me a long, doubtful look and told me to wait. Well, I waited. I saw her interviewing other students, better dressed, cleaner, ever so much more promising-looking than I, without a look at me. But I didn't go away. That solid, three-story brick building—all just to provide a chance to study for people who had never had a chance to study—how could I go away, even if I were not welcome? I waited. After several hours of watching that teacher admitting other students, she finally had an idea about me and told me briefly, dubiously, 'The classroom next to this one needs to be cleaned before the Institute opens tomorrow. Do you suppose you could sweep it out? There's a broom over there in the corner.'

"In all my life I never had an order which so uplifted my heart. Could I sweep it out? Oh, Mrs. Ruffner!

"I swept that classroom three times. I moved every piece of furniture and swept under each one. There was a closet. I swept that. Joyfully I swept every corner clean. I found a dust cloth. I dusted everything in the room, I turned the cloth and dusted everything again, and again. I was in the middle of my fourth dusting when the teacher opened the door and stepped in. She was a Yankee. She knew what to look for. She took a clean handkerchief from her pocket, shook it out, and passed it over the top of a desk. After one startled look at me, she rubbed the seat of a chair with it.

"I stood at ease, my head high, fearing nothing. I did not need anybody's permission to feel sure of myself. I had been asked to perform a task. I had done it.

"She passed her testing handkerchief over a window sill, and turned to face me. She was a Yankee and wasted no words. She put the handkerchief back in her pocket, and in a matter-of-fact voice said, 'You're admitted to Hampton.'

"I had been set an entrance examination. And thanks to Mrs. Ruffner I had passed it."

His name was Booker T. Washington.

ESSAY

How "Flint and Fire" Started and Grew

I feel very dubious about the wisdom or usefulness of publishing the following statement of how one of my stories came into existence. This is not on account of the obvious danger of seeming to have illusions about the value of my work, as though I imagined one of my stories was inherently worth in itself a careful public analysis of its growth; the chance, remote as it might be, of usefulness to students, would outweigh this personal consideration. What is more important is the danger that some student may take the explanation as a recipe or rule for the construction of other stories, and I totally disbelieve in such rules or recipes.

As a rule, when a story is finished, and certainly always by the time it is published, I have no recollection of the various phases of its development. In the case of "Flint and Fire," an old friend chanced to ask me, shortly after the tale was completed, to write out for his English classes, the stages of the construction of a short story. I set them down, hastily, formlessly, but just as they happened, and this gives me a record which I could not reproduce for any other story I ever wrote. These notes are here published on the chance that such a truthful record of the growth of one short story, may have some general suggestiveness for students.

No two of my stories are ever constructed in the same way, but broadly viewed they all have exactly the same genesis, and I confess I cannot conceive of any creative fiction written from any other beginning . . . that of a generally intensified emotional sensibility, such as every human being experiences with more or

less frequency. Everybody knows such occasional hours or days of freshened emotional responses when events that usually pass almost unnoticed, suddenly move you deeply, when a sunset lifts you to exaltation, when a squeaking door throws you into a fit of exasperation, when a clear look of trust in a child's eyes moves you to tears, or an injustice reported in the newspapers to flaming indignation, a good action to a sunny warm love of human nature, a discovered meanness in yourself or another, to despair.

I have no idea whence this tide comes, or where it goes, but when it begins to rise in my heart, I know that a story is hovering in the offing. It does not always come safely to port. The daily routine of ordinary life kills off many a vagrant emotion. Or if daily humdrum occupation does not stifle it, perhaps this saturated solution of feeling does not happen to crystallize about any concrete fact, episode, word or phrase. In my own case, it is far more likely to seize on some slight trifle, the shade of expression on somebody's face, or the tone of somebody's voice, than to accept a more complete, ready-made episode. Especially this emotion refuses to crystallize about, or to have anything to do with those narrations of our actual life, offered by friends who are sure that such-and-such a happening is so strange or interesting that "it ought to go in a story."

The beginning of a story is then for me in more than usual sensitiveness to emotion. If this encounters the right focus (and heaven only knows why it is the "right" one) I get simultaneously a strong thrill of intense feeling, and an intense desire to pass it on to other people. This emotion may be any one of the infinitely varied ones which life affords, laughter, sorrow, indignation, gaiety, admiration, scorn, pleasure. I recognize it for the "right" one when it brings with it an irresistible impulse to try to make other people feel it. And I know that when it comes, the story is begun. At this point, the story begins to be more or less under my conscious control, and it is here that the work of construction begins.

"Flint and Fire" thus hovered vaguely in a shimmer of general emotional tensity, and thus abruptly crystallized itself about a chance phrase and the cadence of the voice which pronounced it. For several days I had been almost painfully alive to the beauty of an especially lovely spring, always so lovely after the long winter in the mountains. One evening, going on a very prosaic errand to a farm-house of our region, I walked along a narrow path through dark pines, beside a brook swollen with melting snow, and found the old man I came to see, sitting silent and alone before his blackened small old house. I did my errand, and then not to offend against our country standards of sociability, sat for half an hour beside him.

The old man had been for some years desperately unhappy about a tragic and permanent element in his life. I had known this, every one knew it. But that evening, played upon as I had been by the stars, the darkness of the pines and the shouting voice of the brook, I suddenly stopped merely knowing it, and felt it. It seemed to me that his misery emanated from him like a soundless wail of anguish. We talked very little, odds and ends of neighborhood gossip, until the old man, shifting his position, drew a long breath and said, "Seems to me I never heard the brook sound so loud as it has this spring." There came instantly to my mind the recollection that his grandfather had drowned himself in that brook, and I sat silent, shaken by that thought and by the sound of his voice. I have no words to attempt to reproduce his voice, or to try to make you feel as I did, hot and cold with the awe of that glimpse into a naked human heart. I felt my own heart contract dreadfully with helpless sympathy . . . and, I hope this is not as ugly as it sounds, I knew at the same instant that I would try to get that pang of emotion into a story and make other people feel it.

That is all. That particular phase of the construction of the story came and went between two heart-beats.

I came home by the same path through the same pines along the same brook, sinfully blind and deaf to the beauty that had so moved me an hour ago. I was too busy now to notice anything outside the rapid activity going on inside my head. My mind was working with a swiftness and a coolness which I am somewhat ashamed to mention, and my emotions were calmed, relaxed, let down from the tension of the last few days and the last few moments. They had found their way out to an attempt at self-expression and were at rest. I realize that this is not at all estimable. The old man was just as unhappy as he had been when I had felt my heart breaking with sympathy for him, but now he seemed very far away.

I was snatching up one possibility after another, considering it for a moment, casting it away and pouncing on another. First of all, the story must be made as remote as possible from resembling the old man or his trouble, lest he or any one in the world might think he was intended, and be wounded.

What is the opposite pole from an old man's tragedy? A lover's tragedy, of course. Yes, it must be separated lovers, young and passionate and beautiful, because they would fit in with the back-ground of spring, and swollen shouting starlit brooks, and the yearly resurrection which was so closely connected with that ache of emotion that they were a part of it.

Should the separation come from the weakness or faithlessness of one of the lovers? No, ah no, I wanted it without ugliness, pure beautiful sorrow, to fit that dark shadow of the pines . . . the lovers must be separated by outside forces.

What outside forces? Lack of money? Family opposition? Both, perhaps. I knew plenty of cases of both in the life of our valley.

By this time I had come again to our own house and was swallowed in the usual thousand home-activities. But underneath all that, quite steadily my mind continued to work on the story as a wasp in a barn keeps on silently plastering up the cells of his nest in the midst of the noisy activities of farm-life. I said to one of the children, "Yes, dear, wasn't it fun!" and to myself, "To be typical of our tradition-ridden valley-people, the opposition ought to come from the dead hand of the past." I asked a caller, "One lump or two?" and thought as I poured the tea, "And if the character of that opposition could be made to indicate a fierce capacity for passionate feeling in the older generation, that would make it doubly useful in the story, not only as part of the machinery of the plot, but as indicating an inheritance of passionate feeling in the younger generation, with whom the story is concerned." I dozed off at night, and woke to find myself saying, "It could come from the jealousy of two sisters, now old women."

But that meant that under ordinary circumstances the lovers would have been first cousins, and this might cause a subconscious wavering of attention on the part of some readers . . . just as well to get that stone out of the path! I darned a sock and thought out the relationship in the story, and was rewarded with a revelation of the character of the sick old woman, 'Niram's step-mother.

Upon this, came one of those veering lists of the ballast aboard which are so disconcerting to the author. The story got out of hand. The old woman silent, indomitable, fed and deeply satisfied for all of her hard and grinding life by her love for the husband whom she had taken from her sister, she stepped to the front of my stage, and from that moment on, dominated the action. I did not expect this, nor desire it, and I was very much afraid that the result would be a perilously divided interest which would spoil the unity of impression of the story. It now occurs to me that this unexpected shifting of values may have been the emergence of the element of tragic old age which had been the start of the story and which I had conscientiously tried to smother out of sight. At any rate, there she was, more touching, pathetic, striking, to my eyes with her life-time proof of the reality of her passion, than my untried young lovers who up to that time had seemed to me, in the full fatuous flush of invention as I was, as ill-starred, innocent and touching lovers as anybody had ever seen.

Alarmed about this double interest I went on with the weaving back and forth of the elements of the plot which now involved the attempt to arouse in the reader's heart as in mine a sympathy for the bed-ridden old Mrs. Purdon and a comprehension of her sacrifice.

My daily routine continued as usual, gardening, telling stories, music, sewing, dusting, motoring, callers . . . one of them, a self-consciously sophisticated Europeanized American, not having of course any idea of what was filling my inner life, rubbed me frightfully the wrong way by making a slighting condescending allusion to what he called the mean, emotional poverty of our inarticulate mountain people. I flew into a silent rage at him, though scorning to discuss with him a matter I felt him incapable of understanding, and the character of Cousin Horace went into the story. He was for the first day or two, a very poor cheap element, quite unreal, unrealized, a mere man of straw to be knocked over by the personages of the tale. Then I took myself to task, told myself that I was spoiling a story merely to revenge myself on a man

I cared nothing about, and that I must either take Cousin Horace out or make him human. One day, working in the garden, I laughed out suddenly, delighted with the whimsical idea of making him, almost in spite of himself, the *deus ex machina* of my little drama, quite soft and sympathetic under his shell of would-be worldly disillusion, as occasionally happens to elderly bachelors.

At this point the character of 'Niram's long-dead father came to life and tried to push his way into the story, a delightful, gentle, upright man, with charm and a sense of humor, such as none of the rest of my stark characters possessed. I felt that he was necessary to explain the fierceness of the sisters' rivalry for him. I planned one or two ways to get him in, in retrospect—and liked one of the scenes better than anything that finally was left in the story. Finally, very heavy-hearted, I put him out of the story, for the merely material reason that there was no room for him. As usual with my story-making, this plot was sprouting out in a dozen places, expanding, opening up, till I perceived that I had enough material for a novel. For a day or so I hung undecided. Would it perhaps be better to make it a novel and really tell about those characters all I knew and guessed? But again a consideration that has nothing to do with artistic form, settled the matter. I saw no earthly possibility of getting time enough to write a novel. So I left Mr. Purdon out, and began to think of ways to compress my material, to make one detail do double work so that space might be saved.

One detail of the mechanism remained to be arranged, and this ended by deciding the whole form of the story, and the first-person character of the recital. This was the question of just how it would have been materially possible for the bed-ridden old woman to break down the life-long barrier between her and her sister, and how she could have reached her effectively and forced her hand. I could see no way to manage this except by somehow transporting her bodily to the sister's house, so that she could not be put out on the road without public scandal. This transportation must be managed by some character not in the main action, as none of the persons involved would have been willing to help her to this. It looked like putting in another character, just for that purpose, and of course he could not be put in without taking the time to make him plausible, human, understandable . . . and I had just left out that charming widower for sheer lack of space. Well, why not make it a first person story, and have the narrator be the one who takes Mrs. Purdon to her sister's? The narrator of the story never needs to be explained, always seems sufficiently living and real by virtue of the supremely human act of so often saying "I."

Now the materials were ready, the characters fully alive in my mind and entirely visualized, even to the smoothly braided hair of Ev'leen Ann, the patch-work quilt of the old woman out-of-doors, and the rustic wedding at the end, all details which had recently chanced to draw my attention; I heard everything through the song of the swollen brook, one of the main characters in the story (although by this time in actual fact, June and lower water had come and the brook slid quiet and gleaming, between placid green banks), and I often found myself smiling foolishly in pleasure over the buggy going down the hill, freighted so richly with hearty human joy.

The story was now ready to write.

I drew a long breath of mingled anticipation and apprehension, somewhat as you do when you stand, breathing quickly, balanced on your skis, at the top of a long white slope you are not sure you are clever enough to manage. Sitting down at my desk one morning, I "pushed off" and with a tingle of not altogether pleasurable excitement and alarm, felt myself "going." I "went" almost as precipitately as skis go down a long white slope, scribbling as rapidly as my pencil could go, indicating whole words with a dash and a jiggle, filling page after page with scrawls . . . it seemed to me that I had been at work perhaps half an hour, when someone was calling me impatiently to lunch. I had been writing four hours without stopping. My cheeks were flaming, my feet were cold, my lips parched. It was high time someone called me to lunch.

The next morning, back at the desk, I looked over what I had written, conquered the usual sick qualms of discouragement at finding it so infinitely flat and insipid compared to what I had wished to make it, and with a very clear idea of what remained to be done, plodded ahead doggedly, and finished the first draught before noon. It was almost twice too long.

After this came a period of steady desk work, every morning, of re-writing, compression, more compression, and the more or less mechanical work of technical revision, what a member of my family calls "cutting out the 'whiches.'" The first thing to do each morning was to read a part of it over aloud, sentence by sentence, to try to catch clumsy, ungraceful phrases, overweights at one end or the other, "ringing" them as you ring a dubious coin, clipping off too-trailing relative clauses, "listening" hard. This work depends on what is known in music as "ear," and in my case it cannot be kept up long at a time, because I find my attention flagging. When I begin to suspect that my ear is dulling, I turn to other varieties of revision, of which there are plenty to keep anybody busy; for instance revision to explain facts; in this category is the sentence just after the narrator suspects Ev'leen Ann has gone down to the brook, "my ears ringing with all the frightening tales of the morbid vein of violence which runs through the characters of our reticent people." It seemed too on re-reading the story for the tenth or eleventh time, that for readers who do not know our valley people, the girl's attempt at suicide might seem improbable. Some reference ought to be brought in, giving the facts that their sorrow and despair is terrible in proportion to the nervous strain of their tradition of repression, and that suicide is by no means unknown. I tried bringing that fact in, as part of the conversation with Cousin Horace, but it never fused with the rest there, "stayed on top of the page" as bad sentences will do, never sank in, and always made the disagreeable impression on me that a false intonation in an actor's voice does. So it came out from there. I tried putting it in Ev'leen Ann's mouth, in a carefully arranged form, but it was so shockingly out of character there, that it was snatched out at once. There I hung over the manuscript with that necessary fact in my hand and no place to lay it down. Finally I perceived a possible opening for it, where it now is in the story, and squeezing it in there discontentedly left it, for I still think it only inoffensively and not well placed.

Then there is the traditional, obvious revision for suggestiveness, such as the recurrent mention of the mountain brook at the beginning of each of the first scenes; revision for ordinary sense, in the first draught I had honeysuckle among the scents on the darkened porch, whereas honeysuckle does not bloom in Vermont till late June; revision for movement to get the narrator rapidly from her bed to the brook; for sound, sense, proportion, even grammar . . . and always interwoven with these mechanical revisions recurrent intense visualizations of the scenes. This is the mental trick which can be learned, I think, by practice and effort. Personally, although I never used as material any events in my own intimate life, I can write nothing if I cannot achieve these very definite, very complete visualizations of the scenes; which means that I can write nothing at all about places, people or phases of life which I do not intimately know, down to the last detail. If my life depended on it, it does not seem to me I could possibly write a story about Siberian hunters or East-side factory hands without having lived long among them. Now the story was what one calls "finished," and I made a clear copy, picking my way with difficulty among the alterations, the scratched-out passages, and the cued-in paragraphs, the inserted pages, the re-arranged phrases. As I typed, the interest and pleasure in the story lasted just through that process. It still seemed pretty good to me, the wedding still touched me, the whimsical ending still amused me.

But on taking up the legible typed copy and beginning to glance rapidly over it, I felt fall over me the black shadow of that intolerable reaction which is enough to make any author abjure his calling for ever. By the time I had reached the end, the full misery was there, the heart-sick, helpless consciousness of failure. What! I had had the presumption to try to translate into words, and make others feel a thrill of sacred living human feeling, that should not be touched save by worthy hands. And what had I produced? A trivial, paltry, complicated tale, with certain cheaply ingenious devices in it. I heard again the incommunicable note of profound emotion in the old man's voice, suffered again with his sufferings; and those little black marks on white paper lay dead, dead in my hands. What horrible people second-rate authors were! They ought to be prohibited by law from sending out their caricatures of life. I would never write again. All that effort, enough to have achieved a master-piece it seemed at the time . . . and this, *this,* for result!

From the subconscious depths of long experience came up the cynical, slightly contemptuous consolation, "You know this never lasts. You always throw this same fit, and get over it."

So, suffering from really acute humiliation and unhappiness, I went out hastily to weed a flower-bed.

And sure enough, the next morning, after a long night's sleep, I felt quite rested, calm, and blessedly matter-of-fact. "Flint and Fire" seemed already very far away and vague, and the question of whether it was good or bad, not very important or interesting, like the chart of your temperature in a fever now gone by.

Afterword

A Note on the Life and Career of Dorothy Canfield Fisher

Given her popular appeal and productivity, Dorothy Canfield Fisher could accurately be considered one of the most successful American writers of the first half of the twentieth century. Why, then, one might ask, is Fisher's work not better known today? And just who was this once world-famous author?

To begin with the latter, more straightforward question, Fisher's life was remarkably full and distinguished. Eleanor Roosevelt called her one of the most influential women of her time, and Clifton Fadiman has recently written that she "helped twentieth-century American literature to come of age."[1] She was the author of more than forty books, including translations, juveniles, and nonfiction on subjects such as the Montessori method of education and the history of her adopted home state of Vermont—in addition to best-selling novels and short story collections (which, for tax purposes, she published under her maiden name). Fisher also played an important part in shaping America's popular literary taste through her position on the Book-of-the-Month Club Selection Committee from its inception in 1926 until 1951. Although she wished to be remembered for her writing, Fisher hardly limited her energies to the literary realm. She established a Braille press and children's hospital in France during World War I, organized the Children's Crusade during World War II, and was involved in many charitable causes throughout her lifetime.

1. Madigan, *Keeping Fires*, ix.

Dorothea (after the heroine of *Middlemarch)* Frances Canfield was born in 1879 in Lawrence, Kansas, the second of two children. The daughter of a university professor and administrator, James Hulme Canfield, and an artist, Flavia Camp Canfield, she was exposed to the world of high culture at an early age and traveled widely. Her early years were marked by stays in Lincoln, Nebraska, Columbus, Ohio, and New York City, as her father relocated for academic appointments. She also made summer trips to Vermont, where her father's relatives lived, and Paris, where her mother kept a studio.

As a youth Fisher developed an interest in languages (she later spoke five fluently) and literature, her formal study of which culminated in a Ph.D. in French from Columbia University. Although she had completed the requisite training for a university teaching career, she never became an academic. She turned down an offer of a professorship at Case Western Reserve University in Cleveland to remain near her family in the East and became secretary of the Horace Mann School in New York. In 1907 she married fellow Columbia graduate John Redwood Fisher and soon after moved to Arlington, Vermont, where she had inherited her great-grandfather's farm.

The Fishers moved to Vermont with the aim of supporting themselves as professional writers. However, when the market for Dorothy's fiction outgrew his own, John became his wife's secretary and editor. He also tended to the practical chores of country living and served in local and state government. The couple raised two children, Sally and Jimmy.

Among Fisher's earliest publications are newspaper articles and short stories that appeared in some of the highest-circulation magazines of the day, including *Everybody's, Harper's,* and *Munsey's.* Saul Bellow, for one, has recalled with pleasure that Fisher "contributed to magazines I read when I was very young." Her nascent work found an audience with women in particular, and the *Woman's Home Companion* later became one of her principal publishers. Fisher's first novel, *Gunhild,* did not receive much attention, but *The Squirrel-Cage, The Bent Twig,* and stories about wartime France contained in *Home Fires in France* and *The Day of Glory* were well received by the public and critics alike. She encountered her greatest success with *The Brimming Cup* in 1921. A study of marriage, the book was called an "antidote" to Sinclair

Lewis's satirical presentation of small-town life in *Main Street.*[2] At the end of that year, *The Brimming Cup* was the second-most-purchased novel in the country, just behind Lewis's. As is noted in this volume's Introduction, the book also offers a critique of racial prejudice against African Americans, the first in a modern best-seller.

Fisher's work remained popular until the time of her death in 1958. Her translation of Papini's *Life of Christ* was a best-seller in 1923, as was her novel *The Home-Maker* the following year. Yale English professor William Lyon Phelps thought highly enough of Fisher's novel *Her Son's Wife* to write to her publisher, "I predict that it will win the Pulitzer Prize for 1926. It deserves it."[3] (Sinclair Lewis won, and declined, the award for *Arrowsmith* that year.) Fisher published her last novel, *Seasoned Timber,* in 1939, but wrote many nonfiction articles and a few stories in the forties. She oversaw the publication of anthologies of her work, wrote a history of Vermont, and continued to write children's books and articles in her last years.

Were it not for her own books, Fisher would hold a place in American literary history for her Book-of-the-Month Club work. Along with four other prominent literary figures on the Selection Committee, she helped choose the "book-of-the-month," which was regularly purchased by more than half of the organization's one million customers. One of the most influential members of the committee, and its only woman, she played an important role in promoting the work of Pearl Buck, Isak Dinesen, and Richard Wright, among others.

By the late teens, Fisher was of a stature to draw mention in F. Scott Fitzgerald's *This Side of Paradise;*[4] the twenties established her as one of the country's most popular writers; and by 1933, in the depths of the Great Depression, the serial rights to her forthcoming novel *Bonfire* commanded a sum of $30,000. It is nevertheless true that Fisher's name has been until only recently relegated to the margins of American literary history. The reasons that her own reputation has not endured as

2. Saul Bellow, "Vermont Tradition," 7; William Allen White, "The Other Side of Main Street," 7.

3. Madigan, *Keeping Fires,* 5.

4. F. Scott Fitzgerald, *This Side of Paradise,* 217.

well as those of many writers she championed through the Book-of-the-Month Club are as complex as the debate over the canon of American literature itself.

In his essay "Race and Gender in the Shaping of the American Literary Canon," Paul Lauter cites three main factors that worked against the advancement of women and African American writers. He explains that in the twenties, influence over "serious" reading shifted from literary clubs headed by women to academic professionals who were white and male; that the dominance of New Critical literary theory produced a "narrowing" of the canon through its valorization of the formal qualities of literature above all else; and that the categories into which American literature has been traditionally divided reflect the values of the categorizers—again, white and male—since historical periods are "experienced differently by women and men, by whites and by people of color."[5] As evidence of the effect these factors had on the shaping of the canon, Lauter makes special mention of Fisher, whose work, he notes, was initially included in Norman Foerster's influential anthology, *American Poetry and Prose,* but dropped—significantly—between the second and third editions (1934 and 1947).

Nina Baym has also singled out New Criticism for having a lasting negative impact on the reception of works by American women authors such as Fisher. In "Melodramas of Beset Manhood," Baym postulates that New Critics used close-reading techniques "to identify a myth of America which had nothing to do with the classical fictionist's task of chronicling probable people in recognizable social situations." According to Baym, the myth "narrates a confrontation of the American individual, the pure American self divorced from specific social circumstances, with the promise offered by the idea of America."[6] Fisher's novels and stories, centering on community, domesticity, and personal relationships, clearly did not fit this prevailing critical paradigm.

5. Paul Lauter, "Race and Gender in the Shaping of the American Literary Canon: A Case Study from the Twenties," 452.

6. Nina Baym, "Melodramas of Beset Manhood: How Theories of American Fiction Exclude Women Authors," 131.

The factors cited by Lauter, Baym, and other canon theorists provide at least a partial response to the question about the diminishment of Fisher's literary rank. Without support from those with the cultural power to canonize them, Fisher's works fell into obscurity in the years following her death. It would be disingenuous, however, to suggest that all of the author's prodigious bibliography deserves preservation. Several of Fisher's novels, for instance, are uneven in quality. Interspersed with their more interesting elements one finds passages of purple prose and an educator's seemingly boundless enthusiasm for the didactic. Yet, if the indeterminate length of the novel at times led Fisher astray, it is no less true that the more compact form of the short story suited her literary talents best.

With the acceptance of more diverse critical approaches and the recognition of previously neglected women writers, Fisher's standing has improved considerably in recent years. The DCF Society, dedicated to the study of the author and her circle, has been formed, Fisher's work has been the subject of discussion at professional meetings, articles have been published in academic journals, and dissertations are underway. It is upon this foundation of scholarship that this edition rests and to which it in large part owes its existence. The same will surely hold true for the important work on Fisher that lies ahead.

Bibliography

Fiction and Nonfiction Works by Dorothy Canfield Fisher

Note: Dorothy Canfield Fisher published fiction (with the exception of her only play, *Tourists Accommodated)* under her maiden name, and nonfiction under the name Dorothy Canfield Fisher (with the exception of her dissertation). Fisher published hundreds of stories and articles in various periodicals, a complete bibliography of which has yet to be compiled.

American Portraits. New York: Henry Holt, 1946.

And Long Remember. New York: Whittlesey House, 1959.

Basque People. New York: Harcourt, Brace, 1931.

The Bent Twig. New York: Henry Holt, 1915. Reprint, Cutchogue, N.Y.: Buccaneer Books, 1981.

Bonfire. New York: Harcourt, Brace, 1933.

The Brimming Cup. New York: Harcourt, Brace, 1921. Reprint, New York: Virago, 1987.

Corneille and Racine in England. New York: Columbia University Press, 1904. Reprint, New York: AMS Press, 1966.

The Day of Glory. New York: Henry Holt, 1919.

The Deepening Stream. New York: Harcourt, Brace, 1930.

Fables for Parents. New York: Harcourt, Brace, 1937.

A Fair World for All. New York: Whittlesey House, 1952.

Fellow Captains (with Sarah N. Cleghorn). New York: Henry Holt, 1916.

Four-Square. New York: Harcourt, Brace, 1949. Reprint, Salem, N.H.: Ayer Publishers, 1971.

Gunhild. New York: Henry Holt, 1907.

A Harvest of Stories. New York: Harcourt, Brace, 1956.

Her Son's Wife. New York: Harcourt, Brace, 1926. Reprint, New York: Virago, 1987.

Hillsboro People. New York: Henry Holt, 1915.

Home Fires in France. New York: Henry Holt, 1918.

The Home-Maker. New York: Harcourt, Brace, 1924. Reprint, Chicago: Academy Chicago, 1983.

Life of Christ, by Giovanni Papini. Trans. Dorothy Canfield Fisher. New York: Harcourt, Brace, 1923.

Made-to-Order Stories. New York: Harcourt, Brace, 1925.

Memories of Arlington, Vermont. New York: Duell, Sloan, and Pearce, 1957.

A Montessori Manual. Chicago: Richardson, 1913.

A Montessori Mother. New York: Henry Holt, 1912.

Mothers and Children. New York: Henry Holt, 1914.

Nothing Ever Happens and How It Does (with Sarah N. Cleghorn). Boston: Beacon Press, 1940.

Our Independence and the Constitution. 1950. Reprint, New York: Random House, 1964.

Our Young Folks. New York: Harcourt, Brace, 1943.

Paul Revere and the Minute Men. New York: Random House, 1950.

Raw Material. New York: Harcourt, Brace, 1923.

The Real Motive. New York: Henry Holt, 1916.

Rough-Hewn. New York: Harcourt, Brace, 1922.

Seasoned Timber. New York: Harcourt, Brace, 1939.

Self-Reliance. Indianapolis: Bobbs-Merrill, 1916.

The Squirrel-Cage. New York: Henry Holt, 1912.

Tell Me a Story. Lincoln, Nebr.: University Publishing, 1940.

Tourists Accommodated. New York: Harcourt, Brace, 1934.

Understood Betsy. New York: Henry Holt, 1917. Reprint, New York: Dell, 1987.

Vermont Tradition. Boston: Little, Brown, 1953. Reprint, Marietta, Ga.: Cherokee Books, 1987.

What Mothers Should Know about the Montessori Method of Education. New York: American Institute of Psychology, 1985.

Why Stop Learning? New York: Harcourt, Brace, 1927.

Work: What It Has Meant to Men through the Ages, by Adriano Tilgher. Trans. Dorothy Canfield Fisher. New York: Harcourt, Brace, 1932. Reprint, Salem, N.H.: Ayer Publishers, 1977.

Selected Introductions by Dorothy Canfield Fisher

Dinesen, Isak. *Seven Gothic Tales.* New York: Smith and Haas, 1934.

Guptill, Arthur. *Norman Rockwell, Illustrator.* New York: Watson-Guptill, 1946.

Kent, Rockwell. *Wilderness.* New York: G. P. Putnam's Sons, 1920.

Thomas, Will. *The Seeking.* New York: A. A. Wyn, 1953.

Tolstoy, Leo. *What Men Live By.* Trans. Louise Maude and Aylmer Maude. New York: Pantheon, 1943.

Wright, Richard. *Black Boy.* New York: Harper and Brothers, 1945.

———. *Native Son.* New York: Harper and Brothers, 1940.

Zoff, Otto. *They Shall Inherit the Earth.* Trans. Anne Garrison. New York: John Day, 1943.

Secondary Sources

Apthorp, Elaine Sargent. "The Artist at the Family Reunion: Visions of the Creative Life in the Narrative Technique of Willa Cather, Sarah Orne Jewett, Mary Wilkins Freeman, and Dorothy Canfield Fisher." Ph.D. dissertation, University of California-Berkeley, 1986.

Baym, Nina. "Melodramas of Beset Manhood: How Theories of American Fiction Exclude Women Authors." *American Quarterly* 33 (summer 1981): 123–39.

Bellow, Saul. "Vermont Tradition." In *A Vermont 14: Commemoration of the Two-hundredth Anniversary of Vermont's Admission to the Union as the Nation's Fourteenth State,* ed. Edward Connery Lathem and Virginia L. Close. Burlington: University of Vermont Libraries, 1992.

Biddle, Arthur W., and Paul A. Eschholz, eds. *The Literature of Vermont: A Sampler.* Hanover, N.H.: University Press of New England, 1973.

Boynton, Percy H. "Two New England Regionalists." *College English* 1 (January 1940): 291–99.

Brickell, Herschel, ed. *The O. Henry Memorial Award Prize Stories of 1944.* Garden City, N.Y.: Doubleday, 1944.

———. *The O. Henry Memorial Award Prize Stories of 1946.* Garden City, N.Y.: Doubleday, 1946.

Carver, Raymond. *Fires.* New York: Vintage, 1984.

Cleghorn, Sarah. *Threescore.* New York: Smith and Haas, 1936.

DCF Newsletter. Published biannually by the DCF Society.

F. M. "Feminism Triumphant." Review of *The Home-Maker,* by Dorothy Canfield Fisher. *Christian Science Monitor* 16 (May 31, 1924): 16.

Firebaugh, Joseph J. "Dorothy Canfield and the Moral Bent." *Educational Forum* 15 (March 1951): 283–94.

Fitzgerald, F. Scott. *This Side of Paradise.* New York: Scribner's, 1920.

Foerster, Norman, ed. *American Poetry and Prose.* 1923. Reprint, Boston: Houghton Mifflin, 1962.

Hackett, Alice Payne. *Seventy Years of Best Sellers, 1895–1965.* New York: R. R. Bowker, 1967.

Humphrey, Zephine. "Dorothy Canfield." *Woman's Citizen* 10 (January 1926): 13–14, 36.

Kutner, Nanette. "If You Worked for Dorothy Canfield Fisher." *Good Housekeeping* 117 (November 1943): 41, 196.

Lauter, Paul. "Race and Gender in the Shaping of the American Literary Canon: A Case Study from the Twenties." *Feminist Studies* 9 (fall 1983): 435–63.

Lee, Charles. *The Hidden Public: The Story of the Book-of-the-Month Club.* Garden City, N.Y.: Doubleday, 1958.

Lovering, Joseph P. "The Contribution of Dorothy Canfield Fisher to the Development of Realism in the American Novel." Ph.D. dissertation, University of Ottawa, 1956.

———. "The Friendship of Willa Cather and Dorothy Canfield." *Vermont History* 48 (summer 1980): 144–55.

Macheski, Cecilia, ed. *Quilt Stories.* Lexington: University Press of Kentucky, 1994.

Madigan, Mark J., ed. *Keeping Fires Night and Day: Selected Letters of Dorothy Canfield Fisher.* Columbia: University of Missouri Press, 1993.

———. "A Newly-Discovered Robert Frost Letter to Dorothy Canfield Fisher." *The Robert Frost Review* 4 (fall 1994): 24–27.

———. "Profile: Dorothy Canfield Fisher." *Legacy: A Journal of American Women Writers* 9, issue 1 (1992): 49–58.

———. "'This allegation we repudiate!': An Unpublished Poem by Dorothy Canfield Fisher." *Vermont History News* 41 (March-April 1990): 35–36.

———. "Willa Cather and Dorothy Canfield Fisher: A Literary Correspondence." Master's thesis, University of Vermont, 1987.

———. "Willa Cather and Dorothy Canfield Fisher: Rift, Reconciliation, and *One of Ours.*" In *Cather Studies,* ed. Susan J. Rosowski. Vol. 1. Lincoln: University of Nebraska Press, 1990.

———. "Willa Cather's Commentary on Three Novels by Dorothy Canfield Fisher." *American Notes and Queries* 3 (January 1990): 13–15.

Mann, Dorothea Lawrence. "Dorothy Canfield: The Little Vermonter." *Bookman* 65 (August 1927): 695–701.

McCallister, Lois. "Dorothy Canfield Fisher: A Critical Study." Ph.D. dissertation, Case Western Reserve University, 1969.

Meral, Jean. *Paris in American Literature.* Chapel Hill: University of North Carolina Press, 1989.

Overton, Grant. *The Women Who Make Our Novels.* Freeport, N.Y.: Books for Libraries Press, 1967: 61–74.

Phelps, William Lyon. "Dorothy Canfield Fisher." *English Journal* 22 (January 1933): 1–8.

Pottle, Frederick A. "Catharsis." *Yale Review* 40 (January 1951): 621–41.

Price, Alan. "Writing Home from the Front: Edith Wharton and Dorothy Canfield Fisher Present Wartime France to the United States." *Edith Wharton Newsletter* 5 (fall 1988): 1–5.

Quinn, Arthur Hobson. *American Fiction: An Historical and Critical Survey.* New York: Appleton-Century-Crofts, 1936: 706–14.

Radway, Janice. "The Book-of-the-Month Club and the General Reader: On the Uses of 'Serious' Fiction." *Critical Inquiry* 14 (spring 1988): 516–38.

Reynolds, Paul R. *The Middle Man: The Adventures of a Literary Agent.* New York: William Morrow, 1972.

Rubin, Joan Shelley. *The Making of Middlebrow Culture.* Chapel Hill: University of North Carolina Press, 1992.

Schroeter, Joan G. "The Canfield-Cleghorn Correspondence: Two Lives in Letters." Ph.D. dissertation, Northern Illinois University, 1993.

———. "Crisis, Conflict, and Constituting the Self: A Lacanian Reading of *The Deepening Stream.*" *Colby Quarterly* 27 (September 1991): 148–60.

Sedgwick, Ellery. *The Happy Profession.* Boston: Little, Brown, 1946.

Showalter, Elaine. "Piecing and Writing." In *The Poetics of Gender,* ed. Nancy K. Miller. New York: Columbia University Press, 1986.

Silverman, Al, ed. *The Book-of-the-Month: Sixty Years of Books in American Life.* Boston: Little, Brown, 1986.

Smith, Bradford. "Dorothy Canfield Fisher." *Atlantic Monthly* 204 (August 1959): 73–77.

———. "Dorothy Canfield Fisher: A Presence among Us." *Saturday Review* 41 (November 29, 1958): 13–14.

Wagenknecht, Edward. *Cavalcade of the American Novel.* New York: Holt, Rinehart, Winston, 1952: 294–99.

Warfel, Harry R. *American Novelists of Today.* New York: American Book, 1951: 79–81.

Washington, Ida H. *Dorothy Canfield Fisher: A Biography.* Shelburne, Vt.: New England Press, 1982.

———. "Isak Dinesen and Dorothy Canfield: The Importance of a Helping Hand." In *Continental, Latin and Francophone Women Writers,* ed. Eunice Myers and Ginette Adamson. Lanham, Md.: University Press of America, 1987.

White, William Allen. "The Other Side of Main Street." *Collier's Weekly* 68 (July 30, 1921): 7–8, 18–19.

Williams, Blanche Colton. *Our Short Story Writers.* New York: Moffat, Yard, 1920: 41–54.

Wilson, Edmund. *The Shores of Light: A Literary Chronicle of the Twenties and Thirties.* New York: Farrar, Straus, and Young, 1952.

Wyckoff, Elizabeth. "Dorothy Canfield: A Neglected Bestseller." *Bookman* 74 (September 1931): 40–44.

Yates, Elizabeth. *Pebble in a Pool: The Widening Circle of Dorothy Canfield Fisher's Life.* Brattleboro, Vt.: Stephen Greene Press, 1958.